D0948359

Dark Matter

Also by Philip Kerr

Fiction:

March Violets

The Pale Criminal

A German Requiem

A Philosophical Investigation

Dead Meat

The Grid

Esau

A Five-Year Plan

The Second Angel

The Shot

Non-Fiction:

The Book of Lies

Fights, Feuds, and Heartfelt Hatreds

Dark Matter

The Private Life of Sir Isaac Newton

A NOVEL

Philip Kerr

McArthur & Company
Toronto

First published in Canada by McArthur & Company 2002

McArthur & Company
322 King Street West, Suite 402
Toronto, Ontario
M5V 1J2

National Library of Canada Cataloguing in Publication

Kerr, Philip
    Dark matter : the private life of Sir Isaac Newton :
    a novel / Philip Kerr.

    ISBN 1-55278-322-7

    1. Newton, Isaac, Sir, 1642-1727—Fiction. I. Title.

    PR6061.E8D37 2002   823'.914
    C2002-903054-4

Cover Design by *Whitney Cookman*
Interior Design by *Elina D. Nudelman*
Printed in Canada by *Transcontinental Inc.*

The publisher would like to acknowledge the financial support
of the Government of Canada through the Book Publishing
Industry Development Program (BPIDP) and the Canada
Council for our publishing activities.

10 9 8 7 6 5 4 3 2 1

To Naomi Rose

The Tower of London

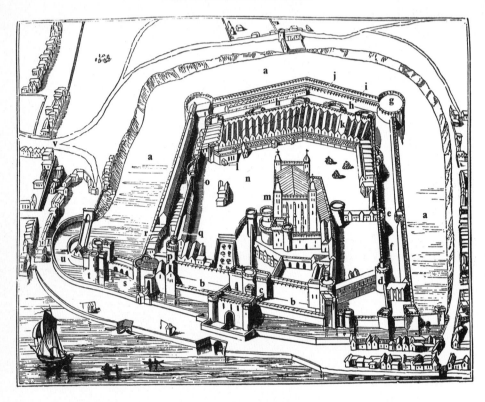

a. Moat

b. Water Lane

c. Bloody Tower

d. Salt Tower

e. Broad Arrow Tower

f. Irish Mint

g. Brass Mount

h. English Mint

i. Warden's House

j. Master's House

k. Brick Tower (home
   of the Master of Ordnance)

l. Chapel

m. White Tower

n. Tower Green

o. Beauchamp Tower

p. Bell Tower

q. Comptroller's House & Yard

r. Entrance to the Mint (and
   Newton's office)

s. Byward Tower

t. Middle Tower

u. Lion's Tower

v. Tower Street to East London

Prologue

ARISE, SHINE; FOR THY LIGHT IS COME, AND THE GLORY OF THE
LORD IS RISEN UPON THEE.

(ISAIAH 60:1)

I swore not to tell this story while Newton remained alive.

On the morning of the twenty-eighth of March 1727—Sir
Isaac Newton having died some eight days previously—I took a
coach from my new lodgings in Maiden Lane, Covent Garden,
with Doctor Samuel Clarke, who was Newton's friend and com-
mentator, to the Abbey to see Newton lie in state like some fab-
ulous Greek hero.

We found him in the Jerusalem Chamber, a great oak-
paneled room with a large open fireplace that lies to the southwest of the Abbey, where there are some tapestries and stained
glass ascribed to the period of Henry III, and marble busts of
Henry IV and Henry V. It is said that Henry IV had a fit while
praying one day in the Abbey and was carried into the Jerusalem
Chamber where he died, thus fulfilling the prophecy that he
would die in Jerusalem.

I cannot answer for whether the likeness of Henry was a
good one, but Newton's embalmer had done his job well and not
made the face up like a whore, which is a very common failing
with these people. His flesh looked quite natural, being florid,
soft and full, as if the man had been only sleeping. And since
there was no perceptible smell, Newton having been dead for a
week or more, which is a long time for a corpse to be out of the

ground, I could readily attest to the efficiency of the embalmer's hand at least, for although Spring was not quite arrived, it had been quite warm of late.

The man I saw, laid out in an open coffin upon a great long refectory table, wore a full-bottomed flaxen wig, a plain white linen stock, and a black three-piece suit. His face was lined, somewhat heavy about the jowls and, despite a keen, aquiline nose that had always put me in mind of the Roman, not unkind. I had thought I might have perceived in the air of his face some of the penetrating sagacity which had once distinguished his composures. Perhaps even some final wisdom. But in death Newton was a quite unremarkable-looking figure.

"He was in great pain with the stone when he died," said I.

"But still quite lucid," replied Doctor Clarke.

"Aye. He was always that. Newton was the most lucid of souls. Newton looked upon all of creation as a riddle, with certain clues that were laid about this world by God. Or perhaps as a kind of cipher which, by great concentration of mind, he might translate. I think he believed that a man who might decipher an earthly code might similarly fathom the heavenly one. He believed nothing unless he could prove it as a theorem or draw it as a diagram."

"Newton has given us the golden thread by which we may find our way through God's labyrinth," said Doctor Clarke.

"Yes," I said. "Perhaps that is right."

After dinner I returned to my lodgings in Maiden Lane. I slept uneasily, alone with my still-smouldering remembrances of him. I could not say that I had known Newton well. I doubt there was any man or woman who could ever have claimed as much as that. For he was not just a rare bird but a shy one, too. And yet I can say that for a while, with the exception of Mrs. Conduitt, I knew him as well as anyone could have known him.

Until I met Newton I was like London before the Great Fire, and gave little thought to the poor repair of my intellectual buildings. But when I encountered his spark, and the strong wind of his mind fanned the flames in the narrow streets of my own poor brain—which were quite filled with rubbish most of them, for I was young and foolish then—the fire took hold so quickly that it raged quite unchecked.

Perhaps, if it had been just the fire ignited by his own acquaintance, something of the man I was might have been saved. But there was also the fire in my heart that was ignited by his niece, Mrs. Conduitt—Miss Barton that was—and, in a case such as this, with fires breaking out in several places at once, and at so great a distance from each other, then the whole conflagration seemed like the result of some great and malevolently supernatural design. For one all too brief and brilliant moment my sky was quite lit up, as if by fireworks. The next, I lay overwhelmed and everything was consumed. My church maimed irreparably; my soul boiled away to nothing; my heart burned to a cold black cinder. In short, my life reduced to ashes.

Of course, after the fire comes the rebuilding. Sir Christopher Wren's many great designs. St. Paul's. Yes, it's true, I had my own projects. The fact that I am a retired colonel might leave one to suppose that something arose from the ashes of my former life. But the rebuilding was difficult. And not entirely successful. Indeed, I sometimes think it would have been better if, like King Priam slain by Neoptolemus in the burning ruins of Troy, I too had died after we parted.

Doctor Clarke did not have the patience to be told as much. Doubtless he was still inclined to believe Doctor Newton was someone who gave sight to the blind. But any soldier will tell you that sometimes you can see too much. Even the most courageous man can become quite untrussed at the sight of the enemy. Could King Leonidas with his one thousand Spartans have held the pass at Thermopylae for two whole days if his men had seen the whole host of the Persian army before them? No, there are occasions when it is better to be blind.

Clarke had said that Newton had given us the golden thread by which we may find our way through God's labyrinth. Well, that is how I first perceived his work, myself. Only the creator of the labyrinth institutes it otherwise, there being no end to the labyrinth, for it is infinite, at which junction one lights upon the awful discovery that neither is there a creator. But I do not like a labyrinth so well as a chasm or an abyss into which Newton, by virtue of his system of the world and falling bodies and mathematics and chronology, lowers us upon a rope, which is a more precarious situation wherein gravity may do its invisible work.

Invisible work. Newton knew all about that. His theory of gravity, of course. His interest in alchemy, for example. And ciphers, too. When I told Doctor Clarke how Newton had believed that a man who might decipher an earthly code might similarly fathom the heavenly one, I could have told Clarke such a story of codes and ciphers and secrets as would have made his wig smoke. But no. Doctor Clarke would not have had the patience to hear such a story as mine, for it is a difficult tale and besides, I am a soldier, without much skill in talk. Moreover, I lack the practice in its recounting since it has not been told before this day. Newton himself swore me to secrecy about this dark matter, as he himself called it. Yet now that the great man is dead I can see no reason not to tell someone. But who? And how would I have begun? I fear I am too cool to have mastered the unaffected eloquence and noble, simple style of history that would hold anyone's attention for very long. It is the Englishman's malady. We are too plain in our speaking to make a good tale in the telling. I must confess there is much about my own history that I have forgotten. It is difficult for me to remember all of this. More than thirty years have passed and there are many aspects to this story that seem to elude my grasp. But perhaps it is me who is lacking, for I do not find myself very interesting; and certainly not in comparison with Newton. How could I ever have thought to understand one such as he? I was not a man of letters. I could better describe a battle than a history such as this one. Blenheim, Oudenarde, Malplaquet. I fought in all those battles. There has been little poetry in my life. No fine words. Just guns and swords, bullets and bawds.

But perhaps I might rehearse the matter in my own head. For one day I should like this story to be known. And if I should happen to be bored, I shall simply order myself to desist and I shall take no offence. I had little thought that in recalling this story I might need to write it down. And yet how else might I improve upon the telling of it, except by writing it?

Chapter One

Michael Maier, *Septimana philosophica*, 1620

THE SUN SHALL BE NO MORE THY LIGHT BY DAY; NEITHER FOR
BRIGHTNESS SHALL THE MOON GIVE LIGHT UNTO THEE: BUT THE
LORD SHALL BE UNTO THEE AN EVERLASTING LIGHT, AND THY
GOD THY GLORY.

(ISAIAH 60:19)

On Thursday, November the fifth, 1696, most people went to church. But I went to fight a duel.

Gunpowder Day was then a cause for Protestant celebration twice over: this had been the day, in 1605, when King James I had been delivered from a Roman Catholic plot to blow up the Parliament; and, in 1688, it had also been the day when the Prince of Orange had landed at Torbay to deliver the Church of England from the oppressive hand of another Stuart, the Catholic King James II. Many Gunpowder Day sermons were preached throughout the City, and I would have done well to have listened to one of them, for a little consideration of heavenly deliverance might have helped me to channel my anger against Papist tyranny instead of the man who had impugned my honour. But my blood was up and, my head being full of fighting, I and my second walked to the World's End Tavern in Knightsbridge where we had a slice of beef and a glass of Rhenish for breakfast, and thence to Hyde Park, to meet my opponent, Mister Shayer, who was already waiting with his own second.

Shayer was an ugly-looking fellow, whose tongue was too big for his mouth so that he lisped like a little child when he spoke, and I regarded him as I would have regarded a mad dog. I no longer remember what our dispute was about, except to say that I was a quarrelsome sort of young man and very likely there was fault on both sides.

No apologies were solicited and none proffered and straight-away all four of us threw off our coats and fell to with swords. I had some skill with the weapon, having been trained by Mister Figg in the Oxford Road, but there was little or no finesse in this fight and, in truth, I made short work of the matter, wounding Shayer in the left pap which, being close to his heart, placed the poor fellow in mortal fear of his life, and me in fear of prosecution, for duelling was against the law since 1666. Most gentle-men fighting paid but little heed to the legal consequences of their actions; however, Mister Shayer and myself were both at Gray's Inn, acquainting ourselves with a tincture of English law, and our quarrel was quickly the cause of a scandal that obliged my leaving off a career at the Bar, permanently.

It was perhaps no great loss to the legal profession, for I had little interest in the Law; and even less aptitude, for I had only gone to the Bar to please my late father who always had a great respect for that profession. And yet what else could I have done? We were not a rich family, but not without some connections, either. My elder brother, Charles Ellis, who later became an MP, was then the under-secretary to William Lowndes, who was himself the Permanent Secretary to the First Lord of the Treasury. The Treasurer, until his recent resignation, had been Lord Godolphin. Several months later the King named as Godolphin's replacement the then Chancellor of the Exchequer, Lord Montagu, to whom Isaac Newton owed his appointment as Warden of the Royal Mint in May 1696.

My brother told me that, until Newton's arrival in the position, there had been few if any duties that were attached to the Wardenship; and Newton had taken the position in expectation of receiving the emolument for not much work; but that the Great Recoinage had given the office a greater importance than hitherto it had enjoyed; and that Newton was obliged to be the principal agent of the coin's protection.

In truth it was sore in need of protecting for it had become much debased of late. The only true money of the realm was the silver coin—for there was little if ever much gold about—which constituted sixpences, shillings, half-crowns and crowns; but until the great and mechanised recoinage, mostly this was hand-struck with an ill-defined rim that lent itself to clipping or filing. Except for a parcel of coin struck after the Restoration, none of the coin in circulation was more recent than the Civil War, while a great quantity had been issued by Queen Elizabeth.

Fate took a hand to drive the coinage further out of order when, after William and Mary came to the throne, the price of gold and silver became greatly increased, so that there was much more than a shilling's worth of silver in a shilling. Or at least there ought to have been. A new-struck shilling weighed ninety-three grains, although with the price of silver increasing all the time it need only have weighed seventy-seven grains; and even more vexing was that with the coin so worn and thin, and rubbed with age, and clipped and filed, a shilling often weighed as little as fifty grains. Because of this, people were inclined to hoard the new coin and refuse the old.

The Recoinage Act had passed through the Parliament in January 1696, although this only chafed the sore, the Parliament having been imprudent enough to damn the old money before ensuring that there existed sufficient supplies of the new. And throughout the summer—if that was what it was, the weather being so bad—money had remained in such short supply that tumults every day were feared. For without good money how were men to be paid, and how was bread to be bought? If all that was not subversion enough, to this sum of calamity was added the fraud of the bankers and the goldsmiths who, having got immense treasures by extortion, hoarded their bullion in expectation of its advancing in value. To say nothing of the banks that every day were set up, or failed, besides an intolerable amount of taxation on everything save female bodies and an honest, smiling countenance, of which there were few if any to be seen. Indeed there was such a want of public spirit anywhere that the Nation seemed to sink under so many calamities.

Much aware of my sudden need for a position and Doctor Newton's equally sudden need for a clerk, Charles prevailed upon Lord Montagu to consider advancing me in Newton's favour for employment, and this despite our not having the fondness which we used and ought to have as brothers. And by and by it was arranged that I should go to Doctor Newton's house in Jermyn Street to recommend myself to him.

I remember the day well, for there was a hard frost and a report of more Catholic plots against the King, and a great search for Jacobites was already under way. But I do not remember that Newton's reputation had made much of an impression upon my young mind; for, unlike Newton, who was a Cambridge Professor, I was an Oxford man and, although I knew the classics, I could no more have disputed any general mathematical system, let alone one affecting the universe, than I could have discoursed upon the nature of a spectrum. I was aware only that Newton was, like Mister Locke and Sir Christopher Wren, one of the most learned men in England, although I could not have said why: cards were my reading then and pretty girls my scholarly pursuit—for I had studied women closely; and I was as skilled in the use of sword and pistol as some are with a sextant and a pair of dividers. In short, I was as ignorant as a jury unable to find a verdict. And yet, of late—especially since leaving my inn of court—my ignorance had begun to weigh upon me.

Jermyn Street was a recently completed and quite fashionable suburb of Westminster, with Newton's house toward the western and better end, close by St. James's Church. At eleven o'clock I presented myself at Doctor Newton's door, was admitted by a servant and ushered into a room with a good fire in it, where Newton sat awaiting my arrival upon a red chair with a red cushion and a red morocco-bound book. Newton did not wear a wig and I saw that his hair was grey but that his teeth were all his own and good for a man of his age. He wore a crimson shag gown trimmed with gold buttons and I also remember that he had a blister or issue upon his neck that troubled him a little. The room was all red, as if a smallpox victim did sometimes lie in it, for it is said that this colour draws out the infection. It was well furnished with several landscapes upon the red walls and a fine globe that occupied a whole corner by the window, as if this room was all the universe there was and he the god in it, for he struck me as a most wise-looking man. His nose was all bridge, as across the Tiber, and his eyes, which were quiet in repose, became as sharp as bodkins the minute his brow furrowed under the concentration of a thought or a question. His mouth looked fastidious, as if he lacked appetite and humour, and his dimpled chin was on the edge of finding itself joined by a twin. And when he spoke, he spoke with an accent I should incorrectly have supposed to be Norfolk but now know to have been Lincolnshire, for he was born near Grantham. That day I met him first he was just a month or so short of his fifty-fourth birthday.

"It is not my manner," he said, "to speak anything that is extraneous to my business. So let me come straight to the point, Mister Ellis. When I became Warden of His Majesty's Mint I little thought that my life should become taken up with the detection, pursuit and punishment of coiners, clippers and counterfeiters. But that being my discovery, I wrote to the Treasury Committee to the effect that such matters were the proper province of the Solicitor General and that, if it were possible, to let this cup pass from me. Their Lordships willed it otherwise, however, and therefore I must stand the course. Indeed, I have made this matter my own personal crusade, for if the Great Recoinage does not succeed, I fear that we shall lose this war with the French and the whole kingdom shall be undone. God knows I have, these past six months, in my own person done my full duty, I am sure. But the business of my taking these rascals is so great, there being so many of them, I find I have sore need of a clerk to assist me in my duties.

"But I want no truckle-head milksop in my service. God knows what disorders we may fall into and whether any violence may be done on this office or upon our persons, for coining being high treason carries the harshest penalty and these miscreants are a desperate lot. You look like a young man of spirit, sir. But speak up and recommend yourself."

"I do believe," I said nervously, because Newton sounded very like my own father who always expected the worse of me, and usually he was not disappointed, "that I should say something to you in reference to my education, sir. I have my degree from Oxford. And I have studied for the Law."

"Good, good," Newton said impatiently. "Likely you will need a quick pen. These mimming rogues are agile storytellers and provide such a quantity of deposition as would leave a man feeling in need of three hands. But let us have less modesty, sir. What of your other skills?"

I searched myself for an answer. What other skills did I possess? And finding myself at a loss for words, with little or nothing to commend myself further, I began to grimace and shake my head and shrug, and started to sweat like I was in the hot steam baths.

"Come, sir," insisted Newton. "Did you not pink a man with your rapier?"

"Yes sir," I stammered, angry with my brother for having apprised him of this awkward fact. For who else could have told him?

"Excellent." Newton knocked the table once as if keeping score. "And a keen shot, I see." Perceiving my puzzlement, he added, "Is that not a gunpowder-spot on your right hand?"

"Yes sir. And you're right. I shoot both carbine and pistol, tolerably well."

"But you are better with the pistol, I'll warrant."

"Did my brother tell you that, too?"

"No, Mister Ellis. Your own hand told me. A carbine would have left its mark on hand and face. But a pistol only upon the back of your hand, which did lead me to suppose that you have used a pistol with greater frequency."

"Well, that's a nice trick, sir. I am trumped."

"I have others here besides. Doubtless we shall have to visit many a kennel where your apparent fondness for the ladies may serve us good advantage. Women will sometimes tell a young man that which they would deny my older ears. I trust that your fondness for the dark-haired woman you were so recently with might permit such stratagems as would gain us information. Perhaps she was the one who did bring you the juniper ale."

"Well, if that isn't Pam," I proclaimed, quite trumped by this, for I had indeed embraced a wench with brown hair that very morning over breakfast at my local tavern. "How did you know she was dark? And that I had some juniper ale?"

"By virtue of the long dark hair that adorns your handsome *ventre d'or* waistcoat," explained Newton. "It proclaims her colouring just as surely as your conversation demonstrates your close acquaintance with the card table. We shall have need of that, too. As much as we shall have need of a man who likes his bottle. If I am not wrong, sir, that is red wine on your cuffs. No doubt you had a good deal of it to drink last night, which is why you were a little sick in your stomach this morning. And why you had need of some juniper ale for your gripes. The smell of that pungent oil in ale upon your breath is most unmistakable."

I heard myself gasp with astonishment that so much of me was plain to him, as if he could see into my mind and read my own thoughts.

"You make me sound the most consummate rakehell that was ever drawn to the gallows," I protested. "I know not what to say. I am quite outhuffed."

"Pray, Mister Ellis," said Newton, "don't take on so. We shall have to daggle a bit, you and I. The business of the Mint requires that I have a man who knows his way around London. That being the case, and to fret you no longer, the position is yours if you want it. The pay is not much. Just sixty pounds a year, to start. Which does not sort well with me, and I confess I am at a vile trouble for fear that the right kind of man will not want the employment and I come to shame because I cannot fulfil the proper duties of my office through lack of an assistant, for whom I have such mighty need. That being the case, it being within my power to do so, I have decided to offer my clerk the Warden's house at the Mint, in the Tower of London, with all the benefits that do pertain to living there."

"That is very generous, sir," said I, beginning to grin like an idiot. For this was more than I could ever have expected. Since leaving Gray's Inn I had taken lodgings in King Street, Westminster, but these were poor quarters and my heart leaped at the thought of a whole house to myself, especially one within the liberties of the Tower, for there a man might avoid taxation altogether.

"Upon my arrival at the Mint last April, I lived there for a while myself before coming here to Jermyn Street, in August. The truth is the Mint is mighty noisy, having the rolling mills going all night, and after the peace and tranquillity of Cambridge, I could not bear with it. But you are a young fellow and it has been my experience that the young have a stronger toleration of noise than their elders. Besides, I have great expectation that my niece will come to live with me in December, and the Mint is a dirty, unwholesome place, with many roguish fellows and where the air is ill, so that I am confirmed not to live there. Come, sir, what do you say? It is a good little house, with a garden."

A whole house, with a garden. This was too much. And yet still I was moved to ask for more. I have mentioned how I had begun to feel the weight of my own ignorance; and it suddenly occurred to me that there was something in Newton's demeanour and conducting of himself that made me believe that I could learn much from him. And I thought to make a condition of it. For I was possessed of the notion that to know the mind of such a man who had penetrated so many scientific and philosophical mysteries would be to know the mind of God. Which would make a change from the minds of whores and gamesters.

"Aye, sir," said I. "I will work for you. But on one condition."

"Name it, Mister Ellis."

"That you will always correct my ignorance of something, for I know you are a learned man. I would wish that you will show me something of the world as you understand it, and to discourse with me on the nature of things in furtherance of my own self-improvement. For I must confess that a university degree got me an understanding of the classics and Sanderson's Logic and not much else. I will work for you, sir. But what in me is dark, I would ask you to illumine. And what is low and base, I would that you might raise and support."

"Well said, sir. It takes an intelligent man to admit his ignorance, especially one with a university degree. But be warned. I was never much of a tutor. In all my time at Cambridge, Trinity College assigned but three fellow commoners to my tuition, and those I took for the fees rather than some desire to be the centre of a modern Lyceum. It is hard for any of us to know how we may appear to the world, but, in truth, I consider myself to have learned only as much as to confirm how little of the world I know. I've a mind that it's this which vexes those rabbinical parts I might possess. But I agree to your condition. I know not what but I'll trepan something into that young head of yours. So, give me your hand on the bargain."

I took Newton's cold thin hand in my own and indeed, I did kiss it, for it now belonged to the master to whom I owed some return of my fortune and prospects.

"Thank you, sir," I said. "I will endeavour to do my best for you."

"I shall write to the Treasury today," said Newton. "They will have to sanction your appointment. But I do not doubt that they will approve my choice. After which you will have to take an oath to keep secret Mister Blondeau's method of edge-marking the coin, although I think it can be no great secret since, I am told, the same machine is shown openly to visitors in the Paris Mint.

"But first let's have some cider, after which I'll write that letter and then we'll take my coach to the Tower where I'll swear you in and show you around the Mint."

And so I was employed at the Royal Mint.

The Mint was within the Tower since 1299, and by 1696 it was as big as many a sizeable town. Two rows of aged wooden buildings, pinned together with clamps of iron, lay between the inner and outer rampires, beginning at the Byward and Bell Towers, extended some five hundred yards along and around the foot of each wall to finish up at the Salt Tower. A narrow cobbled road, illuminated by lanterns and patrolled by sentries, led between the timber-shored buildings which, some of them, were several jetties high and accommodated houses, offices, barracks, stables, wash-houses, melting-houses, smithies, mill rooms, storehouses, taverns and a sutters selling all kinds of victuals.

As Newton had told me, the noise of metalworking was enough to box a man's ears, and walking about the Mint we had to shout to each other to make ourselves heard; but to this must be added the cannons that from time to time were fired, the sound of horses and iron wheels on the cobbles, the bellman cries and voices of the soldiers who were stationed there and who cursed as freely as Templars, the dogs that barked, the ravens that cried out like the throat-rattles of dying men, the fires that roared, the cats that howled, the doors and gates that slammed, the keys that jangled, and the wooden signs that creaked in the high wind, for it had been exceedingly stormy of late. Bedlam could not have seemed more noisy than the Royal Mint. My first impression was of some infernal place such as Virgil might have described when Aeneas visits the underworld and, standing between the Bell and Byward Towers, where I could hear the low moaning of wild beasts in the nearby Lion Tower, which stood outside the westward entrance, I almost thought myself before the very forecourt and in the opening of the jaws of hell. Yet the Tower was an exciting place and I was pleased to be there, for I always had a great appetite for history; and visiting the Tower as a boy I little thought I should ever have worked there.

We walked north, up Mint Street, with Newton all the while acquainting me with the work of the moneyers who operated the coinage presses, and the assayers who checked the fineness of the bullion, and the melters and the engravers.

"Of course," he said, "many of them are villains up to their necks in illegal coining and fit to be hanged. Blank coins are often stolen, as are dies and guinea stamps. At least two men who were in the service of the Mint have been hanged. And another two who were in the service of the Mint are in Newgate Prison, under sentence of death.

"My advice is to trust none of them, from the highest to the lowest. The scoundrel who is Master of the Mint is Mister Neale, although he is so seldom here you would think he would blush to hold the office. But I doubt that you will have sufficient opportunity to know him well enough to recognise his many failings."

At this point Newton bowed stiffly to a man who came out of one of the offices—a small and consumptive fellow who whooped like a trumpet when he spoke; and as soon as he was gone out of earshot my master enjoined me not to trust him either.

"He is mighty friendly with the Tower Ordnance—the garrison of soldiers with whom we are constantly at odds for the privileges of the Mint. For they regard us as interlopers, although in truth we have been here almost as long as they. But this Tower has too many people in it, and there's the crux of the problem.

"Until recently the Ordnance had occupied the Irish Mint, which is near the Salt Tower, at the far end of this road we are on. They had seized the Porter's house and some clerks' dwellings, and built a barracks on a vacant site. But this Great Recoinage has enabled us to get them out of the Mint again, and back within the inner rampire of the Tower, where the common soldiers now take turns to sleep in a bed, so that they now hate us most bitterly. Trust none of them, nor their officers, for they wish us all ill."

Newton caught sight of a haughty-looking man who stood watching us from the top of the Beauchamp Tower.

"And there is the great architect of their resentment. Lord Lucas himself. He is the Lord Lieutenant of the Tower, a position that enjoys many ancient and peculiar privileges and, but for the office exercised by myself, he might call himself the most powerful man in this castle. Above all other men, do not trust him. He is a drunken Borachio and so arrogant I do believe he must wipe his arse with gilt paper."

A little farther on, around the corner of Devereaux Tower, we came abreast of the Smithy, wherein as stern and nasty-looking a rogue as ever I saw, left off shoeing a horse for a moment to fix a most unforgiving eye on Doctor Newton and, by association, myself.

"Upon my soul," said I, when we had walked past, "if that fellow doesn't have the most disinheriting countenance."

"He is a most inveterate knave and no friend to the Mint either. But put him out of your mind for now, as here is the King's Clerk's house, and next to it the Master's house, and next to that the Deputy Warden, Monsieur Fauquier's house."

"Fauquier? He sounds like a Frenchman."

"He is one of those Huguenots," explained Newton, "so lately expelled from his own country by the French King, Lewis. I think that there are several such refugees here in the Tower. The French Church, which is the centre of their community, is but a short walk from the Tower, in Threadneedle Street. Fauquier is a man of considerable substance and, I believe, a diligent one. But do not think to find him in this house—him, or any of these others I have mentioned. It is one of the perquisites of preferment in the Mint that officers may sublet their official residences to whomsoever they wish and for their own personal gain."

It was now that I perceived how in giving me his own official residence, Newton was giving up the good income he might have derived from the letting of it.

Newton stood still and pointed to a neat two-storey house that was built along the wall underneath that part of the outer rampire known as the Brass Mount—so called because of the piece of brass cannon installed there and which, I soon discovered, was often fired in celebration of royal birthdays, or visits by foreign dignitaries.

"This is the Warden's house," said Newton, "where you shall live." He opened the door and ushered me inside and, looking around at the furniture and the books, which belonged to Newton, I thought that the house would suit me very well. "The house is quite cosy although there is, as you can see, some damp—which I think is inevitable from our proximity to the river—and much dust. The vibration of the cannon brings it down, so it can't be helped much. You are welcome to use this furniture. It was brought from Trinity, most of it. None of it is any good, and I care little for it, but I would have you look after these books. There is scant room for any more books in my new house, and yet I would not part with these. Since you are bent upon self-improvement, Mister Ellis, you will doubtless want to read them. You may even find one or two of them to your liking. And I look forward to hearing an opinion of them which, sometimes, is as good as reading a book again oneself."

Going outside again, Newton showed me a little walled garden, rather ill-tended, that curved around the base of the Jewel Tower and which, being the Warden's garden, was mine to enjoy as well.

"You might grow some vegetables here," suggested Newton. "If you do, make sure to offer me some. Otherwise, this is a very pretty place to sit in summer if you be not afeared of ghosts, although, in truth, working for me you will have little time for such idle fancies. I myself am very sceptical of the general appearing of spirits, but there are many within these Tower walls who make the greatest warrants of having seen one apparition or another. I count this nonsense, mostly. But it is no great secret that many have died most cruelly in almost every part of this fortification, which explains much general superstition hereabouts, for such a terrible history will always play upon ignorant men's fancies. It is even put about that your predecessor was quite frightened away by a spirit, but it goes against my mind and I am more likely to believe that he was in league with some of these coiners and ran away for fear of being apprehended, and hanged. For his disappearance almost coincided with my arrival in the Mint, which makes me much suspicious."

The news that I had a predecessor who had disappeared troubled me a little so that I had a mind to know more, for the possibility now presented itself that my new position might be more hazardous than previously I had believed.

"But what was his name?" I asked. "Were not enquiries of him made? It is a sad thing to see how uncertain a thing my predecessor's reputation was and how little is to be presumed of his honesty. I trust if I disappeared, you might give me a rather better opinion."

"Your concern does you credit," admitted Newton. "His name was George Macey. And I do believe some enquiries of him were made."

"But pray sir, is it not possible that Mister Macey should be lamented as a victim, as condemned for a villain? By your own reckoning these are desperate men you have been dealing with. Might he not have been murdered?"

"Might, sir? Might? This was six months ago, when I was still finding my way around this strange place. And I can frame no hypothesis after such an interval of time. For to me the best and safest method of philosophising seems to be, first, to inquire diligently into the evidence of things and to proceed later to hypothesis for the explanations as to how they are. What might or might not have happened is of little concern to me. The investigation of mysteries and difficult things by the method of analysis ought ever to precede the method of composition.

"That is my method, Mister Ellis. To know it is to hit my constitution exactly, sir. But your questions do you justice. I will continue to appreciate your honesty, sir, for I would not make you my creature. But always speak to the point. And make your earliest study my scientific method, for it will stand you in good stead, and then you and I shall get on very well."

"I will study you and your method most diligently, sir," said I.

"Well then, what think you of the house and garden?"

"I like them very well, Doctor Newton. I think I was never so lucky at cards as I have been in entering your employment."

This was true. I had never lived on my own. At the Bar I had shared rooms with another man; and before that, I had been at the University of Oxford where I had lived in college. And it was a great pleasure to close the door of a whole house behind me and be by myself. For all my life I had been obliged to find a space away from brothers and sisters, students and pupil barristers in order that I might read, or dream. But the first night I spent in my new house at the Tower was very nearly my last.

I had gone to bed early with a number of essays on the amendment of English coins that had been written by the leading minds of the day, including Doctor Newton, Sir Christopher Wren, Doctor Wallis, and Mister John Locke. These had been commissioned by the Regency Council in 1695 and Newton had suggested they would give me a good grounding in the various issues surrounding the recoinage. These did not encourage me to stay awake, however; my evening's reading was as tedious as anything I had seen since abandoning my legal studies; and after an hour or two, I put the candle in the fireplace and pulled the quilt over my head with scarcely a thought for the superstitious fancies that had beset me earlier.

I do not know how long I was asleep. Perhaps it was as little as half an hour, perhaps much longer, but I awoke with a start, as if I had pulled myself out of the grave and back into life. Immediately I was possessed of the certainty that I was not alone; and holding my breath I became convinced that the dark shadows of my bedchamber were animated with the respiration of another. I sat up and, my whole body swayed by the beating of my own heart, I listened as closely to the tenebrous atmosphere as if I had been the prophet Samuel himself. And by and by I was able to distinguish the sound in my own bedchamber as of someone sucking air through a quill, which made my hair stand on end.

"For God's sake, who is there?" I cried and, swinging my legs out of bed, I went to fetch the stub of candle from the fireplace to light another and illuminate the gloom. In the same instant out of the shadows spoke a voice that chilled me to the bone.

"Thy Nemesis," said the voice.

I had a brief glimpse of a man's face and was about to answer when, in a most inhuman manner, he attacked me, forcing me back onto the bed where, with all his weight upon my chest, he set about trying to gouge at my eyes with his thumbs, so that I cried out murder. But the strength of my assailant was formidable and although I caught him a couple of good blows about the head, the power of his attack never faltered and I thought for certain that I should be murdered and if not killed then blinded. Desperately, I forced his hands away from my eyes only to have him fasten them about my throat. Sensible of the fact that I was surely being strangled, I kicked out, in vain. A moment or two later I felt a great weight lifted from my chest and assumed that my soul had begun its upward motion to heaven before, finally, I realised that my attacker had been pulled off me and was now under the restraint of two members of the Ordnance, although he tolerated their hold upon him with such calm that I wondered if these two sentinels detained the right man.

A third member of the Ordnance, one Sergeant Rohan, helped me to come to myself with a little brandy so that I was at last able to stand and confront my assailant in the light of the lantern the Yeoman Warders had brought with them.

"Who are you?" I demanded to know in a voice hardly my own, it sounded so hoarse. "And why did you attack me?"

"His name is Mister Twistleton," reported the strangely spoken Sergeant Rohan. "And he is the Tower Armourer."

"I did not attack you, sir," said Mister Twistleton with such a show of innocence that I almost believed him. "I don't know who you are. It was the other gentleman I attacked."

"Are you mad?" I said, swallowing uncomfortably. "There is no other gentlemen here. Come sir, what harm have I done to you that you should attack me?"

"He's mad all right," said Rohan. "But as you can see for yourself, there's no harm in him now."

"No harm in him?" I repeated with no small incredulity. "Why, he very nearly murdered me in my bed."

"Mister Ellis, is it?" asked Sergeant Rohan.

"Yes."

"He'll not trouble you again, Mister Ellis. I give you my word on it. Mostly he's close kept in my own house, under my cognizance, and never troubles nobody. But tonight he slipped out when we wasn't looking and fetched up here. We were out looking for him when we heard the commotion."

"It's lucky for me you did," said I. "Another minute and I wouldn't be talking to you now. But surely he belongs in Bedlam. Or some other hospital for the distracted and lunatic."

"Bedlam, Mister Ellis? And have him chained to a wall like a dog? To be laughed at like an animal?" said one of the Yeoman Warders. "Mister Twistleton is our friend, sir. We couldn't let that happen to him."

"But he's dangerous."

"Most of the time he's exactly as you see him now. Quite calm in himself. Don't make us send him there, Mister Ellis."

"Me? I don't apprehend how any of you are under my compulsion, Mister Bull. His care is your own affair."

"It won't be if you report the matter, sir."

"Christ Jesus have mercy upon us," shouted Mister Twistleton.

"You see? Even he asks your indulgence," said Rohan.

I sighed, exasperated at this turn of events: that I should be attacked in my own bed, near strangled and then asked to forget all about it, as if this had been some foolish schoolboy prank and not a case of attempted murder. It seemed a perfect mockery of the Tower's reputation for security, how a lunatic should be allowed to wander about the place with no more restraint than some wretched raven.

"Then I must have your word that he will be kept under lock and key, at least at night," said I. "The next person might not be so lucky as I was."

"You shall have my word," said Rohan. "Right willingly."

I nodded my grudging assent, for I seemed to have little choice in the matter. From what Newton had told me, relations between the Mint and the Ordnance were already quite bad enough without my becoming the author of yet more bad feeling. "What was it that put him out of his wits?" I asked.

"The screams," said Mister Twistleton. "I hear the screams, you see. Of them as have died in this place. They never stop."

Sergeant Rohan clapped me on the shoulder. "You're a good fellow, Mister Ellis," he said. "For a Minter, that is. He'll not trouble you again, I promise you that."

In the days and weeks that followed, I often saw Mister Twistleton about the Tower and always accompanied by a member of the Ordnance; and in truth he always seemed well enough not to be shut up in a madhouse, so that I congratulated myself how I had made a most charitable judgement in the matter; and it was several months afterward before I wondered if I had not made a dreadful mistake.

With public matters in a most sad condition and the country hardly fit to be governed, the Mint worked twenty hours a day, six days a week. As did Newton, for although he had nothing to do with the organising and stimulating of the recoinage, he slept very little, and on the rare occasions when he was not about the business of hunting coiners and clippers, he would occupy himself with the devising of a solution for some mathematic problem or other that would have been set by one of his many mischievous correspondents—for it was their most earnest desire to catch him out in his calculations. But there was always plenty for us to do, and soon we were frequent visitors to the Fleet Prison or to Newgate, to take depositions of evidence from various rogues and scoundrels, many of whom suffered the full penalty of the law.

I mention just one of these cases now, not because it pertains to the telling of this horrible and secret story, which greatly vexed my master for almost a whole year, but to show how many other legal matters at the same time were occupying his virtuoso mind.

The Lords Justices of England ruled the country in the absence of the King, who was fighting the French, with no great success, in Flanders. They had received a letter from a William Chaloner, a most clever and egregious forger, who alleged that money had been coined in the Tower containing less than its proper weight of silver, that false guineas had been made there, and that blanks and guinea stamps had been stolen out of the Mint. My master was ordered by their Lordships to investigate these allegations, which he was obliged to do, although he knew full well that Chaloner was Mercury himself when it came to rhetoric and that he had sold their Lordships a worthless jade. In the meantime, Peter Cooke, a gentleman lately condemned to death for coining, sought to bilk the hangman by telling us that the same Chaloner had been his accomplice, as were others.

How these scoundrels did peach upon each other, for my master had no sooner heard from Cooke, than Thomas White, another villain squeamishly affected by sentence of death, accused John Hunter, who worked at the Mint, of supplying official guinea dies to Chaloner. He also named as coiners Robert Charnock, a notorious Jacobite who had been recently executed for his part in the treasonous plot against King William of Sir John Fenwick; James Pritchard, of Colonel Windsor's regiment of horse guards; and a man named Jones, about whom little or nothing was known. White had been convicted on the evidence of Scotch Robin, who had been an engraver at the Mint, and was a very leaky fellow, most lachrymose; and although my master suspected his sincerity, he always managed to betray at least one more of his friends under Newton's close questioning.

It was a source of no small wonder to me, that a man who had kept himself close-closeted in Cambridge for a quarter century should prove such an expert interrogator. Sometimes Newton seemed stern and unforgiving and promised White that he would hang before the week was out if he concealed any other criminals; and then, at other times, my master did counterfeit to White such friendship and mirth that a man might have thought they were cousins. By these advocate's tricks, which Newton seemed to know by instinct, White named five others, which earned him another reprieve.

Most of these rogues made a good conscience of their deeds and accomplices, but a few tried to keep up the lie, and had the cunning to cry a great while and talk and blubber that they knew nothing at all. Newton was not a man who was easy to trick and with those who tried he was most unforgiving, as if anyone that filled his mind with false information was guilty of something even more heinous than coining. With Peter Cooke, who had sought repeatedly to trick my master most vexatiously, the Doctor proved he could be as vindictive as the Three Furies.

First, we visited the wretched man in his Newgate dungeon, as did several hundred others—for it is the custom in England to view the condemned man, as a visitor to the Tower might look at the lions in the Barbican. Second, we attended the foolish miscreant's condemned sermon, where Newton fixed his eye upon Cooke, who sat alone in his segregated pew, in front of his own open coffin. And still not full-gorged with his revenge, for so I perceived it, my master insisted that we go to Tyburn and see Cooke make his terrible end.

I remember it well, for it was the first time that I saw a man hanged, drawn and quartered, which is a beastly business. But it was unusual besides because Newton seldomly attended the executions of those he prosecuted.

"I think it is right and proper," he said by way of justifying himself, "that, as officers of the law, occasionally we should oblige ourselves to witness the fate to which our investigations lead some of these transgressors. So that we may conduct ourselves with a proper gravity, and that we shall not make our accusations lightly. Do you not agree, sir?"

"Yes sir, if you say so," I said weakly, for I had little appetite for the spectacle.

Cooke, who was a brawny fellow, was drawn on a hurdle in his shift to the place of execution, with the halter wound around his waist and the noose in his hand. To my way of thinking he kept his countenance well, although the hangman rode with him upon the hurdle, and all the time held the axe which Cooke knew would shortly sever his limbs. I shook merely to contemplate the instrument of torture.

We were almost an hour at Tyburn, Cooke delaying the time by long prayers, one after another, until finally, half fainting with fright, he was dragged up the ladder by the hangman, who fixed his halter upon the beam and then threw him off, whereupon the mob set up such a roar of excitement and pressed toward the scaffold that I thought we would be crushed.

The hangman had judged it nicely, for Cooke's toes touched the scaffold so that he was quite alive when the hangman cut him down and, knife in hand, fell upon his victim like one of Caesar's bloody assassins. The crowd, much quietened, groaned as one when the hangman, gutting Cooke like an old goat, sliced open his belly, stuffed in his hand and drew it out again holding a handful of steaming tripes, for the day was cold; and these he burned on a brazier in front of the still visibly breathing man who, but for the noose still constricting his neck, would surely have screamed out his agonies.

Newton did not flinch at the sight and, studying his countenance for a few seconds, I saw that although he took no pleasure in this sad spectacle, nor did he show any signs of lenity either; and I almost thought my master regarded the whole spectacle as he would have observed the dissection of a human cadaver in the Royal Society, which is to say as some kind of experimental procedure.

Finally, the hangman struck off Cooke's head and, prompted by the Sheriff, held it up for the encouragement of the crowd, declaring it to be the head of Peter Cooke, a villain and a traitor. So ended this terrible morning of blood.

From Tyburn we took a hackney to Newton's house for dinner where Mrs. Rogers, the housekeeper, had cooked us a chicken. Newton's appetite was undiminished by the cruelty of the punishment we had witnessed which I was moved to discuss, finding I had little stomach for eating, the sight of another man's stomach ripped open being still so vivid in my mind.

"I cannot think the law is best served by such severity," I declared. "Should a man who coins be punished in the same way as one who plans to kill the King?"

"One is just as disruptive to the smooth governing of the realm as the other," declared Newton. "Indeed it might even be argued that a king might be killed with little disruption to the country at large, as in ancient Rome where the Praetorians killed their emperors like boys kill flies. But if the money is bad, then so the country lacks a true measure of prosperity and by that same sickness shall it quickly perish. But it is not for us to discourse upon the justice of the punishment. It is a matter for the courts. Or the Parliament."

"I should as soon be murdered in my bed as treated thus."

"Surely 'tis always better to be executed than murdered, for any condemned man has an opportunity to make his peace with Almighty God."

"Tell that to Peter Cooke," said I. "I should think he would have preferred to make a quicker end of it, and trusted God's proper judgement afterwards."

The exceedingly stormy weather of November gave way to a fierce frost in early December, in the midst of rumours about French naval preparations for a landing in Ireland. My master and myself had spent all morning in the office, this being close by the Byward Tower and over the entrance to the Mint. Like everywhere else in the Tower it was a damp little place, which a large fire did little to dispel so that I frequently suffered from a most pernicious cough. Frequently our documents were mildewed so that I was often obliged to dry them in front of the fire.

The office itself was furnished with several comfortable chairs, two or three desks, some shelves and a close stool. There were two windows: one that overlooked Mint Street and the other the moat, wherein we would empty our chamber pot. This moat was ten feet deep and some thirty feet in width, and, in ancient times, had once been filled with snakes, crocodiles, and alligators from the Royal Menagerie.

On this particular morning two dredgers operating under the licence of the Lord Lieutenant—it being one of the Tower liberties that anything which fell into the moat was the property of the Tower and, by extension, of the Lord Lieutenant—were dragging the filthy water. We paid little attention to them at the time, being much concerned with rumours of a new forging process having been perfected in relation to the golden guinea coin, this information being laid before my master by Humphrey Hall, who was one of Newton's extensive web of informers, and a most reliable and diligent fellow. But presently news reached us that one of the dredgers had fetched out of the moat a man's body, the condition of which was such that it was strongly suspected he had been murdered, for the feet were bound together and very likely he had been weighed down.

"That is interesting," remarked my master, who, on hearing these facts, left off stroking the office cat, Melchior, to look out of the window.

"Is it?" I remarked. "I am surprised that more people don't fall in, the moat being surrounded only by a low picket fence that would not deter a goat."

But Newton's curiosity was hardly deterred by my remark. "It may have escaped you, Ellis, but people who fall in rarely take the trouble to weight themselves down," he said scornfully. "No, this interests me. Why would someone dispose of a corpse in the moat when the river Thames is so close at hand? It would surely have been a much simpler matter to have carried the body down to Tower Wharf and then to have let the river's tides and eddies work their transporting effect."

"I offer no hypothesis," said I, railing him with his own philosophy, which he took in good part. And there we might have left it. However, many Mint workers—who were easily provoked to fear—hearing of the discovery of a body, stopped their machines, which obliged my master to put aside his own business with Mister Hall and, accompanied by me, to go and investigate the matter himself.

The body had been taken to an empty cellar in the Tower along Water Lane, which ran parallel to the river and was the only road between the inner and outer rampire that was not occupied by the Mint. Gathered outside the cellar door, the stench of the much putrefied corpse having quite overpowered them, were one of the Constable's officers, several Tower warders, the carpenter, and the two dredgers who had found the body. The Constable's man, Mister Osborne, who was a poxy-looking fellow always standing on his office and often drunk, which sometimes prevented him from standing at all, was instructing the carpenter to fashion a cheap coffin; but seeing my master he stopped speaking, and most insolently rolled his eyes and looked mighty vexed.

"Zounds, sir," he exclaimed, addressing Doctor Newton. "What business have you here? This is a matter for the Ordnance. There's nothing that need concern the Mint, or you, this man being already dead and quite beyond any hanging."

Ignoring this insult, Newton bowed gravely. "Mister Osborne, is it not? I own I am quite at a loss. I had thought to offer my assistance with the identification of this unfortunate soul, and how he came by his death, for many of us in the Royal Society have a small acquaintance with anatomical science. But I perceive that you must already know everything there is to know about this poor fellow."

The others smirked at Osborne upon hearing this, for it was plain that Osborne knew nothing of the kind and would plainly have conducted his inquest in a most indifferent and very likely illegal manner.

"Well, there's many a man drinks too much and falls in the moat," he said, with no great certitude. "No great mystery about that, Doctor."

"Do you say so?" said Newton. "It has been my own observation that wine and beer are enough to trip up a drunken man; so that tying his legs together is usually quite superfluous."

"You've heard about that, then," he said, sheepishly. Osborne removed his hat and scratched his close-cropped head. "Well, sir, it's just that he doesn't half stink, being quite rotten. It's as much as a man can do to be alongside of the poor wretch, let alone investigate his person."

"Aye sir," echoed one of the Tower warders. "He's quite picquant to the eyes and nose, so he is. We thought to get him boxed up and then to stand him in the chimney to keep the stink out, while the Constable made a few enquiries around the parish."

"An excellent idea," said Newton. "Only first let me see what enquiries may be answered from his person. If you will permit it, Mister Osborne?"

Osborne nodded. "My duty suggests that I do permit it," he grumbled. "And I shall wait upon you."

"Thank you, Mister Osborne," Newton said handsomely. "I shall trouble you for some of your rolling tobacco to chaw which will take away the cadaver's smell from our nostrils. Some candles, for we will need plenty of light to see what we are about; and some camphor, to help take the stink off the room."

Osborne cut off a chaw for my master and myself and would have put away his knife, but that Newton asked to borrow that, too, and he handed it over willingly enough before going to fetch the candles and the camphor. While he was gone,

Newton addressed the two dredgers and, offering each man a new-minted shilling, suffered them to answer a few questions about their occupations.

"How do you dredge?" he asked.

"Why, sir, with a drag net which you use while rowing the peter. That being the boat, sir. There's an iron frame around the mouth of the net which sinks to the bottom and scrapes along as the peter pulls it forward, collecting into the net everything that comes in its way. Mostly we are river finders, sir. There's more in the river. But sometimes we try our luck in the moat, as is our licensed prerogative so to do. You always know by the weight when you find a body, sir, but that's the first time we ever found one in the moat."

"This would be where in the moat, exactly?"

"On the east side of the Tower, sir. Just below the Devereaux Tower."

"So then, within the bounds of the Ordnance." Seeing the man frown, Newton added, "I mean that part of the Tower which is not occupied by the Mint."

"Yes sir."

"Was the body deep down?"

"Yes sir. Quite deep, but not on the bottom. We dragged it and for a while it did not budge. But then it came up, sudden like, as if it had been weighted, for as you will see for yourself, sir, the ankles are still tied by a piece of rope that has broken off something else, most likely a heavy object."

"You searched the pockets?"

The dredgermen nodded.

"Find anything?"

Each looked at the other.

"Come, man, you shall keep whatever you found, or be well compensated, my word upon it."

One of the dredgers dipped a grimy hand into his pocket and came out with a couple of shillings which Newton examined most carefully before returning them to their keeper.

"Do you see many corpses fetched out of the river?"

"A great many, sir. Them as shoot London Bridge, mostly. As the saying goes, it was made for wise men to go over and fools to go under. Take my advice, gentlemen, and always get off your skiff and walk around the bridge rather than try and go under it."

Mister Osborne returned with the candles and camphor, and took them into the cellar.

"One last question," said Newton. "Can you tell how long a man has been in the water?"

"Yes, your honour, and notwithstanding the weather, which affects the dignity of a man's corpse greatly. The summer, being a cool one, has not much altered the pace of decomposing so much as the rats. But by and by, even the rats lose their stomach as the tallow in a man's body stiffens and swells and sticks to his bones after the skin has become softened and quite rotted away, so that he doth almost resemble a body consumed in a fire, except that he be white instead of black."

"So then," prompted Newton, "by your expert reckoning, what is your estimate of this one?"

"Why, your honour, six months, I reckon. No more, no less."

Newton nodded and handed each man the shilling he had promised, and me my chaw of tobacco.

"Have you chawed before, Mister Ellis?" he enquired.

"No sir," I replied, although I might well have added that it was about the only bad habit I had not picked up when I was studying for the Law. "Not even for the toothache."

"Then have a care to spit often, for it's not well known that tobacco contains an oily liquid called nicotiana which is a deadly poison, and that all men who chaw are merely experimenting with its toxic effect. But it may be that your stomach shall be churned whether you chaw or no."

So saying, Newton went into the cellar and I followed him to find Osborne lighting the candles to illuminate the scene.

"Thank you, Mister Osborne, that will be all for the present."

But for the stench, the corpse seemed hardly human at all, more like some ancient Greek or Roman marble statue, in a poor condition of repair, that now lay on its side upon an oak table. The face was quite unidentifiable, except for the expression of pain that still clung to what remained of the features. That it was a man was clear enough, but in all else I could have said nothing about him.

"What can you observe about that knot?" asked Newton, looking at the rope which bound the corpse's feet together.

"Very little," said I. "It looks common enough."

Newton grunted and took off his coat, which he handed to me; then he rolled up his sleeves, so that I saw how his forearms were much scarred; but also how he was fascinated by this cadaver, and what it seemed to represent, for while he cut away what remained of the dead man's clothing with Mister Osborne's knife, he told me what he was doing.

"Make sure you observe nature's obvious laws and processes," he said. "Nothing, Mister Ellis, can be changed from what it is without putrefaction. Observe how nature's operations exist between things of different dispositions. Her first action is to blend and confound elements into a putrefied chaos. Then are they fitted for new generation or nourishment. All things are generable. Any body can be transformed into another, of whatever kind, and all the intermediate degrees of quality can be induced in it. These principles are fundamental to alchemy."

It was as well he told me what it was to which he referred, as I had possessed not the remotest idea. "You are an alchemist, sir?" I said, holding the candle closer to the body.

"I am," he said, removing the last shred of clothing from the corpse. "The scars on my arms that you noticed when I rolled up my sleeves are burns from more than twenty years of using a furnace and a crucible for my chemical experiments."

This surprised me, for the law against multipliers—as were called those alchemists who tried to make gold and silver—had not been revoked until 1689, but seven years before, until when, multiplying had been a felony and therefore, a capital offence. I was somewhat troubled that such a man as he should have admitted his former felony with so much ease; but even more so that he appeared to believe such arrant quackery.

Newton began to examine the cadaver's teeth, like a man who intended to buy a horse. "You seem a little disconcerted, Ellis," said he. "If you intend to vomit, then please do it outside. The room smells quite bad enough as it is."

"No sir, I am quite well," I said, although my chaw was beginning to lighten my head a little. "But are not many alchemists in league with the devil?"

Newton spat a stream of tobacco juice onto the cellar floor as if he hoped my opinion might be lying there.

"It is true," he said, "that there have been many who have tried to corrupt the noble wisdom of the magi. But that is not to say that there be no true magicians." He paused and, averting his face from close proximity to the corpse for a moment, drew a deep breath before coming close to the open mouth of the skull; then stepping back he breathed out again, and said, "This man lacks the molars in his upper left jaw."

"What is a molar?" I enquired.

"Why, the back grinding teeth, of course. From the Latin *molaris,* meaning a millstone. I have also observed that the second and third fingers of his left hand are missing."

"There's a great deal that is missing from this poor fellow," I offered. "Ears, nose, eyes . . ."

"Your powers of observation commend you, Mister Ellis; however, both amputations have occurred in precisely the same location, that being the tip of each finger. It is very singular to this individual. As is the *modus mortis*. For the condition of the chest is most extraordinary. The ribcage has been quite crushed, as if he was broken by some great compression. And do you see the strange position of the legs? The lower legs pressed onto the thighs, and the thighs up toward the belly?"

"Indeed it is curious," I admitted. "Almost as if he had been rolled up into a ball."

"Just so," Newton murmured grimly.

"Do you think it is possible— No, it will only vex you, Doctor."

"Speak, man," he exhorted me.

"It was merely an hypothesis," said I.

"You will allow me to be the judge of that. It may be that you will have confused it with an observation. Either way, I should like to hear what you have to say."

"I wondered if this be not another poor victim of the Mighty Giant. Indeed, I heard one of the warders utter the same thought."

This Mighty Giant was a most notorious and as yet undiscovered murderer who was much feared, having killed several men by crushing their bodies horribly.

"That remains to be demonstrated," said Newton. "But from what I have read of his previous victims, the Mighty Giant—if there be such a man, which I doubt—has never thought before to dispose of a body, nor indeed to bind the feet with rope."

"Why do you doubt he exists?" I asked.

"For the simple reason that giants are so few and far between," said Newton, continuing to inspect the body. "By their very definition they stand out from the crowd. A man who has killed as often as the Mighty Giant must then be rather more anonymous. Mark my words, Mister Ellis, when that particular murderer is apprehended, he will be no more a giant than you or I.

"But what is here undeniable is that this man was killed with great cruelty. It is as plain as the truth of alchemy here demonstrated."

"I do not understand," I admitted. "How is that truth of alchemy to be demonstrated from a corpse, master?"

"To be explicit, the living body is a microcosmos. Having lived out its span of life, permeated by heat and air, it comes back through water to final dissolution in earth, in the never-ending cycle of life and death."

"There's a merry thought," I said. "I wonder who he was."

"Oh, there's no wonder about it," said Newton, and grinning at me now, he did add, "This is your predecessor. This is George Macey."

Before leaving the cellar, Newton bade me say nothing of this to anyone for fear that the information should further delay the recoinage in the Mint.

"There is enough silly superstition among the moneyers already," he declared. "This would only confound them further and put them in greater fear, for they are the most damnably credulous men I ever saw. If the identity of this poor fellow were generally known, all reason would cease at once. And this place should grind to a halt."

I agreed to say nothing of what he had told me; nevertheless I was somewhat disturbed by the alacrity with which my master lied to Mister Osborne and the other Tower warders, when we were outside the cellar again.

"I owe you an apology, Mister Osborne. Alas, the fellow is much too decomposed to say anything about him, except that it was not the Mighty Giant who killed him."

"But how can you tell, Doctor?"

"I have paid some attention to the reported details of these particular murders. In all cases, the victim's arms were broken. But it was not so with our anonymous friend from the moat. This man's injuries were exclusively to the torso. If he had been held in the embrace of this Mighty Giant, as is already rumoured, I should have expected broken arms as well as ribs. You may box him now, if you wish."

"Thank you Doctor."

"I think, Ellis," said Newton, spitting the remains of his chaw on the ground, "that you and I need a drink, to take away the taste of this damned tobacco and, perhaps, to settle our stomachs."

It was only as we started back along Water Lane toward the Stone Kitchen, which was the name of the tavern in the Tower, that the implications of Newton's lying began to impinge upon my Christian conscience.

"Sir, you are quite sure it was George Macey?" said I, as we started back along Water Lane. "I could barely determine that it was a human male, let alone have identified the poor fellow."

"There can be no doubt about it. I met him but once or twice; however, it did not elude my notice that Mister Macey lacked several teeth on his upper jaw. But, more importantly, the upper joints of his second and third fingers were missing from his left hand. It is an injury most peculiar to this Tower, and more precisely this Mint."

"It is?"

"Perhaps, when you have become better acquainted with the practice of coining, you will recognise that the moneyer who feeds the coining press with blanks must be mighty nimble-fingered. There can be hardly one of them who has not lost one or more finger joints. Prior to his clerkship, Macey was himself a moneyer. These observations, added to the dredger's expert opinion as to how long the body had been in the water, and the finding of two new-minted shillings on the victim's person, such as the ones I myself gave the two dredgers, must equal the conclusion I have described. Even though the coins had been a long time in the water, the milled edges were quite unmistakable."

"Why, then, sir, if it is George Macey—."

"You may rest assured of it."

"Then what of his eternal rest in Christ? Does he not deserve a good Christian burial? What of his family? Perhaps they would wish a stone to remember him by? To say nothing of this matter would surely be wrong."

"I can't see that it matters very much to him, can you?" He smiled, as if vaguely amused by my outburst. "I believe there was a whore in Lambeth Marsh he liked to visit. But I shouldn't think she would want to pay for a funeral. And as for his rest in Christ, well, that would all depend on whether or not Macey was a Christian, would it not?"

"Surely there can be no doubt of that," said I. "Did he not, as I did, lay his hand upon the Bible and swear the oath of secrecy?"

"Oh, he may have done. Not that that proves anything, mind. After all, most of the Bible was written by men who had no knowledge of Jesus Christ. No, the plain fact of the matter is that Macey was no more a Christian than was the prophet Noah. I told you that I only met Macey once or twice. But on each occasion I discoursed with him long enough to learn the true nature of his religious views. He was of the Arian persuasion, which is to say that he believed that Jesus Christ and our

Lord God are not of one substance, and that there was no human soul in our Saviour. Therefore he would hardly have wanted a Christian burial, with all its attendant idiosyncrasies."

"But that is heresy," said I. "Isn't it?"

"Indeed, many would say so," murmured Newton. "But you should concern yourself more with why Macey was killed and where, than with the fate of his immortal soul. For it is plain that he was murdered in the Tower, and by people from the Ordnance who were in a great hurry to be rid of his body."

"Why do you say that?" I asked.

"For the present I would merely ask you to recall the knot that was tied around poor Macey's feet. Common enough, you thought. But in reality, much more singular. It is made by twisting two parts of rope in opposite directions, forming two side-by-side eyes through which the base of a hook may be passed so that a sling or weight may be hung from the hook. The knot, called a cat's paw, is used to attach a rope to a hook and is quite versatile, but I have seldom seen it used outside of this Tower. I have other reasons, also, for believing the Ordnance was involved, which we will investigate as soon as we have wet our whistles."

The Stone Kitchen was a miniature Babylon of vice and iniquity which did not lack its own scarlet woman, for the wife of the landlord was a whore that could persuade the Minters and warders that went there to do more than just drink away their pay. She, or one of her female friends, was not infrequently to be seen taking some fellow into a dark corner of the inmost ward for a threepenny upright; and once I even saw this bawd plying her wares behind the Chapel of St. Peter ad Vincula. Indeed I am certain of it, for I confess that I myself did, once or twice, go with her; and others. In truth there were many places in the Tower where a jade from The Stone Kitchen might fetch a man off for a few coppers; and it was just one of several reasons why my master seldom ventured through the tavern's door, for he also abhorred drunkenness and the fights that excessive drinking sometimes occasioned between Minters and the Ordnance. I, on the other hand, often frequented the place when my master was back in Jermyn Street, for it was certain that The Stone Kitchen was the cosiest place in the Tower, with a great hearth and an enormous skillet that usually contained an excellent stew, because for all her lewd ways and probable distempers—during the summer her cunny parts smelt as frowzy as a Scotsman's dog—the landlady was an excellent cook.

As we came through the door Newton surveyed the occupants of the tavern with Jeremiah's disapproving eye, which earned us the greeting of a low murmuring groan and a lesser consort of cat-calls; and perhaps it need be stated again that Newton lacked a facility with ordinary people, so that there were times when he resembled old Mister Prig.

We sat down near the fire, for it was cold outside, and warmed our hands and feet; and having ordered two mugs of hot buttered ale, we looked about the tavern at the Minters who had finished their shifts, and the warders who had come off duty. For myself I nodded at some of the faces I recognised: a surveyor of the meltings; an engraver; a moneyer; and the Tower barber. I even nodded at Mister Twistleton who, wild-haired and white-faced, sat meekly pressed between Yeoman Warder Bull and Sergeant Rohan, and looked like nothing so much as the pages of a book bound with a robust leather cover; he smiled back at me and then continued to study a paper with which he seemed to be much diverted.

And of course I smiled at the landlady who brought our buttered ales, and caressed me with a most venereal eye, although she was kind enough not to speak to me with any great familiarity in the presence of my master, which would have caused me some embarrassment.

Newton regarded all of these with the suspicion of a
Witchfinder-General, and sitting amidst those brawny boozers
of the Mint and the Ordnance, whose conduct was a scandal to
sobriety and whose faces contained much roguery, I swear he
fancied each tankard a coiner's cool accomplice.

We drank our ale and kept our own counsel until Jonathan
Ambrose, a goldsmith contracted to the Mint as a melter and
refiner, and already much distrusted by Newton on account of
how his cousin had been hanged as a highwayman, approached
us with a show of contempt and proceeded to subject my master to a most insulting speech.

"Doctor Newton, sir," he said, almost sick with intemper-
ance. "I declare, you are not much loved in this place. Indeed, I
believe you are the most unpopular man in this Tower."

"Sit down, Mister Ambrose," yelled Sergeant Rohan. "And
mind your tongue."

Newton remained seated and ignored Ambrose, seemingly
unperturbed; but, sensing some trouble, I got up from our bench
to interpose my body between the goldsmith and my master.

"God's whores, it's true, I say," insisted Ambrose. He was a
tall fellow with a manner of speech that made me think he spoke
side-saddle, for his mouth was all to one side of his nose when
he was talking.

"Sit down," I told Ambrose and gently pushed him away.

"Pox on't, no," snarled Ambrose, his mouth a slavering
diagonal of distaste. "Why should I?"

"Because you are drunk, Mister Ambrose," said I, moving
him still further away, for he had begun to point most belliger-
ently at Newton, as if his forefinger had been a javelin. "And you
are most importunate."

"Have a care, Doctor," said Ambrose, craning his neck
across my shoulder. "People die in this Tower."

"I think we've had enough out of you, Jonathan Ambrose," declared the landlord.

It was now that Ambrose aimed a blow at my head. It was easily ducked, but I had a mind to pay him back for his insolence and, aiming at his ear, struck him in the mouth with my fist. I was not much of a man for bare knuckles, but the blow knocked Mister Ambrose off his feet and onto the table in front of Mister Twistleton, which earned me a cheer from the men in The Stone Kitchen, as if we had been in the Bear Garden in Southwark. And while the landlord set about the simplified task of ejecting Ambrose from the tavern, I helped Mister Twistleton to collect his paper from the floor, although this was naught but the jumbled-up alphabets of a child.

"Perhaps," said Newton, rising to his feet, "we had better be going, too."

"Sorry about that, gentlemen," said our landlord. "He's barred from this moment hence."

"I think," replied Newton, "that if every sober man in the Tower should be called to account for the nonsense he speaks in his drink, then you should soon have no customers, Mister Allott. So let's have no talk of barring anyone, and think no more of this business. Here's five shillings to buy a drink for all that's in here."

"Very generous of you, sir."

And with that, we took our leave of The Stone Kitchen.

When we were outside again, there was no sign of Mister Ambrose, and Newton let out a breath and smiled at me.

"You are a useful fellow to have around, Ellis," he said. "I can see I made the right choice. You are quite a Hector."

"It was nothing," I said, following him along Water Lane. "The fellow needed a dry basting. I was glad to do it. He threatened you, sir."

"No, no," insisted Newton. "He warned me. That is something very different."

Instead of proceeding to the Mint, we walked along the south wall of the White Tower, in what was the inmost and oldest ward of the Tower, to the Coldharbour Building and the museum which was there. Inside this place was a splendid collection of mounted armour-clad figures that purported to show the line of Kings upon the throne of England; and a gallery that displayed various instruments of torture and execution. It was these cruel machines and implements that Newton wished to look at now.

I had not seen the rack before, however I had, of course, heard stories of its use, and shuddered as I looked upon it, finding it only too easy to think of myself bound to the two opposite windlasses like some hapless victim of the Holy Inquisition—for it was stated on a nearby placard that all of these instruments had been captured from the wreck of a Spanish Armada ship and had been intended to help in the work of reconverting the people of England to Roman Catholicism.

"God bless Sir Francis Drake," I murmured. "Or else this rack should have made us all Papists by now."

On hearing this, Newton laughed. "I hold no candle for Roman Catholics," he said. "But, mark my words, Rome can teach Englishmen nothing about cruelty."

"But is the rack not still used in Spain?" I replied.

"It may be so," admitted Newton. "And would explain why so little science emanates from that country. God knows how many great scientific minds were stunted when Galileo, the greatest mind of the century, was tried for heresy. However, it is not the rack that we have come to see, but this much more portable instrument of torture which, if I am right, was used about six months ago, on poor George Macey."

Newton pointed at a curious metal implement that was as

tall as a man and shaped like a keyhole, with manacle holes for a man's head, hands and feet. Newton leaned forward to blow away only a light covering of dust from the object, which action he repeated upon the beam of the rack, thereby setting up a veritable cloud of grime.

"Observe, if you will, how much less dusty this instrument of torture is than the rack."

Now, from his pocket, Newton produced a magnifying glass that he did sometimes use to read, with which he proceeded to examine the black metal surface of the machine most closely.

"But what is it?" I asked. "I cannot fathom the mechanism."

"This is the Scavenger's Daughter, also known as Skeffington's Gyves, or shackles, and invented by a former Lord Lieutenant of this Tower. The Scavenger's operation is, in all respects, the very opposite action to the rack; for while that draws apart a man's joints, this, on the contrary, binds a man into a ball, the human body being almost broken by the compression. This torture was more dreadful and more complete than the rack, so that in some extreme cases the box of a man's chest was burst and death resulted soon thereafter. Also, it is much more portable than the rack since it may be fetched to a prisoner, rather than the other way around."

"And you believe this is how poor Mister Macey met his end?"

"His injuries are certainly consistent with it having been used," he said. "Yes."

Newton was still in possession of Mister Osborne's knife and used this to scrape something off the manacles onto a piece of paper which he showed to me. "If I am not mistaken, this is dried blood. But we shall examine it under a microscope later on."

"You have a microscope? I have never seen through a microscope," I admitted.

"Then you are to be envied. For the first sight of natural phenomena under the microscope is always most breathtaking."

"If you are right," said I, "and this is blood, then George Macey must have been privy to information that others wished desperately to know, or else they should not have tortured him so cruelly."

"Mint workers are always in possession of some secrets," said Newton, "although I hazard that there's not one of them, Macey included, who wouldn't give up what he knows for a few guineas. No, it is more tempting to conclude that Macey was tortured for information he did not possess, otherwise the excruciating pain of this device would surely have persuaded him to talk much earlier on, and certainly before receiving any mortal injuries."

"That's a terrible thought," I said sickly. "To be tortured for information you had would be bad enough. But how much worse it would be with nothing to betray."

"Your instinct for self-preservation does you a dubious credit," said Newton, and, folding away the paper with the suspected dried blood, he offered me a wintry smile. "It persuades me that I need not utter another salutary to remain silent about this matter. Whoever killed George Macey would doubtless slit our throats as easily as other men would slice a cucumber.

"Come, let's away from here, lest some should see us and feel disquiet at our proximity to this machine."

Leaving the Storehouse, Newton declared his wish to visit my house and use his microscope which, he said, would assist our further enquiry. But outside the door to the Warden's house we found Mister Kennedy, who was another of the Mint's informers, and two gentlemen I did not recognise.

Mister Kennedy was a most forbidding-looking fellow, having a false nose made of silver to cover the gaping holes of the nostrils of the one that was lost: from an accident in the mill room, he said; but there were, I knew, plenty who speculated that the real accident had been received in the cunny parts of a whore. This feature, however, lent Mister Kennedy a villainous aspect that enabled him to mix with some of the worst rogues in London. He, having received a shilling from one of the two gentlemen for having brought them to Newton, now withdrew, leaving them to introduce themselves. It was the taller, older and less modish of the pair who did the talking:

"Sir," he said, bowing gracefully, "this is indeed an honour. Permit me to introduce myself. My name is Christopher Love. Perhaps you have read my work on the chemical teachings that are being done in the University of Leyden?"

"I regret I have not had that pleasure," Newton said gruffly, for he hated being sought out by new disciples while he was about the business of the Mint.

"No matter," said Doctor Love. "This is the Count Gaetano, from Italy, who is a most adept and notable philosopher in his own country, and has done great work in the secret art."

The Count, attired in powdered silk and wearing the largest feather I had ever seen on a man's hat, contrasted sharply with the scholarly black of his companion, whom I judged to be in the fiftieth year of his age. He bowed with more panache than an Irish actor and then spoke most haltingly to my master, in an accent that was as thick as the braid upon his sleeves.

"Sir, I should be greatly honoured if you would be my guest for dinner. At your convenience, sir. Very much."

"I am not insensible of the honour you do me, Count," answered Newton. "However, I accept very few invitations."

"The Count appreciates you are a busy man," said Doctor Love.

"Very much."

"Nevertheless he feels he has something which would be of very great scientific interest to you."

"Very much."

And so saying, Doctor Love removed from a square of velvet a gold ounce, which he presented to Newton.

"Before my very own eyes," explained Doctor Love, "the Count used a tincture of his own discovery to convert what had been a miserable piece of lead into this golden ingot."

Newton examined the gold with a show of deep feeling.

"I took it at once to a goldsmith," continued Doctor Love, "who declared it to be the purest gold he had ever seen."

"Indeed," said Newton, weighing the gold piece in the palm of his hand and all the while looking greatly affected.

"Who could be better than yourself, Doctor Newton, Warden of the Royal Mint and England's greatest scientist, to put this gold to the test? And if you were convinced that it was real, we considered that you might care to witness the Count's process of transmutation for yourself."

"Very much," said Newton; and the assignation of a definite time for this demonstration having been made, the two alchemists were persuaded to take their leave of us, and we were at last allowed to go inside the house, whereupon Newton handed me the gold piece.

"It certainly looks and feels like real gold," said I. "I think should like to see a real transmutation. If such a thing is possible."

"We have other business before us now." And, finding his microscope, Newton placed the instrument on the table by the window, and a mirror and a candle next to it to better illuminate the specimen.

"See if you cannot find Mister Leeuwenhoek's book," he told me, placing the scraping from the Scavenger on a slide. "Or Hooke's *Micrographia*."

But I could not find either book.

"No matter," said Newton, and, producing a pin from his lapel, pricked his own thumb so that a small ruby of blood did ooze out. This he pressed onto another slide, compared the two, and then invited me to look myself.

Gradually I was able to distinguish a dim but magnified image that Newton assured me was his own blood. It was one of the most remarkable things I had ever seen. The blood from Newton's thumb seemed to be almost alive.

"Why, sir, it is composed of thousands of small objects," I said. "But only some of them are red. And these do flow in a liquid that is almost transparent. It is like looking closely into a pond on a bright summer's day."

Newton nodded. "These minute portions are called cells. And it is believed that these are the ultimate elements in all living matter."

"I did not think it possible that a man might be reduced to something so small. Looking at it so close, human life seems somehow less miraculous. As if we ourselves might not add up to much more than what floats in the village pool."

Newton laughed. "I think we are a little more complicated than that," he said. "But pray tell me what is your opinion of the sample we took from the Scavenger?"

"It is without doubt the same, sir. And yet it does not move. It is as if the life that animates the pond has departed."

"Quite so."

"It is blood, then," said I. "What shall we do?"

"Do? Why, nothing at all. I will at my leisure think of this some more and see what might go to explain it. Until then, put this matter from your mind lest these discoveries of ours, weighing on your thoughts, shall spill off your tongue."

Two or three nights afterwards—Newton having tested the sample of gold himself, and confirmed him in his first opinion, which was that the ounce of gold was genuine—I accompanied him to Doctor Love's house in Soho, where Count Gaetano received the news about his sample with modest smiles and humble shrugs, almost as if he expected his demonstration was a foregone conclusion and that Newton was already congratulating him on his transmutation. Doctor Love had laid on a splendid dinner, but before we could partake of a mouthful of it, Newton, already bored with the conversation of these two philosophers, looked at his watch and declared that he was anxious to proceed with the transmutation.

"What say you, Count?" asked Doctor Love. "Are you ready?"

"Very much."

We accompanied Doctor Love and the Count to a workshop at the back of the house where the furnace was already heated so that the shop felt like an oven. At this point Newton opened a bag he had brought with him that now revealed a crucible.

"To avoid all imposition," he explained, "I have brought along a crucible, some charcoal and some quicksilver with which I am certain no gold has been mixed. I was sure you would agree that it is always important to approach all hermetic matters with as much scientific rigour as possible."

Count Gaetano smiled broadly. "Very much," he repeated, and, taking these items from Newton, set about his transmutation.

"While you work, Count," said Newton, "perhaps you will favour me with some particulars about your preparation of the Mastery?"

"I'm afraid that must remain a secret for now, sir," said the Count.

"Of course. How long will the work take?"

"No more than several minutes," replied Doctor Love. "The process is remarkable."

"Indeed it must be," observed Newton. "For every sage I have ever read testifies that several months are required to effect a transmutation."

"Several months to learn the secret of the Magistery," the Count said firmly. "But once the great secret is known, the work is simplicity itself. Now, sir, if you will stand over there."

"I confess I am fascinated," said Newton, moving away from a metal close-stool that stood in the corner.

The Count placed about half an ounce of lead into Newton's crucible and heated it on the furnace; and presently, the lead having liquefied, he cast his tincture upon it and we saw the lead duly enveloped.

"Gentlemen," said the Count, "please to stand back a little and cover your eyes, for there will be a great flash of light and perhaps you will be blinded a little."

We stood back from the crucible. For several minutes nothing happened, so that finally I was tempted to look through my fingers, at which point there was a blinding flash and a strong smell of cinnamon, and, as the Count had predicted, I was blinded by a green spot in front of my eyes for several minutes. But when my sight was recovered and I inspected the crucible once more, I saw to my astonishment that the whole mass had been converted into what looked to be the finest gold.

"I should not have believed it if I had not seen it with my own eyes," said I.

"That much is certain," said Newton.

The Count poured the molten gold into an ingot, and, it having cooled sufficiently, he set the ingot in water and then polished it up for our inspection.

Newton placed the small ingot in the pan of a balance to determine the weight, and smiled. He handed me the ingot, and while I stared in wonder at the miracle I had seen, he inspected the crucible from which it had been poured.

"My doubts are removed," he said firmly. "Sir, you are a rascal. I thought it proper to remove my doubts about your demonstration by marking the lip of the crucible I gave you. That mark having now disappeared—"

"It was the heat of the fire that consumed it, surely," protested Doctor Love.

"The mark was most indelible, being a fine groove I chiselled in the stone of my own crucible this very afternoon. I am certain that this crucible containing the gold was substituted for the one I marked and which contained the lead. As soon as the Count advised us to cover our eyes, I was suspicious. He waited just long enough before curiosity overtook us and we peeped to see what had happened. At that moment he threw some phosphorus into the crucible, which blinded us long enough for him to make the substitution. I smelt the fault, however, for phosphorus is most offensive to the nostrils; but it can be rendered less offensive by first dissolving it in oil of cinnamon."

"Sir," said the Count, gesturing most innocently with his hands. "You are very much mistaken."

"Am I?" said Newton and, catching hold of the Count's wrist, quickly inspected his fingers' ends, which were most painfully blistered, before the Count snatched away his hand with what looked like a mighty show of guilt. "My late friend Mister Boyle once had occasion to demonstrate phosphorus to me. I seem to recall that his own hands were similarly blistered from handling phosphorus with his bare hands. But I will freely admit I am mistaken if a search of this laboratory finds no evidence of fraud."

The Count, who was still all innocence, silently invited Newton's scrutiny. My master hardly hesitated and, advancing swiftly across the laboratory, lifted up the lid of the close-stool in the corner to reveal the second crucible containing the melted lead and bearing Newton's mark.

"How ever did you know that it was there?" I asked, amazed.

"Before beginning his demonstration, the Count asked me to move away from its proximity, for fear that I should perhaps hear him open it. Moreover, this commodious Ajax is made not of wood, but entirely of metal, which struck me as curious, until now."

"But what about these two mountebanks?" I asked. "How are we to proceed against them?"

"Sadly, no crime has been committed here," said Newton. "However, you two gentlemen would be well advised not to repeat your fraudulent demonstrations in London. For then I should be under compunction to denounce you to all men of learning."

The Count smiled thinly and narrowed his eyes so that I began to perceive how he was less of a bombast and more of a desperado than I had earlier supposed.

"And you, sir, would do well to stay out of my way," he said quietly. "For if you called me a liar in front of other gentlemen of quality, I should not have very much hesitation in challenging you, Doctor."

Doctor Love was no less threatening than his rascally Italian friend. "In Italy," he said, "the Count is a most notorious swordsman and has killed three men in affairs of honour."

"Come, Ellis," said Newton. "I think we must be leaving now. We have seen all that we needed to see." And with that we left, for which I was very glad, since the atmosphere in that laboratory had grown doubly hazardous.

"What a pair of charlatans," muttered Newton, when we were outside again. "That they should have thought they could trick me."

I told my master that I did not think the Count looked like a man lightly to be thwarted. "You must be more cautious,

Doctor," I said. "I think we were lucky to get out of there without a fight."

"This world is full of rogues," said Newton. "Forget him. He'll not trouble us again."

Taking pity on my still empty stomach, Newton invited me to his house, in Jermyn Street, which was but a walk away from Soho. And I have mentioned this matter only because it was on this night that I met Miss Barton, which was as near to a genuine transmutation as I ever beheld, for after I met her, my feelings were become gold and it seemed to me that, by comparison, all fondnesses I had felt for other girls were as dull as lead.

"My niece, Miss Barton, who has come to live with me, will welcome the company," he explained while we walked down from Soho toward Piccadilly. "She is the daughter of my half sister, Hannah, who was married to a Northamptonshire cleric, the Reverend Robert Barton. But he died, some three years ago, and left little money for his three children; I have taken upon myself the cost of their upbringing. I have told her I am a dull stick, but she wishes to see London; and besides, Northampton, the nearest town to where she lives, is a dull place, much destroyed by the fire of 1675, and the society there not fit for a girl of Catherine's intelligence. Or loveliness. I am told by Lord Montagu, who has met her, that she is a great beauty. But I will also value your opinion, Ellis, for I believe you to know more about women than almost anything else."

"Why, sir, have you never met her yourself?"

"Of course I have. But I confess I understand little of that quality in a body and its mechanical action upon another human mind and its senses."

"A man might think you were describing not a girl but a problem of geometry, sir," I said, laughing. "I don't think beauty is to be apprehended as a matter of mathematics."

"That," said Newton, reaching his front door, "is only your opinion."

The young woman to whom I was now introduced was perhaps eighteen or nineteen, and it was hard to perceive in her any great similarity to her uncle, which was perhaps not so surprising given that her mother was only Newton's half sister. She was pretty, of that there could be no dissent; but in truth, during the first few minutes of our acquaintance, I considered her not altogether so great a beauty as milord Montagu had opined. And it took me several marvellous minutes to understand how it was that beauty rests on more than just a pretty face; there was also the matter of her very obvious intelligence to be take into account. For her excellent mind—most other ladies I had met were much more obviously shy and retiring than Newton's precocious niece—caused Miss Barton's lovely features to be much animated with thought, and being added to her prettiness, the effect of each was doubled, so that her great beauty was my inevitable impression. So great a beauty that by and by I found I was very pleased with her and soon found myself too much minding her. By her conversation she was clever and witty beyond her bigness and age and exceedingly well bred as to her deportment, having been a scholar at the local school in Brigstock these nine or ten year.

After we had eaten supper, she said, "My uncle tells me that, prior to entering his service, you were training to become a lawyer, Mister Ellis."

"Yes, that was my expectation, Miss Barton."

"But that you fought a duel which obliged you to leave off your studies."

"Yes, that is true, I did, although I am near ashamed to mention it to you, Miss Barton."

"Nonsense," she railed. "I never met anyone who fought a duel. You are my first duellist, Mister Ellis. But I confess I have met dozens of lawyers. Northamptonshire is quite riddled with them. Is that the sword with which you fought?"

I looked down at the hilt of my sword. "Yes, it is."

"I should like to see it. If I asked you nicely, would you show it to me?"

I looked at her uncle.

"I have no objection," he said.

No sooner had he spoken thus, than I had drawn my sword and, kneeling before her, presented it to Miss Barton upon the sleeve of my coat. "Have a care, miss, it's very sharp."

"I did not think you looked like the kind of man to carry a blunt sword, Mister Ellis." She took hold of the hilt, raised my sword, and fenced the air for a moment or two. "And did you kill him?"

"If I had, I would not be standing here now," I said. "I merely pricked him, in the pap."

Miss Barton inspected the point of my blade in the firelight. "To think that this has drawn a man's blood," she breathed; and then: "I should like to learn to fence."

"With your uncle's permission, Miss Barton, I should be happy to instruct you."

"No," he said flatly. "It is out of the question. Child, what would your mother say?"

She shrugged, as if what her mother said was of no import, and then handed me back my sword. "No matter," she said. "I didn't come to London to have gentlemen prick me with their rapiers."

"Not for the world," said I.

"Indeed, no," echoed Newton.

"Pray tell, what was your quarrel about, Mister Ellis?" she enquired.

"With whom?"

"Why, the gentleman you fought a duel with, of course."

"A matter of such little import that I would blush to tell you, Miss Barton."

"If I defeated you in a duel, would you tell me then?"

"I should have little choice but to do so. Even so, I should only whisper it, for fear of earning your uncle's scorn."

"Then we shall duel, you and I. Will you challenge me?"

"Willingly, if it will amuse you; yes, I challenge you. Which gives you choice of weapons."

"Then I choose drafts."

"Be careful, Mister Ellis," advised Newton. "She does not lack for skill."

To play drafts with Miss Barton was to understand how much she took after her uncle—whom I had often played at the Tower—for if I gave either of them first move, they were sure to beat me wholly, which, at the hand of Miss Barton, I did not much mind, her being so childishly pleased by winning. After our first game, she demanded her forfeit.

"Come now, pay up. The explanation why you duelled, Mister Ellis."

I was pleased to have lost, for it gave me the opportunity to whisper in her exquisite ear, which was as close to her sweet-smelling neck as I could have wished to be, short of kissing it.

Hearing it she laughed out loud, and then insisted we play again; and I confess I had never in my life been quite so happy to lose five games of drafts in a row.

My master took to inviting me for supper, once a week, saying that he pitied any man such as I who was obliged to cook for himself, but I think that he saw that Miss Barton and I enjoyed each other's company, which left him time to read, or to work upon a mathematical problem; I even went to communion with them on Christmas Day. And, by the Twelfth Day of Christmas, this pretty young woman occupied my first thought in the morning and my last thought at night, and I regarded her most fondly.

However, I said nothing to this effect, at least not yet, thinking that my loving this beautiful girl should be to the discontent of her uncle, my master. And indeed I endeavoured mightily to put her out of my mind and not to love her at all except that she offered several provocations to my doing so, such as giving me a book of her favourite poems she had copied out in her own hand, and nicknaming me Tom because she said I reminded her of a cat of that name she had once owned, which was most pleasingly familiar; and once, presenting me with a lock of her hair which I kept in a little box by my bed. So that very soon thereafter she was in my head a thousand times each day.

And for the first time in a long time I was happy. For love is mostly optimism.

I never knew as wise a man as Newton. And yet he was as ignorant of the female sex as Achilles. Perhaps, had he had more knowledge of the world and girls, he might have governed her behaviour in a way that would not have left me encouraged as much as I was. And things might have turned out very differently between Miss Barton and myself.

Sometimes it is not so easy to distinguish where love ends and lunacy begins; and I fancy there are a great many Bedlamites who are love's loyal yeomanry.

Chapter Two

Michael Maier, *Viatorium*, 1618

Then Jesus said unto them, Yet a little while is the light with you. Walk while you have the light, lest darkness come upon you: for he that walketh in darkness knoweth not where he goeth.

(John 12:35)

*J*anuary 1697 was an exceedingly cold month, as cold as I could ever recall and, my master assured me, the coldest he could remember since 1683, when he had stayed indoors and written his *Universal Arithmetick*—his most elementary work. I tried to read it, but did not succeed. Perhaps the cold slowed my intellectual parts, just as it slowed the production of new coin. For the money was still scarce, despite the very best endeavours of the moneyers, and although everyone talked of a peace with France, nothing came of it. And all the time more Jacobites were arrested, so that the country did seem mighty unstable. Meanwhile, James Hoare, the Comptroller of the Mint who had died, was replaced by Thomas Molyneux and Charles Mason, who my master said were both corrupt, and in truth they did soon feud with each other and prove to be ineffectual.

I have mentioned how Newton's spy, Humphrey Hall, brought us information that some coiners were rumoured to have perfected a new process in application to the gold guinea coin; and it was this business that caused us to be involved in the next part of my story which Newton swiftly came to call his dark matter. Mister Hall's discourse had greatly disturbed my master, a guinea being a much more serious thing to forge than a silver crown, or a shilling, and yet we lacked the evidence of a counterfeit coin. But on the night of Saturday the thirteenth of February, this shortcoming remedied itself.

I was early to bed and asleep when I woke to find Mister Hall in my bedchamber with a candle in his hand.

"What is it, Mister Hall?" I asked, rather alarmed to find him there because, for all the fact that he was most reliable, Mister Hall was also rather stern of countenance and old and quiet, so that he stood at the foot of my bed like Charon waiting to ferry my spirit over the marsh of Acheron. Charon's price was one obol, but it was a guinea that Mister Hall wanted to talk about.

"I believe we have found what we are looking for, Mister Ellis," he said in his stagnant, muddy voice. "The head keeper at Newgate has heard that a prisoner, whose name is John Berningham, has been boasting of having paid for his garnish with a false guinea."

Garnish was what the keepers called the bribes they extracted from prisoners awaiting trial, for their better treatment; and this they paid for with rhino, or quidds, both of which meant ready money, or cash: since joining Newton's service I had been obliged to learn a whole dictionary of criminal cant, or else I should never have understood the very depositions I wrote down; and there were times when Newton and I found ourselves speaking to each other like a couple of convicts.

"I thought we ought to go and investigate it now," added Mister Hall, "for fear that the man will be released, or that we shall lose the guinea."

"Of course," I said. "I'll come with you."

So I made myself ready presently, and straightaway Mister Hall and myself walked to Newgate with much ado, the ways being so full of ice and water by people's tramping of the recent snow.

From a distance, Newgate looked well enough, being recently restored after the Great Fire, with a handsome pilastered exterior which, when inspected closely, would have yielded the explanation as to why it was also called the Whit, for, upon the base of one pilaster, sits a carving of Dick Whittington's cat. And yet the Whit did not easily forgive such close inspection. Those foolish enough to linger in the gateway risked being pissed upon or struck with a chamber pot pitched from the upper windows and, approaching the entrance, I, out of habit, so much scrutinised these same windows that I watched not where I was going and put my foot in a great heap of dog turds, which mightily amused those wretches at the begging grate on Newgate Street who otherwise cried out for alms. I never passed these disembodied hands that reached through the grate without thinking of the gates of the infernal city of Dis, in Dante's *Inferno,* where howling figures threatened Virgil and the Pilgrim from the walls and, for all that I bridled under the laughter of these wretched men and women, yet I pitied them also, for, truly, Newgate is a habitation of misery and quite the worst place in London.

Inside was yet more pandemonium, there being a great many dogs and cats, poultry and pigs, to say nothing of the roaches and rats that there abound, so that the smell of animals and their excrements being added to the reek of ale and strong water that were brewed there, as well as the smoke of fires and the cold and the damp, can make a man's head ache for want of good air.

There were four quarters to Newgate: the Condemned Hold in the cellars; the Press Yard; the Master's Side; and the Keeper's Lodge, where ale and tobacco were sold and where we met Mister Fell, the head keeper. Fell was a knavish-looking fellow, with a badly pox-marked face and a nose that resembled a small potato gone to seed, sprouting several greenish hairs from his nostrils.

"Gentlemen, gentlemen," he said, grinning boozily. "Will you have some comfort? Some mum, perhaps?"

We had some of his mum, for the comfort in his strong water smelled none too palatable, and we drank each other's health with more optimism than was warranted in that foul place.

"'Tis a great pleasure," Mister Fell said to me, "to be the messenger of important information to a gentleman such as yourself, sir, who is the friend of Doctor Newton, who does so much to keep us all in work." He laughed unpleasantly, and added, "I shall not keep you in suspense. Except to say that you must excuse me if my first enquiry relates to the squeamish matter of compensation, for nobody can help the frailty of poverty, sir."

His poverty I doubted, for I knew that, as head keeper, Fell could make at least several hundred pounds a year in garnish. But I humoured him for the want of his information.

"If your information be good, I'll warrant you'll be well rewarded by my master."

Fell delved into his pockets, scratched his arse for a moment, and then retrieved a gold guinea which he polished briefly on his filthy coat and then laid down upon the table.

"But if my guinea be not good?" he said. "What then? Will it be replaced by a proper yellow boy?"

"You have my word upon it, sir," I replied, and scrutinised the coin most carefully. "But what makes you think it is bad? Faith, sir, it bears my own examination well enough, although, in truth, I'm not as well acquainted with golden guineas as I should care to be."

I handed the coin to Mister Hall, who bit the coin hard with no discernible damage. "Aye, sir," he said. "It looks and tastes all right."

"Why, sir," said Mister Fell, "to look at and to chew upon, it passes well enough, don't it? But then answer me this: Why would a man say a guinea was not real if it were indeed a true coin?"

"You make a good point, Mister Fell," I said. "Pray tell me more of this man you mention."

"Yesterday evening there was a fight at The Cock, in Threadneedle Street. Mister Berningham bought his chop at a butcher's shop in Finch Lane and, as was his wont, took it to The Cock to be cooked, but eating it liked it no more than if it had not been cooked at all, and quarrelled with the landlord; and, drawing upon him, ran him through the belly with his sword, whereupon he was arrested and brought here.

"He paid fifteen shillings for four weeks food, lodging, and strong waters, for I told him it would likely be that long afore his case came before the court. And five shillings in advance for his wife to come and visit him. He said she would come on Sunday afternoon. But later on, in his cups, he boasted to a prisoner named Ross, who keeps his ears sharp for me, that the yellow boy he had presented was counterfeit. Which put me in mind of Doctor Newton and yourself, sir, you two gentlemen being so very diligent in the enquiry of such felonies, sir."

"You did right, Mister Fell," said Mister Hall.

"Indeed, sir," said I. "And we are obliged to you for your trouble. With your permission I should like to borrow this guinea to show to Doctor Newton. It shall be returned unless, if it proves to be counterfeit, it will certainly be replaced. And if your information leads to the arrest and conviction of its man-ufacturer, I daresay you will be rewarded as well."

Mister Fell nodded slowly. "You may borrow it, sir. And I am very glad to have been of assistance to you."

"Shall you require a receipt, Mister Fell?"

"No need of that, sir," he grinned. "I have a fixed confidence in you and the Doctor, sir, as men of honour. Besides, we have two witnesses here that it's my guinea what you are borrowing."

"Did Mister Berningham say when his wife would visit on Sunday?"

"He did, sir. At around five o'clock, and that I should keep an eye our for her, as she was a lady, and not used to the Whit."

"I'm obliged to you, Mister Fell."

When at last I got home and to bed again I had a very restless night of it being too excited to sleep soundly, for the next day being St. Valentine's Day, I was now possessed of the perfect excuse to be at my master's house in the morning. It being the custom for a woman to take as her valentine and kiss the first person she saw, naturally I hoped to see Miss Barton in advance of any other and so become her valentine.

I rose from my bed at five o'clock since it was also Sunday and I decided I must arrive in Jermyn Street before eight o'clock as, very soon after that, Miss Barton would likely accompany her uncle to St. James's Church. Finding myself lousy I washed myself with cold water and found in my head and my body above a dozen lice, little and great, which I did not wonder at after my visit to Newgate. Being the Lord's Day there were no boats to carry me down to Westminster, nor any hackneys, although I should not have taken one, the fare being one and sixpence, and I was obliged to walk from the Tower to Piccadilly, which is a good distance, and took me almost two hours.

Upon arriving in Jermyn Street, I presented myself at my master's door and knocked, but Mrs. Rogers, the housekeeper, would not open the door until I answered whether I was a man or woman.

"It is I, Christopher Ellis," said I.

"Wait there, sir," Mrs. Rogers told me.

And by and by the door was opened by Miss Barton herself. "I am mighty relieved it is you, dear Tom," she said, using my pet name. "Quite careless of such important matters, my uncle has invited the Dean of St. James's Church for dinner, and

I do not think I would have wanted him as my valentine. He has breath like a stews, and I should have had a sermon and no embrace."

"Then it is well that I came," I said, and stepping into the parlour, Miss Barton let me kiss her, being the first time this had happened. This kiss was the most chaste I had had in many a year, and yet it did give me more pleasure than any other I had ever received; and which made Newton laugh out loud, something that I had not seen before that day.

That being done, to Miss Barton's no less evident pleasure, upon our mirth subsiding, Mrs. Rogers fetched me some bread, a piece of hot salt beef and a tankard of hot buttered ale, and, much refreshed by my breakfast, I acquainted my master with the other reason for my attending him so early in the morning.

"And here was I thinking you had walked all the way here from the Tower solely on my account," she said, affecting some disappointment. "Christopher Ellis, I do believe you have no more romance in your body than my uncle."

But Newton expressed great satisfaction at the story of the golden guinea and, upon examining the coin, declared that we should, by experiment, test it in a crucible as soon as possible.

"But before then I should be grateful if you would escort Miss Barton and Mrs. Rogers to Church, this morning," he said. "For it will require the work of a whole morning in my laboratory for me to build the heat up in the furnace."

"I should be delighted, sir, if Miss Barton is not too disappointed in me."

She said nothing.

"Or perhaps," continued Newton, now addressing his niece, "you had hoped to have the Dean all to yourself over dinner. For I was going to ask Mister Ellis to stay and dine with us."

Miss Barton closed her eyes for several moments, and then

opening them again, she did give me her sweetest, most engaging smile.

And so I escorted Miss Barton and Mrs. Rogers to St. James's Church, which gave me great pleasure, although it was the first time I had been in church a month of Sundays, and I had to endure a most tedious sermon of the Dean about Jacob wrestling with an Angel of the Lord, which was only made easier to bear by the content I found in having such a handsome girl as Miss Barton to look upon, and have squeeze my hand once or twice during the prayers.

After church we returned to Newton's house and, leaving Miss Barton and Mrs. Rogers in the kitchen for a while, I sought my master out in his laboratory which was in a basement cellar with a window that gave onto a small back garden. This laboratory was well furnished with chymical materials such as bodies, receivers, heads, several crucibles and a furnace that was by now as hot as the lowest part of hell and which made my master sweat mightily.

At the sound of my footsteps he glanced around and waved me toward him with a cry of satisfaction. "Ah, Mister Ellis," he shouted over the roar of his furnace. "You are just in time to see my own freakish trial of the pyx," he said, placing Mister Fell's guinea in a heated crucible. The trial of the pyx was the ancient ordeal by which the purity of gold and silver in the new-minted coin was tested by a jury of the Company of Goldsmiths.

"To my way of thinking, a man's trying to turn lead into gold is as absurd as expecting bread and wine to become the body and blood of Jesus Christ. It is what they represent that should inspire us. Nature is not merely chemical and physical, but also intellectual. And we should accept the spirit of enquiry that is implicit in this *opus alchemyicum* you see before you now, as another man might accept the *opus divinum* of the mass. Both are journeys toward understanding. We are all seekers after truth. But not all of us are vouchsafed the grace of faith that provides all the answers. Some of us must find those answers for ourselves. For some the answer in the darkness is the light of the Holy Spirit; while for others the discovery is in the fact that hidden in Nature's darkness lies another light. To this intellectually illuminating end my whole life has been dedicated.

"Now let us see what has become of this guinea."

Newton fell to inspecting the contents of his crucible while I thought about what he had said. What his meaning might be, I was not completely able to penetrate into at the time, but later on I saw that he aimed at something beyond the reach of human art and industry.

"Look there," he said and, holding the crucible with a pair of tongs, showed me the melted metal.

"Is it counterfeit?" I asked. "I cannot tell. Even now it looks to me like real spanks."

"You see, but you do not observe. Look more closely. There is not one but four, possibly even five, metals present here: I know not yet what they may be, but I've a strong fancy this coin is mostly copper. Which brings us much trouble, for I have never seen such an ingenious facsimile, not these past nine months. If there be many more like it besides . . ." Newton left off speaking and shook his head gravely, as if the prospect was too terrible to countenance.

"But how was it done, master? Do you think this is the same process that Humphrey Hall spoke of?"

"I do indeed," said Newton. "The process was devised in France, during the last century. I am not privy to understanding all the secrets thereof, but the key is thought to be, as in many, mercury. In truth, no one knows more about mercury than me. About three years ago, I almost poisoned myself through breathing the vapours of mercury—although this effect is not well known. Mercury demands respect. It is not something that may be used with much safety, and this will assist our investigations, for there are many outward signs of mercury's abuse."

"What are we to do?"

"What would you have me do?"

"I should question John Berningham about this false guinea. We may perhaps persuade him to make a clean breast of it."

"That will take a while," said Newton. "So very often one such as he will lie and keep on lying until he feels Jack Ketch breathing down his neck. It would be better to know much more of this matter before we questioned him. You say that he paid to have his wife visit him?"

"Yes sir. An ounce of silver for the privilege, in advance."

"Then she may be the key that will open the door." Newton looked up. "But I hear that the Dean has arrived, and I must play the host."

Putting on our coats, we went back upstairs for dinner. The Dean was a more congenial dining companion than he was a preacher, and kept Newton occupied with divers matters of theology while Miss Barton and I made eyes at each other. And once or twice she did even rub my shin with her stockinged foot, while all the time discussing the Dean's sermon, which made me think she was more wicked than I had ever suspected.

After dinner Newton stood up from the table and announced that he and I had Mint business to attend to, and, reluctantly, I took my leave of Miss Barton.

"Are we going to the Mint?" I asked, when we were outside the house in Jermyn Street.

"Did not Mister Fell, the keeper at Newgate, say that Mister Berningham's wife would visit him at five of the clock?"

"He did. I confess I had quite forgotten that."

Newton smiled thinly. "Evidently your mind has been much preoccupied with other, frivolous matters. Now then, if I may have your full attention, sir. You and I will repair to Newgate and while I question Scotch Robin and John Hunter—it may be that they were not the only two rogues employed by the Mint who could have stolen a golden guinea die—you shall keep vigilant for this Mrs. Berningham; and seeing her, follow her, for doubtless her husband will have kept his place of lodging secret."

We made our way to Newgate, where my master, being recognised from one of the upper storey windows, and much hated among the prisoners for his great diligence, was obliged to dodge a bole of shit that was thrown at him, and with such adroitness that I did perceive how, for all his fifty-four years, he was a most athletic man when the occasion demanded it. Entering at the gate, he made light of the ordure bole, saying that it was as well that it had been an apple that fell on this head and not a turd, otherwise he should never have thought of his theory of universal gravitation, for he would have had nothing in his head but shit.

Berningham was in quod on the Master's Side, which consisted of thirteen wards, each as big as a chapel, and here I loitered on a wooden bench outside the door that held Berningham, like any common cull or warder. While there I was solicited by two or three of the whores that plied their trade in the prison; and sometimes by one of the children who lived there—a small, almost toothless boy that offered to sell me a newspaper that was several days old, and to fetch me some "washing and lodging," which was another name the occupants of that terrible place did have for gin. Finally I took pity on the lad and gave him a halfpenny for his enterprise, which was at least more bearable than that of the jades who offered me a threepenny upright in some quiet corner of the Whit. All of this I bore until the cull I had garnished with another coin tipped me the wink that a most handsome-looking woman—although she wore a vizard—whom he admitted to her husband's ward, was the lady in question. To keep her observed was no great skill, for over her grey moiré suit she wore a thickly wadded cloak of bright red cloth that made her stand out like a cardinal in a Quaker church.

Mrs. Berningham stayed with her husband for more than an hour, after which, and hiding her face again, she left the ward and returned to the main gate, with me skulking after her as if I were some Italian in a tragedy of revenge. By and by we both found ourselves out of the Whit again, whither she walked south down Old Bailey, and again I followed her, whereupon, to my surprise, I found my master fall into step beside me, for he was an even better skulker than might be supposed of one who had become so famous.

"Is that Mrs. Berningham?" he asked.

"The same," I replied. "But what of Scotch Robin and John Hunter? Did you question them?"

"I left them both with much food for thought," said Newton. "I said that as ever I hope to see heaven I would make certain each of them would meet the cheat before Wednesday if they did not tell me who might have stolen a die. I shall return tomorrow for an answer. For I have always thought that if a man does but reflect upon the prospect of hanging for one night, it greatly loosens his tongue."

Mrs. Berningham remained very visible in her red hooded cloak, although it was become quite dark and mighty cold besides, which made us glad to hurry after her as she turned east onto Ludgate Hill, for we had no wish to let her out of our sight. But then, turning the corner ourselves, we saw that Mrs. Berningham was surrounded by three ruffians carrying cudgels in their hands, and who seemed to speak very roughly to her, so that I feared they intended to do her some harm. And I shouted at the fellow to desist. At this the villain who was the largest and most ruffianly aspected of the three advanced on me brandishing his cudgel most menacingly.

"I can see that you need a little mortifying, gentlemen," he growled, "to help you to remember to mind your business."

I drew the two German double-barrelled Wender pistols I kept about my person whenever I went to the Whit, cocked my piece, and then fired above his head, thinking that this would put him off. But when he continued to advance it was plain to me that the fellow had been fired upon before, and so I was obliged to shoot again, only this time with more aim and, upon his cry and dropping off his cudgel, I was sure that my ball had struck him in the shoulder. Cocking my other piece, I fired twice at one of the others who came on after their comrade, but missed him altogether, for he was moving quickly, and seeing this villain, similarly undeterred, seem as if he meant to have at my master with a plug bayonet, I had at him with my rapier and pinked him on the thigh, which caused him to yelp like a dog and leave off soon enough. Whereupon the three withdrew in various stages of disorder and I even thought to give chase until I saw that my master was lying on the ground.

"Doctor Newton," I cried, kneeling down beside him with great anxiety, and thinking him to have been run through with that bayonet after all. "Are you all right?"

"Yes, thanks to you," said Newton. "I slipped on the cobbles when that debauched rogue tried to stab me. Look to the lady, I am quite well."

I found Mrs. Berningham not much agitated and very pretty besides, her vizard having fallen off during the quarter; but seeing me with my sword still drawn, she seemed to realise what danger she must have been in and suddenly looked fit to swoon so that I was obliged to gather her up in my arms and, with my master leading the way, carry her back up Old Bailey, and place her in the little chariot that was waiting upon us at a short remove from the Whit.

"Pray, madam, tell us where you live so that we may convey you home with safety," said Newton.

Mrs. Berningham dabbed at her lightly powdered cheeks and nose with a *mouchoir* and said, "I am much indebted to you two gentlemen, for I honestly believe those ruffians meant to do more than merely rob me. I live on Milk Street, off Cheapside, close by the Guildhall."

She was a handsome, red-haired woman, with green eyes and good teeth and a dress that showed the tops of her bubbies most fetchingly, which made me feel most amorous toward her. But for Newton's presence in the coach I think she might have let me kiss her, for she smiled at me and held my hand to her bubbies several times.

Newton instructed his coachman to drive to the address, which took us east along Newgate Street, this being a more direct route to Milk Street than the way she had earlier taken on foot.

"But why did you not come this way before, madam?" Newton asked suspiciously. "Instead of going down Old Bailey and onto Ludgate Hill. You were most conspicuous to us, from the minute you left the Whit."

"You saw me leave the Whit?" Mrs. Berningham glanced out of the window as a cloud cleared from the sky, and in the suddenly moonshine light, I did think she coloured a little.

"Ay, Mrs. Berningham," said Newton.

Hearing her name, for she had not mentioned it herself, Mrs. Berningham dropped my hand, and stiffened visibly.

"Who are you?"

"Never mind that for now," said Newton. "When you left the Whit, where were you going?"

"If you know my name, then you'll know why I was at the Whit," she said, "and why I should want to pray for my husband. I went down Old Bailey intending to go to St. Martin's Church."

"And did you also pray for your husband before visiting him?"

"Why, yes. How did you know? Did you follow me there, too?"

"No, madam. But I'll warrant your attackers did. For it was clear they were waiting for you. Did you recognise them?"

"No sir."

"But I fancy one of them said something to you, did he not?"

"No sir, I think you are mistaken. Or else I do not remember."

"Madam," Newton said coldly, "I never misrepresent matter of fact. And there is nothing I dislike more than contention. I am right sorry for your trouble, but let me speak plainly with you. Your husband stands accused of the gravest crimes, for which he might easily forfeit his life."

"But how can this be? I am reliably informed that the landlord whom John stabbed will soon recover. Surely, sir, you exaggerate the gravity of this matter."

"What? Do you persist in fencing with us, Mrs. Berningham? The stabbing is a mere bagatelle, of no interest to me or my friend here. We are officials of His Majesty's Mint, and of graver import is the matter of a counterfeit guinea coin which your husband knowingly passed off as genuine, and for which he will surely hang unless I am disposed to intervene on his behalf. Therefore I beseech you, for his sake, and for yours, to tell us everything you know of this false guinea. And, that being done to my satisfaction, to prevail upon your husband to have like to do the same."

Mrs. Berningham sighed most profoundly and handled her fur tippet as if, like a Catholic rosary, it might afford her some spiritual guidance in forming her resolution. "What must I do?" she whispered, quite distracted. "What? What?"

"All that is possible to do for your husband, Doctor Newton's influence may effect," I told her, and gently took her hand in mine. "It would be vain to suppose there are any other ways of helping him now. You must unburden yourself of all you know of this matter, madam."

"It's not much that I know, except that John has been a fool."

"Unquestionably. But tell us about your assailants," said Newton. "What words were spoken?"

"He said that if John should peach, then I should get worse than the beating was coming to me now. That the next time they would kill me."

"And that was all he said?"

"Yes sir."

"But you knew what it was to which he referred?"

"Yes sir."

"Then it's plain you did recognise them after all."

"Yes sir. My husband was sometimes in their company, but he told me not their names."

"Where was this?"

"At a mum house in Leadenhall Street," she said. "The Fleece. Or sometimes they were at The Sun."

"I know both of those places," said I.

"But in truth," she continued, "they were ruffians and he paid them little heed. There were others with whom he seemed better acquainted. Gentlemen from the Exchange, or so I thought them."

"The Royal Exchange?"

"That was my own apprehension, but now I am not so sure. John was to use false guineas to pay some merchants, which I was much against, thinking he would be caught. But when he showed me the guineas I could not conceive of anyone thinking them to be anything other than genuine, which, I am ashamed to confess, made me quite leave off my objections. Indeed, sir, I am still at a loss to know how the ridge was culled, since it was my husband's practice to mix good and bad coin."

"He is not much of a dissembler, this husband of yours. In his gin cups Mister Berningham boasted that the ridge with which his garnish had been paid was false."

Mrs. Berningham sighed and shook her head. "He never did have a head for strong waters."

"These other men you thought were from the Exchange. What were their names?"

Mrs. Berningham was silent for a moment as she tried to remember. "John told me, only . . ." She shook her head. "Perhaps I will remember tomorrow."

"Mrs. Berningham," Newton said crossly, "you say much, but you tell us very little of consequence."

"It has been," she sighed, "a most vexatious evening."

"'Tis true," I said in her defence. "Look here, the lady is encrusted with distress."

"In time, Mister Ellis, you will learn that the licence of invention some people take is most egregious indeed. For all we do know, this woman is as culpable as her husband."

Whereupon Mrs. Berningham appeared mightily grieved and began to cry, which only served to make Newton more impatient, for he did tut and look up at the ceiling of the coach and moan as one with the stomach-ache and then yell out to the coachman to make haste or else he would go mad. And all the while I held Mrs. Berningham's hand and tried to comfort her so that finally she once again composed herself sufficient to comprehend what Newton next had to say to her.

"The man we are looking for, madam," he said carefully. "The man who did forge the guinea which your husband was foolish enough to pass off. He is very likely French. He is perhaps a man with teeth *à la Chinoise,* which is to say that they are black and quite rotten and, had he ever spoken with you, his breath would have seemed most foul. Perhaps you would also have noticed his hands, which might have trembled like a milk pudding, and to which you may even have attributed his great thirst for ale or beer, but never wine, for the man I am looking for drinks not for enjoyment but from necessity, wanting moisture as much as doth the parched ground in summer."

To my surprise, for I had never heard this description before Newton gave it utterance, Mrs. Berningham started to nod, even before my master had finished speaking.

"But, Doctor Newton," she exclaimed. "Surely you have met my husband."

"I have not yet had that pleasure," said Newton.

Mrs. Berningham looked at me. "Then you must have described him to the Doctor."

"No, madam," said I.

"Then how do you seem to describe him so well? For 'tis true, he has not been well of late."

"It is no matter for now," said Newton.

Newton's coach drew up at Mrs. Berningham's address in Milk Street and we set her down, whereupon my master cautioned her to return to the Whit only in daylight when her safety might be better assured.

"But how did you know Berningham's appearance?" I asked, when she had gone up to the door of her house. "A man you have never seen nor heard of before. And yet Mrs. Berningham recognised him from your description."

And upon my asking, Newton smiled a quiet little smile so that I thought how he seemed rather pleased with himself. "'He giveth wisdom unto the wise and knowledge to them that know understanding. He revealeth the deep and secret things: he knoweth what is in the darkness and the light dwelleth with him.' The Book of Daniel, chapter two, verses twenty-one to twenty-two."

I confess that I was a little piqued at Newton's enigmatic resort to the scriptures, for it seemed to confirm in my mind that he enjoyed confounding me, which made me feel and no doubt look mighty ill-humoured, so that my master patted my knee, like a spaniel methought, although his speech was full of much warmth and good intent toward me.

"Oh come, sir, this will not do. I would know if I am to improve myself."

"Rest assured, my dear young friend, that you who have saved my life shall know my complete confidence. The description was furnished easily enough. Whoever forged that guinea has had a prolonged acquaintance with mercury, which produces in a man all the ill effects that were described: the blackened teeth, the tremulous hands, the great thirst. I might also have mentioned the unsoundness of mind. These effects are not generally known. I only discovered them myself as a result of a great distemper with which I was afflicted during the year of 1693, when I almost lost my mind through much experimentation in my laboratory.

"All of which leads me to suppose that the lady tells us much less than she knows."

"How is that?"

"She told us that her husband was merely passing off the bad coin as good, when the substance of the matter is that he did forge them himself. Berningham is almost certainly the man who has perfected the *d'orure moulu* process for making fake gold. But it may be that she still hopes to save him from the gallows, although I have always thought that hanging and marriage go very much together as a fate."

Newton instructed his coachman to drive to the Tower and from thence back to Jermyn Street.

"I have a favour to ask of you: that Miss Barton shall be told nothing of tonight's adventure. She is a sensitive child, prey to all sorts of imaginings, and it would greatly inconvenience me if every time I went abroad, she were to detain me with questions regarding the safety of my person. My duties on behalf of the Mint are the only matters on which I am happy for my niece to remain in complete ignorance."

"Depend upon it, sir. I shall be the very model of discretion where that young lady is concerned."

Newton bowed his head to me.

"But," I said, "since I now dare to enjoy your complete confidence, sir, I would take advantage of that to remind you of a matter in which my own continuing ignorance is an affront to me. I would ask if you have had any further thoughts regarding the death of George Macey, of whose murder you bade me to remain silent. And, if you have, I would be grateful if you would share them with me, for I do confess that my own predecessor's death still much occupies my thoughts."

"You do well to remind me of it," said Newton. "But I have not lacked for diligence in obtaining more information.

"Macey was, by several accounts, a most diligent man, but not an educated one, although he does seem to have made an attempt at improving himself. None of this amounted to very much, however, and it seems that Macey often had recourse to consult the mind of a man I suspect was one of Macey's informers, a goldsmith by the name of St. Leger Scroope. Oddly it is a name that I seem to be familiar with, although I have been unable to fathom why. And since Mister Scroope was to have been out of the country until about this time, I confess I have not pursued the matter any further, and therefore your reminder is most opportune. We shall try and visit Mister Scroope tomorrow, at his place of business in the Strand. It may be that he can shed some further light on a letter written in a foreign language that was rumoured to have come into Macey's possession, about which, according to Mister Alingham, the Tower carpenter who was a friend of his, Macey was much exercised to comprehend."

Out of the coach window I saw the familiar castellated outline of the Tower appear in the moonshine like King Priam's city bathed in the glow of Zeus's silvery eye. The coach pulled up at the Middle Tower, close by the Barbican wherein the lions restlessly groaned, and set me down upon the esplanade. Before closing the door behind me, Newton leaned out into the cold and feral-smelling night, for the wild beasts below did much pollute the air with their excrements, to speak to me one last word before I took my leave of him.

"Meet me outside the water tower at York Buildings tomorrow morning at nine o'clock, when we shall call upon Mister Scroope. And after that we may visit this Berningham fellow at the Whit."

Then Newton rapped on the roof of the coach with his stick and the little red chariot was rattling away to the west, along Thames Street.

I turned and approached the guard near the Byward Tower, who was well away from his post, and for a moment I stopped to talk with him, for it was always my habit to try to improve relations between the Mint and the Ordnance. We spoke of how to keep warm on duty, and which Tower was the most haunted, since I never walked about the Tower at night without being afeared to see some spirit or apparition. For shame I could not help it; and yet to speak in my own defence, so many dreadful things had happened there that if anywhere be haunted it might be the Tower. The guard believed that the Jewel Tower, also known as the Martin Tower, was a place of many ghostly legends. But we were soon joined in this conversation by Sergeant Rohan, who knew the Tower as well as any man.

"Every quarter has its own ghostly legends," opined Sergeant Rohan, who was a great burly figure of a man, almost as wide as he was tall. "But no part is so scrupulously avoided as the Salt Tower, which, it is said, is much disturbed by spirits. As you know yourself, Mister Twistleton, the Armourer, saw a ghost there, which is what lost him his wits. I myself have heard and felt things there I know not how to explain, except to say that their origin be malign and supernatural. Many Jesuit priests were tortured there, in the lower dungeon. You may see the Latin inscriptions carved upon the wall by the hand of one."

"What happened to him?" I asked.

"He was taken to York in 1595," said Rohan, "where he was burned alive."

"Poor fellow," said I.

Rohan laughed. "Think you so? He was a very fanatical sort of Roman Catholic. Doubtless he would have done the same to many a poor Protestant."

"Perhaps so," I admitted. "But it is a very poor sort of philosophical argument that we should do unto others before they do unto us."

"I doubt there are many philosophers who could know what a needful capacity for cruelty most Roman Catholics have," insisted the Sergeant. "Dreadful things were done to the Protestants in France during the *dragonnades* of 1681 and 1685, when King Lewis's soldiers were quartered in the homes of Huguenots and allowed full licence to behave as cruelly as they wished in order that many might make converts to Rome. Believe me, lad, there were no conceivable cruelties which these brutal missionaries did not use to force people to mass and to swear never to abandon the Roman religion. Old men imprisoned, women raped and whipped, young men sentenced to the galleys, and old mothers burned alive."

"You speak as if you witnessed these cruelties yourself, Sergeant," I observed.

"Twenty years I've been at war with the French," said the Sergeant. "I know what they are capable of."

After a few minutes spent debating this issue with Rohan, who was most obstinate in his hatred of Jesuits, I wished Sergeant Rohan and Mister Grain good night and left the Byward with a borrowed lantern, which did little to allay the apprehension of seeing a ghost that our talk had increased in me.

Walking quickly home to the warden's house, I thought much about those Jesuits who had been tortured, perhaps with the same Skeffington's Gyves that had been used on George Macey. It was easy to imagine some tormented priest haunting the Tower. But reaching home and being warm in bed, with a good candle in the grate, I began to think again that ghosts were idle fancies and that it was probably better to be afeared of those living men who had murdered my predecessor and who were still at liberty to kill again.

The next morning, I took a wherry boat from London Bridge to York Building stairs. Upon alighting, I and others found the mud on the jetty quite frozen over, which was so hazardous to our company that I thought fit to complain to the watermen that the steps should have been salted and kept free of ice so that passengers might step off a boat without threat to life or limb. At this the watermen, who were weatherbeaten, strong-looking men, merely laughed, and, sore from the previous evening—for I still had the apprehension that I had been the butt of the Ordnance's joke—I started to draw my sword; but then I saw my master standing by the water tower and thought better of pricking their arses.

"You were right to contain your anger," he said, when at last I was safely on the embankment beside him, "for there's not a more independent lot of men in London. They are generally temperate, for a drunken waterman would hardly be trusted, and yet they can be most violent. If you had drawn your sword you would very likely have found yourself in the river. A seven-year apprenticeship makes a poor man most obdurate in defence of his rights and knowledgeable of his proper duties, which, alas, do not include the cleaning of the jetties. For the Thames, being a tidal river, would make a mockery of anyone that swept these walkways free of mud. High tide was but one hour before you landed."

Bridling under my master's lecture, I said that I had no idea he knew so much about London watermen and the tides that affected their trade.

At this he smiled thinly. "About watermen I know only what most people know about all London workmen: that they are a blight. But about tides I know a great deal," he said. "You see, it was I who first explained them."

And as we took a short coach ride up to the Maypole in the Strand, Newton proceeded to tell me how by propositions mathematically demonstrated he had deduced the motions of planets, the comets, the Moon, and the sea.

"So it is the gravitational effect of the Moon that makes the tides?" I said, summing up his own much longer account of this celestial phenomenon. Newton nodded. "And you received all this from the fall of an apple?"

"In truth, it was a fig," he said. "But I cannot abide the taste of figs, whereas I am most fond of apples. I have never been able to tolerate the idea that it was the fruit I despise most in the world that gave me my idea of how the world moves. And it was only the germ of my idea. I remember thinking that if the power of gravity could extend to the top of a tree, how much farther might it extend? And indeed, I perceived that the only limit to its power was the size of the bodies themselves."

It was clear that Newton saw the world in a different way from everyone else; which made me feel mightily privileged that

I enjoyed such a great man's confidence. Perhaps I was beginning to understand a little of the excellence of his mind; but this was enough to appreciate that it was only my failure to grasp a little more of the actual theories themselves that stopped him and me from becoming friends. In truth, we were always separated by such a wide river of knowledge and ability that he was to me like a man must seem to an ape. In all respects he was a paragon, a human touchstone that might try gold, or good from bad.

The question of why the name of St. Leger Scroope had seemed familiar to my master was answered almost as soon as we arrived at his place of business, in a house at The Bell, near the Maypole. A servant answered the door to us by whose manner of dress—for he wore a small cap upon his head—I took to be a Jew; and having enquired our business, he nodded gravely, and then went to fetch his master.

Scroope himself was a tall man, at least six fingers higher than me, with a black periwig, a beard turned up in the Spanish manner, and fine clothes which were as rich as gold and silver could make them. I thought Scroope recognised my master immediately, although he waited until the Doctor had explained the purpose of his visit before giving expression to this knowledge.

"But do you not know me, Doctor Newton?" he asked, smiling strangely; and seeing Newton's eyes narrow as he struggled to find Scroope in his remembrances, the goldsmith's face took on a disappointed aspect.

"I confess, Mister Scroope, that you have the advantage of me, sir," stammered Newton.

"Why then, that it is a first for me, sir, for I never yet knew any man who could best you." Scroope bowed handsomely. "Pray, let me remind you, sir. I was your fellow commoner at Trinity College, Doctor Newton, assigned to your tuition, although I neither matriculated in the university, nor graduated from it."

"Yes," agreed Newton, smiling uncertainly. "I remember you now. But then you had not the beard, nor the wealth, I'll hazard."

"A man alters much in twenty-five years."

"Twenty-six, as I recall," said Newton. "Also that you were much neglected by me, although you were not unusual in that respect."

"Science will thank you for that neglect, sir. I was not a very diligent student, and events have proved that you were better employed with your opticks and your telescope. Not to mention your other chemical studies." At this Scroope smiled knowingly, as if my master's devotion to alchemy had not been such a great secret after all.

"You are very gracious, Mister Scroope."

"It is easy to be gracious to one whom all of England honours." Mister Scroope bowed once more, which made me think him a most obsequious fellow, better suited to fawning on a king than smithing gold. "But my conscience has its own particular mortification," added Scroope, whose civilities began to grow tiresome to me. "For I left no plate to the college, as was expected from a fellow commoner. Therefore, to assuage my embarrassment, sir, I should be grateful if you would accept some baubles on behalf of the college."

"Now?" asked Newton. Scroope nodded. "I should be honoured."

Scroope left us alone for a moment while he went to fetch his gift.

"This is most unexpected," said Newton, handling Scroope's walking stick with some interest.

"Is this one of the three students you ever had?" I asked, remembering what he had told me upon our first acquaintance.

"I am embarrassed to say that he is."

"Oh fie. I think Mister Scroope has more than enough embarrassment to cover both your consciences."

"I was a very dull fellow at Cambridge," admitted Newton. "Dull and most inhumane. But I am a better man since I came to London. This work in the Mint has broadened my horizon. And yet it is not as broad a horizon as perhaps that of Mister Scroope. I fancy he sometimes visits places where a man must be doubly vigilant."

"How do you mean, sir?" I asked.

"He wears a sword, like most gentlemen. And yet he has also been at some pains to conceal a sword inside this stick. Do you see?"

Newton showed me how the body of the stick ingeniously concealed a blade, two or three feet long, so that the handle of the stick was also the handle of a short but useful-looking rapier. I tried the blade against my thumb.

"He keeps it sharp enough," I said.

"You would not need to take such precautions unless you had some tangible danger to fear," he argued.

"Are not all goldsmiths subject to such dangers?" I suggested. "They have more to lose than just their lives. I wonder that you do not carry a sword yourself."

"Perhaps you are right," allowed Newton. "Perhaps I might carry a sword. But I do not think I shall ever need to carry two swords."

Mister Scroope returned to the room bearing four silver cups with a *repoussé* decoration which, with some pomp, he presented to Trinity College in the person of my master, who, despite his duties at the Mint, was still the Lucasian Professor of Mathematics at Cambridge University.

"These are very fine," said Newton, examining the cups with increasing pleasure. "Very fine indeed."

"I've had them down in my cellars for a number of years, and I think it's time they were properly appreciated. They are ancient Greek, recovered from a Spanish treasure ship. As well as a goldsmith, I have also been a projector of schemes with your own Mister Neale."

"Mister Neale who is the Master of the Mint?" asked Newton.

"The same. Several years ago we did recover a wreck, the *Nuestra Señora de la Concepción,* which carried much gold and silver. Those cups were but a small part of my share."

Newton continued to examine the cups with much interest.

"The cups purport to tell the story of Nectanebus, the last native King of Egypt, who was also a great magician. You may read of him in the history of Callisthenes."

"I shall do so at my earliest opportunity," said Newton, and then bowed gravely. "On behalf of Trinity College, you have my thanks."

Scroope nodded back, allowing himself a smile of some satisfaction, and then poured us some burnt wine from an equally fine silver jug that a servant fetched into the room where, the civilities completed, at last we sat down. The wine greatly warmed me for, despite the huge log that was burning on two brass firedogs that were as big as wolfhounds, I was still cold to the marrow from my river journey.

"And now, sir, pray tell me, what it is that brings you here?"

"It is my information that you had the acquaintance of Mister George Macey."

"Yes, of course. George. Has he returned?"

"Regrettably he is still not accounted for," said Newton, who neatly sidestepped the lie by this equivocating answer. "But, if I may ask, how was it that you and he were acquainted at all?"

"The wreck of which I spoke, that Mister Neale and I invested in, was brought to Deptford, where I and Mister Neale went to see the treasure brought ashore, and to take our shares. But this was not before Mister Neale, in his capacity as the Mint's Masterworker, had first removed the King's Share.

Mister Macey accompanied Mister Neale and assisted him in these official duties. This was several years ago, you understand.

"Not long afterward, a second expedition was promoted to search for the rest of the treasure that the first had been obliged to leave behind. Mister Neale invested, I did not, preferring to use the great sum I had made to establish myself in business as a gold and silver smith. I have no skills in working metals. I am no Benvenuto Cellini. I prefer to have others do that work for me. But there are significant profits to be made. And I have been very successful doing it."

"That much is evident," said Newton.

"That being said, the second expedition was not successful, and Mister Neale lost some money, for which he blamed me, in part. However Mister Macey and I remained friends."

At this point Mister Scroope glanced awkwardly at me, as if there was something else he should like to have said, which Newton's keen eyes quickly detected.

"You may speak freely in front of Mister Ellis," he said. "He has my total confidence and, as an officer of the Mint, has taken an oath of secrecy. My word upon it."

Scroope nodded. "Why then," he said, "to tell it plainly, upon occasion I was in the habit of passing certain information to Mister Macey. Doubtless you will appreciate how, in my business, one hears things about coiners and clippers and other dishonest fellows who undermine the Great Recoinage and, by extension, the prosperity of the realm."

"That is my greatest concern also," declared Newton. "Their Lordships at the Treasury have made it very plain to me that we may lose this war against France if we do not put a stop to this heinous practice of coining. That is why I am so diligent in these matters. It is given out by the general population that I do what I do to further my own preferment. But I tell you plain,

Mister Scroope, it is because I would not have this country defeated by France and ruled by a Roman Catholic."

Scroope nodded. "Well, sir, I should be glad to perform the same service for you, Doctor, as I did for Mister Macey, should you so desire. Indeed I should be honoured, for poor Macey and I became quite close confidants as a result."

"I am grateful to you, sir," said Newton. "But pray tell me, did Macey ever bring you a letter, written in a foreign language perhaps, that he asked you to translate for him? It is likely he would have been much exercised about its contents."

"Yes, I think there was such a letter," admitted Scroope. "And although this was six months ago, I have come to believe that both the time of this visit—which was to be the last time I saw him—and the content of the letter—which, although it was very short, I do remember but inexactly—were connected with his vanishing."

Scroope appeared to rack his brains for a moment, which made my master leave off prompting him for a closer account of the letter.

"The letter was not addressed to him. That much he told me. And it was written in French. I think it said something like 'Come at once or my life is forfeit.' Which seemed to interest him a great deal, for I have not yet told you that the letter was discovered by him in the Mint, and I believe George suspected that there was some great plot afoot there to disrupt the Great Recoinage. More than that he did not say. And I did not ask."

"But did you not think to come forward with this information?" asked Newton.

"For a long while after he disappeared, it was given out that Macey had stolen some guinea dies," said Scroope. "Therefore I had no wish to draw attention to myself by saying that George had been my friend. Nor could I say very much without revealing myself to have been an informer. My relationship with George Macey was based on many years of trust. But these two men I knew not at all."

"But you knew Mister Neale," said Newton. "Could you not have told the Master Worker himself?"

"Doctor Newton, if I may speak frankly with you, Mister Neale and myself are no longer friends. And in truth, I trust Mister Neale not at all. He has too many projections and schemes for one who occupies such a public office. He may have lost his enthusiasm for wrecks and colonies, but he has other, no less hazardous, schemes which may leave him compromised. It is my own information that he is much concerned with arrangements for another lottery using the duties on malt as collateral."

"That, sir, is my own information, also." Newton nodded wearily. "But I thank you for your candour."

"To be candid with one such as yourself, sir, is an honour. And affords me the expectation that we shall meet again, when, if I can, I shall be delighted to be of service."

Upon our leaving, Newton said something to Scroope's servant, in a language I did not understand, and for a moment the two men conversed in what I took to be Hebrew; and after this we took our leave of Mister Scroope, for which I was much relieved, thinking him a very pompous fellow.

"An interesting man, this St. Leger Scroope," said Newton when we were in the coach once more. "Very obviously a rich and successful man, and yet also a secretive one."

"Secretive? I don't know how you deduce that," I said. "He seemed a very preening sort of fellow to me."

"When we left, his velvet shoes were quite ruined with mud," said Newton. "Yet when we arrived they were noticeably clean, with new soles. Since the road in front of his premises is cobbled over, with no mud on it at all, I should suppose that he has a back yard, and that there was something out there that he was most concerned we should not see. Sufficiently concerned to ruin a pair of new velvet shoes."

"He might easily have got them muddy while fetching these silver tankards," I said, objecting to Newton's deduction.

"Really, Ellis, it's time you paid more attention to your own eyes and ears. He himself said that he fetched the tankards from his cellar. Even the cellars in the Tower are not as muddy as that."

"But I don't see what it proves."

"It proves nothing at all," said Newton. "Merely what I said: that for all his generosity and apparent outwardness to us, Mister Scroope is a man who carries two swords and has something to hide."

"Was that the Hebrew language you spoke?" I asked.

"It was Ladino," said Newton. "The man is a Spanish Marrano. The Marranos were Jews who managed to enter England under the guise of Protestants fleeing from persecution in Spain."

After which he told me, with much apparent satisfaction, of how well the Jews had done in England.

"Egad, sir," I said with some exasperation, for then I believed the Jews to have been Christ's murderers. "You speak of them in such terms that one might think you approved of them."

"The God we honour and worship is a Hebrew God," said Newton. "And the Jews are the fathers of our Church. We may learn much from a study of the Jewish religion. Therefore I say to you that not only do I approve of the Jews, I also admire and do honour unto them.

"When you entered my service, my dear Ellis, you asked that I should always correct your ignorance of something and to show you something of the world as I understand it. This hatred people have for the Jews is based on a lie. For it is my opinion that much of modern Christian doctrine is a lie; and that scriptures were corrupted by the opponents of Arius in the Council of Nicea, during the fourth century. It was they who advanced the false doctrine of Athanasius, that the Son is of the same body as the Father, even though that idea is not in scripture. Once this misconception has been disposed of, it may be seen how the Jews are no more to be despised."

"But, sir," I breathed, for fear that the coachman might overhear us, "you speak against the Holy Trinity and the divinity of Our Lord Jesus Christ. All this is heresy to our Church."

"To my mind it is the worship of Christ that is heretical. Jesus was merely the divine mediator between God and man, and to worship him is mere idolatry. Jesus became God's heir not because of his congenital divinity but because of his death, which earned him the right to be honoured. Just as we honour Moses, Elijah, Solomon, Daniel, and all the other Jewish prophets. Honoured, but nothing more than that."

Newton had an expert's knowledge of theology, and I knew he could have disputed doctrine with the Archbishop of Canterbury. And yet I was profoundly shocked to discover just what he believed, or, to put the case more correctly, what he did not believe. The beliefs of Galileo, heretical in the eyes of Rome, were as nothing compared with those of my master, for Newton's Arianism was, like Roman Catholicism, specifically excluded from the Toleration Act of 1689 that offered religious freedom to all faiths. Even a Jew enjoyed more religious freedom than an Arian.

My astonishment was tempered by the sense of trust that Newton had now put in me. For immediately I saw how Newton's enemies would have taken delight in the public exposure of his avowed heresy, which would also have destroyed his position in society. I could not imagine how an avowed heretic such as he might have been allowed to remain as the Lucasian

Professor at Trinity. At the very least he would have lost his place in the Mint. Possibly he might have suffered an even worse fate. It was only two years since a young man of just eighteen years had been hanged for denying the Holy Trinity in Scotland, despite his having recanted and done penance. Of course the Edinburgh clergy, like all the Scots, were the most bigoted opponents of anti-Trinitarianism. But even in England the penalties for dissenting opinions could be severe. Although heresy was not punishable at English Common Law, a man's blasphemous tongue could be branded with a hot iron, and his person whipped and pilloried. Therefore to be made the trustee of such a grave secret was confirmation indeed of the great faith Newton now placed in me. This pleased me greatly; but I confess I never foresaw how being exposed to Newton's heretical creed would begin to work upon my own Christian conscience.

From the Strand we returned to the Whit, where Newton explained that it was his intention to press Scotch Robin and John Hunter for information in the matter. When I asked why we did not simply question John Berningham, he explained that he still had hopes that Mrs. Berningham might yet work her uxorious way with her husband. Immediately we arrived at the Whit, Newton had Scotch Robin and John Hunter brought up from the Condemned Hold in the cellars to the Keeper's Lodge, one after the other. Scotch Robin was a mean, red-haired fellow with a scowling fist of a face and a wen on the side of his scurvy-looking neck as large as a plover's egg. To me he looked such an obvious jailbird the wonder was that he had ever been permitted to work in the Mint at all.

"Have you considered what I said to you last night?" Newton asked him.

"Aye, I have," said Scotch Robin, and nonchalantly draped his shackles across his shoulders so that his hands hung about his neck like one almost indifferent to his fate. "But I've asked about, and I reckon I've got a bit more time than you told me. It seems that Wednesday's not a hanging match."

"It's not a regular hanging day, that's true," admitted Newton, colouring a little. "But you would do well to remember that yours could hardly be called a regular hanging. Not with all the attendant barbarities that the law requires the executioner to inflict upon your body. Do not take me lightly, Robin. I am a Justice of the Peace in seven counties of England. I have sworn to uphold the Law, and I will do so in the very teeth of Hell. And I can assure you that it is well within my power to go before a judge this very afternoon and obtain a special warrant for your immediate execution."

"For the love of Christ," flinched Robin. "Have you no pity?"

"None for such as you."

"Then God help me."

"He will not."

"Is it you who says so?"

"He came not to Saul, who was a King and the Lord's anointed. Why should he come to a wretch like you? Come, sir," insisted Newton, "I grow weary of your prevarications. I did not come here to debate theology with you. You'll dance for me or in the Sheriff's picture frame with a rope about your neck."

Robin hung his head for a moment and at last uttered a name.

Then Newton was Draco himself with John Hunter, who said that he would only co-operate with my master's investigation on condition of a full pardon for all his past mistakes and the sum of twenty-five guineas to start a new life in the Americas.

"What?" sneered Newton. "Is it true? You still hope to profit from your crimes? Have you no shame? Am I bound to satisfy you, sir? Do you hear him, Mister Ellis? It seems he thinks it is not enough that I save him from a wry neck and wet pair of breeches. The Law trades not with ignorant vulgars such as you, sir. I shall only tell you that if you intend to save your life, you must be quick in informing, for I intend to lose no time. And when I am at last satisfied that you have done this, I shall petition the Lords Justices to deliver you from darkness. But hinder me, sir, and the day after tomorrow I shall deliver you to the hangman myself, my word upon it."

At which Hunter battered his own forehead with his chain darbies while all the air and bluster now seemed to go out of him. Then he smiled a wry smile and remarked that he had meant no harm.

"I don't like the black air of the cell," he said. "Forgive me, sir. I was only trying to find a Jacob, I mean a ladder out of there. Any man would have done the same. But it's a different kind of ladder I'd be mounting if I thwarted you, sir. I can see that now. And a darker kind of air at the top of it, I'll warrant. Therefore I'll peach. I'll help you nail the man you want. The man what is still in the Mint, who is as ready to steal guinea dies to order as a physician is to let blood."

Then Hunter named one Daniel Mercer, who was known to both Newton and myself as an engraver whom we thought to be an honest man. This was the same man whom Scotch Robin, who was himself an engraver, had named.

I read over the deposition I had taken and had Hunter sign it, as Scotch Robin had signed his, before having the cull return him to the Condemned Hold, for Newton still thought to extract yet more information from these two at some time in the future.

"Shall we obtain a warrant for Daniel Mercer's arrest?" I asked, when we were alone.

"By heaven, no," said Newton, fixing me with that eye of his: an eye that had stared into the eternal and the infinite. "We shall leave him at his liberty in the hope that we may observe this body's orbit, so to speak. We shall have him watched, by Mister Kennedy, and decide what his motion argues. The matter may receive greater light from hence than from any means that might be available to us while he was in this dark place. He may still draw us to the main intelligence behind this scheme, as salt of tartar draws water out of air."

We returned to the Tower where we left a note for Mister Kennedy, he that was Newton's best spy, and briefly walked about the Mint, now operating with more noise than a battle-field. We were not long there before Doctor Newton saw Master Worker Neale coming toward us, and remarked upon it as one who looked upon a Tory arrived in a club for Whigs.

"It is he, I swear. Hang me if it isn't. What on earth brings him here, I wonder?"

"Who?" said I, for this was the first time I ever clapped eyes on Mister Neale, who was notionally in charge of the Mint but whose appearances there were as rare as hen's teeth.

"This, Ellis, is Mister Neale, who goes by the title of Master Worker, although I think he would count it some kind of mis-fortune indeed if ever he had to work at all. Indeed I think it would quite spoil the purchase of his office altogether if the busi-ness of this Mint were to intrude upon his pleasures and projec-tions. For as I have told you he leaves the general management of this Mint to the joint comptrollers, and the chief clerk."

Seeing us now, the Master Worker saluted us most affably and walked toward us, while all the time Newton fulminated like salt-petre in a crucible upon Mister Neale's lack of diligence.

I judged Mister Neale to be about sixty years of age, somewhat fat, but handsomely dressed with wig and silk coat abundantly powdered, bullion-fringed gloves, a fine beaver hat, and a fur-lined cape. But by his conversation I found him to be an easygoing sort of fellow, the very kind of man I would once have chosen for to accompany to a tavern, and mighty merry besides in inveighing against Lord Lucas, the Tower's Lord Lieutenant, which was all the opinion he and Newton held in common.

"This is unexpected," said Newton, with a bow. "What brings you here, Mister Neale?"

Mister Neale was accompanied at a distance by a middle-sized fellow who somehow seemed familiar to me. This other man was about forty years old, with a hooked nose, a sharp chin, grey eyes and a mole near his mouth; he wore an expensive wig, and a diamond pinkie on his finger; and yet he looked most unaccountably shabby and more melancholy of countenance than perhaps he ought to have.

The Master Worker introduced his glum companion as Mister Daniel Defoe, to whom the Master Worker had let his official house that was in the Tower.

"But I thought it was already let," objected Newton. "To Mister Barry."

"It was, it was," chuckled Mister Neale. "However, another gentleman played me at cards and, having lost all of his money, persuaded me to take the lease as his bet. Which he then lost. But no sooner had I won it back myself than I lost it again to this friend of mine here." Neale grinned railingly at Mister Defoe who nodded back at him silently.

"Mister Defoe, this is the famous Doctor Newton, a very great scientist. If you stay in the house yourself you'll see a lot of him about the Mint. He is, by reputation, most diligent in his duties as the Warden."

"Diligence is but the father of good economy," said Mister Defoe, bowing to Newton.

"Mister Defoe, I trust you will be very comfortable in your new house," said Newton.

"Is it always this noisy?" asked Mister Defoe.

Newton glanced around, almost surprised. "I confess that I hardly notice the noise, unless someone mentions it first. One become used to it, I suppose."

Even as we spoke a cannon fired up on the outer rampire, which made Mister Defoe almost jump out of his own skin.

Newton smiled. "One never becomes used to the sound of the cannon, I'm afraid."

By and by, these two men took their leave of us, upon which Newton sighed most profoundly and shook his head.

"I thought this a better venture than a church living," he said. "But with men like that around, their pockets full of false dice and fees from all sides, I'm not so sure. Did you not think Mister Defoe looked like the most dishonest gentleman you ever saw?"

Even as I replied that I did think there were more honest-looking men in the condemned hold of Newgate, and that doubtless Mister Defoe would fit in well with some of the crook-fingered types that were already in the Tower, I remembered where it was that I had seen Mister Defoe.

"I believe I have seen that gentleman before," said I. "It was when I was still at Gray's Inn. He was before the King's Bench for debt, and threatened with the sponging house. I remember him only because of the peculiar circumstances of the case, which pertained to a scheme for the raising of sunken treasure by means of a diving bell."

"A diving bell?"

"Yes sir, to enable a man to breathe under water."

Newton's interest was piqued. "I would wish to know more

about our new neighbour," he admitted. "See what else you may discover about him. For I don't much like having bankrupt men in a place like this. And at the very least I should like to be told if he be friend, or he be foe."

I smiled, for it was rare indeed that Newton did make a joke. "I will, master."

Walking on a way, near the engraver's house, we saw Richard Morris, who was another engraver, and Newton spoke with him awhile about a great many things, so that I almost did not notice how he subtly enquired after the health of Daniel Mercer, who now stood accused by Scotch Robin and John Hunter.

"He is well, I think," said Mister Morris. "His uncle in America is lately died. But he is left some money, and does not seem too much put out."

"A little money will often soften a man's grief," said Newton.

"It's most convenient to have an uncle in America leave him money," said Newton when we were alone in our office. "For there's nothing attracts attention like a sudden bout of spending."

"I had the same thought," I said.

After this we had dinner, which I was very glad of, and while we dined we talked of other matters pertaining to the Mint as well as religious affairs, for I was keen to know more of why my master disputed Our Lord's divinity; and I said that it was a strange thing indeed, for one who had been a professor at Holy Trinity College in Cambridge for so many years, not to believe in the very doctrine which had inspired the founding of that same college. But, hearing this, Newton became silent, as if I had accused him of hypocrisy, and I was glad when, by and by, his steel-nosed intelligencer in the mill rooms, Mister Kennedy, visited our office, as requested.

"Mister Kennedy," said Newton. "What do you know of Daniel Mercer?"

"Only that he is an engraver, whom I had thought to be an honest man. I know him to look at, I think. But not to speak to."

"You said you *thought* he was an honest man?"

"In truth, 'tis only your enquiry makes me think that it might be otherwise, sir. I've not seen or heard anything that might make me think otherwise. If I had, I assure you I would have told you straightaway."

"I know you are a good fellow, Kennedy." Newton placed a bright new guinea on the table in front of him. "I should like you to perform a service for me. I should like you to spy on Daniel Mercer."

"If it be for the good of the Mint, sir," said Kennedy, eyeing the guinea. He made it sound as if he had not spied for us before, when he had done so, many times, and for less money than was being offered to him now.

"It is. He is named from inside Newgate by Scotch Robin and John Hunter."

"I see." Kennedy sniffed loudly, and then checked that his metal nose, held onto his face by a length of string tied behind his head, was straight. "They might think to save their skin, of course, by naming an innocent man."

"It does you credit to say so, Kennedy. But they were each questioned apart, and named Mercer separately, without any prompting from me."

"I see." Kennedy picked up the guinea.

"Mercer is suspected of stealing guinea dies. I should like you to tell me if you think it be true or not. Who his confederates are. And where they are to be found." He nodded at the guinea in Kennedy's grimy hand. "There will be another like it if your evidence may be used in court."

"Thank you, sir." Kennedy pocketed the guinea and nodded. "I'll do my best."

After this, Newton went to the Treasury while I returned to my house all the afternoon and night, writing up the depositions I had taken in several other cases that were pending—which work I was at till midnight, and then to supper, and to bed.

At about three of the clock I was awakened by Thomas Hall, the special assistant to Mister Neale, who appeared before me in a highly agitated state.

"What is it, Mister Hall?" I asked.

"Mister Ellis. Something terrible has happened. Mister Kennedy has been found dead in the most horrible circumstances."

"Mr. Kennedy? Dead? Where?"

"In the Lion Tower."

"Has there been an accident?"

"I cannot tell, but it may be that you should fetch Doctor Newton."

So I made myself ready presently and accompanied Mister Hall to the Lion Tower, that was formerly known as the Barbican, which stood outside the main westward entrance to the Tower. It was a bitterly cold night and I was shivering inside my cloak, the more so when I was informed of the dreadful fate that had befallen Mister Kennedy, for it seemed he had been half eaten by a lion in the Tower menagerie. Amid much loud roaring, for the animal had only just been driven back to its cage with pikes and halberds, I entered the Lion Tower, which was most popular with visitors to the Tower since the Restoration. This tower was open to the elements, having no roof, with the animal cages arranged around the perimeter with a large exercise yard in the centre, where I beheld a scene of almost indescribable carnage.

A great deal of blood lay upon the ground so that my shoes were soon sticky with it, and in a corner of the yard was what remained of Mister Kennedy's body. Although his neck was quite bitten through and his mouth gagged, his face was easily recognisable, if only by the absence of his false nose which lay on the ground nearby, glinting in the bright moonshine like a dragoon's decorative cuirass. He was badly mauled, with great claw marks on his belly through which his guts were clearly visible, and was missing an arm and part of a leg, although it was no great mystery to whence these had been removed. Several members of the Ordnance were standing about holding pikes while the animal keeper busied himself with bolting the cage to which the murderous lion had now been returned.

One of the warders was known to me, being Sergeant Rohan, and I entreated him that the body might not be moved or the scene much trampled over until my master should have had an opportunity to examine it.

"Rightly, Mister Ellis," growled the Sergeant, "this is the proper province of the Ordnance, not the Mint. Lions don't fall within your proper jurisdiction, except when they appear upon a silver crown."

"True, Sergeant. However, the man who has been killed was employed in the Mint, and his death may very likely have a strong bearing on its business."

Sergeant Rohan nodded, his big face only part illuminated by the torchlight, so that his mouth was covered by darkness. "Well, that's as may be. But Lord Lucas will decide the matter. If he can be woken. So I reckon the quicker you can fetch your master here, the better. Let the two of them dispute the matter like a couple of Titans, I say, and we'll stay out of it, eh?"

I nodded.

"A proper mess, isn't it?" he continued. "I seen men bayoneted, men blown to bits with cannonade, men cut to pieces with swords, but I never seen a man chewed by lions before. It gives me a new respect for the courage of them early Christian martyrs. To die for Christ facing such beasts as these, why it's an inspiration. Aye, that's what it is."

"Yes, indeed it is," I said, although I immediately wondered what my master would have said of those early Christians of whom the Romans made such a spectacle in their arenas. Were they also mistaken in Newton's eyes?

Leaving Sergeant Rohan still contemplating Christian courage, I ran to Tower Street, where I thought to hire a horse from The Dolphin or The King's Head in order that I might ride to Jermyn Street, for I had no expectation that I might find a hackney coach at that hour. And yet I did find one setting down a passenger at a house opposite the Custom House, and although the driver was reluctant to take me, it being so late and him intent on going home to Stepney, which is in quite the opposite direction, I persuaded him with the promise of his being handsomely rewarded. And within the hour I was back at the Tower in the same hackney with Newton to learn that Lord Lieutenant Lucas was still not come, and it was being reported that he was too drunk, which delighted my master.

After some words with Sergeant Rohan, Newton walked about the menagerie like an architect who was desirous of knowing every inch of the space that was to be considered in his mind's eye. Presently he asked one of the wardens for a bowl of water and a towel to be brought and, taking off his coat, which he gave to me, rolled up his shirt sleeves, in spite of the cold. Then he fetched some clean straw and knelt beside the body to examine its condition.

First he removed the cloth that had gagged poor Kennedy's mouth and, searching inside a mess of bloody pulp and broken teeth with his fingers' ends, Newton found a smooth stone. This he wrapped carefully inside his handkerchief which he then handed to me for safekeeping.

"Why would anyone—?" I said, beginning a question that I saw no need to finish framing when I saw Newton's querulous expression directed at me.

"You know the proper method, Mister Ellis, therefore please abstain from idle queries which do little to assist my examination."

So saying, Newton turned Kennedy over onto what remained of his belly to examine a cord that was tied around his one surviving wrist.

"Where is the other arm?" he said coldly, as if I myself might have taken it.

"I believe one of the lions still has it, sir."

Newton nodded silently and then examined Kennedy's pockets, from which he withdrew several items which he entrusted to me. At last he seemed to have finished, and rinsed his hands in the bowl of water that had been fetched. Finally he stood up and, drying his hands, looked about the menagerie. "Which lion?" he asked.

I pointed across the yard and Newton followed the line of my finger to one of the cages where, under the eyes of the animal keeper and several Tower warders, the lion was still making a quiet feast of Mister Kennedy's leg. Putting his coat back on, Newton walked over to the cage and, removing a storm lantern from the wall, shone the light into the arched vault behind the bars that was the lion's abode.

"I can see the leg well enough," he remarked, "but not the arm."

The keeper pointed at the back of the vault. "There it is, sir," he said. "I'm afraid we've had no luck recovering either of the unfortunate gentleman's limbs, sir."

" 'The slothful man saith, There is a lion in the way,' " murmured Newton.

"Beg pardon, sir?"

"Proverbs, chapter twenty-six, verse thirteen."

"Exactly so, sir," said the keeper. "Rex, that's the name of the lion. He refuses to give them up. Mostly it's horse meat they eats, the lions. But he's found a taste for human flesh and no mistake."

"My eyes are not as keen as they were," said Newton. "But is that a piece of cord tied around the wrist?"

"It is," said I.

"Then it was murder all right. Someone brought Mister Kennedy down here, tied his hands, and then released the lion from its cage. How is the door fastened?"

"With those two bolts, sir."

"No lock and key?"

"These are animals, sir. Not prisoners." But even as the keeper spoke, the lion looked up from its human feast and roared fiercely at us, as if it might have disputed that remark. It was a fearsome-looking beast, a big male with mighty fangs, and its fur and great mane now much stained with blood.

"Mark well the colour of that lion," Newton said to me. "It is quite red, is it not?"

At the time I thought this interested him because red was his favourite colour, and it was only later on that he explained how he perceived the significance of the red lion.

"Who found the body?" he asked.

"I did, sir," said the keeper, whose posture was that of a man whose head was permanently bowed in prayer, so that Newton addressed all his questions to the man's shiny pate. "I sleep with the Ordnance, sir. In the Tower barracks. I put the key there as usual, at about eight o'clock, sir. I went out of the Tower to a local tavern, sir, as is my wont, for I don't much like The

Stone Kitchen. Then to bed. I awoke to hear the animals roaring when they should have been asleep. And thinking that something was amiss with them, I came to take a look and found the bloody mess you see now, sir."

"The door to the Lion Tower, Mister Wadsworth. Is it locked at night?"

"Aye, sir. Always. The key hangs in the guardroom at the Byward Tower. Except tonight. When I went to fetch it, the key was gone. I thought someone else had gone ahead of me to investigate the commotion. But I was the first to get here, and I found the key in the door, and the door locked."

"Who was the guard on duty there tonight?" asked Newton.

"I believe it was Thomas Grain, sir," answered the keeper.

"Then we shall want to speak to him."

"You will do nothing of the sort, sir," said a loud and imperious voice. "Not without my permission."

Lord Lucas, the Lieutenant of the Tower, had arrived, a most odious, haughty and quarrelsome fellow, whose jealousy of the Tower liberties made him a mighty unpopular man in the Mint and in the surrounding boroughs.

"As your Lordship pleases," said Newton and bowed with mock courtesy, for he hated Lucas with as much venom as he hated all stupid people who got in his way—especially those that were supposed to be his betters—although I think his lordship was too crapulent with drink to have noticed Newton's insolent manner.

"Egad, sir. What the devil do you think you're doing, anyway? Any fool can see what happened here. A fellow don't exactly need to be a member of the Royal Society to see that a man has been killed by a lion." He looked at Sergeant Rohan. "Eh, Sergeant?"

"That's correct, milord. Any man as has eyes in his head can see that, sir."

"Accidents will happen when men and wild animals are in close proximity to one another."

"I do not think it is an accident, Lord Lucas," said Newton.

"A plague on you, Doctor Newton, if this isn't any of your damned business."

"The dead man is from the Mint, my lord," said Newton. "Therefore I am obliged to make this my business."

"The deuce you say. I don't care if he's the King of France. I'm the law in this Tower. You can do what you please in the Mint, sir. But you're in my part of the Tower now. And I'll grind this damned music box whatever way I like."

Newton bowed again. "Come, Mister Ellis," he said to me. "Let us leave his Lordship to probe this matter in his own fashion."

We were making our way back to the door when Newton stopped and bent down to look at a black shape he noticed on the ground.

"What is it, Doctor?" I asked.

"The sad-presaging raven," answered Newton, collecting a dead but still lustrously plumed black bird off the ground, "that tolls the sick man's passport in her hollow beak."

"Is that the Bible, sir?"

"No, my dear fellow, it's Christopher Marlowe."

"There are plenty of ravens about the Tower," I said, as if there were nothing remarkable about a dead raven; and indeed, the Tower's population of ravens was severely controlled since the time of King Charles II when the Royal Astronomer, John Flamsteed—who was also much disliked by my master, for Newton believed that the theory of the moon was in his grasp but could not be completed because Mister Flamsteed had sent him observed positions of the moon that were wrong, so that he did apprehend some intended practice in the matter—had complained to the King that the ravens were interfering with his observations in the White Tower.

"But this bird's neck was wrung," he said, and replaced the dead raven on the ground.

At the Byward Tower he questioned Thomas Grain, the guard, in defiance of the Lieutenant's orders. Grain had no instructions not to speak to us, and therefore he answered the Doctor's questions freely enough.

"In the normal course of events, the keeper hung the key in the guardroom at about eight of the clock."

"How did you know it was eight of the clock?" asked Newton.

"By the toll of the curfew bell, sir," answered Grain, jabbing his thumb over his shoulder to the rear of the Byward. "In the Bell Tower. Curfew's been eight of the clock since the time of William the Conqueror."

Newton frowned for a moment and then said, "Tell me, Mister Grain. Does the key to the Lion Tower form part of the ceremony of the keys, when the main gate is locked?"

"No sir. It stays here until morning, when Mister Wadsworth, the keeper, collects it."

"Is it possible that anyone could have come in here and removed the key to the Lion Tower without your noticing?"

"No sir. I'm never very far away from these keys, sir."

"Thank you, Mister Grain. You've been most helpful."

From the Byward, Newton and I returned to the Mint, and straightaway Newton ordered the two sentinels, who were nominally under his command, to search for Daniel Mercer and to bring him to the Mint Office. As soon as they were gone I told my master that the previous evening I had seen Mister Grain standing on the bridge over the moat, about halfway between the Byward and the Middle Tower, which was about thirty feet away from the keys.

"We spoke for almost ten minutes," I said. "During that time anyone could have taken a key. Therefore if it was possible last night, then it must have been equally be possible tonight."

"Your logic is irresistible, sir," he said quietly and, collecting the cat, Melchior, off the floor, set to stroking him thoughtfully as another man might have smoked a pipe.

Then, by candlelight, we examined those items we had found about Mister Kennedy's person. As well as the stone Newton had removed from the dead man's mouth were several crowns, a pair of dice, a rosary, a lottery ticket, a pocket watch, some rolling tobacco, and a letter which appeared to have been written by a lunatic but which greatly interested my master. While he examined this, I threw the dice and observed out loud that Mister Kennedy had been a serious gambler.

"What leads you to that conclusion?" asked Newton. "The lottery ticket? The dice? Or both together?"

I smiled, for here I was on familiar ground. "No sir. These dice alone would have told me as much. They are cut perfectly square by a mould and have their spots made with ink, instead of being holes filled with wax, such as would prevent any deceit. No novice would take such precautions."

"Excellent," said my master. "Your powers of observation do you credit. We shall make a scientist of you yet."

He tossed the letter he had been perusing onto the table in front of me. "See what your new powers of observation can make of that, Mister Ellis."

tqbtqeqhhnuquczrpsvxwkxfklevqkkoiwvihgklgkbyaothhx

zjbdxrnynsvmfzxmxnweghpohpaaphnxednxoschombafq

jfqwnsfradgkgejfmulqmqxyidrgyidsuysmvrastkilhihrzltp

nbxveukudvojuyjxvvewafyrmxyfjxrlkmluzfiidsbbvelwcq

dhmvszoqnzbntwdpasqkhpbcrdhoywqralextjtoigppffhdt

qwtstsaldjbmtakqhumhbclbhtqruwbzkaauochgqokomqv
cwyhmfkydzvsiendssrrrswgcrykvjabuvshqhgqbnqnbedm
opfbzx

I looked with puzzlement at the jumble of letters and shook my head. "It is meaningless," I said. "A fanciful arrangement of letters that has some whimsical purpose, perhaps. I might say that it was some child or illiterate person's perverse conceit, except that the letters are well formed."

"Mister Kennedy could read and write well enough. Why would he have such a thing upon his person?"

"I cannot say."

"And you are still convinced it is some crotchet-monger's whimsy?"

"Most certainly," I replied firmly, too tired to perceive that he was making a straw man of me; and, what was more, one he was about to shy with wooden balls.

"It matters not," he said patiently. "I do believe mathematicians are born, not made. Such things are plain to me. In truth, I see things in numbers that most men could not ever see, even if they could live to be a hundred."

"But these are letters," I objected. "Not numbers."

"And yet one may discern that there must be some numerical order in the frequency of the appearance of these letters. Which makes this more than mere whimsy, Ellis. This is most likely a cipher. And all ciphers, if they are properly formed and systematic, are subject to mathematics; and what mathematics has made obscure, mathematics will also render visible."

"A cipher?" I heard myself exclaim.

"Why do you sound so surprised?" asked Newton. "All of nature is a cipher, and all of science a secret writing that must be unravelled by men who would understand the mystery of things. This cryptic message, together with the clues we found at the scene of Mister Kennedy's murder, indicate that this will be a most interesting and unusual investigation."

"I am the stupidest person in the world," I said. "For I confess I saw no clues."

"Perhaps that is too strong a word for the things we observed in the Lion Tower," Newton said patiently. "Most specifically the stone in the dead man's mouth, the red lion, and the raven. All of these are possessed of a significance that only one who was versed in the golden game might understand."

"Do you mean that alchemy is somehow involved?"

"It is a strong possibility."

"Then tell me what these things mean."

"That would take too long." Newton picked the stone off the table and turned it over in his hand. "These things are a message, just as surely as the cipher in this paper, and both must be understood if we are to solve this matter. The meaning of these alchemical signs may be merely allegorical; but I'm certain this cipher contains the key to everything. These are no ordinary coiners with whom we are dealing, but men of learning and resource."

"And yet they were careless to leave that written message on Mister Kennedy's body," said I. "Even if it is a cipher. For ciphers can be broken, can they not?"

Newton frowned, and for a moment I almost believed I had said something else that disagreed with him.

"As always, your thinking troubles me," he said, quietly, and folding the cat's ears. "You are right. They might be very careless. But I rather think that they are confident that the cipher will not yield its secret easily. For the message is so short, otherwise I might begin to divine the method in it. And yet by thinking upon this matter continually, I may yet play Oedipus to this particular riddle."

A heavy step was heard upon the stairs, at which Newton

pronounced that the sentinel was returned and that he would be very surprised if Daniel Mercer was accompanying him. An instant later the sentinel came into the Mint office and confirmed what my master had suspected, that Daniel Mercer was not to be found in the whole Tower of London.

"Mister Ellis," said Newton, "what should be our next course of action?"

"Why, sir, to search for him at his place of lodging. Which I have already made a note of from the employment records in the Mint, after Scotch Robin and John Hunter named him as a likely culprit. Mercer lives across the river, in Southwark."

We left the Tower at around five of the clock and walked across London Bridge though it was no fair weather and still very cold. Despite the early hour, we found the bridge already congested with people and their animals journeying to the market at Smithfield, and we were obliged to push our way through the arches underneath the tall and elaborate houses that sometimes make the bridge seem more like a series of Venetian palazzos than the city's only thoroughfare across the Thames.

At the southern end of the bridge, on the Surrey Shore, we came past the footbridge by the Bear Garden, walked around St. Mary Overies and, near The Axe Tavern, between a tanner's shop and a currier—for Southwark was home to all sorts of leather workers—we found the house where Daniel Mercer had his lodgings.

Mercer's landlady, who was a most lovely-looking woman, suffered us to come indoors where she told us that she had not seen Mister Mercer since the day before and was now much concerned at his continuing absence. Hearing this, my master counterfeited much anxiety on Mercer's behalf and, explaining that we were come especially from His Majesty's Mint, begged to see his rooms that we might find some clue to his whereabouts and perhaps thereby assure ourselves that the injury to his person we suspected had not been received. At which Mrs. Allen, for that was the woman's name, straightaway admitted us to Mister Mercer's lodgings, and with tears in her eyes so that I thought she and Mercer were pretty close.

A table covered with green felt occupied the centre of the room, beside a chair on which lay a fine beaver hat, and in the corner stood an uncomfortable-looking truckle bed which was the twin of the one on which I had slept at Gray's Inn. Such is the life of a bachelor. On top of the table lay an egg, a sword, and several books much torn up, as if the reader had been piqued by the writer, which is a thing I have sometimes been tempted to do myself with a bad book.

"Have you admitted anyone else in here since you last saw Mister Mercer?" Newton enquired of Mrs. Allen.

"It's strange you should ask that, sir," said Mrs. Allen. "Last night, I awoke and thought I heard someone in here, but when I came to look to see if it was Mercer, there was no one. And the room looked as you see it now. Which was not at all as Mercer would have left it, for he is a most careful man in his habits, sir, and is very fond of his books, so he is. It is all most alarming and strange to me, sir."

"Does the sword belong to Mister Mercer?" he asked.

"One sword looks much like another to me, sir," said Mrs. Allen and, folding her arms as if she was afraid to touch it, stared at it most circumspectly. "But I reckon it's Mercer's right enough. His father's sword, it was."

"The green tablecloth. Do you recognise that?"

"Never seen it before in me life, sir. And Lord only knows what a goose egg is doing on the table. Mercer couldn't abide the taste of eggs."

"Do you lock your door at night, Mrs. Allen?"

"Always, sir. Southwark isn't Chelsea yet."

"And did Mister Mercer have a key?"

"Yes sir. But Mercer was never in the habit of lending it."

"And was your door locked when you rose this morning?"

"Yes sir. So that I almost thought I must have dreamed I heard someone in here. And yet I am certain Mercer would not have torn up these books. These books were his chief enjoyment, sir."

Newton nodded. "I wonder if I might trouble you for some water, Mrs. Allen?"

"Water, sir? You don't want water, not on a cold morning like this one. It is too heavy to be good for the health and will give you the stone if you're not careful. We can do better than that for gentlemen such as yourselves. Will you take some good Lambeth ale, sir?"

Newton said we would, and with great pleasure, although it remained plain to me that in asking for water his intention had only been to remove the woman from Mercer's room so that he might search it. This he proceeded to do and all the while commented on the appearance of the room, which he found mighty interesting.

"The emerald table, egg, sword, without doubt this is another message," he said.

The mention of the sword prompted me to pick it up and examine it with the same judicious care Newton himself might have brought to the matter. He himself drew open a small cabinet drawer and examined a box of candles while I brandished the rapier in the air as Mister Figg, my fencing master, had once taught me. "This is an Italian cup-hilted rapier," I said. "Ivory grip. The hilt deep-cut and well-pierced and engraved with some scrolling foliage. The blade of the lozenge section signed by Solingen, although the bladesmith's name is illegible." I tried the edge against my thumb. "Sharp, too. I should say this is a gentleman's sword."

"Very good," said Newton. "If Mrs. Allen had not told us the sword belonged to Mercer's father, we should now know everything about it."

Newton, who was still examining the candles thoughtfully, caught sight of my disappointment, and smiled at me. "Never mind, my dear young fellow. You have told us one thing. That Mercer had seen better days than is evident from his present circumstances."

I waited for him to make some disclosure about the candles, but when he did not, my curiosity got the better of me, and I did look at them myself. "They are beeswax," said I. "I would have expected tallow candles in Southwark. Mercer was not one for economy. Perhaps he had not lost a taste for better living."

"You are improving all the time," said Newton.

"But what do they signify? What is their meaning?"

"Their meaning?" Newton replaced the candles in the drawer and said, "They are for light."

"Is that all?" I grumbled, seeing that he had mocked me.

"Is that all?" He smiled a most damnedly supercilious smile. "All things appear to us and are understood through light. If fear of the darkness had not plagued the heathen, he would not have been blinded by false gods like the Sun and the Moon, and he, too, might have taught us to worship our true author and benefactor as his ancestors did under the government of Noah and his sons, before they corrupted themselves. I have given much to understand light. Once I almost sacrificed the sight in one eye to its understanding by experimentation. I took a blunted bodkin and put it between my eye and the bone as near to the backside of my eye as I could. And pressing my eye with the end of it, so as to make the curvature in my eye, there appeared several white, dark, and coloured circles. Which circles were plainest when I continued to rub my eye with the point of the bodkin; but if I held my eye and the bodkin still, though I continued to press my eye with it, yet the circles would grow faint and often disappear until I resumed them by moving my eye or the bodkin.

"Light is everything, my dear fellow. 'God saw the light, that it was good: and God divided the light from the darkness.' As we must do, always."

Mrs. Allen returned, for which I was grateful as I did not much care to be preached at, even by one such as Newton. For what manner of man was it that was prepared to risk blindness in search of understanding? She brought two mugs of ale which we drank and then took our leave, whereupon I, having given some thought to the early occurrences of this day, suggested to Newton it was possible those alchemical symbols he had interpreted were perhaps a kind of warning to those who threatened the Sons of the Art and their hermetick world. To which Newton proceeded to give a most dusty answer:

"My dear young man, alchemists are seekers after truth, and all truth, as I am sure you will agree, comes from God. Therefore I cannot concede that those who have committed murder are true philosophers."

"Why then," I said, "if not true philosophers, then what of false ones? It seems to me that Doctor Love and Count Gaetano might easily contemplate such wickedness. Those who are prepared to corrupt the ideals of alchemy for their own ends are perhaps the kind of men who would not shirk from murder. Did the Count not threaten you?"

"That was all bluster," said Newton. "Besides, it was me they threatened, not poor Mister Kennedy."

"Yet when first we met them outside my house," I said, persisting in this argument, "was it not Mister Kennedy who accompanied them? And had they not by their own admission recently come from the Lion Tower? The circumstances would seem to afford some evidence against them, master. Perhaps Kennedy had some private business with Doctor Love and the Count, that gave them a grievance against him."

"It may be," allowed Newton, "that there is some truth in what you say."

"Perhaps if they were invited to offer some account of where they were last evening, they might acquit themselves of any suspicion."

"I do not think they will be disposed to answer any question I may have for them," said Newton.

We crossed the bridge once more, where I bought some bread and cheese, for I was mighty hungry. Newton did not eat, for he was invited to dinner by a fellow member of the Royal Society, which was one of his few ways of keeping abreast of its learned activities, since he refused to go to its meetings himself so long as Mister Hooke remained alive.

"You had better come with me," said Newton. "So don't eat too much. My friend keeps an excellent table to which I fear I shall not do polite justice. You will help to remedy that defect in my manly parts."

"Is it me you want, or my appetite?" said I.

"Both."

We walked to Newgate with Newton complaining about the amount of building work that afflicted the city; and he remarked how, with one town added to an old one, soon there would be no countryside left, only London, which was quickly becoming as vast a metropolis as ever had existed, to the affright of those who lived there and were obliged to suffer its dirt and its general lawlessness; so that it was clear to me how he did not love the city much at all; and although he had told me he had grown tired of Cambridge, yet I often thought he hankered for the peace and quiet of that university town.

Bad news did await us at the Whit, for John Berningham, that had forged the gold guineas, was sick in the stomach and fit to die. Such was the number of prisoners awaiting trial or punishment in Newgate that it was easy enough to fall ill there and then to perish, for no physician would set foot in the place. But Berningham's sickness was of a most violent and convulsive nature that made my master suspect he had been poisoned. And, questioned by my master, the cull who guarded the ward wherein poor Berningham was confined observed that he had started to vomit soon after a visit from his wife the previous evening.

"That is most coincident," said Newton, scrutinising the contents of Berningham's pisspot as if the proof might be found there. "It may be that she has poisoned him. But I fancy there's a quick way we can prove it, at least to our own satisfaction."

"How?" I asked, looking in the pot myself.

"How? That is simple. If Mrs. Berningham has left her lodgings in Milk Street, then I'll warrant she's as guilty as Messalina, and this poor wretch is poisoned right enough."

"I cannot believe that lady would do such a thing," I protested.

"Then we'll soon find out which of us understands women better," said Newton, and started to leave.

"But is there nothing we can do for poor Berningham?" I asked, tarrying by the fellow's grimy cot.

Newton grunted and thought for a moment. Then, removing a shilling from his pocket, he beckoned a girl toward him.

"What's your name, girl?"

"Sally," said the girl.

Newton handed her the shilling. "There's another shilling in it if you look after this man exactly as I tell you." To my surprise, Newton bent down to the fireplace and removed a piece of cold charcoal, which he then broke into small pillular fragments. "I want you to make him swallow as many pieces of char-coal as he can eat. As in the Psalms of David. 'For I have eaten ashes like bread and mingled my drink with weeping.' He must eat as much as he can manage until he dies or until the convulsions cease. Is that clear?"

The girl nodded silently as once again Berningham was overcome with a fit of retching so strong that I thought his stomach would fall out of his mouth.

"Very likely it is already too late for him," Newton observed coolly. "But I have read that charcoal absorbs some vegetable-based poisons. For I think it must be vegetable-based, there being no blood in his water, and that is sometimes indicative of something like mercury, in which case I should recommend he be fed with only the white of an egg."

Newton nodded as if he had only suddenly remembered useful information that had been long forgotten to him. This was a distinctive characteristic of his. I was always left with the impression that his mind was as vast as a great country house, with some rooms containing certain things that were known to him, but seldom visited, so that sometimes he seem surprised at what knowledge he himself possessed. And I remarked upon this as we walked along Cheapside to Milk Street.

"As to myself," he replied, "it very much appears to me that the most important thing I have learned is how little I do know. And sometimes I seem to myself to have been only like a boy playing on the seashore, diverting myself with smooth pebbles or pretty shells while a great ocean of truth lies undiscovered before me."

"There is much that still lies undiscovered in this case," said I. "But I have the impression, from all our activity, that we shall soon discover something of significance."

"I trust you shall be right."

For my own part I could have lived very contentedly without the discovery that lay before us now, which was that no such person as Mrs. Berningham or anyone answering her description lived, or had ever lived, at the house in Milk Street where Newton's coach had set her down but thirty-six hours earlier.

"Now that I do think of it, I cannot remember that she went through the front door at all," Newton admitted. "You have to admire the jade's audacity."

But the realisation that she had tricked us disappointed me, for I had entertained high hopes of her being innocent of her husband's poisoning, which her never having lived there at all seemed after all to confirm.

"Who would have thought that I was a keener judge of women than you?" railed my master.

"But to poison your own husband," I said, shaking my head. "It is quite unconscionable."

"Which is why the law takes such a dim view of it," said Newton. "It's petty treason, and if she's caught and it be proved that she did murder him by poison, she'll burn for it."

"Then I hope she is never caught," said I. "For no one, least of all a woman, should suffer that particular fate. Even a woman that murders her husband. But why? Why would she do such a thing?"

"Because she knew that we were on to her husband. And hopes to protect someone, perhaps herself. Perhaps others, too." For a moment he remained in thought. "Those fellows whom you did suspect of accosting her near the Whit."

"What about them?"

"Are you quite sure that they meant her harm?"

"What do you mean?"

"By the time I saw them, you had engaged with them."

I took off my hat and scratched my head sheepishly. "It may be that it was only their weapons and rough voices did persuade me that they meant her some harm. In truth I cannot recall that any of them laid a hand upon her."

"I thought as much," said Newton.

We returned to the Tower, where we were straightaway summoned to the Lord Lieutenant's house, which overlooked Tower Green in the shadow of the Bell Tower. And in the Council Chamber where, it was said, Guy Fawkes was put on the rack, Lord Lucas met us with Captain Mornay of the Ordnance and told us that we were to address any questions regarding the death of Mister Kennedy to the Captain who, in accordance with the law, had been ordered to impanel a jury of eighteen men from the Tower that it might be determined whether his death be an accident or not.

"As sure as iron is most apt to rust," said Newton, "I tell you this was no accident."

"And I tell you that the jury will decide the matter," said Lord Lucas.

But Newton's obvious irritation quickly gave way to anger when he learned that all eighteen of the men who were impanelled for the jury had already been drawn from the Ordnance and that there was to be no representation of the Mint.

"What?" he exclaimed, being most agitated. "Do you intend to have this all your own way, Lord Lucas?"

"This is a matter for our jurisdiction, not yours," said the Captain.

"And do you seriously think that his death could be accidental?"

"The evidence for murder is very circumstantial," said Captain Mornay, who was a most cadaverous-looking officer, for his face was most white, so that I formed the apprehension not that he powdered it, but that he might be ill. His eyes were the largest I had ever seen upon a man and very evasive, while his hands seemed very small for one of his height. In short, the whole proportion and air of his being was so peculiar and inexactly formed that, but for his uniform, I should have taken him for a poet or a musician.

"Circumstantial, is it?" snorted Newton. "And I suppose he tied his hands himself?"

"Pray, sir, correct me if I am wrong, but since one of Mister Kennedy's arms was no longer attached to his body, there is nothing to prove that his hands were ever tied at all."

"And the gag? And the stone in his mouth?" insisted Newton. "Explain those if you will."

"A man may chew a stick, sir, to help him bear the pain if he knows he is to be cut by a surgeon. I have myself seen men suck musket balls to make spit in lieu of drinking water. I have even seen a man tie his own blindfold before being shot by a firing party."

"The door to the Lion Tower was locked from the outside," said Newton.

"So Mister Wadsworth has said," answered Lord Lucas. "But with respect to you, sir, I know him better than you. He is a most intemperate, addle-pated fellow who is just as likely to forget his head as where he left a key. It's not the first time that he has been negligent of his duties. And you may be assured that he will find himself reprimanded for it."

"Are you suggesting that Mister Kennedy might have committed suicide?" Newton asked with no small exasperation. "And in such a dreadful way? Why, milord, it's preposterous."

"Not suicide, sir," said Lord Lucas. "But it is plain to anyone who has ever visited Bedlam that folk who are troubled by virulent lunacies may often pluck out their own eyes and gouge themselves. Perhaps they may even feed themselves to a lion."

"Mister Kennedy was no more mad than you or me," said Newton. "Why then I at least, for you, milord Lucas, begin to show some signs of delusion in this matter. You too, Captain, if you persist with this impression."

Lord Lucas sneered his contempt, but Captain Mornay, who was Irish, I thought, seemed rather taken aback at this imputation.

"I'm sure there is nothing in what I have said to put me upon a level with a person of that stamp," he said.

"And now, gentlemen," said Lord Lucas, "if you will all excuse me, I have work to do."

But Newton had already bowed and was walking out of the Council Chamber. Captain Mornay and I followed suit, with the Captain almost apologetic to me.

"I am sure I should be very sorry to affront that gentleman," he said, nodding at the figure of my master ahead of us. "For I believe he is a very clever man."

"He knows things which I never expected any man should have known," I replied.

"But you understand, I have my orders and must carry out my duty. I am not free to think for myself, Mister Ellis. I am sure you can receive my meaning." At which he turned on the heel of his boot and walked off in the direction of the Chapel.

Catching my master, I reported this brief exchange of conversation.

"Lord Lucas would have me thwarted in all things," he said. "I think he would side with the French if I were their opponent."

"But why does he dislike you so much?"

"He would hate whoever was charged with conducting the affairs of His Majesty's Mint. As I told you before. This Great Recoinage has turned the garrison out of the Mint, although it was not of my doing. But I did issue all Minters with a document that protects them from the press-gang and from any exercise of the Tower liberties upon their persons, which Lucas much resents. But we shall make a fool of him yet, Mister Ellis.

Depend upon it, sir. We shall find a way to make him look a proper idiot."

⌒

Before dinner I went to The King's Bench to make enquiries of Mister Defoe, that had taken the Master Worker's house in the Tower. For since he was to live amongst us in the Mint, my master wished to know what kind of a fellow he was. And I discovered that Mister Neale's friend was an occasional pamphleteer who also went by the name of Daniel de Foe, and Daniel De Fooe, and that he had once been made bankrupt in the enormous sum of seventeen thousand pounds, for which, prior to my seeing him in court, he had been imprisoned in the Fleet. Before his bankruptcy he had been a liveryman of the Butcher's Company, a member of the Cornhill Grand Jury, and a projector in several enterprises, none of which had prospered. Currently he was acting as a trustee for the national lottery that Neale managed; but as well as this, he owned a brickmaker's yard in Tilbury, and acted as the accountant to the commission on glass duty, collecting the tax on glasses and bottles, although not the window tax. But he still owed a lot of money, for the principal debt remained undischarged, so that I wondered how he was ever permitted to remain outside of the debtor's prison, let alone work for Neale.

All of this I told to Newton when we met for dinner outside York Buildings off the Strand, which was where his friend, Mister Samuel Pepys, of the Royal Society, lived.

"You have done well," said Newton. "I myself have discovered he is spying on me, for I am certain he followed me here today."

"A spy?" Instinctively I looked around, but could see no sign of Mister Neale's strange friend. "Are you certain, sir?"

"Quite certain," replied Newton. "I saw him first when I got down from my carriage to leave some depositions with Mister Taylor at the Temple. He was speaking to some of the whores who go there. From there I went to the Grecian, and leaving there just now to come and meet you here, I saw him again. Which goes beyond all coincidence."

"Why would Mister Neale wish to spy on you, Master?"

Newton shook his head impatiently. "Neale is nothing," he said. "But there are some powerful men behind Neale who might wish to discredit me. Lord Godolphin and other Tories who hate all Whigs, like Lord Montagu, and their creatures, like you or I. Perhaps it would explain why our Mister Defoe is permitted to remain out of the debtors' prison."

Newton looked up at York Buildings, which were several modern houses that occupied the site of a great house that was once owned by the Archbishops of York.

"It would be well if Mister Defoe did not see us go in here," he said. "For my friend Mister Pepys has his own fair share of Tory enemies."

And so we went into the New Exchange nearby and meandered in a most haphazard fashion about its walks and galleries for several minutes, until Newton was convinced that we would be lost to anyone trying to follow us.

In York Buildings our host lived as comfortably as any man I ever saw. He was a most convivial man in his sixties who was a former President of the Royal Society and, until the accession of King William to the throne, had been Secretary to the Admiralty. I liked him immediately for he made me most welcome, as if he and I had been long acquainted. Mister Pepys lived very handsomely, but it was as well I had been asked to do that gentleman's table the justice it deserved, for our host ate and drank almost as little as my master, explaining that he was troubled with the stone which obliged him to leave off eating and, more particularly, drinking, rather sooner than he often had a mind to.

"And who keeps your house in the Tower, Mister Ellis?" asked Mister Pepys. "Some pretty wench, I'll be bound."

"Sir, I cannot yet afford a servant. But I manage well enough. It is a fine little house I have. Thanks to the Doctor."

"Yes, I know the one. Indeed there is very little about the Tower I do not know."

Mister Pepys then proceeded to tell us a most curious story that involved the Tower.

"During the December of 1662 I spent several days digging for buried treasure in the Tower, for it had been rumoured that Sir John Barkstead had, while he was Oliver Cromwell's Lieutenant of the Tower, placed the sum of seven thousand pounds in a butter firkin, and then hidden it somewhere in the Tower. But the search came to nothing.

"Then, not long after my retirement from the Admiralty, in 1689, my enemies reappeared with the aim of having me eliminated beyond recall to any government office. I was imprisoned in the Tower for six long weeks. I was not close-confined, which afforded me the opportunity to study the Tower records. These are kept in St. John's Chapel at the White Tower. There, to my great fascination, I soon discovered that Barkstead, who was hanged in 1662, had spent a prodigious amount of time working among the Tower records; and, in particular, with those documents that dealt with the Templars.

"The Templars were an order of warrior monks who were accused of heretical practices by Philippe the Fourth of France; but it was generally held that King Philip envied the Order its enormous wealth and influence, and that the charges were falsely trumped up as an excuse to rob the Order. Many Templars were burned as heretics but a large number escaped. It was supposed that as many as eighteen galley ships containing the treasure of the Templars set sail from La Rochelle in 1307. The ships were never heard of again.

"Strenuous efforts were made to arrest those Templars who came to England," continued Mister Pepys, "and many of these were imprisoned in the Tower. It is said that, fearing the secret of their treasure might forever be lost, the Templars made a map showing its location. This map was never found although a commentary made by a Jew who had seen the map was said to exist that purported to describe the treasure and what was on the map.

"Now before he was come to serve the Commonwealth, Barkstead was a goldsmith in the Strand, in a shop he purchased from Jews. I now believe that this was when he discovered the existence of that same commentary and that upon learning of the existence of Templar treasure, Barkstead did everything in his power to make himself Lord Lieutenant of the Tower, with the sole aim of finding the treasure for himself.

"It was a secret he shared with no one, not even his mistress, who nevertheless suspected something from his assiduous endeavours with the Tower records, and finally he told her that a great sum of money was buried in the basement of the Bell Tower. And yet none of Barkstead's notes, which may still be found in the Tower records, make any mention of the Bell Tower. Only the White Tower, where many of the Templars were held. It was there that Barkstead concentrated his efforts."

"Did you say the north-east turret?" remarked my master, frowning. "Until comparatively recently the Astronomer Royal, Mister Flamsteed, under the patronage of Sir Jonas Moore, Surveyor to the Ordnance, occupied that north-east turret as a makeshift observatory."

"It is my belief," said Mister Pepys, savouring his own conversation as I had savoured his excellent French wine, "that Flamsteed and Moore were looking for something else beside the stars."

"But upon what basis did they conduct their search?" I asked. "Did they find the map? Or the commentary?"

"Sir Jonas Moore was a good friend of the librarian," explained Mister Pepys. "Moore was Official Surveyor to the Ordnance in the Tower since 1669. No man knew the Tower better than he. I was well acquainted with Moore until his death, in 1679. But I never knew the secret of his wealth, which came late in his life. It was given out that the money came from the official and unofficial remunerations he received from his surveying work in Tangier. But I never believed that, for the sums of money were too great.

"When Moore became Surveyor of the Ordnance in 1669, it is my belief that William Prynne, who was the Keeper of the Tower Records, confided something of the secret of the Templar treasure to him, shortly before his own death in that same year. It is also my belief that soon thereafter, Moore stumbled accidentally upon a small part of the treasure and that he spent the last ten years of his life trying to find the rest of it, with Flamsteed's help."

"But, sir, pray explain," I said. "I thought you said that the treasure of the Templars was taken to Scotland."

"It was only a rumour that it went to Scotland, and it is more likely that part of the treasure was in London during the early fifteenth century. Following the battle of Tewkesbury in 1471, Marguerite of Anjou used the treasure to buy her life and Richard, Duke of Gloucester, took it to his family estates in Greenwich Park and hid it there."

"Greenwich Park," exclaimed Newton. "God's teeth, this story is the best I ever heard, Mister Pepys. Are you suggesting that our Royal Observatory at Greenwich was chosen because of its proximity to some buried treasure?"

"The pre-eminent sponsor of the new observatory was Sir Jonas Moore," said Mister Pepys. "It was Moore who acquired the site and who, with the Master General of the Ordnance, organised the Observatory's construction using money raised from the sale of army surplus gunpowder in Portsmouth. It was Moore who made certain that it was Flamsteed who became Astronomer Royal, and it was the Ordnance who paid and continue to pay his salary."

"Do you suspect that Flamsteed still searches for the treasure?" I asked.

"I am certain of it," replied Mister Pepys. "As certain as I am that he cannot ever find it. Moore found only a small part of the greater whole of treasure that still remains intact. And this leads to the second part of my story."

Newton laughed cruelly. "No sir, I swear you cannot think to amuse me any further than you have already done so. Flamsteed plays Sir Perceval in search of the Holy Grail."

"For once you say more than you know." Mister Pepys smiled. "In 1682, I visited Scotland with the Duke of York, where I made the acquaintance of the Duke of Atholl. It was his eldest son, Lord Murray, who declared for King William and fought Viscount Dundee at the Battle of Killiecrankie in 1689. Dundee was killed whereupon Murray found a grand cross of the Order of the Temple of Sion around the dead man's neck. Murray had a most exact copy of the cross fashioned which he recently gave to me as a keepsake. It is why I asked you here today, to show it to you."

Here Mister Pepys produced, from the pocket of his coat, a saltire cross the size of a man's palm which he handed over for Doctor Newton's inspection. It appeared to be made of silver and was covered with markings which greatly interested my master.

"Why was it thought this was to do with the Order of Templars?"

"Because it was known that Dundee wore a cross of that

name. I had hoped you could make some sense of it, Doctor, for it was generally held that this saltire constitutes the key to finding the treasure."

"The markings are interesting," conceded my master. "But what are these tiny holes for, I wonder? You say this is an exact facsimile of the original?"

"Exact," said Mister Pepys.

Newton held the cross up to the window and muttered something beneath his breath. "How very fascinating," he said, eventually. "This merely seems to be a cross. In truth it is something altogether different."

"But if it be not a cross," said Mister Pepys, "then pray, what is it?"

"It's a constellation of stars," Newton explained. "The positions of these holes, especially the three holes at the centre of the cross, indicate as much being most distinguishing of Orion, the hunter and master of our winter skies. It is quite unmistakable."

Newton handed the cross back to Mister Pepys.

"Beyond that," he said, "I can tell you very little. However, it may be that the positions of the holes, taken in conjunction with the numbers and symbols that also appear on it, may indicate a position on a map."

Mister Pepys nodded with a great show of wonder. "No sir," he said. "You have told me more than I ever hoped to know."

"I am glad to have been of some small service to you," said Newton, and bowed his head slightly to Mister Pepys.

"This discovery has increased my resolve to discover how the cross may be employed to find the Templar treasure," declared our host.

"Then I wish you good fortune in your endeavours," said Newton.

We took our leave of Mister Pepys soon after, and made our way back to the Tower.

"I'm damned if that wasn't the most fascinating story I have ever heard," said I.

"'Tis certain the Tower has many secrets," admitted Newton.

"Would not such a secret be worth killing for?"

Newton stayed silent.

"A treasure in the Tower. Yes indeed. A powerful inducement to commit murder."

"You know my philosophy, Ellis," said he. "We must make an observation before we may hypothesise. Until then, I will thank you to keep your idle speculations to yourself."

Arriving back at the Tower, Newton declared an intention to fetch something from my house; and so I accompanied him to unlock the door, it being my habit so to do since the murder of Mister Kennedy. Entering my house, Newton fetched his reflecting telescope from the same wooden box that housed his microscope, and placed it upon the table. The telescope itself was much smaller than I had supposed, being no more than six inches long and mounted on a small globe so that it resembled some kind of miniature cannon such as would have demolished the walls of a child's toy castle.

"I have a mind to see the view from the north-east turret in the White Tower," he declared, carrying the telescope out of the door.

We entered the White Tower and climbed up the main stairs to the third floor, where I lit a lantern, and then up a narrow stone stair to the north-east turret. Newton set his telescope down on a table near the window, and having adjusted the telescope on its plinth, he then peered in a small hole at the top so that he seemed to look back down the body of the telescope toward the polished mirror at its base. And while Newton observed—I knew not what precisely—I walked idly around the turret as might have done one who had been imprisoned there.

I confess, my thoughts dwelled not on bloody murder nor on the treasure of the Templars, but on Miss Barton, for it was several days since I had seen her, so that being in the turret of the White Tower served to remind me of how I was separate from her and, being separate, was not happy until I could see her again. Each hour that I did not see Miss Barton made me feel as if I was dying; but, in truth, death was never very far from my thoughts when I was at the Tower, for there was hardly a walk, a wall, a tower, or a turret that did not have a tale to tell of cruel murder or bloody execution, and so I tried to keep the image of Miss Barton before me as some tormented Jesuit priest might have conjured a picture of the Blessed Virgin Mary to ease his pain.

"What do you hope to see?" I asked Newton finally.

"Orion," he said simply.

"Is this something to do with the treasure?"

"It is something to do with what Mister Pepys told me, which is an altogether different affair."

"And what might that be?"

But he did not answer, so, for a time, I went down onto the second level and the Chapel of St. John the Evangelist, where I hoped to divert myself by looking upon the shelves of state records in imitation of Mister Pepys and Mister Barkstead who had once searched there for clues to buried treasure.

It being late, the present Keeper of the Records was not to be found and I wandered among the shelves that were arranged behind the simple stone capitals of the outer aisles. Upon these lay books and records which I was now resolved thoroughly to know whenever I found myself with sufficient time. Underneath the tribune gallery stood a great refectory table upon which lay an open book that I perused idly. And, doing so, was much surprised to discover a bookplate that proclaimed the book to be from the library of Sir Walter Raleigh. This book, which I examined for the love of the binding, it being most fine, disturbed me greatly, for it contained a number of engravings, some of which seemed so lewd that I wondered that the book was ever read in a chapel. In one picture a woman had a toad suck at her bare breast, while in another a naked girl stood behind an armoured knight urging him to do battle with a fire; a third picture depicted a naked man coupling with a woman. I was more repelled than fascinated by the book, for there was something so devilish and corrupt about the pictures it contained that I wondered how a man like Sir Walter could have owned it. And upon returning soon thereafter to the north-east turret, I thought to mention that it seemed indecent to leave such a book lying around so that any might examine it.

At this Newton left off looking through his telescope and straightaway accompanied me back down to the second floor, where, in the chapel, he examined the book for himself.

"Michael Maier of Germany was one of the greatest hermetick philosophers that ever lived," he remarked as he turned the book's thick vellum pages. "And this book, *Atalanta Fleeing*, is one of the secret art's great books. The engravings to which you objected, Mister Ellis, are of course allegorical, and although they are in themselves difficult to understand, they serve no indecent purpose, so you may rest assured on that count. But it was open, you say?"

I nodded.

"At which page?"

I turned the pages until I came upon the engraving of a lion.

"In the light of what happened to Mister Kennedy," he said, "the page being open at the Green Lion may be suspicious."

"There is a bookplate," I said, turning back the pages. "And I showed him Raleigh's bookplate.

Newton nodded slowly. "Sir Walter was imprisoned here for thirteen years. From 1603 until 1616, when he was released in order that he might redeem himself by discovering a gold mine in Guiana. But he did not, and upon his return to England he was imprisoned in the Tower once again, until his execution in 1618. The same year as this book."

"Poor man," I exclaimed.

"He merits your pity, right enough, for he was a great scholar and a great philosopher. It is said that he and Harry Percy, the Wizard Earl, being rightly minded, where possible, to avoid any hypothetical explications, carried out some experiments in matters hermetick, medical and scientific in this very Tower. Thus the book may indeed be accounted for, but not why it is being read now. I shall make sure to ask the Keeper of the Records who has been examining this book when next I see him. For it may that it shall give us some apprehension of who might have murdered poor Mister Kennedy."

Chapter Three

Michael Maier, *Atalanta fugiens*, 1618

THIS THEN IS THE MESSAGE WHICH WE HAVE HEARD OF HIM, AND
DECLARE UNTO YOU, THAT GOD IS LIGHT, AND IN HIM IS NO
DARKNESS AT ALL.

(FIRST EPISTLE OF JOHN 1:5)

*U*pon leaving the White Tower, where Newton had observed Orion through his telescope, he and I returned to the office, where we fell to discussing the murder of poor Mister Kennedy and the disappearances of Daniel Mercer and Mrs. Berningham for whose arrests Newton now wrote out the warrants.

"Yet I do not think we shall find them," he said as he handed me the papers. "Mrs. Berningham is very likely on board ship by now. While Daniel Mercer is very likely dead."

"Dead? Why do you say so?"

"Because of the message that was left at his lodgings. Those hermetick clues that we found upon the table almost told me as much. And because none of his own possessions were taken away. The new beaver hat that lay upon the chair would have cost almost five pounds. A man does not leave such a hat behind when he leaves somewhere of his own accord. No more would he have left a good warm cloak in such cold weather as this."

As usual the logic of Newton's arguments was inescapable.

I was about to suggest to my master that I should like to go to bed, for it was quite late, when there was a loud knock at the door and old John Roettier entered the Mint office.

John Roettier was one of an old family of Flanders engravers who had worked in the Mint since the restoration of

King Charles. His was an odd situation: he was a Roman Catholic whose brothers Joseph and Phillip had gone to work in the mints of Paris and Brussels and who had been replaced by Old John's two sons, James and Norbert. These two were recently fled to France, with James accused of having joined in a treasonous conspiracy to kill King William. All of which left the old man alone in the Mint, cutting seals and suspected by the Ordnance of being a traitor on account of his religion and his treacherous family. But Newton liked and trusted him well enough and accorded him the degree of respect that was due to anyone who has given public service for many years. He was a slow, steady sort of man, but straightaway we perceived that he was greatly perturbed by something.

"Oh sir," he exclaimed. "Doctor Newton. Mister Ellis. Such a horrible thing has happened. A murder, sir. A most dreadful horrible murder. In the Mint, sir. I never saw the like. A body, Doctor." Roettier sat down heavily on a chair and swept an ancient-looking wig off his head. "Dead, quite dead. And most awful mutilated, too, but it is Daniel Mercer, of that I am certain. Such a sight, sir, as I never saw until this night. Who would do such a thing? Who, sir? It is beyond all humanity."

"Calm yourself, Mister Roettier," said Doctor Newton. "Take a deep breath in order that you might give some air to your blood, sir."

Old Roettier nodded and did as he was bid; and having drawn a deep breath, he replaced the wig upon his head so that it looked like a saddle on a sow's back and, gathering his wits, explained that Daniel Mercer's body was to be found in the Mint, at the foot of the Sally Port stairs.

Newton calmly fetched his hat and cloak and lit the candle in a storm lantern. "Who else have you told about this, Mister Roettier?"

"No one, sir. I came straight here from my evening walk about the Tower, sir. I don't sleep so good these days. And I find a little night air helps to settle me some."

"Then snug is the word, Mister Roettier. Tell no one what you have seen. At least not yet. I fear this news will greatly disrupt the recoinage. And we shall try to keep this from the Ordnance as long as possible, lest they think to interfere. Come on, Ellis. Stir yourself. We have work to do."

We came out of the office and walked north up the Mint, as if we had been going to my house, bracing ourselves against a cold wind that stung our faces like a close razor. Between my own garden and an outhouse where Newton kept some of his laboratory equipment, the Sally Port stairs led up from the Mint to the walls of the Inner Ward and the Brick Tower, where the Master of the Ordnance now lived.

Old Roettier had not exaggerated. In the sinuous light of our lanterns my master and I beheld such a sight as only Lucifer himself might have enjoyed. At the foot of the stairs, so that he almost looked as if he might have missed his footing in the dark and fallen down, lay the body of Daniel Mercer. Except that his head had been neatly severed and now lay on its neck upon one of the steps; and from this the two eyes had been removed, which lay upon a peacock's feather of all things, which itself lay beside a flute. While on the wall were chalked the letters

updrtbugpiahbvhjyjfnhzjt

Newton's face shone in the lantern light as if it had been made of gold and his eyes were lit up like two jewels, so that I could easily see how, far from disgusted by the dreadful scene that lay in front of us, he seemed much excited by it. And almost as soon as he contemplated Mercer's body, Newton muttered the word "Mercury" so that I had the apprehension that the meaning of the feather and the flute were already apparent to him.

"Go to your house," he told me, "and bring pen and paper. And fetch another lantern also."

Trembling—for the murder had been done close by where I lived, which made me fearful—I did as I was bid. And when I returned Newton asked me carefully to copy down what had been chalked upon the stairwell, which I did as if it had been an important deposition and not the meaningless jumble of letters that I thought it to be. Meanwhile Newton went up to the top of the stairs and walked back and forth between the Brick Tower and the Jewel Tower; and upon finishing my copying, I joined him on the wall. Seeing his two lanterns held low down for his eyes to search the ground, I asked him what he was looking for.

"A great effusion of blood," he said. "For it is impossible to behead a man without it. And yet there is none on the stairs. Not even a trail." He straightened. "Nor here also. We must go back down the stairs to Mint Street and search there."

In the street there was no trail of blood either. But Newton paid close attention to some wheel-tracks upon the ground.

"Within the last half hour some kind of cart has delivered a heavy load and gone away again," he remarked. "It passed right by this place."

I looked at the wheel-tracks but could distinguish almost nothing of what my master seemed to see so clearly. "Why do you say so?"

"Half an hour ago there was a great shower of rain that would have effaced these tracks. Observe the inward-bound tracks being very much deeper than the outward-bound ones, so that we may deduce there was a very considerable weight on the inward-bound cart. Therefore it is plain he was not murdered here but somewhere else. Likely he was brought here in the cart and then placed upon these stairs, with all the trimmings we see before us now." And so saying he laid both his lanterns close to Mercer's headless body and scrutinised it and the head most carefully.

My own eyes were drawn irresistibly to those of poor Mercer, and to the peacock feathers on which they lay like some sacrificial offering.

"This is much like the story of Argus," I observed, with no small timidity, fearing Newton's scornful laughter. Instead he looked up and smiled at me.

"Do, pray, go on," he urged.

"Argus who was slain by Mercury," I explained. "At the instigation of Jupiter. For it was the many-eyed Argus who did guard Io, who was the object of Jupiter's lust, but who had been turned into a cow by Juno." Seeing Newton nod his encouragement, I continued with my classical interpretation of this scene of murder. "Mercury played his flute so that Argus did fall asleep, and while he was sleeping Mercury killed him and stole Io. That might explain the flute, master."

"Good," said Newton. "And the feather?"

"I cannot account for it."

"No matter. It is hermetick and not easily interpreted by one who is not adept. Knowledge of the secret art is akin to skill in music. The death of the giant Argus is the dark matter or blackness, for *argos* is Greek for shining or white. His hundred eyes are set on the tail of Juno's bird. Which explains the peacock feather. The peacock feather is also the emblem of the evil eye and is considered unlucky."

"It certainly was for poor Mister Mercer," I said, although I thought myself not much enlightened by Newton's hermetick explanation. In truth I was most unnerved by a coincidence I could see: for the sight of Mercer's gouged-out eyes prompted me to recall the attack that Mister Twistleton had made upon my own eyes not long after my living at the Warden's house; and thinking how the matter now seemed more pertinent than of late, I mentioned the circumstances of the attack to Newton, who sighed, most exasperated.

"I wonder that you did not think to speak to me of this before now," he remarked. "Did not the murder of Mister Kennedy give you some cause for concern that the perpetrator might have been some lunatic person?"

"I confess that it did not," I said. "In truth, since that time, Mister Twistleton has seemed a little less troubled in his mind, or else I should have mentioned it sooner."

"Is there anything else you have perhaps omitted to inform me of?" Newton asked. "A man carrying a bloodied axe, perhaps? Or a peacock missing its tailfeathers that you have seen?"

"Now that I come to think of it, there is something," I said. "Something else about Mister Twistleton."

"This is the misery of a keen mind," groaned Newton. "To be blunted on the wits of others."

"Your pardon, sir, but I recall how, when I struck Mister Ambrose in the Stone Kitchen, he fell upon Mister Twistleton, and knocked a paper on the floor. And just now I have recollected how, at the time, Mister Twistleton occupied himself with the perusal of a sort of confounded alphabet of letters. Much like the one upon this wall. And in the letter we found on Mister Kennedy's body."

"It's very well that you remember this, sir, and so I do heartily forgive your earlier omission. But we'll think on this again." Stroking the peacock feather, Newton was silent for a moment. "I have seen a rendering of this story before," said Newton. "In a book by a Flemish gentleman named Barent Coenbers van Helpen. It was titled *L'Escalier des Sages*, which means 'The Stairway of the Wise,' and is a very fine work of the philosophy."

"Is that why the body was placed on these stairs? Is this supposed to be a stairway to the wise?"

"It may be so," said Newton. "And yet I suspect that the close proximity of the Warden's house now occupied by you, my dear fellow, also touches upon this matter. For why else would Mercer have been killed in some other place and then brought here, if not to teach us something?" Almost absently Newton picked a piece of straw off the dead man's waistcoat, and then another off his breeches. "But it is a mystery exactly what that might be."

"Are we in any danger?"

"Where there are mysteries there are always dangers," said Newton. "Even God hides his mysteries from the wise and prudent of this world, and it is not every man who can fit his understanding to the revelation of truth.

"Come," he said, and leaving the stairs we fetched a sentinel from the Mint Barracks, to take charge of Mercer's body. Then we walked back to the Moneyer's stables. Inside the stables Newton looked at bales of straw most carefully, even the loose straw, as if, like some hard Egyptian taskmaster, he wondered if it were possible to make bricks without it. Finally he seemed to find what he had been looking for, which was a small quantity of bloodstained straw, although, he said, it was not enough to identify the stable as the place of murder.

"But very likely it may help to confirm to us how the body was transported about," he said.

For good measure he also inspected the straw in the Comptroller's stables, but, finding no trace of blood there, we went to the smith's shop, where the Ordnance kept some of its horses.

Mister Silvester, who was the smith, was a most knavish fellow. He had black swinish eyes, a furious slit of a mouth, and a braggart's voice and manner that hardly stopped short of belligerence. He looked like a pig grown ill-tempered and heavy from being fattened at the mast of a ship. Following Newton about the stable, Silvester, who was still ignorant of Daniel Mercer's murder, asked him what he thought he was doing.

"Pray what does it look like, Mister Silvester?" replied Newton. "I am examining the quality of your straw, of course."

"There's nothing wrong with my straw, Doctor Newton. It ain't damp. It ain't mildewed."

"But where does it come from?" Newton enquired.

"From the Ordnance's own barn in Cock and Pye fields, every morning. I wouldn't let my horses eat anything that wasn't good. And I'd like to meet the man who says different."

"I've seen all I need to see," said Newton. "Thank you, Mister Silvester, you have been most helpful.

"That's a right squirt-tailed fellow," he said of Silvester, as we returned to the Moneyer's stable, where we had found the small quantity of bloodied straw. "Always ready to shit on someone."

There were twelve horses in the Mint. Six horses were assigned to each of two rolling mills, with four horses yoked to a capstan that drove simple gears which turned two horizontal iron cylinders situated on an upper floor. Here fillets of gold and silver were passed between the rolls until they were thin enough to permit the cutting of blanks. It was hard work for the horses, but they were well cared for by two horsekeepers, one of whom, Mister Adam, Newton questioned closely about his straw.

"What time is your straw delivered from the barn at Cock and Pye fields?"

Mister Adam, who was altogether more respectful of Newton, straightaway removed his cap as soon as he was spoken to, revealing a pate that was much scarred with the pox so that it looked like a chequer board.

"Well, sir, it's the Ordnance that's supplied from there, not the Mint. Our straw comes mostly from Moor Fields. Every-thing we have is separate from the Ordnance so as you would think they were France and we were England, which ain't so very far from the truth being as how there are so many of them Huguenots in this here London Tower."

"I see," said Newton. "And what time is straw and animal feed delivered?"

"All times, sir. On account of how horses is the most important creatures in this place, for without them fed well and properly watered, the Mint would grind to a halt, sir. Or would not grind at all, if you see what I mean."

"Very well," Newton said patiently. "Then pray tell me, Mister Adam, when was your last cartload delivered? And by whom?"

"That would have been about six of the clock, sir. I heard the bell from the chapel. But as to the fellow what delivered it, sir, I really couldn't say who he was, inasmuch as I'm sure I never saw him before. Not that that's so very out of the ordinary. We get all sorts coming and going, and at all hours of the night."

We came away from the stables not much enlightened; and seeing a candle in the window of the Master's house, Newton thought to enquire of Mister Defoe if he had seen or heard anything untoward. But upon his knock, the Master's door was opened not by Mister Defoe, but by Mister Neale himself; and what was more, we were afforded a clear view of the four men who sat around the dinner table, all of them smoking pipes, so that the room stank like a Dutch barge. These were Mister Defoe, Mister Hooke, who was the Doctor's scientific nemesis, and Count Gaetano and Doctor Love, the two rogues who had sought to trick my master with their fraudulent transmutation of gold.

Several more sentinels trotted past on their way to the Sally Port stairs, which looked like shutting the stable door after the steed was stolen; and seeing them, Mister Neale advanced into the street.

"What means this commotion, Doctor?" he asked. "Is there a fire?"

"No sir, another murder," replied Newton. "One of the engravers. Mister Mercer has been found dead, on the Sally Port stairs."

"Is the culprit known?"

"Not yet," said Newton. "I knocked at this door in the hope that Mister Defoe might have seen or heard something."

Mister Defoe, coming to the door, shook his head. "We have heard nothing."

The Master looked at Mister Defoe and then at the other men who stood stiffly around the table, and gave off an air of private and sinister intrigue like a dog gives off a smell of meat.

"To think that while we played cards, a murder occurred within a few yards of this door," said Mister Neale. "It's unconscionable."

"Indeed it is, Mister Neale," said Newton. "But I believe I have the matter in hand. An investigation is already under way."

Neale shook his head. "This will do little to facilitate the recoinage," he said. "'Tis certain to disrupt the business of the Mint."

"That is also my first concern," said Newton. "Which is why I have taken charge of the matter myself. I am confident that we shall apprehend this villain before long."

"Well, then, I resign the matter to you, Doctor; and most cheerfully, for my stomach is so squeamish and watery that I cannot abide the sight of a corpse. Goodnight to you, Warden."

"Goodnight to you, Master."

When Mister Neale had closed the door, Newton looked at me and raised his eyebrows most meaningfully. "That," he said quietly, "is a pretty parcel of rogues, and no mistake."

"But why did you not warn Mister Neale about Doctor Love and Count Gaetano?" I asked.

"Now is hardly the time for that," said Newton. "We have data urgently requiring our collection; and only out of that will arise knowledge of what has here transpired. Besides, from the reeking mist of tobacco smoke in that room, it was clear to me that the Master's door had not been opened in a good while. Ergo, none of them could have deposited Mercer's body here."

Walking away from the Master's door, Newton glanced up at the outer ramparts that lay above the King's Clerk's house, the Master's house, and my own house opposite, and watched as one of the Ordnance sentries walked a cold beat along the wall.

"Whoever stood upon that wall at six o'clock might have seen a hay cart stopped on front of the Sally Port stairs," he said. "That was the same time that we were in the White Tower, for I remember looking at my watch before beginning my observations."

"Why not ask him?" I said, indicating the sentry on the wall.

"Because it was not he who was on guard," Newton replied with a certitude that surprised me.

"But he would surely know the name of the man he relieved," I said, accepting my master's word on the sentry's identity. "Should we not ask him now, before Lord Lucas is informed?"

"You are right," said Newton. "Lord Lucas will only try to obstruct our enquiries, and the business of the Mint. He is a fly in a cow turd that thinks himself a king."

We went up to the outer rampire, where the cold wind snatched away my hat so that I was obliged to chase after it lest it blow over the wall and into the moat.

"Look you there now," said the sentry, a little surprised at our being there. "It is a naughty night to see the sights, gentlemen. Best you hold your hat in your hand, sir, unless you've a mind to make a present of it to the moon."

"What is your name?" asked my master.

"Mark, sir," said the man slowly, his eyes whirling about as if he was not quite sure of this fact. "Mark Gilbert."

Up close, he looked to be rather small for a soldier and somewhat round-shouldered, although his countenance and manner were of one who seemed alert enough.

"Well, Mister Gilbert, this night a body most cruelly murdered has been discovered in the Mint."

Gilbert glanced over the wall before spitting down into the Mint.

"And it is imperative that I question all who may have seen something of what happened down there tonight."

"I've seen nothing out of the ordinary, sir," Gilbert said. "Not since I came on duty."

"And when was that?"

Before answering, Gilbert spat again so that I had the apprehension that he spat to loosen up his cogitations.

"Five o'clock, sir," he said.

"And yet you were not walking your beat on this wall at all times since then," said Newton. "Did Sergeant Rohan and Major Mornay not stand here for a while, also?"

Gilbert frowned that Newton should know this. "Sergeant Rohan relieved me for half an hour, sir. That's true. But I didn't see no officer."

"But why did Sergeant Rohan relieve you at all? It is not common, surely, for a sergeant to relieve an ordinary soldier?"

"True, sir. I cannot say why he did that. And yet I was mighty grateful, for it is that cold, sir. At the time I did think this might be the reason, sir. And Rohan is a good sort for a Frenchie."

"Sergeant Rohan is a Huguenot?"

"Yes sir."

"Do you say so?" Newton walked along the wall some way, leaving me with Gilbert.

"Who got murdered, then?" he asked me.

"Daniel Mercer," I replied.

"No," said Gilbert. "Danny Mercer? He wasn't a bad cove, for a Minter. But murdered, you say?"

"It may be so," I said, for I could see no purpose in alarming the fellow, and in truth I was watching my master more closely than I was listening to Mark Gilbert. Newton had walked along the rampart as far east as the Brass Mount, and back again, pausing only to pick up something from the wall beneath his feet.

"Come," he said, brushing past me on his way back to the stairs. "Quickly. We are in haste. Thank you, Mister Gilbert."

Then we repaired to the Byward Tower, which was the entrance to the Tower, where Newton questioned the porter, who confirmed that, provided a man was not carrying a sword or a pistol, no searches were made of those who entered the castle; and that coaches and carts were not searched until leaving, in case, like Captain Blood, they tried to steal the royal jewels. From which explanation it was plain enough to see that it would have been a simple matter to have transported a headless corpse into the Mint in a haycart.

Thence we walked down Water Lane and, entering the inner ward, made our way toward the Grand Storehouse, where, the porter had informed us, Sergeant Rohan might be found. As we drew level with the Chapel Royal of St. Peter ad Vincula, we saw two men coming toward us in the dark who we only latterly recognised as Sergeant Rohan and Major Mornay.

"Doctor Newton?" said Mornay. "What means this rumour? It's given out that another body has been found."

"Aye, Major. Daniel Mercer. In the Mint."

"Mercer?" said Mornay. "I don't think I knew him. Was he one of yours, Doctor?"

"Yes, Major," said Newton. "He was one of the engravers."

"This is most vexing," said Mornay.

"Aye, for me, too, who must investigate it according to my own judgements."

"Lord Lucas will need to be kept informed."

"And he will be," allowed Newton. "But only when I believe I know enough myself not to be wasting His Lordship's valuable time. He has great affairs to dispatch, I daresay, great affairs."

"Yes, most certainly," agreed Major Mornay with something less than certitude.

"But perhaps you and the Sergeant may help me expedite my enquiries in one small matter, for you may have seen something when you both met on the Brass Mount earlier this evening. Mercer's body was left upon the Sally Port stairs at around that time."

"You are mistaken, Doctor," said the Major. "We were not on the Brass Mount."

Newton smiled his chilliest of smiles. "The world loves to be deceived." He removed his hat and, sighing loudly, stared up at the star-encrusted sky. "But myself, I trust not the guise of the world, Major Mornay. And I do not care to be deceived when I have the evidence of my own senses to rely upon. So I say again, you and Sergeant Rohan met upon the Brass Mount and I ask you to tell me if you saw anything untoward happen below you in Mint Street."

"I must be gone," said the Major stiffly. "I have no leisure to throw away on your conversation, Doctor Newton. You have had my answer, sir."

"Before you go, Major," said Newton, "would you like your belt buckle back?"

The Major reached for the buckle of his own sword belt and, finding it gone, gasped when he saw it held like a magician's coin in Newton's outstretched hand.

"Silver, is it not?" asked Newton.

"How did you come by that, sir?" he asked, collecting it from Newton's hand.

"I found it on the outer rampire," said Newton. "Close to the Brass Mount. I believe it fell from your belt when Sergeant Rohan struck you to the ground and then wrestled you to your feet again."

"It is not possible we were observed," whispered Major Mornay.

"Tell me, Major, is it common practice in the Army for sergeants to strike their officers with impunity?"

"I think you are mistaken, sir," said Sergeant Rohan. "I struck no officer."

"No more did you threaten him, I suppose."

"It was a private matter," said Mornay. "Between two gentlemen."

"Nay, sir, between an officer and a sergeant. Tell me, Major, are you still carrying the letter the Sergeant gave you?"

"Letter?"

"And you, Sergeant. Are you still in possession of the Major's guinea?"

"What manner of a man are you?" Rohan asked, much disturbed, as if he almost believed it to be some kind of witchcraft that Newton knew so much about their affairs.

"I am a man that sees much and understands more," said Newton. "Think on that when next you and Major Mornay discourse your hidden matter. Was that what you argued about? The most secret of secrets?"

"I know not what you mean, sir," answered Sergeant Rohan.

"I cannot imagine that you could mistake me. I was plain enough. Even for a Frenchman to understand."

"I'll give you no further account of my actions, sir," said the Sergeant.

"There's nothing but impudence can help you out now," said Newton.

"Come, sir," Rohan said to Mornay. "Let's away, lest this gentleman be foolish enough to call me a liar to my face." Whereupon the two soldiers walked away toward the Bloody Tower, leaving me almost as surprised as they were themselves.

Newton watched their retreat with something like delight, rubbing his hands together. "I think that I have put the bear in the pit, so to speak."

"But was it wise, Doctor, to provoke them so?" I asked him. "With two murders done here or hereabouts?"

"Three," said Newton. "Let us not forget Mister Macey."

"And did you not counsel caution to me, for fear that it might hinder the recoinage? Or perhaps something worse?"

"It is too late for that, I fear. The damage is done. And it has been in my thoughts this past half an hour that some disruption to the recoinage was surely intended by this murderer."

"When this gets out, it may be the Minters will be too afeared to come to the Tower."

"Indeed that is so. I shall speak to Mister Hall, and advise him that the wages of the Minters should be increased to take account of their fears."

Newton glanced back at the two retreating figures of Rohan and Mornay.

"But I think that those two should be provoked, for they are much too conspiratorial. Like Brutus and Cassius. Perhaps now they will reveal their design in some way, for it seems certain there is some great secret in this Tower."

"But, Master, how ever did you know these things? Their argument. The buckle. The letter. I think that they must have suspected you of some sorcery."

"It was only the sorcery of two polished copper plates," said

Newton. "The one convex, the other concave, and ground very true to one another."

"The telescope," I exclaimed. "Of course. You saw them from the north-east turret of the White Tower."

"Just so," admitted Newton. "I saw them as I said, arguing most violently, so that I was surprised to see them again, much reconciled. If one thing is clear to me in this dark matter it is that Sergeant Rohan knows something that holds Major Mornay in thrall to him, or else he should have been arrested and flogged for striking an officer. I must question them both again, and separately."

"There was a moment when I swear I thought the Sergeant would strike you. I thought I should have to speak to him by way of my sword."

"I'm right glad to have the both of you around," offered Newton. "Especially in as cold and dark a place as this. Why, a man might think himself come down to hell. We must find out more about Sergeant Rohan and Major Mornay. It shall be your earliest concern."

We walked back to the Mint, where we discovered that the night shift of Mint workers had already gathered in the Street outside the Warden's Office, and now loudly declared themselves of the opinion that the Mint was not a safe place in which to work, and that, French War or not, the King's Great Recoinage could be hanged.

"We'll all of us be murdered if we stay here much longer," said one. "What with Lord Lucas and his general provocations of us Minters, and now these horrible killings, this is no longer a fit place for God-fearing men to work."

"We must nip this in the bud," murmured Newton, "or else the war will be lost for lack of coin to pay the King's troops."

Newton listened patiently to their remonstrance; and at last he raised his hands to quell the general clamour, and spoke to the disgruntled Minters.

"Listen to me," he pleaded. "You have more to fear from the French than from this murderer, for he will soon be caught, you have my word upon it."

"How?" shouted a man.

"I will catch him," Newton insisted. "Even so, it is only proper that you should be properly compensated for your continuing devotion to the Great Recoinage, in the face of these heinous crimes. I will speak to their lordships and demand that you should receive a boon for your important work here. Any man who stays to work will receive an extra five guineas when this great work shall be completed. Even if I have to pay that boon out of my own pocket."

"Does that include the day shift?" asked another.

"Including the day shift," said Newton.

The Minters looked at one another, nodded their assent, and then gradually drifted back to their machines, at which point Newton let out a sigh of relief.

"And all the time, the Master of the Mint plays cards," said I. "I do not think the King can know what a loyal servant he has in you, Doctor."

"We must hope their lordships agree with you," smiled Newton. "Otherwise I shall be considerably out of pocket. You have the copy of what was written on the wall of the Sally Port stairs?"

I handed Newton the paper, which he put away in his sleeve.

"It will be my evening's endeavour," he said, "to solve this conundrum, for I don't like to be dunned and teased about things which are at base mathematical. For in any cipher I think that the frequency of vowels and consonants depend upon the rules of number, with the former being more frequent than the latter."

It was plain to see that he relished the task that now lay before him, much as the prophet Daniel might have enjoyed revealing the will of God to Belshazzar when the fingers of a man's hand did write upon the plaster of the wall in the great king's palace. For my own part, however, I was very tired and, despite the close proximity to my house of a headless corpse, and the clamorous noise of the Mint being now resumed, I was looking forward to my bed.

I awoke, if awakening is how it can be described, for I hardly slept at all, at the mercy of a slight fever. But I attempted to play the Stoic and reported to the office as usual, where Newton told me that we were going to visit Bedlam.

"To see your friend Mister Twistleton. Enquiring about him this morning I discovered that he was taken there last night at Lord Lucas's order. After Mercer's body was discovered. Is it not strange?"

"But do you hope to question the man?"

"Why not?"

"He is mad, sir."

"Nature seldom bestows an enduring and constant sanity even on her most advantaged sons. And if Mister Twistleton's madness be of the kind that makes him speak whatever comes into his head, then we may find that we are able to order his thoughts for ourselves."

We went by coach to Moorfields and the Bethlehem Royal Hospital, which was a most magnificent building designed by the same Robert Hooke whom Newton regarded as his great scientific rival, and therefore, I was not at all surprised to hear my master speak most dismissively of the shape and pattern of the hospital.

"Only a madman would make a madhouse look like a palace," he complained. "Only Hooke could perpetrate such a fraud."

But there was nothing palatial about Bedlam's hellish interior.

We passed through the entrance, flanking either side of which stood statues of Melancholy and Madness, as if some horrible Gorgon had stared into the eyes of two mindless brothers, which was a better fate, to my mind, than that which lay inside, where all was screams and echoing laughter and such a dreadful picture of human misery and distasteful imbecility as would have given only Beelzebub comfort. And yet raw minds went there to make sport and diversion of Bedlam's miserable inhabitants, many of whom were chained and placed in cells, like the animals in the Lion Tower. To my untutored eye—for I knew nothing about caring for mad folk—the atmosphere was that of an enduring Tyburn holiday, for there was cruelty and callousness, drunkenness and despair, not to mention a great many whores who plied their trade in the hospital among the visiting public. In short, the picture was a facsimile of the world at large, disjointed, supped full of horror and pleasure both, and such as would have caused any man to doubt the existence of God in his Heaven.

We found Mister Twistleton rattling his chains and wheedling charity behind an iron barricade. His naked shoulders already bore the unmistakable weals of a nurse-warder's whip, and what wits he still possessed were much agitated by the noise and clamour of his new surroundings. And yet he recognised me immediately, and kissed my hand in a way that caused me to apprehend he believed we had come to fetch him back to the relative safety of the Tower.

"How are your eyes, Mister Ellis?" he asked me straightaway.

"Much recovered, Mister Twistleton, thank you."

"I am sorry I gouged them. Only I don't much like being looked at. I feel people's eyes on me, as some men feel the heat of the sun. When I attacked you, I mistook you for this other gentleman, who I think is Doctor Newton."

"I am he, Mister Twistleton," Newton said kindly, and held the poor man's hand. "But pray, why did you wish to gouge my eyes?"

"My own eyes are not so good. But your eyes, Doctor, are the hottest eyes I have ever felt. It was like God himself staring into my soul. An't please your honour, I'm sorry for thinking it, as now I perceive that your eyes are not as unforgiving as once I had thought."

"Is it forgiveness that you seek? If so, I give it to you freely."

"I'm beyond all forgiveness, sir. I did a terrible thing. But I am justly punished, for as you can see, I am quite out of my wits. Even my legs will not obey my mind, for I find I can walk very little."

"What was this terrible thing you did?" I enquired.

Mister Twistleton shook his head. "I can't remember, sir, for I have made myself mad to forget it. But it was something awful, sir. For I never stop hearing the screaming."

"Mister Twistleton," said Newton, "was it you who killed Mister Mercer?"

"Danny Mercer is dead? No sir. Not I."

"Or perhaps Mister Kennedy? Did you lock him in the Lion Tower?"

"Not me, sir. I'm a good Protestant. I bear no man any ill will, sir. Not even Roman Catholics. Not even the French King, Lewis, who would murder me if he could."

"Why would he murder you?"

"To make me a good Catholic, of course."

"Do you know a secret?" asked Newton.

"Yes sir. But I have sworn an oath never to reveal it to any-one. Yet I would tell you, sir. If I could remember what it was that I must never reveal." The poor wretch smiled. "But I think it might touch upon weapons. For I was the Armourer, I think."

"Was it to do with alchemy perhaps?"

"Alchemy?" Mister Twistleton looked puzzled. "No, sir. The only metal I have ever drawn from a fire were the musket balls I made myself. And I have seen very little real gold in my life."

Newton unfolded a copy of the encrypted message that we had discovered on the wall of the Sally Port stairs beside Daniel Mercer's body. "Does this mean anything to you?" he asked.

"Oh yes," said the poor lunatic. "It means a great deal to me, sir. Thank you. Here, wait a minute, I have a message for you, I think." And having searched the pockets of his breeches, he produced a much-folded and dog-eared letter and handed it to Newton, who examined it for a moment, and then let me see that it contained a similarly confounded alphabet of letters as the previous messages that we had discovered. It might even have been the very same letter Mister Twistleton had been read-ing when I had seen him in The Stone Kitchen.

"But what is the meaning?" enquired Newton.

"The meaning?" repeated Mister Twistleton. "Blood, of course. Blood is behind everything. Once you understand that, you understand all that has happened. That's the secret. You ought to know that, sir."

"Is there yet more blood to be shed?"

"More? Why, sir, they haven't hardly started, sir." Mister Twistleton laughed. "Not by my chalk. There's lots of killing to come. Lots of blood. Well, it's like this, see? It depends on whether there be peace or war." He tapped his nose. "More than that I can't say, because I don't know. Nobody knows when such a thing comes about. Maybe soon. Maybe not. Maybe never at all. Who can say? But you will help, sir. You will help get us started. You may not know it yet. But you will."

"Mister Twistleton," Newton said gently, "do you know the meaning of the phrase *pace belloque?*"

He shook his head. "No sir. Is that a secret, too?"

I shook my aching head wearily, and withdrew my hand from the madman's increasingly tight grasp. "This is madness indeed."

"Madness, yes," said Mister Twistleton. "We will make everyone in London mad. And then who will cure it?"

Seeing that we were about to take our leave of him, Mister Twistleton became quickly agitated: his humour became more frantic, and within less than a minute he was raving and foaming at the mouth. This seemed infectious, for at once other lunatics began to rant and rave, and they had soon set up such a chorus of Pandemonium as would have put Hell in an uproar, with Satan himself fit to complain to the Steward about the damned noise. Immediately several nurse-warders descended upon the inmates with whips, which was a piteous sight to behold, and which prompted my master and me to advance swiftly toward Bedlam's exit, eager to be out of that festering air.

Walking through the portico under the melancholy eyes of Mister Cibber's statues, Newton shook his head and sighed with relief.

"Of all things, I most fear the loss of my mind," he said. "During my last year at Cambridge I got a distemper that much seized my head and kept me awake for several weeks so that my thinking was much discomposed."

These symptoms were becoming increasingly familiar to me, for my ague seemed to be worsening; and yet I said nothing to my master beyond enquiring if it were indeed possible for a man to be put out of his wits by seeing a ghost, as Sergeant Rohan had told me.

"There's no question of a ghost," said Newton. "Mister Twistleton has the pox. Did you not see the ulcerated lesions on his legs? You might also have noted his atrophied eyes, his trembling lips and tongue, and his partial paralysis. These are most symptomatic of advanced syphilis."

"I think," I said weakly, "that I should like to wash my hands."

"Oh, there's no time for that," said Newton. "We have to go and see some hatmakers."

"Hatmakers?" I sighed wearily. "Unless you do think to have yourself a new hat, sir—although I must confess I do think you the least hat-minded man I ever met—why on earth should we want to visit some hatmakers?"

To which Newton replied, "What? 'Gavest thou the goodly wings unto the peacocks? or wings and feathers unto the ostrich?'" And seeing me frown, he added, "Job, chapter thirty-nine, verse thirteen."

In the coach, Newton patted my leg and, exuding some delight, showed me the letter Mister Twistleton had given to him. To my tired eyes, the paper, which showed a familiar but disorderly mixture of letters—

tqbtqeqhhnuquczrpsvxwkxfklevqtogkxzzlalcsulixpdmctz
xlzlbizgtpajpdnfpadykforlfbpfoxlduyxwmilldsdlnriieoerx
qxnuiæbpaaafyagfokseicrlexuxtjplttlcgvvmmuqluzgvyqs
swncebkmyetybohlckuasyfkthyizmhzbkvzhydumtksrnpjl
yxdloqmhnfyczeszrvepnbrvhyleedufuivdehfgdrwdeeuh
mmonheybbiktaopigbojcxdgcuouvmnkibhvonxnlzsiefzw
krrvsfdedzhmmnsheasgdtpyhriwqupnefiogzrirpmjpnqc
dlnxqtpfydgmpluynicsbmkhwvsqtexgzidypjtndgizfkkmb
kaoprtdsxyhlmwfflxxæaklrdcsnnyuouflurtqtnnwzbxyjg

wdkcwxylkiajmcykakxkhziqimunavbolltadvfwpfmgwcmz
uszpdqaktiemptpcyvkeygeyffhskntduvnfykrshmorrvuok
gnbuutclafcpnwwekrkcezaxbpluæzgtlqwbypuufzqxdziifs
kszrktncnuljdvfedpgnohprzdoosyskxshdkdgwktgqwtavd
hrusmocxiipiyrlmwopohkd

—yielded no obvious meaning, but Newton declared that he discerned the same pattern that he had beheld in the previous messages we had discovered.

"But Mister Twistleton is a lunatic," I objected.

"Without question," agreed Newton.

"Then I fail to see why you are taking his letter so seriously."

"For the simple reason that Mister Twistleton did not write it."

"But how can you tell?"

"For several years I have made it my amusement to try and infer a person's character, dispositions and aptitude from the peculiarities of his handwriting," explained Newton. "One may even determine the state of a man's health: for example, whether or not he is suffering from some defect in his eyes, or whether he is afflicted with some kind of paralysis.

"Considering the bold strong hand of these letters and the obvious ill health of Mister Twistleton, it is evident that the author of this message was anything but mad. There is a further point of subtler interest, which is that the author of this particular letter has studied Latin."

"How on earth do you determine that?"

"The letters *a* and *e* occur together three times within the coded text; and where they do, the author of the message observes the convention of running them into one another as æ. This indicates a diphthong, which is but a complexion or coupling of vowels, and indicates a Latin pronunciation. For example, it shows that we should pronounce the *C* in the word *Cæsar* with a hard *k*. Therefore I have no doubt that we shall find that the author of this message has been a scholar of sorts, which would exclude Mister Twistleton, whose education has been of a more rudimentary nature."

"But how do you know that? It is possible he might have had some Latin."

"Do you not remember how in response to all his ravings about war and peace, I asked him the meaning of the Latin *pace belloque?*"

"Yes, of course. 'In war and peace.' That was why you asked him that. I wondered."

"He did not know. And it was not because his wits are disordered, but because he did not know. Ergo, he has not Latin." Newton sighed. "You are very dull today, Ellis. Are you quite well? You do not seem like yourself, sir."

"My headache is troubling me," I said. "But I'll be all right," I added, although I did begin to feel quite ill.

We arrived in Pall Mall where the foppish Samuel Tuer, a Huguenot milliner, regarded the two of us entering his shop like a couple of Minerva's birds, being doubtless used to more exotic peacocks, like the gaudy beau in his shop who was examining a hat with the same care and attention that Newton or myself would have devoted to a counterfeit coin. Listening to Newton's question about plumes, Mister Tuer tossed open the lid of a little enamelled snuff-box and charged his fastidious nostrils with a pinch and then sneezed an answer to the effect that James Chase, a featherman in Covent Garden, provided him with all of the ostrich and peacock plumes for his hats, being the biggest and best supplier of feathers in London.

A short while later, arriving at the premises of Mister Chase, which was a large aviary with all varieties of ducks, crows, swans, geese, chickens, and several peacocks, Newton produced the long single feather he had brought from the Tower with its rainbow eye ringed with blue and bronze, and, explaining that he had come on the King's business, continued thus:

"I am told you are the largest supplier of exotic plumes in London."

"That is true, sir. I am to feathers what Virginia is to tobacco, or what Newcastle is to coals. I supply everyone—coachmakers, penmakers, furniture-makers, bed-makers and milliners."

"This is the feather of a blue Indian peacock, is it not?"

Mister Chase, who was a tall, thin and birdlike man, examined the feather but briefly before confirming that Newton was correct.

"Yes sir. That's a blue, right enough."

"Can you tell me anything more about it?"

"Never been on a hat, by the look of it, for it is untrimmed. It's a rare enough bird, the peacock, although a few rich folks like them. But peacocks has a bad disposition, sir, and must be kept apart from other fowl. Apart from the fact that this feather is from one of my birds, I can tell you very little about it, gentlemen."

"It is one from one of your birds?" repeated Newton. "How can you tell?"

"Why, from the calamus, of course." Mister Chase turned the feather upside down to show the horny barrel end, upon which there appeared a single blue stain. "All our feathers is marked thus," he said. "As a sign of quality. Whether it be a swan's feather for writing, or an ostrich plume for a ladies' head-dress."

"Is it possible you would know to whom you supplied this particular feather?" asked Newton.

"Nearly all of my peacock plumes go to Mister Tuer, or Madame Cheret, who are both of them French milliners. Huguenots, sir. They've been good for the feather business.

Occasionally I sell a few to ladies what want to make their own hats. Although not very often. Mister Tuer says there are plenty women who'll make a dress, but not many who want to make a hat.

"I did sell some to a new customer the other day. A man I had never before seen. What was his name? I cannot recall. But not at all the type of man to be a hatmaker."

"Can you remember anything else about him?" enquired Newton.

Mister Chase thought for a moment and then said, "He looked like a Frenchie."

"What, a Huguenot?"

Mister Chase shook his head. "Looked like one. Foreign-sounding name, I thought, although I can't remember what it was. But to be honest with you, sir, the French are really all the foreigners I know. He could just as easily have been Spanish, I suppose. Not that he spoke like a foreigner. No sir, he sounded English. And educated, too. But then some of these Huguenots parlez-vous English pretty well. I mean, you would think Mister Tuer an Englishman, sir."

"An Englishman, of sorts," said Newton.

After we took our leave of Mister Chase, Doctor Newton looked squarely at me and said he believed I had need of a dish of coffee; and so we went to The Grecian, a coffee house which was popular with the fellows of the Royal Society. Quite soon after we arrived and had received our coffee, which did seem to revive me for a while, a man of about thirty years old came and sat beside us. I took him for a scholar, which was not so wide of the mark, for he was himself a fellow of the Royal Society and tutor to the children of the Duke of Bedford. His accent seemed to proclaim his Frenchness, although he was in fact a Swiss Huguenot.

Newton introduced the man as one Nicholas Fatio de Dullier, and although it was quickly plain to me that they had once been close friends, my master exhibited a coolness to Mister Fatio which made me suspect that they had quarrelled and that there was now some distance between them; and Mister Fatio himself regarded me with a degree of arch suspicion that I would have called jealousy but for the suggestion this might have raised against my master's own character; because it could hardly be ignored that Mister Fatio was delicate to the point of being effeminate.

By now I had discovered that I had little appetite for coffee after all, and the thick smoke in The Grecian was doing nothing to improve my light-headedness; consequently my recollection of the conversation that passed between my master and Mister Fatio is hardly circumstantial. But from the outset it was clear that Mister Fatio sought to recover some of Newton's former confidence.

"I am most glad to have found you here, Doctor," he said. "Otherwise I should have been obliged to write to you, and tell you that yesterday a man sought me out at the home of the Duke, to ask questions about you. I think he said his name was Mister Foe."

"I have met him," said Newton. "Mister Neale introduced us at the Mint."

"Mister Neale, the Master Worker?"

"The same."

"Why, this is very strange. I had it from Mister Robartes, in this very coffee house, that Mister Neale has asked Hooke to introduce an Italian chemist, the Count Gaetano, to the fellows of the Royal Society. It is said that the Count has perfected a method for the transmutation of lead into gold. Mister Neale has already confirmed the purity of the Count's transmuted gold, and it awaits only Hooke's imprimatur for the introduction to go forward to the society."

"Faith, this is good news," said Newton. "For the Count is a scoundrel and can no more work a transmutation than you can raise the dead, Fatio."

Mister Fatio bristled and for a moment looked most womanly so that he would have given us a gale with his fan if he had held one in his little white hand; and which I might have enjoyed, for suddenly I felt such a want of good air as a man with a halter about his neck.

"You are sick, sir," said Newton, perceiving my want of health. "Come, let me help you to the door and a more wholesome draught. Fatio? Make some enquiries concerning this Count Gaetano with your friends on the Continent, and you will earn my gratitude." And with that Newton helped me to my feet, for it was much as I could do to stand.

Outside The Grecian I stood swaying like a rotten tree, so that Newton was obliged to offer me his arm; and beckoning his carriage, he offered the following remarks about his friend.

"Do not deceive my good opinion of you, Ellis, by apprehending anything unseemly in my relationship with Mister Fatio, for I know what other men think of him. But he has a good heart and an excellent mind, and once I did love him as a father might love his own son."

I remember smiling at Newton and assuring him that nothing would alter my high opinion of him; and then I think I must have fainted.

Newton fetched me to his own home in Jermyn Street and put me in a bed with fine white Holland sheets, where Mrs. Rogers and Miss Barton might nurse me, for the fever was now become an ague that left me feeling as weak as a basketful of kittens and full of shakes and sweats and the headache and pains in my legs so that I felt like some plaguey person in all symptoms save the buboes that distinguish that awful pestilence. But when the fever broke, and I saw who was my nurse, I thought I had died and was gone to heaven. For Miss Barton was sitting next to a window, reading in the sunlight, with her hair much like gold, and her eyes as blue as cornflowers; and when she did see that I was awake, she smiled and put down her book straightaway, and held my hand.

"How are you feeling, dear Tom?" she asked, using her fond name for me.

"Better, I think."

"You have had an ague. And have been in a fever now for almost three weeks."

"So long as that?" I heard myself croak.

"But for my uncle's remedies, you were fit to have died," she explained. "For it was he who effected your cure. Soon after Mister Woston, our coachman, brought you to Jermyn Street, my uncle went to an apothecary in Soho to fetch Jesuit's bark, and also some dried meadowsweet, which he then ground to a powder in a pestle, for he had read that these sometimes served as an ague remedy. And so it has proved, for you are restored to us."

She mopped my brow with a damp cloth, and then helped me to drink some beer. I tried to sit up, but found I could not.

"You must stay still, for you are very weak, Tom. You must rely on me and Mrs. Rogers as if we were your own hands."

"I cannot allow it, Miss Barton," I protested. "It is not proper that you should look after me."

"Tom," she laughed, "don't take on so. I am a woman who has brothers. There is nothing to be ashamed of."

It was some time before my condition improved enough to take proper cognisance of what had happened to me. By which time it was Lady Day. But Newton would not hear of my coming back to his service until I was fully recovered. Nor would he answer any of my enquiries relating to the investigations we had been working on. Instead he brought a piece of blackboard to my room which he did set upon a painter's easel and, with the aid of some chalk, would, upon occasion, attempt to explain his system of fluxions to me. He meant well, of course; and yet I had not the brain for it, and these lectures in mathematics merely served to increase my resolve soon to be well again despite the fact that with Miss Barton nursing me I had good reason to lie abed thinking myself to be a man much blessed by being ill. For she baptised me with her love, and resurrected me with her tender care. When I was feverish, she mopped my brow. There were days when I lay awake and just looked at her for a whole afternoon. Other days I remember not at all. I have not the words to describe my love for her. How is love described? I am no Shakespeare. No Marvell. No Donne. When I was too weak to feed myself, she fed me. And always she read to me: Milton, Dryden, Marvell, Montaigne, and Aphra Behn, of whose work she was especially fond. *Oroonoko* was her favourite—although I myself did think the end much too gruesome. That book contains the history of a slave, and 'tis no exaggeration to say that by the time I was strong enough to return to the Mint, I was hers.

It was the eighth day of April, a Thursday, when I went back to work. I do remember that, and easily enough, for I could not have forgotten that milord Montagu was become the Earl of Halifax, and had replaced milord Godolphin as Lord Treasurer. And it was several days after before the business of the Mint permitted me the opportunity to enquire of Newton what had become of our investigation into the murders of Daniel Mercer and Mister Kennedy, for we had not spoken of these matters at all while I had been ill.

"As to the cipher," said Newton, "I confess I have had no success with it, and it has become clear to me that more mes-

sages would be required in order to fathom the numerical struc-
ture that is its foundation. Mister Berningham died. Despite the
ministrations of that prison drab, he succumbed to the poison
he had been given. Very likely the girl did not do exactly as I told
her. Doubtless she thought it madness to feed a man pieces of
charcoal. And yet it might have cured him.

"I have had Mister Humphrey Hall keep a close eye on
Count Gaetano and Doctor Love with very little to report
except that Hooke continues to make himself their creature;
and I would almost be unhappy if we were to discover some evidence of their having murdered Kennedy and Mercer before
they have had a chance to murder Hooke, or, at the very least,
his reputation.

"As to Sergeant Rohan and Major Mornay, I had both of
them followed by two of our agents. It seems that like the
Sergeant, the Major is also a Huguenot, as are several others in
the Tower, both in the Mint and in the Ordnance. Naturally I
was already aware of John Fauquier, the Deputy Master of the
Mint, was also a Huguenot. But I did not know there were so
many others."

"It is said," I remarked, "that the Huguenots are so numer-
ous that there are as many in London as there are Roman
Catholics. I have heard as many as fifty thousand."

"The centre of their community is the Church of the
Refuge in Threadneedle Street," said Newton. "Some attend the
Austin Friars Chapel in the City. Others the French Conformist
Church of the Savoy in Westminster. But all the Huguenots from
this Tower, whether they are Mint or Ordnance, attend Threadneedle Street. I myself went to a service at the French church of
La Patente in Spitalfields where I found much to admire, since
many of these Huguenots do embrace anti-Trinitarian views
which are familiar to me. And yet they are most secretive. I was
required to state my belief that Christ was a mere man, though

without sin, before they would permit me to remain during their worship, for they are very fearful of spies. And not without good reason, I think. I have heard it said often enough that they do harbour secret Papists in their midst. My own agents say the same, but that is based on nothing more substantial than their own ignorant fancy, for our spies think all Frenchmen are, when weighed in the balance, found wanting."

"That was also my own opinion," I told him. "Certainly I know that there were a great many Huguenots who fought for King William at the Battle of the Boyne, including General Ruvigny himself. But I confess I have little apprehension of the true character of their persecutions. And why so many of them are here at all."

"But you must have heard of the Massacre of Saint Bartholomew," protested Newton.

"I have heard of it," I said. "But I am unable to describe what happened."

Newton shook his head. "I would have thought the circumstances of the massacre were familiar to Protestants everywhere. What history are they teaching young people these days?" He sighed. "Well then, let me enlighten you. On the night of August the twenty-fourth, 1572, a large number of Protestants were in Paris to see the Huguenot Henry of Navarre, the future French King and grandfather of the present French King, Lewis, married to Marguerite, who was a member of the ruling French Catholic family of Valois. The treacherous Valois family saw opportunity to extirpate Protestantism from France, and took it. Ten thousand were massacred in Paris and many more in the provinces; and it is generally accepted that as many as seventy thousand Huguenot Protestants were murdered by the Roman Catholics. Many Huguenots sought refuge in England."

"But that was in 1572; surely by now they would be much integrated into English society?"

"Henry himself was spared, and eventually became the King of France; and by the Edict of Nantes, did establish religious toleration for Protestants in France. Which persisted until about ten years ago, when this same edict was revoked by his own grandson, and now many more Huguenots are fled to England again. Now do you understand?"

"Yes. I see. But that you say there are several Huguenots here in this Tower still surprises me. One might think that the security of the Mint would demand that only Englishmen should garrison this place."

"Did I say several?" said Newton. "I meant many." He collected a sheet of paper on which appeared two lists of names. "In the Mint, Mister Fauquier, Mister Coligny the assay master, Mister Vallière the melter, and Mister Bayle the moneyer. In the Ordnance, Major Mornay, Captain Lacoste, Captain Martin, Sergeant Rohan, Corporals Cousin and Lasco, and Warders Poujade, Durie, Nimmo, and Lestrade.

"There may be others not yet known," continued Newton. "Those who have sought refuge in England since 1685 and the revocation of the Edict of Nantes are easier to see than those whose families have been here since the defeat of La Rochelle in 1629. Major Mornay was born in this country. As was Mister Bayle, the moneyer. Being more English than French of course may make them weaker links in the Huguenot chain."

"Do you think that they conspire to do something? Could they have murdered Daniel Mercer and Mister Kennedy?"

"I cannot hypothesise. That is what we must find out. It is true that there is much to connect French Protestantism and the Huguenots with the hermetic world of alchemy. But I do not believe that there is anything in these Huguenots that would make them any more protective of alchemy than I am myself."

"That may be so," said I. "But what about the Templars of whom your friend in the Royal Society, Mister Pepys, spoke when we dined with him? Were the Templars not French, too? Might it not be that these Huguenots are the heirs to the Templars and their own secret? Would not such a treasure be worth killing for? It seems to me that there are many secrets hereabouts."

"Enough, enough," groaned Newton. "You trouble me with your incessant speculations."

"What would you have me do?"

"We must keep these Huguenots under our eye," said Newton. "And hope that they may reveal themselves. Particularly Major Mornay. I fancy that the more we know about him, the better equipped we shall be to question him again. He is not nearly as strong a character as Sergeant Rohan, who, it seems, was once a galley slave in King Lewis's navy. We'll not break down his defences, I'll warrant. Meanwhile you must learn to be patient, my dear fellow. Nothing is to be gained here by acting with haste. Relations between Mint and Ordnance are delicately poised. And this Gordian knot must be unravelled if we are still to have use of the rope afterward."

For the next three weeks I worked with a whole network of Newton's agents to keep the Huguenots who were in the Tower under our scrutiny. Mornay was a frequent visitor to an address in the Strand that was the home of Lord Ashley. Ashley was a Whig and the Member of Parliament for Poole, in Dorset. Sergeant Rohan often attended the courts at Westminster Hall. There he would listen to whatever case was being heard, and the real purpose of his going there seemed to be that he should meet a tall clerical man from whom he seemed to take orders, and who wore a great hat with a black satin hatband and a long, rose-coloured scarf. Bowlegged and bull-necked, the fellow proved too elusive and we lost his trail somewhere in

Southwark, so that for a while, at least, he continued to elude identification.

While I was shadowing Sergeant Rohan through the many shops that lined both sides of Westminster Hall, a curious incident occurred which left me better acquainted with him and possessed of a higher estimate of his character.

I had for only a moment taken my eyes off the Sergeant to survey one of the many trading madams who are usually to be found there, possessed of legal papers that help to foster the impression that they come to be clients instead of finding clients for themselves, and was chagrined to discover that I had lost him. Reflecting that I was perhaps not best fashioned to make a spy, for I was too easily distracted by strumpets, I was making my way to the great door of the Hall when, while eyeing another of these pretty jades, I collided with the person of the Sergeant himself. And he, apprehending the true reason for my want of attention to where I was going, was most amused, clapping me on the shoulder and, demonstrating an affability and complaisance I found surprising, he invited me to a nearby tavern. So I went, thinking I might learn something more of his character that might be to our advantage; and learn something of him I did, although not in any way I might have supposed.

"Your Mister Newton," he said, fetching us two pots of Byde's best. "He's a clever one. I don't know how he came to suspect me for a mutineer, but it ain't at all like he thinks between the Major and me. We're old friends, him and me—old enough to forget rank when we quarrel, as all friends do now and then. When you've served with a man, fought alongside him in a fight, saved his skin a few times, it gives you a certain privilege. The possession of an advantage, so to speak. A debt, some might call it."

"You saved Major Mornay's life?"

"Not so much saved, as kept him alive. He and I were captured at the Battle of Fleuris, in Flanders, fighting for King William. It was the King's first defeat in the Low Countries. That was in 1690. The French General, Luxembourg, was a cruel fellow and all his prisoners were sentenced to serve as convicts in King Lewis's galleys, for life. Three days later, the Major and me arrived at Dunkirk, where we were placed in the galley ship *L'Heureuse*. Do you know what that means?"

I shook my head.

"It means Fortune," said the Sergeant. "And I can tell you there is precious little of that to be found in a French galley ship.

"Let me tell you about a galley, young fellow. It has fifty rowing benches, twenty-five on each side, six slaves chained to a bench. That's three hundred men. No one who has not seen the work of a galley slave can possibly imagine it. I myself have rowed for twenty-four hours without a moment's rest, encouraged by the whips of the *comites* who commanded us. If you fainted you were flogged until you started to row again, or until you were dead, and then your body was thrown to the sharks. Turks did most of the flogging." The Sergeant grinned as he recollected the cruelties he described. "There's no Christian who can flog a man quite like a Turk. Who can flay a man to the bone with a rope's end, dipped in pitch and brine.

"The strongest and the weakest were put together, which is how I came to row with the Major. I was at the head of a bench with the Major next to me. Dogs was what the ship's captain called us, and like dogs was how we lived. He was a man of most Jesuitical sentiments and hated all men of the reformed faith. Once he ordered one of the Turks to cut off a man's arm with which to beat another. For some reason, the captain took against the Major, and singled him out for an especially harsh beating. But for me, the Major would have died. I gave him half my biscuit and applied vinegar and salt to his weals to stop the beginning of a mortification to his flesh. And somehow, he survived.

"There were many cruelties we endured, and many hardships: the heat in summer; the cold in winter; the beatings; the starvation; the cannonades from other ships. One time we were raked with langrage shot, which is a long tin box filled with bits of chain and old metal that's stuffed down the barrel of a gun. A third of the men in the galley were blasted to pieces. All the wounded were thrown overboard for the sharks.

"Two years the Major and I survived in that Catholic ship of damnation. Once you asked me why I hate Catholics so much. Well here's why: We were visited by the Mother Superior of an order of Catholic sisters who offered us Huguenots our freedom if we would make an abjuration of our faith. Many of us did, only to discover that she had lied and that it was not within her power to give us freedom. It was the Captain that had put her up to it. His idea of a joke, I suppose.

"Two years, my friend. In the galleys, that's a lifetime. We thought our sufferings would never end. But then one day there was a battle. Admiral Russell, bless him, defeated the French at Barfleur, our ship was taken, and we were freed."

Sergeant Rohan nodded and then finished his ale; and I thought his story explained much that lay between himself and Major Mornay. Stunned by his tale—in truth I have hardly done it justice—I paid little attention to the curiosity about my master and his habits he now demonstrated; so that I answered many of his questions with scant regard for the danger it occasioned my master.

Which later on was to cause me great personal grief.

For all Newton's obvious intelligence, we seemed no closer to identifying the perpetrators of these atrocities than we had before I had fallen sick. It was fortunate therefore that the murders remained largely unknown outside the castle walls. At the request of the Lords Justices, Doctor Newton and Lord Lucas were ordered to keep secret these atrocities for fear the general public might apprehend some threat to the Great Recoinage and perceive that this might fail, as the Land Tax and the Million Act had failed before it. With the Army still in Flanders and King William still unpopular in the country at large, his son the Duke of Gloucester so frail, and Princess Anne—who was second in line of succession—childless despite her seventeen confinements, there was great fear of national insurrection at home. And nothing was perceived to inflame discontent as much as the continued debasement and scarcity of the coin. The closing date for receipt of the old coin at full value—June twenty-fourth—was fast approaching, but there was so little of the new in circulation that the Lords Justices had secretly given out that any news that bore ill upon the Mint and the recoinage was to be suppressed.

Yet there was much curiosity—no, *concern*—as to the results of Doctor Newton's investigations. And his easily ignited and touchy character being well known in Whitehall, it was given to my brother (who, as I have said, was under-secretary to William Lowndes, the Treasury's Permanent Secretary) to make some enquiries of me as to what progress was being made with my master's investigations. At least this was what he said in the beginning. It was only toward the end of our meeting that I learned the real purpose of his speaking to me.

We met at Charles's office in Whitehall while Newton appeared before their Lordships in order to recommend a pardon for Thomas White, whose execution for coining had been deferred thirteen times on Newton's motion in return for information.

Even then my brother and I did not enjoy cordial relations, although I was grateful to him for finding me employment. But

I was damned if in return I was going to become his creature, and had made this plain almost as soon as I was appointed to the Mint. As a result Charles saw me as an embarrassment and a possible hindrance to any substantial preferment in the Treasury, and spoke to me as he might have spoken to his servant. Which was how he spoke to most people, now that I come to reflect upon it. He had grown rather fat and self-important, and reminded me very much of our father.

"How is your health?" he asked gruffly. "Doctor Newton told me you were ill. And that you were taken care of."

"I am much recovered now," said I.

"I would have come to see you, brother, but I was detained here."

"I am well enough now, as you can see."

"Good. So then pray tell me, what is happening in the Tower? By the by, is it one murder or two? Milord Lucas is adamant that there has been but one, and that it is nothing to do with the Ordnance."

"There have been three murders," I said, enjoying the look of consternation that creased my brother's face.

"Three? God's sores," breathed Charles. "Well then, are we soon to be enlightened as to who has committed these crimes? Or must we await Doctor Newton's pleasure in this matter? Perhaps he intends to keep these things to himself as he kept silent about his theory of light for so long. Or perhaps he no longer has the brain for it. It is given out at Cambridge that he only took the position because his mind was gone."

"Does one need a brain to work at the Treasury?" I said provocatively. "I'm not sure. However there is nothing wrong with Newton's mind. And I resent your implication that he is being deliberately secretive in this matter."

"So what should I tell the Permanent Secretary?"

"I care not what you say to the Permanent Secretary."

"Shall I tell him that?"

"It is you who would be judged by it, not me."

"And yet you owe me this employment."

"As you never cease to remind me."

"But for me, Kit, you would have no prospects at all."

"Did you do it for me, or did you do it for yourself?"

Charles sighed and looked out of the window, which was heavily rained upon, as if God did think to become a window cleaner.

"Am I my brother's keeper?" he muttered.

"You have not yet given me liberty to answer your questions. I will tell you what you wish to know. But you must not speak ill of a man for whom I have the greatest respect. Just as I would not do anything but speak well to you of Mister Lowndes or Milord Montagu."

"Halifax," he said, reminding me of Montagu's new peerage. "Milord Montagu is now the Earl of Halifax."

"Be not so damned high," I continued. "Or take such offence at me, brother. Offer me some wine and some courtesy and you shall find me a turd become honey."

Charles fetched us both some wine and I did drink and then talk.

"In truth, brother, there are so many different possibilities that I can scarce devise which to tell you first. Well then, to speak in strict chronology, it may be some forgers who are behind these murders, for one of the dead men, Daniel Mercer, had been named by others now clapped up in Newgate for coining. There is a murderous gang who are possessed of an ingenious method of forging golden guineas, and it may be that this same Mercer was murdered in order to silence him as to his involvement. The agent we set to watch this Mercer, called Kennedy, was also murdered.

"And yet there are secret alchemical aspects to the appearance of these murders that make Newton think there may be some hermetic part to their commission. This is most strange and most bloody, and I trust you will not pick a hole in my damned coat if I tell you it is also very frightening. Whenever I am in the Tower I have the constant apprehension that something untoward is about to happen to my person."

"That's not unusual," remarked my brother. "At least not in the Tower."

I nodded patiently, thinking to get out of his office soon without picking another quarrel with him.

"Then there has been some talk of the Templars and buried treasure, which would provide almost anyone with motive enough to kill men who might have held a candle to, or hindered, its discovery, I know not which. But it's plain that there are many who have searched for a treasure already. Barkstead, Pepys—"

"Samuel Pepys?"

I nodded.

"Damned Tory," he said.

"Flamsteed, God alone knows who else."

"I see."

"Then there are a number of French Huguenots in the Tower."

"Not just the Tower. The whole country's rotten with Frenchies."

"They are full of secrecy, and arouse Newton's suspicions by virtue of their secretive ways."

"When does a Frenchman not arouse suspicion?" demanded Charles. "It's their own fault, of course. They think we dislike them simply because we are their historical adversaries. But the truth is we dislike them because of their damned insolence and the airs they give themselves. Roman Catholic, Protestant, Jew or

Jesuit, it makes no difference to me. Without exception I wish all Frenchmen to hell." He paused. "What's the favourite horse?"

"Newton is a most scientific gentleman," I said. "He will not hypothesise without proper evidence. And it is pointless trying to get him so to do. One might as well stick an enema up a bottle and expect it to shit. But he is most diligent in his enquiries and although he says little, I think that he weighs these matters very carefully."

"I am right glad to hear it," said Charles. "Three damned murders in what's supposed to be the most secure castle in Britain? Why, it's a scandal."

"If anyone can fathom these mysteries, it is he," I declared. "Just to be near him is to feel his mind vibrate like a Jew's trump. But I dare not ask him too much, for he is easily put out of countenance and I become obnoxious to his opinion."

"So he and I share something in common, do we?" railed my brother.

"As soon as he has arrived at some conclusion himself, I feel he will tell me, for I have his confidence. Yet not before. *Omnis in tempore,* brother."

Charles picked up his quill and, holding it over a blank sheet of paper, hesitated to write.

"Well, that's a pretty report for Mister Lowndes," he said, and then threw aside the quill. "God's blood if I can't think what to write. I could as well describe his damned *Principia.*" He made a bad-tempered noise. "I looked at it, and could make neither head nor tail of it. It is amazing to me that something so clever can make me feel so stupid. Have you read it?"

"I have tried."

"I can't understand how one book can create such a stir when I can find no one who has actually read it."

"I don't believe there are a dozen men in all of Europe who

could say they understood it," said I. "But they are such a dozen as might stand head and shoulders above mere mortals. And all of them are agreed it is the most important book that ever was written."

Charles looked pained, as well he might, for I knew he had even less of a mind for these things than I had myself.

"Of course he's very clever," grumbled Charles. "I think we all know that. It says it in his Treasury file. But he's a strange bird. His devotion to his duty is well known and much admired. But he cares not for praise, I think. Only to be told that he is right. Which he already knows well enough by himself. And which makes him a damned awkward customer to employ in Government. He is too independent."

"He is a strange bird, it is true," said I. "But one that flies so high that it all but disappears from the sight of ordinary men. I think he is an eagle that soars up to the very limits of our world and perhaps beyond, to the moon and stars, to the very sun itself. I never knew his like. No man ever did."

"S'blood, Kit, you make him sound like one of the Immortals."

"It is certain that his name and reputation shall evermore endure."

"Would that reputation was so durable," said Charles. "God's sores, if he is so certain of posterity, then I do wonder how it is that he needs people like me to warn him that the world is thickly stocked with his enemies. For there are those who would wish that the Warden could be less diligent in the pursuit of his duties. Certain Tory gentlemen who would like to see him removed from office and who search for some evidence of his malpractice."

"Then why did they appoint him? He himself asked for his forensic duties to be given to the Solicitor General, did he not?"

"There were some who thought that a man who had spent

twenty-five years hidden away at Trinity would know little of the world. And would make a most pliable Warden. Which is why they agreed to his appointment. Do not mistake me in this, brother. I am on his side. But there are others who would find some corruption against him. Even if none were there, if you see what I mean."

"Faith, he's the least corrupt man I ever met," said I.

"If not his corruption," continued Charles, "then perhaps his deviation from what is considered orthodox. I hope you perceive my meaning here."

At this I stayed silent for a while, long enough to find my brother nodding at me as if he had found Newton out. "Yes," he said. "I thought that might quieten you, brother. Your master is suspected of holding certain dissenting opinions, to put it mildly. And there are others who are inclined not to put it mildly. Tongues have wagged. The word 'heresy' has been mentioned. And he'll be dismissed if it be proved against him."

"This is idle gossip."

"Aye, gossip. But when in this world did gossip ever go ignored? Listen closely, Kit. For this was the main purpose of my asking you here today. That you might gently warn your master to be much on his guard and prepared for the moment when his enemies shall move against him. As they certainly shall, before long."

All of which I did relate to Newton when I did see him in our office back at the Mint.

"I have suspected as much for some time now," admitted Newton. "Nevertheless I am greatly indebted to your brother. To be warned thus is to be forearmed. However, I must conclude that no concrete thing has yet been found against me, but only a heap of froth and mischief."

"What will you do?" I asked.

"Why, nothing," exclaimed Newton. "Except my duty. You too. We must put it away from our minds. Do you agree?"

"If you wish it."

"I do, most heartily." He paused and, collecting the cat Melchior from the floor, set about stroking his fur like a feeder from the Shake-bag Club smoothing the goose-green plumage of his champion cock. I thought to leave him awhile alone with his thoughts, but then he said:

"This Major Mornay. We must look closely at him, as through a prism, and see if he be refrangible or no."

"You have the advantage of me, Doctor," I told him. "For I confess I know not what you mean by that word."

"What?" exclaimed Newton. "Is it possible that you are ignorant of my *experimentum crucis*?"

I confirmed that I was, and so we went to my house, where Newton searched in an old brass-bound chest from which he fetched a prism of his own manufacture and showed me how the ordinary daylight was a complex mixture of colours, and how, by holding a second prism within the spectrum he had made with the first, colours could be diverted or deflected from their previous course, like streams of water. This diversion Newton called *refraction,* and the property of refraction he called refrangibility. All prismatical colours were immutable and could not be altered by projecting upon them other colours.

"Thus you may perceive a very useful object lesson for those of us whose occupation it is to discover matters artfully or criminally concealed: that all is never as it seems; and that purity is sometimes an illusion."

Newton allowed me to hold the second prism and to divert the colours in various directions to my heart's content.

"It may be that Major Mornay can be similarly refracted

from his normal course," I suggested, understanding his original meaning. "But what shall we use for a prism?"

"Something broad," mused Newton. "Something strong and pure. Yes, I do believe I have just the instrument we need. You, my dear fellow. You shall be our prism."

"Me? But how?"

"Has Major Mornay ever noticed that he has been followed?"

"Never. He does not seem to be a particularly observant man."

"Then you must help him. Let the Major see that he is followed and then observe how he is refracted. Will he go away from Lord Ashley's house without going in? Will he remonstrate with you? Whom will he tell that he is being followed? And what will happen then? It may prove to be a tedious and dangerous task to do as it ought to be done, but I cannot be satisfied till we have gone through with it."

"I am not afraid," said I. "I shall carry both my pistols and my sword."

"That is the spirit," urged Newton, and clapped me on the shoulder. "If he asks why you are following him, say that you are not. It will only serve to divert him yet further. But be careful not to fight with him, though. If you kill him we shall learn nothing."

"And if he kills me?"

"For Miss Barton's sake, please don't be killed, Ellis. She would hold me responsible and I should never hear the end of it. Therefore I say to you, if you pity me, Ellis, then keep yourself safe."

"I will, sir."

This information pleased me enormously, of course; and for the rest of the afternoon I diverted myself with a most elegant fancy in which Miss Barton pressed my most grievously wounded body to her bare bosom as Cleopatra mourned Mark Antony. Since my recovery from the ague, I saw her but once a week, at the weekly suppers at Newton's house; this was hardly enough to satisfy one who loved her as much as I; yet there was no proper way for us to meet more than this; and so I did construct many baroque but harmless fantasies of her such as this one.

But not all my fantasies of Miss Barton were so innocent as this one.

That very same evening, when Mornay came off duty, I followed him out of the Tower and straightaway I made myself as plain as a pikestaff. Not that it mattered, for he was quickly away in a hackney and heading west along Fleet Street, which I pursued in a hackney of my own. At one of the many alleys on the east side of the Fleet Ditch, between Fleet and Holborn bridges, his coach stopped. A minute later my own coach pulled up and, having handed the driver a shilling, I looked around for Mornay, but not finding him in sight, was obliged to ask the driver who had set him down. The driver snorted loudly and then shrugged.

"He didn't come to get married, I can tell you that much," he said sourly. "Look, mate, I just drive them. Once they're out the back of that coach they're invisible."

"I'll tell you for a penny," offered the links boy who had carried a lighted taper in front of my coach to light our way through the dark streets.

I handed over a coin.

"He's gone for a bit of trumpery," said the boy. "There's a nice buttered bun along the alley, name of Mrs. Marsh, who keeps a nunnery where the vows ain't so strict, if you know what I mean, sir. Just ask one of those other bunters if you want to find the place."

The Fleet Alley was an unsavoury sort of place, though I knew it well enough from the time when I had read for the Bar. As well as being the location for many marriage houses where couples went that thought to avoid paying as much as a guinea's tax for the privilege of getting married in a church, the Fleet was a popular area with prostitutes, especially at night, when the trade in illegal marriages dropped off a bit. Even as I walked up the alley, several jades drew open their dresses most brazenly and, showing me their cunny parts, invited me to partake of their frowzy-smelling flesh. I have seldom cared for a threepenny upright, not even when money was scarce, for this sort of buttock often works with a twang to rob you when you are engaged with cock in cunny, so to speak. But I jested with these squirrels awhile until one of them directed me along the cobbled alley where, next to a most boisterous tavern, was the jettied frame of a house whose double-height windows, separated by friezes embellished with a number of indecent grotesques, lit up the whole alley like a giant lantern.

I was divided in my own mind as to whether or not I should go in; but finally I decided that it was safer in than out and knocked upon the door, in which, after a moment or two, a lattice opened to reveal a woman who asked me my business. This was a common enough precaution in London. At that time it was not so very long since a Shrove Tuesday riot when some of London's apprentices had pulled down a bawdy house with ropes, and most cruelly beaten the jilts that poured out of it like rats. But I knew the code well enough. Better than I could have described the importance of a judgement in any case at law.

"I hear you admit of very few," I said, with no small humility, for some of these pussies do think most highly of themselves and the power they possess between their legs. "But I am a gentleman and can present expense in advance should you wish." And so saying I held up my purse and jangled my coins with much intent.

"Five shillings," said the whore. "To do what you would."

I handed over my ounce and waited for the jilt to draw the bolts. After a moment or two the door opened and I was admitted to a small hall by Mrs. Marsh herself who, though quite presentable, was, like many of her kind, the strangest woman in her conversation. Helping me off with my cloak—which she called a toga—and taking my hat—which she called my calm—she then pointed to my sword.

"You had better leave the tail as well," she said. "And the brace of wedges," she added, meaning my two pistols. "Here, have you come for a fuck or a fight?"

Having assured her that my intentions were strictly amorous, I enquired of her as to whether my friend Major Mornay was already in the house.

"If you mean that officer of Guards, yes. Only we call him Monsieur Vogueavant."

"Why? Is he so much in the front of fashion?"

"No, it's on account of his little partiality," said Mrs. Marsh.

"I confess I did not know he had one," said I.

"Then you don't know much about your friend," she said.

"In England," said I, "I believe that is how one remains friends with someone."

"True," she admitted, with a smile.

I followed her through to the parlour, where all sorts of girls sat and lay around in various stages of undress. Mrs. Marsh offered me a chair and fetched me a glass of ale. But looking around the room I could not see the Major and asked her where he might be.

"Upstairs, I'll warrant," she said. "See anything you fancy, dear?"

Even as she spoke, a servant came into the parlour carrying a large silver plate which he placed upon the table, and a young girl, having made herself naked, lay upon it and struck indecent postures for my amusement. It is certain that life has some strange tricks up its sleeve to play upon us for our general confoundment. If there be such a thing as the devil, he knows how to make sport of our inmost thoughts and feelings. For it could hardly be ignored that the girl who struck these wicked postures, and showed me her bumhole and the inside of her cunny, was like the very twin of Miss Barton, and I was repelled and fascinated by the prospect of her nakedness. This was the same sweet girl that I loved; and yet it was not. Could I ever look upon Miss Barton again and not remember this brazen whore that touched her own bubbies and rubbed her cunny parts so lasciviously? But things were about to become yet more vexatious, for, seeing my interest in the girl that postured, and thinking that by affording me the liberty to do what I wanted with her she might get me out of her house all the more quickly, Mrs. Marsh took the girl by the hand and raised her up from the silver platter and brought us both upstairs, where she left us alone in a bedchamber.

The girl, who told me her name was Deborah, was most lovely and, drawing back the bedclothes, invited me to lie with her; but I had no courage to meddle with her, for fear of her not being wholesome, until she sold me a length of sheep's intestine with which I could sheath my manly parts, whereupon I fucked her. It was most ignoble of me, but all the time I stayed mounted upon her and gazed upon her face, which demonstrated much enjoyment, I told myself that this was indeed Miss Barton and that I was taking my carnal pleasure of her flesh. So that when at last I ejaculated within her, it felt like the best I had ever had, and I shuddered all down my shanks like some horrid dog, before collapsing upon her breast in the manner of one shot through the heart.

For a moment the whim of doing it thus amused me greatly.

"Want to go again, dear?" asked Deborah.

"No," I said. "Not yet."

And then the sadness came. Of course, it is normal for a man to feel this way. But this was a sadness like no other I had ever felt, for I sensed that I had somehow tarnished the bright perfection that was the regard I had for Miss Barton. And I felt the remorse of it most acutely. So that when I heard a man cry out in pain, I almost thought the sound came from within my own breast. It was Deborah's laughter that persuaded me the sound had come from somewhere else; and when I heard the man cry out again, this time he seemed to have been prompted by another, sharper report.

"Why does that man cry out?" I asked.

"Oh, that's just Monsieur Vogueavant," said Deborah, trying to coax my cock to crow again. "Vogueavant's French for 'stroke.'"

"I had quite forgotten him," I confessed.

"And he is beaten with a whip."

"A whip? Good Lord, where is there pleasure in that?"

"Not so as you would notice. I've beaten him myself upon occasion. But I care not for it. It's warm work. Warmer than this. For Monsieur Vogueavant has a tolerance of pain like no other man I have ever met. And one must lay on hard to please him. The English perversion, they calls it, but Monsieur Vogueavant learned his taste as a galley slave on a French ship. His back tells the story well enough, for I never saw the like."

Once again I heard Mornay cry out in response to the sting of the whip.

"And the Major has himself beaten in order that he should recollect his experiences? How monstrous."

"I believe that it is more confused than that. He himself told me that he is beaten so that he will never forget his hatred of the French, and of Roman Catholics in particular."

I was properly confounded by this information, which at least served to take my mind off the insult I had privately done to Miss Barton, and would have said more about the disgusting things men will have done to them in pursuit of pleasure, yet I feared Deborah's abusing me for a hypocrite and so I kept silent. Which was more than she did, for momentarily she was troubled with some wind in her cunny parts, and I was moved by her farts to take my leave of her bed.

I had just started to piss in her pot, which be another good precaution against the clap, when I heard Mornay's door open, followed by the sound of his boots stamping downstairs; and I made haste to dress and go after him.

"Why do you rush so?" asked Miss Barton's facsimile.

"Because he does not know that I am here. And I know not where he goes now."

"Oh, I can tell you that," said Deborah. "He goes over the water to the Dutchman's house in Lambeth Marshes."

"To do what, pray?"

"It ain't to have his fortune told by gypsies. It's a wicked place he goes. What a man with money cannot obtain there, let him not search for it anywhere else in this world of ours. He wanted to take me there once. Offered me a guinea to go with another woman, he said. Well, I don't mind that so much. It's safer than going with a man. Just licking another girl's cunny and moaning a bit. But I've heard tales about that place. Called The Dutchman's. Some of the poor molls who go to work there are never seen again."

Having for a shilling obtained some directions to this house of evil repute, I went outside onto Fleet Street, took coach, and went down to White's Stairs in Channel Row, where, hearing a wherryman shout "Southward, ho!," I joined a boat that was crossing the river.

The moon edged out from under a black flap of sky like a curling yellow fingernail. Halfway across the river a mist descended upon our boat that was like some floating pestilence.

In the distance, the windows of the leaning houses on London Bridge were lit up like a necklace of yellow diamonds.

So far I was making a sorry job of plaguing my quarry; and I hardly knew how I was going to tell Miss Barton's uncle where my pursuit of Major Mornay had taken me. Nor knew how I would present my expenses. Would any man wish his ward to associate with a fellow that had visited such places? Especially a man like Newton, who took a dim view of all licentious behaviour and was only concerned with higher things—a man for whom the body and its needs hardly seemed to matter except as the possible medium for some scientific experiment. Every time I looked Newton in the eye, I thought of him probing it with a bodkin. What did such a man know of human frailty?

Our boat rocked on, making, it seemed to me, very little progress across the grey water, and somewhere above our heads, a seagull hovered like some invisible screaming demon. Gradually, we neared the other side of the river where the mist lightened and the skull-shaped hulls of ships loomed across our boat. A dog barked in the distance as I stepped off the boat at the King's Arms stairs, and then all was quiet.

Lambeth was a large unruly village on the Surrey bank of the Thames, with most of the buildings grouped around the palace and the Parish Church of St. Mary, and behind these, the black masts of ships. It was separated from Southwark, with its many small metalworking shops to the east, by the marshes where many crooked houses and lonely taverns were situated. As soon as I landed I drew my sword, for it was much darker on the south side of the River, with one or two ruffianly-looking men about. I walked east, along the Narrow Wall, as Deborah had directed, until I came to the sawmills, where I turned my footsteps south, across a stinking, muddy field, to a small row of houses. Here, next to the sign of the star, which is often said to indicate a place of lewd purpose, I found the house I was looking for. I peered in at a grimy-looking window, and seeing the orange tongue of a candle, I knocked.

The door was opened by a woman who looked comely enough, although she also seemed somewhat hard and yellowish in the face, and her eyelids almost motionless; and having saluted her and paid the ten shillings she asked, which was a large sum, I went inside. A sweet, heavy aroma filled air that was thick with pipe smoke.

The woman took my cloak, and as she hung it on a peg I recognised the Major's hat and cloak. He was here after all. "So," she said, in a whistling accent that made me think she must be Dutch. "Will you take a pipe first, or see the show?"

I have never much liked smoking, for it gives me the cough; and I replied that I would see the show. She seemed a little surprised at this, but led me through a tattered green curtain and down a flight of stairs to a low, mean room, surrounded with greasy-looking mirrors, that was stopped from any light save a few candles, where five dull-looking men sat in the shadows and, like a theatre audience, awaited some kind of performance. I knew not what this might be, and thought another posturer was probably expected. Of Major Mornay there was no sign, and I presumed he must have gone to smoke a pipe first. Meanwhile I made no attempt to conceal myself and took a most prominent seat so that Mornay, when eventually he came in, might easily see me.

My breath came uneasily to me down in that loathsome room, for the atmosphere was filled not just with smoke but also with foreboding, as if something dreadful was about to happen. And yet, curiously, I did almost feel at my ease.

After a good deal of waiting, two women brought a nun into the room and treated her most cruelly, spitting upon her and slapping her before eventually stripping her naked; whereupon they made her lie belly-down upon the bare floor without any garment. Her arms and legs were drawn with cords to a post in each corner of the room; and all the while the poor, dull-eyed nun bore her torments without protest, as if she cared little what happened to her. As I was myself. I know not if she was a real nun or no, except to say her hair was cut very short, which is, I believe, a sign of the nun's renunciation of the world; but she was most comely, being no more than twenty years of age, and the sight of her naked body and privy parts stirred me much.

It was now that the Major came downstairs, and I remarked to myself how he seemed to be almost ill, or drunk; but despite my very obvious position, he sat down without even seeming to notice I was there.

After she was properly secured, one of the other men stood up from his chairs and started to whip her, all the time cursing her for a damned Roman Catholic whore, and other words most obscene, so that I began to apprehend some real danger to the girl's life. And standing up myself, I remonstrated with these men most openly, calling them monsters to mete such treatment to a woman, and entreating them all to desist, although I looked only at the Major so that at last he recognised me, and with such anger in his yellow-looking eyes that it quite froze my blood. It may have been his eyes, but it was more likely the sound of a piece cocked and the chill of a pistol pressed against my cheek that was so disconcerting.

"What's this girl to you, then?" asked a man behind me, whose voice persuaded me that he also must be Dutch.

"Nothing," I replied. "I care not for Galloping nuns, Quests, or Beguines, but she is human and, being so young, seems hardly to deserve such abuse."

"Abuse you call it," laughed the man. "Why, we ain't hardly started yet."

At this point the Major ran quickly out of that terrible room and up the stairs. Meanwhile the naked girl on the floor looked up at me with a most peculiar indifference, as if she cared very little for my intervention, so that I wondered if she did not mind her pain, or even enjoyed her flogging, like the Major.

"Surely she doesn't deserve such cruelty?"

"Doesn't deserve it?" said the voice. "What has that got to do with anything?" The voice behind me was silent for a moment. "What are you doing here?" it said at last.

I pointed upstairs. "I came with him. Major Mornay. He brought me. Only I came with little understanding of what I was to see, for he did not warn me of anything."

"It's true," said the Dutch woman who had admitted me. "He did arrive not long after the Major."

The man holding the pistol stepped in front of me so that I could see him. A most ignoble ruffian he was, with a forehead villainous low, and boils like barnacles; his red eyes were fierce, and yet his hand trembled upon the pistol which now he waved up the stairs.

"Your friend has left," he said quietly. "Perhaps you had better leave as well."

I moved toward the stair, glancing back all the time at the girl on the floor, whose back and bottom were already striped like a maypole.

"She cares not what happens to her," laughed the man. "It's the price she pays to satisfy her cravings. I wouldn't worry about her if I were you."

And still the girl said nothing; and endured her whipping, which commenced as soon as I had mounted the stairs, without so much as a murmur.

I hardly knew whether to believe him or not, but leave I did, although I was part minded to mount the stairs and return with my pistol in my hand to see that nothing more happened to the girl. I might have shot the one with the boils, but the other men were armed as well, and I do not doubt that they would have killed me. And for a while I was haunted by the possibility that the girl was a real *fille dévote* monstrously abused and perhaps even killed for their delectation, since the men all had murder in their faces, and most obviously regarded Roman Catholics with such malice that they would hardly have shirked the commission of such a wicked crime.

Much relieved to be out of that evil house, and somewhat light-headed, too, for the cloying smoke had been as thick as the river fog, I took a deep breath of cold air, and thinking Major Mornay to be long gone, I started back the way I had come, toward the wall and the river. I had not gone ten paces when he stepped out from the door of a vile-looking tavern and, trembling with anger, confronted me.

"Why are you following me, Mister Ellis?" he asked and, drawing his sword, advanced upon me with such obvious intent that no other course lay before me but to draw myself and prepare to answer his attack. True, I had promised Newton not to fight, but I could hardly see how I was now to avoid it. I snatched off my hat for ease of movement and vision, although I would have parried his first thrust easily enough had I been wearing St. Edward's Crown, for it was plain to see that Major Mornay was indeed drunk. Which at least explained why he had taken so long a time recognising me.

"Put up your sword," I told him. "Or I shall be obliged to wound you, sir."

With some ferocity he redoubled his attack, so that I was obliged to fence with him in earnest. And still not troubled by any of these attacks, I allowed him to meet me, hilt upon hilt, where, so close to me that I could smell the smoke that still lay upon his breath, he asked his question a second time.

"Why are you following me, Mister Ellis?"

Thus I did almost not notice how he had armed his free hand with a dagger, and I barely had time enough to step back before he lunged at me with his second blade, only to be caught in the flesh of his left upper arm with the tip of my rapier. The dagger clattered to the ground and Mornay dropped his guard so that, bating my own sobriety, I might easily have run him through. Indeed I almost wanted to kill him, for I dislike a man who brings a knife to a sword fight. Instead I retreated several paces, which allowed Mornay to turn and flee into the darkness of Lambeth Marshes.

After a moment or two I collected his dagger off the ground, glanced at its curious shape, and then slid the blade into the neck of my boot. I hardly knew if I should feel pleased with myself. I had not killed him, he had not killed me, and there was surely some cause for rejoicing. But would Newton find much to learn from the way the Major had been "refracted," if that was how his vile and intemperate behaviour might be described? It seemed more likely that Mornay would inform Lord Lucas, who would use the news and bruit of our quarrel to make another complaint to the Lords Justices about the conduct of the Mint. This hardly grieved my heart, for I was suddenly very tired, and thought myself very fortunate not to have been murdered. In view of my own licentious behaviour that might have been just, for I had clearly dealt sacrilegiously with Miss Barton in my heart, and I resolved never to do the like again.

The next morning Newton examined Mornay's dagger with interest, polishing it up like some back-street bravo, while I related a purgated version of my evening's adventures in pursuit of the Major. I left out the fact that we had fought with swords; while my explanation of how I had struggled with my own lust drew the following advisement from Newton's ascetic lips, for I doubt he ever kissed anything other than Miss Barton's forehead, or a book he had particularly enjoyed.

"By being forcibly restrained lust is always inflamed," he observed gravely. "The best way to be chaste is not to struggle with unchaste thoughts, but to decline them, and to keep the mind employed about other things. That has always been my own experience. He that's always thinking of chastity will nearly always be thinking of women, and every contest waged with unclean thoughts will leave impressions on the mind as shall make those thoughts apt to return more frequently. But pray continue with your story. I am all fascination."

"It is finished, more or less," I replied. "Outside the house in Lambeth Marshes he ran away and dropped that dagger behind him."

"But you have left out the story of your sword fight," protested Newton. "I am keen to hear that most of all. Tell me, is the Major badly wounded?"

"He drew on me," I stammered. "And I was obliged to defend myself. I only pricked him in the arm and I daresay he'll recover soon enough. But how did you know, master? Did he inform Lord Lucas? Is it bruited about the Tower? Has His Lordship already complained?"

"I am quite certain that Major Mornay will not inform Lord Lucas," said Newton. "What? A Major in the Ordnance bested by a mere clerk of the Mint? His reputation could not bear the ignominy."

"Then," I said with no small exasperation, "how did you know that we fought?"

"Simple. You have cleaned your sword. The cup upon its hilt now gleams like a communion chalice when yesterday it was as dull as pewter. I recollect that the last time you cleaned that rapier was when you drew it in Mrs. Berningham's defence. I daresay that when you had bettered the Major with your sword, he drew this dagger and attempted to prick your ribs with it."

"The fight happened just as you say," I admitted. "I don't know why I thought to hide it from you. You seem to know everything without the need to be told of it first. It's quite a trick."

"It's no trick. Merely observation. *Satis est.* That is enough."

"Well then, I should like to be as observant as you."

"But there is nothing to it, as I am often telling you. But it will come in time. If you live that long. For I believe you have had a fortunate escape. It's clear from what you have told me, and from what is written on this blade, that Major Mornay and, very likely, several others besides are religious fanatics."

"I saw no engraving on the blade," I said.

"You would have done better to have polished up this dagger than your own sword," said Newton, and handed me back the dagger, the blade of which now shone like firelight.

"'Remember Religion,'" I said, reading one side of the blade. "'Remember the murder of Edmund Berry Godfrey,'" I continued, reading the other.

"This is a Godfrey dagger," explained Newton. "Many of these were forged following Sir Edmund Berry Godfrey's murder, in 1678." My master searched my face for some sign that I recognised the name. "Surely you must have heard of him?"

"Why, yes," I said. "I was but a child at the time. But he was the magistrate who was murdered by Roman Catholics during the Popish plot to kill King Charles II, was he not?"

"I abhor Roman Catholicism in all its aspects," said Newton. "It is a religion full of monstrous superstitions, false miracles, heathen superstitions and foul lies. But there was no more wicked lie perpetrated against the safety of the realm than that Popish Plot. It was given out by Titus Oates and Israel Tonge that Jesuit priests conspired to murder the King at Newmarket races. I don't doubt that there were Jesuits who conspired to do much to restore the Roman Catholic faith to this country. But murdering the King was not one of their designs. Nevertheless, many Catholics were hanged for it before Oates was found to be a vile perjurer. He ought to have been hanged himself but for the fact that the law does not prescribe the penalty of death for perjury. Instead, Oates was whipped, pilloried and sent to prison for life."

"Did Oates murder Sir Edmund Berry Godfrey, then?"

"Who killed him is a more abiding mystery," said Newton. "Some have thought that he was killed by a villain whom he had sentenced to prison as a magistrate, and who bore him a grudge. We are no strangers to such situations ourselves. I have even heard talk that Godfrey was one of those Green Ribboners that did seek to make the country once more a Republic; and that he was murdered when he threatened to betray them. But I myself favour another, simpler opinion.

"It is my belief that Godfrey strangled himself by leaning upon a ligature; he was by all accounts a most melancholy man, and feared being discovered a traitor and punished accordingly. Finding his body, Godfrey's two brothers feared the shame and the loss of Godfrey's money, for he was a rich man, and a suicide's estate is forfeit to the state, being *felo de se*. Therefore they mutilated his body and blamed it on Roman Catholics.

"What is certain is that no one will ever know the truth now. But there are many who still persist in the belief that he was murdered by Catholics. Major Mornay's opinion seems clear enough. His possession of this dagger and his conduct in the stews would seem to indicate that his detestation of Catholics knows no bounds."

"What then shall we do?"

Newton's brow gathered in a knot above his eyes and one slender finger stroked his long nose as if it had been a small shock dog, so that he did look most shrewd.

"We shall return this dagger to him," he said quietly. "And in doing so we shall further provoke him. It is a simple matter of motion, as are many other things to which proof, one day I shall find a pencil of black lead and sum it up for you on a page of paper, so that you might understand the world. For every body continues in its state of rest, or of uniform motion in a right line, unless it be compelled to change that state by forces impressed upon it. That's as true of Major Mornay as it is of the planets and the comets. But we must also be prepared. We must be vigilant. For to every action there is always opposed an equal reaction."

"But, sir, this is your great theory, is it not?"

"Well done, Ellis. But it is no theory. It's as much codified fact as the laws of England. More so, for I have the mathematical proofs that do render these laws immutable."

"I would understand what they mean for the world," I said. "If I could."

"Then understand only this," said Newton, and dropped the Godfrey dagger to the floor so that the point was left sticking in the boards. "The fall of this dagger is the same as the fall of the moon. The force that draws this dagger also draws the moon. The force that draws the moon also guides the planets and everything that is in the heavens. For the heavens are here on Earth. That, my dear fellow, is gravity."

The heavens are here on Earth? Perhaps this Earth is all the Heaven there is.

At first I only turned my back on Jesus. And that was Newton's doing, for there was very little in the New Testament to which he did not take some exception. The Old Testament he could only accept in parts. The Book of Solomon was very important to him. As was Daniel. And Ezekiel. But that a man might choose those books that suited him and reject those that did not seemed to me a very strange kind of religious faith.

For a long time I believed that it was Newton's opinions of holy scripture that had shaken the tree of my life and caused the apple of my religious faith to fall to the ground, where it started to rot and perish. But this was only part of the story. Because of Newton, asking questions became second nature to me. And I began to perceive that it is our duty to ask whether these religious things be true; and if true, whether they be good or not. If we wish to find God we must banish all ignorance of ourselves, our world and our universe.

Strangely it was those silver cups that Mister Scroope had given into Newton's keeping for their Cambridge college that first caused me to question the Pentateuch itself. The cups told the story of Nectanebus, the last native King of Egypt, who was a magician and made models of his own soldiers and those of the enemy and set them in a tank of water to work a trick so that his enemies should be engulfed in the waters of the Nile. And this made me think that when Moses led the children of Israel out of Egypt and all the Pharaoh's armies were drowned in the Red Sea, it was no more than a story borrowed from the Egyptians. Which shook me, for if the Pentateuch was not true, then everything else that followed in the Bible could be no more than myth or legend. Thus it was that gradually I came to think that if one part of the Bible might be questioned and found wanting, then why not the whole?

Perhaps I might still have believed in God. But it was my master's science that caused me to deny the existence of God himself. It was Newton's mathematics that reduced the cosmos to a series of algebraic calculations, while his damned prisms ripped apart God's rainbow covenant with Noah. How could God remain in heavens that were so keenly observed through a telescope and precisely described as a series of fluxions? Like some satanic geometer, Newton pricked the bubble of God's existence and then divided his heavenly kingdom with a simple pair of compasses. And seeing all such mysteries conquered, my own thoughts crashed to earth from the ethereal sky like a flaming cherub, with hideous ruin. O how fall'n! how changed. It was as if once I had thought myself an angel but, finding my wings clipped by the sharp scissor blades of science, I discovered I was merely a raven on Tower Green, raspingly lamenting its cruel fate. Regions of sorrow, doleful shades, where peace and rest can never dwell, hope never comes that comes to all.

In the officers' quarters at the Ordnance, Major Mornay was wearing his arm in a sling. He was being shaved by Mister Marks, the Tower Barber, and was attended by Mister Whiston, the broker, Lieutenant Colonel Fairwell, Captain Potter and Captain Martin. For all his previous evening's debauches, he seemed to be in good humour, for we had heard his voice outside the door; but even as we entered, he left off telling the brave story of how he had received the wound in his arm and, colouring like a beetroot, stared upon us as if we had been two ghosts.

"*Olim, hero, hodie, cras nescio cujus,*" Newton remarked with a cruel smile,

Once upon a time, yesterday, today, tomorrow, I know not whose, by which I assumed my master meant the Major to know that he was well aware that Mornay had lied about how he had come by his wound. And yet it was not a direct statement to that effect, for this might have provoked Mornay too far, perhaps into challenging Newton to a duel. My master was no coward; but he had seldom held a sword, let alone a pistol, and had not the slightest intention of being challenged. I suffered no such constraints, however, although Newton had cautioned me to give only utterance to that which he prompted.

"What do you mean by that?" Major Mornay asked Newton, his speech faltering like an admission of high treason.

"Mean? Why, nothing at all, Major. Nature has cursed me with a manner that doth sometimes seem like impertinence. It is only the disadvantage of intellect, for I think that Nature is best pleased with simplicity and affects not the pomp of super-fluous words or thoughts."

"To what do I owe the pleasure of your visit, Doctor?" He took a cloth from Mister Marks and wiped his face carefully.

"We came to return you this dagger," said Newton.

Mornay hardly glanced at the blade now in Newton's hand, its handle extended, politely, in the Major's direction, and then, briefly, at me, so that he did lie most brazenly.

"I own no such dagger," said Mornay. "Who says I do?"

"Perhaps you do not recognise it," said Newton, "since I have cleaned it for you. Otherwise one could not mistake such a dagger, to be sure. For it has a most noble sentiment engraved upon the blade. It says, 'Remember Sir Edmund Berry Godfrey. Remember religion.'"

"Amen," said Captain Martin.

"Amen indeed," said Mornay. "Nevertheless it is not my dagger."

Newton remained all smiles. "If you say so, Major, then it must be true, for you are a gentleman. And yet we should certainly not relinquish the evidence of one man's good eyes for the vain fictions of another man's devising." Newton pointed at me. "This humble clerk saw you drop this dagger last night, outside a house in Lambeth Marshes."

"I was nowhere near Lambeth Marshes last night."

Seeing that I was about to contradict Mornay's bare-faced lie, Newton did hold me by the arm and shake his head so slightly that I think only I perceived it.

"One of you two gentlemen must be mistaken."

"The mistake is not mine," said Mornay.

Newton let go my arm, which I took to mean that I was at last allowed to speak.

"Nor mine," said I.

"Why, then, one of you—I know not which—must be a liar and a shameroon," said Newton.

"Fetch a Bible," I said, hardly caring that the Bible had little value for me now. "Let me swear. The dagger is his."

"Have a care, sir." Newton spoke gravely to me. "For you do say as much as that Major Mornay is a liar to his face, in front of all his brother officers, for which, as a gentleman, he would surely demand the satisfaction of proving his word against yours by force of arms."

"I do say it. Most vehemently. Major Mornay is a liar. I saw him drop the dagger just as you have described."

Mornay rose from his chair, his mouth opening and closing like a cormorant.

"Were I not incommoded by my wound, I should not hesitate to challenge you, Mister Ellis."

"Perhaps," said Newton helpfully, "Mister Ellis could waive his privilege of choosing weapons. I believe the Major is right-handed. In which case he might challenge you safely, so to speak, were he to be assured that pistols would be your choice of weapons."

"Then let him be reassured," said I. "If he seeks satisfaction of me, he has my word that I should choose to fight with pistols."

There followed a longish silence with all eyes on Major Mornay, who swallowed loudly several times before, finally, stammering out a whey-faced challenge with less bravado than a toothless old gammer.

"We accept your challenge," said Newton. "I shall act as Mister Ellis's second and await your instructions." And so saying, he bowed gravely. Then did I, before taking our leave of these now-bemused officers.

Walking back to the Mint office, feeling like a numb eel, I steeled myself for a jangle with Newton, for I was right angry to find myself manoeuvred by him like a jolly-boat. And as soon as we were alone, I argued with him on the impropriety of his conduct to me.

"Well, I like that," I remarked. "I think a man might be allowed to pick his own quarrels and to issue his own challenges."

"He challenged you," said Newton, correcting me.

"Only because you painted him into a corner."

"If I had left the matter to you, my dear fellow, the matter could never have come to a head quite so neatly."

"Neatly, do you say? It's not a year since a duel almost cost me my liberty. Or had you forgotten how I came into your service, Doctor? Suppose I kill him? What then? Suppose he kills me? Suppose he's a better shot than he's a swordsman? Damn it all, sir, I thought you intended to trip him into some confession."

"There will be no fight," said Newton. "He has no stomach for it. That much was easily apparent."

"Very little that involves you is ever easily apparent to me," I said bitterly. "In this, as in all matters, I am your creature."

"Nay sir, not creature," said Newton reproachfully. "I create nothing. I merely attempt to extend the boundaries of what we know. And just as the Ancients put their faith in the god Pan and his pipe, so now and then, you must do the same and let me play a tune with you. My fingers may move upon you, but the music is yours, my dear fellow, the music is yours."

"Then I like not this tune. It's easier to govern a rapier point than a pistol ball. And I am not such a good shot that I can comb his hair with lead. If I shoot him, I might very likely kill him. And what of you, sir? My second. Have you no thought for your position? Duelling is illegal. Sir William Coventry was sent to the

Tower merely for challenging the Duke of Buckingham to a duel. To say nothing of your safety. You know, it's not unknown for seconds to engage and take their shares, even though the main protagonists may wish it otherwise. You may be killed, sir. And then what would become of Miss Barton?"

"And I say again that it will not proceed so far. For it is plain to me that Major Mornay is actuated by the will of others in this Tower. Perhaps his old friend from the French galleys, Sergeant Rohan. His challenge was not governed by them, and I believe they will now show themselves as they seek to reach an accommodation with us. For a duel would only draw attention to them in a way that cannot serve their secrecy. What is covert always abhors a scandal. For, as you say, that is what we will have if a duel is fought between Mint and Ordnance."

I know not what he expected. I doubt that he knew himself. For all his scientific method, it seemed a most unscientific course of action on which we were bound. Later on that day he dressed the matter up yet further and called it an experiment, but I could not believe it effectual for determining truth, and by my own thinking it was more akin to goading a bear with a hot iron. What is certain is that neither one of us had anticipated that which happened next; and for this Newton felt some shame and rightly so, since it seems to me that no one should make an experiment, so called, without having some idea of the possible outcomes. If that is science, then I want no part of it, since where is the common sense in it? To my mind it is like a girl who lets you bundle with her but does not have the apprehension that you might try and go even further. For when one seeks to discover something, sagacity would always seem to be a better guide than accident or otherwise the quest must result in things one did not seek at all.

PHILIP KERR

Such as a man's death, for example.

Major Mornay's body was discovered hanging in the Mint that same evening. I say "in the Mint" advisedly, for the circumstance of his death provoked yet another bitter argument between my master and Lord Lucas. Mornay was found hanged, having apparently tied a rope around a crenellation atop the Broad Arrow Tower, so that when he threw himself off the battlement his feet almost touched the ground in the Mint Comptroller's garden; and indeed it was the wife of one of the Mint Comptrollers, Mrs. Molyneux, who found the Major's body.

Newton was summoned straightaway by Mister Molyneux, who then returned to his house to comfort his poor wife, who was most upset by her discovery. My master was still contemplating the body as might an artist who proposed to sketch the scene for a painting of Judas Iscariot, when Lord Lucas and some other members of the Ordnance arrived on top of the Broad Arrow Tower and, declaring that the Major's death was properly a matter for the Ordnance—for it was given out immediately that it was Mornay who was dead—they sought to draw the rope still bearing him by the neck, back up the wall of the inner rampire. Which made Newton much aggrieved, and producing the ivory-handled table knife that he sometimes carried about his person, he cut through the rope so that the body fell into the Comptroller's rhubarb, which, although medicinal, had not the power to revive the poor Major from his lethal condition.

Seeing himself cheated of the jurisdiction—for as Newton reminded His Lordship, possession is nine points of the Law—Lucas's noble face took on an apoplectiform look and he thundered all sorts of revenges he would take on Newton when next he saw the Lords Justices, which Newton ignored as one who did not hear these threats at all. Instead he gave even closer inspection to the rope around Mornay's neck than the Major's previously elevated position had allowed.

"This is too bad," he sighed. "The poor fellow."

I had not liked the Major—he had tried to gouge me with his dagger, after all—but I, too, pitied him now as I pity all who murder themselves, for the Law makes suicide a most uncomfortable grave. And I murmured something in Newton's earshot to that effect.

"I have attended a sufficient number of executions within the course of my duty to know how a man's neck is affected by hanging," said Newton. "I have observed that the neck breaks but rarely, and most often that death be occasioned by simple strangulation. The lungs are deprived of air; but just as importantly, if William Harvey's book is to be believed, the brain is most mercifully deprived of blood.

"When a man is cut down before disembowelling, the rope hardly has time to draw tight, as occurs with a normal hanging. And yet I have noted how the geometry of his punishment always leaves its mark upon his neck, so that it may be observed how a man who slowly strangled upon the rope may be distinguished from one who hardly dangled at all.

"The level of tightening of the ligature in a hanging is always much higher than in strangulation and less likely to encircle the neck horizontally. Commonly it may be observed around the larynx in the front rising to a suspension point at the knot with its characteristic open angle behind or under the ear on one or t'other side, or at the back of the head. This means that with most hangings the impression caused by the noose will naturally be deepest opposite the suspension point.

"And yet here observe if you will," he told me, "that the neck bears the fine impression of the rope in two different places."

I looked at Mornay's neck as Newton had instructed, trying to ignore the turgid tongue that protruded from his mouth
like a third lip, and his eyes, which were as horribly prominent
as a couple of weeping chancres, and thus I saw, as he proposed, not one but two rope marks upon the Major's broken
neck.

"What does this mean?" I enquired uncertainly. "That the
rope slipped when he threw himself off the Tower?"

"No," Newton said firmly. "That he was strangled before he
was thrown off the Tower. And since strangulation is rarely sui-
cidal, we must conclude that he was murdered."

"Must we?"

"Yes indeed," he insisted. "The first mark which identifies
the strangulation shows even on the back of the neck where the
skin is thick and the tissues are tough, and could only have been
made by extreme violence and, as its corollary, a most desperate resistance. Moreover this mark is horizontal as would denote
someone attacking the Major from behind.

"Now contrast the second mark, which is much more ver-
tical and shows almost no resistant damage. This suggests that
the man was dead when it was made."

All of which made me think that Newton knew as much
about how a man might hang as Jack Ketch himself, so that his
arguments seemed to be quite without answer, except to say that
I could utter no objection to his findings. And, as ever, I was
astonished how much he seemed to know about nearly everything. But perhaps it was only fitting that the man who
explained gravity should be so well informed—even, it must be
said, animated—on the subject of hanging; and since then I have
often considered the possibility that he was morbidly fascinated
by the gallows. For my own part I find hanging a very unpleas-
ant sight, and said as much to Newton.

"All the doctors I have talked with," said he, "inform me

that there is no pain at all in hanging, for it stops the blood's circulation to the brain and so ends all sense in an instant."

"I have yet to see the man turned off a ladder who bears his experience with a smile on his face."

"What?" exclaimed Newton, and leaving off his examination of the Major's neck, he set about an inspection of his hands, as if, like some ancient chiromancer, he might divine the origins of the poor man's fate. "You think that we should let rogues walk free who also deserve to hang?"

"I think that there is much difference between a flash ballad and a capital crime."

"Oh, you would have made a fine barrister," teased Newton. And then, holding up one of Mornay's hands, he asked me to note the fingers. "Look at his fingernails," he said. "Torn and bloody. As if he struggled against the rope. A real suicide would meet the means of his own end with greater equanimity. It may be that the Major's murderer bears the scars of his crime. Perhaps some scratches on his hands and face."

Newton prised open the dead man's jaws and, pushing aside his tongue, searched his mouth. But finding nothing, he began to search the dead man's pockets.

"I regret that I did not foresee this circumstance," admitted Newton. "This is my fault. I confess I did not think they would kill their own confederate. My own consolation is that by proving this is murder and not suicide, I shall save him from a dishonourable burial. But am I mistaken or did he not try and kill you last night? Why should you be sorry for him?"

"I am sorry for anyone who meets such a fate as this," said I.

Newton paused. "Ah, but what have we here?" His long lean hands produced a letter which he unfolded.

"Now we have something," he said, mighty pleased at this new discovery. "For this is written in the same code as those other messages before."

He showed me the letter, which appeared thus:

vahtvjrqcyubxqtmtyqtowbbmhwdjpmgulmplyaklyualrek
kmjbatapffehyztmweenlolkymnolcoevkbbdmhfffjamiocc
cqsaayuwddogscaostanxmcadppbokwqdsknuvkhlpjrzrg
waxcifdtjgxtbohbjxkpeuqwfmchvwmvhqycrwmkrrwgapr
xjjovzhhryvqpbzlnklplzaysagxsgckbvtxzbhfptmhldqchyy
czgwraebbbntvzmbsrzbmsxnqtbaxqcipkbacmtizrrmiqyi
qdsjuojbsh

"Excellent," he said, pocketing the letter upon my returning it to him. "Our material is accumulating. Now, at last, we may make some progress in this case."

"With three people murdered, let us hope so."

"Four," said Newton. "You have a habit of forgetting George Macey."

"I had not forgotten," I said. "How could I when the manner of his death was so memorable? But at your own instruction I had put it out of my mind. Or at least one part of my mind. And yet for all its singularity, I sometimes think his death can hardly be associated with these others."

Newton only grunted, and seeming much preoccupied with the poor Major's death, he walked slowly back to the Mint office—not along Water Lane, which would have been more direct, but up Mint Street; for although he did not say, I knew that he wished to avoid a further confrontation with Lord Lucas—with me following at a distance respectful to his deep thoughts.

Upon reaching the Mint office I fetched us both a cup of cider—of which he was most fond—and I observed that Newton thought some more. He sat down in his favourite chair by the fire, and removing his wig, which was always a sign that he wished his brain to be most comfortable inside his head, he held his lace stock with both hands and twisted it like a garrotte, as if he meant to squeeze something useful out of his head.

For a while I believed he did recriminate himself some more, or that his thoughts were directed toward the cipher, for although he did not examine the letter he had taken from the Major, I knew his mind was capable of holding what was written there almost at a glance. But when, after more than an hour with the cat upon his lap, he spoke again, it was to utter one word.

"Remarkable," he said.

"What is, sir?"

"Why, the murder of Major Mornay, of course."

"With respect, Doctor, I have been sitting here considering how unremarkable it is. Compared with the others that went before."

"What was it you said about George Macey?" he asked.

"Why, sir, nothing. I have been silent this past hour."

"Back in the Comptroller's garden, sir. What were you talking about?"

"Only that it seemed hard to believe that Macey's murder had any connection with these three subsequent murders, sir."

"Why do you say so?"

"Its very lack of any distinguishing features, sir."

"But do you find many such features attending the murder of Major Mornay?" he asked.

"Well, sir, there is the coded letter. We first encountered the code with Kennedy, and then with Mercer."

"Apart from that, what else?"

I thought for a moment. "I cannot think of anything," I admitted.

"That is what is so remarkable about this latest murder," said Newton. "Its singular lack of features. No dead ravens. No stones in the dead man's mouth. No peacock feathers. No flute.

Nothing except the body itself and this enciphered letter. It is as if the Tower's murderer had become mute."

"Indeed, sir. But perhaps our murderer has nothing to say to us. And but for the presence of another message in code, one might almost think Major Mornay was murdered by someone different from the man who killed Mercer and Kennedy. Or for that matter from the person who killed George Macey."

Newton lapsed into another of his long silences, which were best answered with silence. And it was at times like these that I put aside the murders that were done in the Tower and, picking up a sampler in my mind, returned with silk thread and tent stitches to further embroider my love for Miss Catherine Barton. Which by now was quite a piece of work. And with my own thoughts thus diverted, I dreamed of being in her company again, for it was that night that I was due to sup with her uncle and his niece; so that I almost thought Newton had looked into my mind and seen what was done there when he said that it was time we went to Jermyn Street, to sup. My heart missed a beat and my ears burned so that I was glad I was wearing my wig and Newton could not see their colour and mock my embarrassment.

The coach journey to Jermyn Street was also conducted in silence, which made me think that for all his avowed hostility to the monastic order, Newton should have made a splendid monk, albeit one like his hero, Giordano Bruno. Bruno was executed as a heretic in 1600 because of his theories of the infinite universe, the multiplicity of worlds, and his adherence to Copernicanism. Newton greatly admired Bruno, who was strongly suspected of Arianism, and certainly the two had much in common, although I do not think they could ever have liked each other. Like Cain, genius cannot abide its own brother.

Nor is genius always as honest as it could be. I already knew how Newton had pretended a show of adherence to Trinitarianism at Cambridge in order to remain the Lucasian

Professor of Mathematics. I was about to apprehend just how much Newton could also counterfeit a show of religious orthodoxy toward his niece, Miss Barton.

In truth she seemed more than pleased to see me accompanying her uncle, for I swear she blushed upon finding me standing in her parlour, and stammered out a greeting most tremulously, which made me feel very good inside, as if I had already quaffed a mug of the hot wine she swiftly prepared for us. She wore a lace commode upon her head, as was most fashionable, an amber necklace, and a silver lace Mantua gown which was open at the front to reveal an embroidered corset, and was most becoming to her.

After supper, Miss Barton sang to her own accompaniment on the spinette, which was as beautiful a sound as I had ever hoped to hear outside of heaven. She had a fine voice, not strong but very pure, although I think that Newton cared nothing for music, whatever its origin. At last he stood up, pulled the periwig from his head, which Miss Barton replaced with an elegant scarlet nightcap of her own embroidery, and bowed slightly in my direction.

"I have a mind to study our cipher," he explained. "So I will say good night to you, Mister Ellis."

"Then I must be leaving, too."

"Shall you go?" asked Miss Barton.

"Pray, stay a while longer, Mister Ellis," insisted Newton. "And keep Miss Barton company. I insist."

"Then, sir, I shall."

Newton retired to his library and, that being done, Miss Barton smiled sweetly at me and for several minutes we sat in silence, savouring our privacy, for this was the first time we had ever found ourselves alone, Mrs. Rogers having long before retired. Gradually, Miss Barton began to talk: about the war in the Netherlands and Mister Dryden's newest book that was a translation of the works of Virgil, and Mister Southern's latest play, being titled *The Maid's Last Prayer,* which she had seen and very much enjoyed. It seemed that she was nervous and sought to find herself at ease in conversation.

"I did not see that one," I confessed, although I might have added that her own uncle kept me too busy ever to go to see plays performed. "But I saw the one before, which was *The Wives' Excuse.*"

"Which I have not seen. But I have read it. Tell me, Mister Ellis. Do you agree that cuckolds make themselves?"

"Not being married, it is a little difficult for me to speak about that condition," I said. "But I should think that a wife would only ever be provoked to cuckold a husband because of his own failings."

"That is my opinion also," she said. "Although I do not think that because a man is married he must be a cuckold. For that would be scandal upon all women."

"Yes, it would."

In similar vein we spoke awhile, although I found it difficult to rid myself of the very vivid memory I still carried of the whore at Mrs. Marsh's house, whose name was Deborah and who resembled Miss Barton as two peas in a pod—which made me sometimes tongue-tied, for I had the apprehension that at any moment Miss Barton might shrug off her Mantua and her silk embroidered corset and mount the dinner table and strike an indecent posture for my amusement.

And, truth to tell, her conversation seemed mighty sophisticated for a girl of her age and somewhat at odds with her youthful beauty and apparent simplicity. She even asked me about the murders in the Tower, which Newton had told her about, and it was quickly clear to me that she was not the modest white violet Newton had led me to believe she was. Indeed her discourse was so lively that I soon formed the impression that her intelligence was almost equal to his own. Certainly she had as much desire to experiment with life as he—perhaps more so, as I was about to discover. But while the garden of her mind was laid out with the same symmetry and logic as her uncle's, much that was planted there had yet to grow to maturity.

"Mister Ellis," she said finally, "I should like you to sit beside me."

I drew my chair close to her, as she asked.

"You may hold my hand if you choose," she added now; and so I did.

"Miss Barton," I said, encouraged by our proximity, "you are the loveliest creature that any man ever beheld." And I kissed her hand.

"Dear Tom," she said. "You kiss my hand. But will you not kiss me properly?"

"With pleasure, Miss Barton," I said, and, leaning forward, kissed her most chastely on the cheek.

"You kiss me like my uncle, sir," she admonished. "Will you not kiss me upon the lips of my mouth?"

"If you will permit it," I said, and kissed her rosebud lips most tenderly. After which I held her little hand and told her how much I loved her.

She made no reply to this declaration of love, almost as if she already knew how much I loved her and took it as no more than her due. Instead she spoke of the kiss, with such forensic choice of language as one might have used to plead in an English court of law.

"That was most enlightening," she said, curling her fingers in mine. "Brief, but stimulating. You may do it again whenever you wish. Only this time, longer please."

When I had kissed her again, she exhaled most satisfiedly, licked her lips as if enjoying the taste I had left there, and smiled brightly. And I smiled back, for I was in heaven. In England it was not at all unusual for young women to take the lead in sexual matters, often with the connivance of their parents. Once or twice I had bundled with a girl in the presence of her mother and sisters. Yet I had not expected one so angelic to be quite so forward.

"You may feel my breasts if you wish," she offered. "Come, let me sit on your lap, so that you may touch them more easily."

So saying, she stood up, untied the ribbons that laced her corset, and, baring her breasts, which were larger than I had supposed, sat down upon my lap. Hardly needing a second invitation, I gently weighed these bubbies in my hand, and kneaded her nipples, which seemed to afford her no small delight. After a while she stood up, and fearing that I might have gone too far, I asked what was the matter.

"The matter, sir," she said, smiling, most lasciviously, "is that." And she pointed to the unmistakable evidence that I too had enjoyed the experience; and kneeling before me, she touched my privy parts through my breeches and asked that she might look upon them.

"I have seen my brothers," she said. "But only when they were boys. And I have never seen the privy parts of a man who was ready for love, so to speak. All that I know, which is very little, is from a book," she added. *"Aretine's Postures.* Which raises as many questions as it supplies answers. And I should like very much to gaze upon Priapus, now."

"What if Doctor Newton should come into the room?" I said.

Miss Barton shook her head and, through my breeches, squeezed my cock most affectionately. "Oh, we won't see him again tonight. Not now he has started to think upon that cipher. He will often cogitate upon such problems all night long. Once Mister Bernoulli and Mister Leibniz suggested a problem to him that kept him occupied until dawn. During that time I spoke to him, entreated him to go to bed, offered him some cider, and yet he paid me no heed at all. It was as if I had not been there."

"But if Mrs. Rogers should disturb us," I protested.

"She has gone to bed," she said. And then: "You studied for the Law, did you not, Mister Ellis?"

"Yes, I did."

"Then you will know what a *quid pro quo* is, sir."

"Indeed I do, Miss Barton."

"Then what about a *quim pro quo*?"

I grinned and shook my head that she did know such a word. But amusement turned to surprise and ecstasy as she lifted her skirts and suffered me to fondle her belly, thighs, and cunny parts. And pressing my mouth to these, I licked her from stem to stern, which drew such gasps from her lips as I thought would wake the house; but each time I tried to draw my head away, she gripped my hair most tightly, and held my mouth there until she was done.

So that when finally I unbuttoned my own breeches to show her my prick and suffered her to look upon me, I was as mighty a figure as ever I have been in my life. So that Miss Barton marvelled that such a thing as human lovemaking were possible.

"To think," she breathed, squeezing my cock in her fist, "that so large a part of a man can go inside a woman's quim."

"One might as well wonder that woman do give birth to infants," said I.

"Yet how vulnerable it is," she continued, marvelling. "How tender wounded looks its head. As if it has been struck hard about the face. And yet how frightening also. For it seems almost to have a life of its own."

"You say more than you know, Miss Barton," I said.

"The seed emanates from the small fissure, does it not?" she asked.

"It does and will if you are not careful," I said.

"Oh, but I want to see the ejaculate," she insisted. "I want to understand everything."

"The ejaculate is most phrenetic," I said, "and I cannot answer for where I would fetch off." Feebly, I added, "On your gown . . ."

"Perhaps if I gathered it in my mouth," she said; and before I could forbid it, she had taken my whole member into her mouth, after which I was quite incapable of resisting her further anatomical enquiry of me, for so it did feel, until I had fetched off in her mouth. Which to my horror, she swallowed.

"Catherine," I said, withdrawing my privy parts from her cool hands, and doing up my breeches again, "I cannot think it safe that you swallowed that."

"Why, Tom, dear, it is quite safe, I can assure you. There is no danger of being brought to bed with a child. A woman's womb may be of her belly, but it is not connected to her stomach." She laughed and then wiped her lips with a kerchief.

I drank a draught of cider to try to calm myself.

"That was most instructive," she remarked. "And most enjoyable. I am most grateful to you. And in truth, now that I have seen and tasted a man's cock in all its glory, there is much that doth seem clear to me."

"I am very glad of it, Catherine," said I and kissed her forehead. "But the only thing clear to me now is how much I do adore you."

For a long while we sat in front of the fire, holding hands and saying very little. I would kiss her and she would kiss me back. And thinking us to be as intimate in all things as it was possible to be with another human being, I now made a terrible mistake.

A mistake that perhaps cost me my life's happiness.

After we were seated again, and we did converse again, I think, again most businesslike, she did turn our conversation to the plays of Mister Otway: in particular *The Soldier's Fortune* and its sequel, *The Atheist,* which, she and I being both Whigs ourselves, neither of us had liked particularly well. If I had left things there, it might have gone well enough between us. In time, we might even have married. But then I made some remark to the effect that I knew not how any man could remain a Christian who came into close contact with her uncle's opinions. At which point Miss Barton seemed to form the impression that some great insult had been done to him, for she withdrew her hand from mine immediately, and the colour she had worn since our bundling quite drained away in an instant.

"Pray, sir," she said coldly, "what do you mean by that remark?"

"Why, only what must be well known to you, Miss Barton. That Doctor Newton believes all received Christian tradition to be counterfeit and a fraud perpetrated by evil men who, for their own purposes, have wilfully corrupted the heritage of Jesus Christ."

"Stop," cried Miss Barton, rising suddenly to her feet, one of which she stamped like an impatient little pony. "Stop. Stop."

Slowly I stood up and faced her, only now too late realising the truth of the matter, which was that for all her uncle's heretical opinions—of which I could now perceive that she knew nothing—her clever discourse, her inquiring mind, and her manifest desire for me, Miss Barton herself retained the simple Christian faith of a village curate's wife.

"How could you say such a wicked thing about my uncle?" she demanded, her eyes moistening suddenly.

I did not compound my offences by asserting that I had merely spoken the truth, for that would have added insult to the box on the ears my words had already given her; and instead I chose to compound them by explaining that it was possible that the unorthodox opinions I had imputed to Doctor Newton were mine and mine alone.

"Can it be that you believe such heinous and wicked things as I have heard you utter tonight?"

What is a lie? Nothing. Nothing but words. Could I have dissembled and preserved the bond that was between us? It is possible. Love, like a cuckolded husband, wishes to be deceived. I could have answered smoothly that I was a true Christian and that I thought my fever had returned, and she might have believed me. I might even have counterfeited a fainting attack and collapsed down upon the floor, as if I had been afflicted with the falling sickness. But instead I avoided her question altogether, which I'll warrant was all the answer she needed.

"If I have offended you, Miss Barton, I am most heartily sorry and beg your pardon, most humbly."

"You have offended yourself, Mister Ellis," she said with a quite regal degree of hauteur. "Not just in my eyes, but in the eyes of Him who created you and in front of whom you will one day stand for judgement and be held to account for your blasphemy." And then, shaking her head, she sighed loudly and added, "I have loved you, Mister Ellis. There is nothing I could not have done for you, sir. As you have already witnessed this evening. You have occupied my every waking thought these past few months. I would have loved you so much. Perhaps in time we might even have married. How else could I have permitted our earlier intimacies? But I could not love anyone who did not love Our Lord Jesus Christ."

This was sore indeed and hardly to be endured, for it was plain to me that she intended our relationship to be at an end; and my only hope of her being reconciled to me now lay with him who had no more understanding of love than Oliver

Cromwell. But still I tried to justify myself, as when one who is condemned although not yet sentenced is asked if he has anything to say.

"Religion is full of rogues," said I, "who pretend to be pious. All I can say, Miss Barton, is that my atheism is honest and hard-wrought. I would that it were different. I had rather believe all the fables and all the legends than that this universal frame is without a mind. And yet I do not. I cannot. I will not. Until I met your uncle I had no other apprehension but that to deny God is to destroy the mystery of the world. Yet now that I have perceived how it is possible to see the mystery of the world explained by a man such as he, I cannot believe other than that the Church is as empty as a fairy ring, or that the Bible is as baseless as the Koran."

Miss Barton shook her head vigorously. "But where does the uniformity in all the outward shapes of birds, beasts and men come but from the counsel and contrivance of a divine author? How is it that the eyes of all creatures are made the same? Did blind chance know that there was light and how it might be refracted, and did it design the eyes of all creatures after the most curious manner to make use of it?"

"The accident of uniformity in creation only seems to be thus," I argued. "As once gravity and the rainbow used to seem which, now explained, are no more accidents than prisms or telescopes. One day all these questions will be answered, but not by reason of a God. Your uncle's hand has pointed out the way forward."

"Do not say this," said Miss Barton. "He does not believe this. For him, atheism is senseless and odious to mankind. He knows that there is a Being who made all things and has all things in his power, and who is therefore to be feared. Fear God, Mister Ellis. Fear him as once you loved me."

It was my turn to shake my head. "Man's nobility is not born of fear, but of reason. If I must be kin to God by fear, then

God is himself ignoble. And if your uncle does not understand this, it can only be because he does not wish to understand, for in all else he is the very spirit of understanding.

"But let us have no more high words, Miss Barton. I can see the insult I have offered you seems very grievous and shall say no more to vex you further."

I bowed stiffly, and adding only that I would love her forever, to which she said nothing, I took my leave, already weary, to walk the several miles back to the Tower. And as I walked I had the smell of Miss Barton's privy parts on my fingers to confirm that for a moment I had possessed her, only then to be rejected; and I was like one who had been shown the gates of Paradise only to have been denied entry. Which gave me no more appetite for my life than Judas, if such a man ever did exist. Indeed I might have hanged myself as Major Mornay was in the beginning thought to have done, but for the fear that now infected me of being nothing afterward.

It is no wonder that the early Christians could go to their martyrdoms with hymns on their lips when a place in Heaven seemed assured. But what was there for atheists, except oblivion? And without Miss Barton there was not even Paradise on earth.

It was two of the clock by the time I reached Tower Hill, and I could not have felt worse if I had been told I was to meet the hangman and his axe there in the morning. In the Lion Tower, one of the big cats moaned most pitiably, which sounded much like my own hopeless spirit, so that I pictured myself pacing up and down within the cage of my own disbelief. I passed through the gates at the Byward, with hardly a word for the sentry, Mister Grain, feeling as much sorrow for myself as any who had ever gone into that unhappy place. And when at last I reached my house, I went straightaway to bed but could not sleep all night.

So at six o'clock, with very little repose and rest, I arose and took a turn about the battlements to clear my head in a brisk wind that blew up the Thames from Deptford. London's early-morning bustle contrasted sharply with my own preternatural calm: barges unloaded cargoes of wood and coal upon the Tower's wharf at the same time that three-masted ships were setting sail for Chatham and beyond; while on the western side, in range of the dozen and a half cannon that were pointed at the City, maids in wide straw hats were putting down large baskets of fruit, bread and vegetables upon the ruined walls of the Tower's old bulwark to sell unto the people that were already walking or riding by. Behind me, the flag of Saint George fluttered and snapped loudly in the unrelenting breeze, like a ship's sail; at seven o'clock the gun on the Brass Mount fired its own salute to another day; and columns of soldiers stiffly marched their clockwork way about the Inner Ward like toys at a fair. And all the while I felt as if the world was passing me by, like a mote in a sunbeam.

My heart full of trouble, I went to the Mint office at around eight o'clock and occupied myself with filing away witness statements in the other cases we still had to deal with; until Doctor Newton came and immediately began to talk about his night's work with the cipher, for it appeared he had not gone to bed at all. But all the time he spoke, my mind was yet at disquiet that I could not be informed how I stood with Miss Barton and if the morning still found her much offended with me.

"I have a solution," he said, with reference to the cipher. "Of sorts."

Chapter Four

Barent Coenders van Helpen, *Escalier des sages*, 1689

AND THERE CAME IN ME FEAR WITH JOY, FOR I SAW A NEW LIGHT GREATER THAN THE LIGHT OF DAY.

(THE APOCALYPSE OF PETER)

I was too upset about what had passed between myself and Miss Barton to be much interested in Newton's solution to the cipher; and yet I feigned some attention while, with much animation, he spoke of it; so that if there was one thing I understood most clearly, it was that Miss Barton had not spoken to her uncle of our disagreement; and since she had avoided mentioning it, quickly I resolved to do the same, although it had occasioned the greatest sorrow to me that I ever knew in this world.

"My hypothesis upon this cipher has been pressed with many difficulties," explained Newton. He sat by the table with his papers spread out, and Melchior the cat upon his lap. "As a blind man has no idea of colours, so had I no idea of the manner by which this cipher worked. I still do not. I confess the key eludes me even yet. But what I think I understand now is how the cipher is related to the murders that were done. That I did not perceive this earlier now seems to me so great an absurdity that I begin to wonder what this employment within the Mint has done to my mind. For I believe no man who has any competent faculty of thinking about philosophical matters should ever fall into such an error.

"Because you, my dear fellow, always desire simplicity in things, I'll explain myself with what brevity I can. Three murders have been accompanied by written ciphers. I have worked upon these with such diligence, you would have thought I did this labour like Heracles. And yet in spite of all my efforts, for all my weapons of divine origin, I am left with only mathematical contradictions. And a contradiction *in terminis* argues nothing more than an impropriety of speech. In other words, the logic in the code is at fault because I suspect that the code has been sometimes used ignorantly, by someone who did not know how the cipher operated.

"It was you, my young friend, who put this in my mind. It was you who mentioned that one might think these murders were done by different people. And so I do believe, but not until last night.

"Now, the murder of George Macey was clear enough in the sense that there was no distinguishing feature save the awful brutality with which it was committed. There were no ciphers, nor any signs of hermetic significance.

"Then things started to become interesting. The murders of Mister Kennedy and Mister Mercer both showed us hermetic signs and written ciphers; and for a long time I also thought that Macey's murder might even have presented some similar features that time and the actions of putrefaction prevented us from observing.

"But with the murder of Major Mornay, our picture changed once more. This time we found a written cipher, but nothing to indicate there was anything remotely hermetic about it. Now here is a curious thing, Ellis: only the second and third murders show any visible consistency; however, it is only the second and fourth murders in which may be demonstrated some mathematical consistency. Because with the third murder, that of Major Mercer, which gave us the shortest message of all— that which was chalked upon the wall of the Sally Port stairs— the cipher was used without any discernible logic, which leads me to suppose that the author of the third murder could not be the author of the fourth. And the cipher that was chalked upon the wall beside Mister Mercer's body was wrong. Or, to put the case another way, that it was used ignorantly, as I have said."

"What about the cipher that Mister Twistleton gave us?" I asked. "Was that used ignorantly too?"

"No, no," said Newton. "That demonstrates the same logic as those other messages that were letters also. It is only the message chalked upon the stairs that is wrong. Therefore I have discounted it altogether." He shook his head wearily. "It has cost me much time. But for that, I might have understood this whole case by now."

Newton pounded the table in the Mint office with his fist, which made Melchior leap off his lap with fright. "If only I had another sample of this cipher," he said, pounding the table again, which shook me out of my silence. "For I am certain I could solve it now."

To his credit, Newton had not accused me of copying the cipher on the wall near Mercer's body incorrectly, for which I was grateful; but nevertheless I was somewhat taken aback at what he seemed to be suggesting.

"But that is almost the same as saying you would wish a fifth murder to be done," I said with some incredulity. "Are not four murders enough?" I shook my head. "Or do you intend to provoke that one, too?"

Newton stayed silent, avoiding my eyes, mistaking all that was welling there for disapproval of him.

"You are taking this too lightly, Doctor," I said, admonishing him. "As if it were a mere mathematical exercise such as that problem Mister Bernoulli and Mister Leibniz challenged you with."

"The brachistochrone?" Newton frowned: this was the name of the mathematical conundrum set by Leibniz and

Bernoulli with which they hoped to defeat Newton. "I can assure you, Ellis, that was no mere exercise, as you describe it. When no man in all of Europe could provide a solution, I solved it."

"But this is murder, Doctor. And yet it seems to me that you are treating it as an intellectual diversion."

"It would take a considerable intellect to divert me," insisted Newton, who coloured a little as he spoke.

"Nevertheless, you are diverted," said I.

"What's that?"

"What could be more diverting for a mathematician than a code? What could be more intriguing for one who is philosophically adept than those hermetic signs of alchemy that accompanied the murders of Mister Kennedy and Mister Mercer?"

"True," admitted Newton. "If only I had more data, I tell you I could solve this problem overnight. Just as I did the brachistochrone."

"Perhaps that is the point, Doctor," said I. "Perhaps you are not meant to solve the code. Perhaps it means nothing at all. Or perhaps God does not mean you to unravel it." I was merely using God's name to discover if it still sounded convincing on my own tongue; but also to provoke him, for I was become increasingly ill-tempered in this conversation, which was a combination of a broken heart and no sleep.

Newton stood up suddenly, as if he had received the effect of a clyster.

"God does not mean me to unravel it," he breathed excitedly. "Or someone else that does play at being God who is the architect of this design." And snatching off his wig he walked about the office muttering to himself: "This will make the pot boil, Mister Ellis. This will make the pot boil."

"What pot is that, sir?"

Newton tapped his forefinger against his temples. "Why,

this pot, of course. Oh, what a fool I have been. Too much conceit, that's what does it. That this should happen to me. Me. I should have been more mindful of Occam's razor."

"No more things should be presumed to exist than are absolutely necessary," I construed.

"Exactly so. It is the principle of William of Occam, our brilliant and rebellious countryman who wrote vigorously against the Pope, as well as much idle metaphysics. He was a great freethinker, Ellis, who helped to separate questions of reason from questions of faith, and thus laid the foundations for our modern scientific method. Upon his razorlike maxim we shall cut this case into exactly two halves. Fetch me some cider. My head has a sudden need for apples."

I poured some cider for my master, which he drank as if he really did seek to stimulate his brain. Then, seating himself again, and taking up pen and paper, he wrote down what he called the bare bones of the case. After which he put more metaphorical ashes upon his head and declared himself properly penitent for his earlier lack of apprehension. And yet I thought that his avowed lack of earlier understanding could hardly compare with my own that still continued unabated; at least until he spoke again.

"This is the second time today I have found myself at fault," he reported. "And I am right glad that only you are here to witness it, Ellis, and not that damned German or that awful dwarf, Hooke. They would be delighted to see me so easily tricked."

"Tricked? How so?"

"Why, it's just as you said yourself. I have been diverted, have I not? Cast your mind back a few months, Ellis. What case were we investigating when Mister Kennedy was killed?"

"Those golden guineas," said I. "The ones that were done with the *d'orure moulu* process. A case that remains unsolved."

"You see, you were quite right. I was diverted. As someone meant me to be diverted. Someone who knew me well, I think.

For those hermetick clues were for my benefit. And I now believe that those other messages—the ones that were enciphered—were for someone else."

"Then why did we first find the cipher when Mister Kennedy was murdered?" I asked. "Alongside other hermetic clues?"

"Because I believe that whoever killed Kennedy had no understanding of the code," explained Newton. "For there is much that is contradictious between our first enciphered message and the second; and yet the underlying elements are the same."

"Are you suggesting that Major Mornay's murderer did not kill the other three?"

"Merely that he did not kill Kennedy and Mercer. For only those two murders have the peculiar alchemical flourishes that were designed to intrigue me. Whoever killed Major Mornay only wanted him dead and out of my sight."

"But why?"

"We should need to solve the cipher to know that," said Newton.

"So you believe that whoever killed Kennedy and Mercer merely wanted to lead you away from those golden guineas."

"Kennedy was killed because he was set to watch Mercer. Mercer was killed because he was being watched. Because he might have given away the names of his fellow coiners."

"This is most confusing," said I.

"On the contrary," said Newton. "My hypothesis agrees with the phenomena very well, and I confess I begin to see the light." He nodded firmly. "Yes, I think it very probable because a great part of what we have seen easily flows from that which would otherwise seem inexplicable."

"If you do not think that Major Mornay's killer is responsible for the deaths of Kennedy and Mercer," said I, "what do you think of him for George Macey's murder?"

"I like him very well for it. But there is no evidence. Therefore I can frame no hypothesis. In truth I have much neglected what I do know about George Macey."

Newton got up from his chair and walked over to the bookshelf where the Mint records were kept, as well as several numismatic histories, account books, law reports, Mister Violet's Commons Report of 1651, and the small library that George Macey had owned, being a Latin primer, a book on mathematics, a book on the French language, and a book of shorthand.

"It is not possible to know much about him now," said I.

"Except that his reading showed a commendable desire for self-improvement," said Newton. "It is always best that a man educate himself. The superior education is the one wrought from private study. Even I taught myself mathematics. And yet I wonder that Mister Macey wished to learn French. My own French is less than perfect. For I like the French not at all."

"Since we are still at war with them," I said, "I cannot fault you for that, Doctor."

Ignoring Melchior, who wrapped his tail around Newton's hand like a whore's shawl, Newton picked up Mister Macey's French grammar, blew the dust off the cover—which was always considerable in the Mint office, from the constant vibration of the coining presses, not to mention the cannon—and turned the pages of the book. To my surprise, for I knew Newton had already examined the book once before, he found a paper that was pressed between the leaves.

"It's a bookseller's account," said Newton. "Samuel Lowndes, by the Savoy."

The Savoy was a great town house on the south side of the Strand, with grounds stretching down to the river. Most of it was given over to a hospital for sick and wounded seamen and soldiers, so that the whole area teemed with men recently returned from the war in Flanders—some of them terribly mutilated by grapeshot or bursting charge; and there were several poor wretches that I saw who were missing limbs or parts of their faces.

The remainder of the building was leased out to a French church, the King's Printing Press, two gaols—both full—some private lodgings, and a number of shops that included Samuel Lowndes, the bookseller.

Mister Lowndes was a slight figure of a man, with an urchin's face and a most obsequious manner so that the minute Newton and I came through his door, he pulled off his apron, put on his wig and coat, and, with wringing hands, waited upon the Doctor in a most servile, cringing way.

"I want a bookseller," muttered Newton. "Not a Lord Chamberlain."

"Doctor Newton," exclaimed Mister Lowndes. "Why, sir, what a very great honour you do my shop by coming into it. Do you search for something in particular, sir?"

"I search for information about a customer you had last year, Mister Lowndes. A Mister George Macey, who worked for His Majesty's Mint in the Tower. As I do myself."

"Yes, I recall Mister Macey. Indeed, now I come to think more upon it, it's almost a year since I have seen him. How is Mister Macey?"

"Deceased," Newton replied bluntly.

"I am right sorry to hear it."

"There were certain circumstances about Mister Macey's death which show the grim character of homicide," explained Newton. "And it touching upon the business of the Mint, we consider it a matter imperative to speak to all who can shed some light as to what his habits were. We have recently discov-

I would be grateful if you could assist me by bending your recollection to other people you might have seen him with; some
names he may have mentioned to you; or perhaps even the
books he bought."

Mister Lowndes looked most discomfited by the news of
Macey's murder; and yet he quickly did as Newton had asked
and straightaway consulted a ledger book that contained a
record of all his customer accounts.

"He was a pleasant man," said Mister Lowndes, turning the
ledger's thick pages. "Not an educated one like yourself, Doctor.
But a conscientious one; and governed by a Christian sense of
duty."

"Very commendable, I'm sure," murmured Newton.

Mister Lowndes found the page he had been searching for.
"Here we are, sir," he said. "Yes, he purchased several books of
a didactic nature, as you can see for yourself. And one that surprised me very much, being so unlike the others. Also, it was
expensive. Very expensive for a man of his means."

Following Mister Lowndes's forefinger upon the ledger,
Newton observed the written entry for a moment and then read
aloud the title and author to which the bookseller did refer.
"Polygraphia, by Trithemius. I know your Latin is good, Mister
Ellis. But how is your Greek, sir?"

"Polygraphia? I think that would mean 'much writing,'"
said I, whose Greek was never much good at all.

"Quite so," agreed Mister Lowndes. "Although the book
itself was written in Latin."

"And yet Macey had no Latin," objected Newton. "The elementary character of the Latin primer he bought from Mister
Lowndes would seem to confirm as much." Newton paused and
tapped his bony finger upon the page of the ledger. "Did he
explain why he wanted this particular book?"

"I seem to recall that he intended it to be a gift for some-one. But who I cannot say."

"Could you perhaps find me another copy of this book, Mister Lowndes?"

"Not for several weeks," admitted Mister Lowndes. "I had to send off to Germany to obtain the copy that Mister Macey ordered. You might, of course, search around St. Paul's. The Latin coffee house near there often holds auctions of rare and expensive books such as the one for which you search."

Newton grunted without much enthusiasm at such a labo-rious prospect.

"But I believe I know where you might have sight of a copy, at least, for I ordered a copy of this same book once before."

Mister Lowndes turned back the pages of his ledger until he found what he was looking for.

"Here we are, Doctor. That other customer was Doctor Wallis. I ordered the same book for him."

"Doctor John Wallis?" repeated Newton. "Do you mean he that is the Savilian Professor of Geometry at Oxford University, sir?"

"Aye sir, the very same. I believe I said as much myself to Mister Macey. He seemed most interested by the news."

"So am I, sir," admitted Newton. "So am I."

Early the next morning we took the flying coach to Oxford, which was a most vexatious journey, with much dangerous water on the road because of recent heavy rain, and there was almost some mischance to the coach, but no time lost, so that we arrived at our destination about thirteen hours after leaving London.

Newton had many friends at Oxford. Chief among these was David Gregory, a young Scotsman who held the Savilian

Chair of Astronomy and who, at very short notice, dined us very well at Merton, which is a very pretty place, and was my own college, which made me feel mighty peculiar, my being back there.

I believe Gregory must have been about thirty-eight years of age when first I met him. He was a typical Scot, being small and whey-faced, and very fond of his bottle and his pipe, so that his rooms stank of tobacco like the most fumigated London coffee house; indeed his body seemed incapable of supporting life by any other breath than the smoke of some sweet-scented Virginia. It was to Newton's influence that the younger Gregory owed his current eminence at Oxford. Over dinner they began to talk of Doctor Wallis.

"But you have not met Wallis before?" asked Gregory. "He was at Cambridge, was he not?"

"We have met, yes. More often we have corresponded. He has been most persistent that I should publish something—nay, anything—in his *Opera Mathematica*. No doubt he is currently reading the letter I wrote to him yesterday, and my arrival here in Oxford, as a sign that I have changed my mind upon the matter."

"So why do you wish to see him?"

"It is the business of the Mint that brings me to Oxford. I was hoping that Wallis might help me with some enquiries. Yet more I cannot say, for it is a delicate matter and most secret."

"Of course," said Gregory, puffing away like a Dutch boatswain. "But I don't think that Doctor Wallis is any stranger to secrecy himself. I have heard it said that he does confidential work for milord Sunderland. I think it is something to do with the war, although I wonder how an eighty-year-old man can help to defeat the French. Perhaps he sets them calculations and bids to bore them into submission."

"Is he still so fond of mathematics?" exclaimed Newton.

"Indeed he is, sir. He is a scholar of real worth, for I have seen him extracting square roots without pen or paper, to seven places."

"I have seen a horse clap its hoof upon the ground seven times," Newton remarked. "But I do not think it was a mathematician."

"He is not your peer," said Gregory. "You have developed mathematics quite astonishingly."

"For my own part," answered Newton, "I think I have barely skimmed the surface of the great ocean of knowledge. Marvellous secrets still remain to be uncovered. It is the challenge of our age to demonstrate the frame of the system of the world. And so long as we continue to distinguish between the formal reason of nature and the act of divine will, I do not see why we should not believe that God himself does not directly inform nature so that the world necessarily emanates from it."

Here Newton did look at me most directly, so that when he spoke again I formed the impression that perhaps Miss Barton had reported our conversation after all.

After breakfast the next day, we received a note from Wallis inviting us to call on him at eleven of the clock, and at the appointed hour we did go to Exeter College to see him. I did not like Exeter as much as Merton, Magdalen, or Christchurch, it being disfigured by large and unsightly chimneys, not to mention much building work being done in the front quadrangle, so that I wondered how Wallis could study there. But this was soon explained when we entered the Professor's rooms and met Wallis himself, since it was quickly evident that Doctor Wallis was a little deaf, which was no great wonder in a man of his age. He was of medium height, with a small head and slightly infirm of gait, and leaned upon a stick and a boy of about fourteen years old, whom he introduced to us as his grandson William.

"There, William," said his doting grandfather. "One day you will be able to say that you once met the great Isaac Newton, whose notions of mathematics are received with great applause."

Newton bowed deeply. "Doctor Wallis," he said, "I was not able to find anything general in quadratures, until I had understood your own work on infinitesimals."

Wallis acknowledged the compliment with a nod, and then told the boy to run along before inviting us to sit and declaring himself mighty honoured that Newton should think fit to visit an old scholar like himself.

"Pray tell me, sir," he asked. "Does this mean that you have reconsidered your decision not to publish your *Opticks* in my book? Is that why you have come?"

"No sir," Newton said firmly. "I have not changed my mind. I am here on the business of His Majesty's Mint."

"It's not too late, you know. Even now Mister Flamsteed sends me an account of his observations, which shall be included. Will you not reconsider, Doctor Newton?"

"No sir, for I fear that disputes and controversies may be raised against me by some confounded ignoramus."

"But perhaps some other may get scraps of your notion and publish it as his own," said Wallis. "Then it will be his, not yours, though he may perhaps never attain a tenth part of what you are already the master of. Consider that it is now almost thirty years since you were master of those notions about fluxions—"

"I think," said Newton, interrupting, "that you have already written me a letter to this same effect."

Wallis grunted loudly. "I own that modesty is a virtue," he said. "I merely wished to point out that too much diffidence is a fault. How should this, or the next age, know of your discoveries if you do not publish, sir?"

"I shall publish, sir, when I am minded so to do."

Wallis tried to conceal his show of exasperation, with little success.

"The business of the Mint, you say?" he said, changing the subject. "I had heard you were Master of the Mint. From Mister Hooke."

"For the present I am merely the Warden. The Master is Mister Neale."

"The Lottery man?"

Smiling thinly, Newton nodded.

"But is the work so very challenging?"

"It is a living, that is all."

"I wonder that you do not have a church living. I myself have the living of St. Gabriel's in London."

"I have not the aptitude for the Church," replied Newton. "Only for inquiry."

"Well then, sir, I am at the Mint's service, although if we are to talk of money, I can tell you there's none in the whole of Oxford." Wallis gestured at his own surroundings. "And I cannot counterfeit anything save this show of worldly comfort. The only silver hereabouts is the college plate, and all sober men of the University are fearful of ruin. This Great Recoinage has been badly handled, sir."

"Not by me," insisted Newton. "But I have come about a book, sir, not the scarcity of good coin in Oxford."

"We have plenty of those, sir," said Wallis. "Sometimes I would we had fewer books and more money."

"I seek a particular book—*Polygraphia,* by Trithemius— which I would desire to have sight of."

"You have come a long way to read one ancient book." The old man got up from his chair and fetched a handsomely bound volume from his bookcase.

"*Polygraphia,* eh? That is an ancient book indeed. It was

first published in 1517. This is an original copy which I have owned these past fifty years."

"But did you not order another from Mister Lowndes of the Savoy?" asked Newton.

"Who told you that, sir?"

"Why, Mister Lowndes, of course."

"I like this discovery not, sir," said Wallis, frowning. "A man's bookseller should keep his confidence, like his physician. What can become of a world where every man knows what another man reads? Why, sir, books would become like quacks' potions, with every mountebank in the newspapers claiming one volume's superiority over another."

"I regret the intrusion, sir. But as I said, this is official business."

"Official business, is it?" Wallis turned the book over in his hands and then stroked the cover most lovingly.

"Then I will tell you, Doctor. I bought another copy of *Polygraphia* for my grandson William. I have been teaching him the craft in the hope that he will follow in my footsteps, for he demonstrates an early aptitude."

An early aptitude in what? I wondered. For writing? Neither Newton nor I yet had any real idea what this book by Trithemius was about.

"Trithemius is a useful primer in the subject, sir," continued Wallis, handing the book to Newton. "Although I do not think his book could long detain a man such as you. Porta's book, *De Furtivis Literarum Notis,* is more suited to your intellectual parts. Perhaps also John Wilkins's *Mercury, or The Swift and Secret Messenger.* You may also prefer to read John Falconer's *Cryptomenytices Patefacta,* which is most recent."

"*Cryptomeneses,*" Newton murmured to me as Wallis took down two more books from his shelves. "Of course. Secret intimations. I did not understand until now." And seeing me remain still puzzled, he added, with greater vehemence, *"Cryptographia,* Mister Ellis. Secrecy in writing."

"What's that you say?" asked Wallis.

"I said I should like to read this one, too."

Wallis nodded. "Wilkins teaches only how to construct a cipher, not to how to unravel one. Only Falconer is practical, for he suggests methods of how ciphers may be understood. And yet I think that a man who wishes to solve a cryptogram is always best advised to trust to his own industry and observation. Do you not agree, Doctor?"

"Yes sir, I have always found that to be my own best method."

"And yet it is hard service for a man of my years. Some-times I have spent as long as a year on a particular decipher-ment. Milord Nottingham did not understand how long these things can take. He was always pressing me for quick solutions. But I must stand the course, at least until William is ready to take over the work. Although there is very little reward in it."

"It is the curse of all learned men to be neglected," offered Newton.

Wallis was silent for a moment, as if much pondering what Newton had said.

"Well, that is odd," he said finally. "For now I remember that someone else from the Mint came to see me about a year ago. Your pardon, Doctor Newton. I had quite forgotten. Now, what was his name?"

"George Macey," said Newton.

"The very same. He brought with him a small sample of a code I had never before encountered, and expected me to work a miracle with it. Naturally. They all do. I told him to bring me some more letters and then I would stand a chance of over-coming the difficulty of it. He left the letter with me, but I had no luck, for it was the hardest I ever met with, though as I said,

I had not enough material to be assured of any success. And I put it aside. I had not thought of it again until now, but I never heard from Mister Macey again."

Upon hearing Wallis mention a letter, I almost saw Newton's cold heart miss a beat. He sat forward on his chair, chewed the knuckle of his forefinger for a moment, and then asked if he might see the letter Macey had left behind.

"I am beginning to understand what this is all about," said Wallis, and fetched the letter from a pile of papers that lay upon the floor. He seemed to know where everything was, although I could see no great evidence of order; and handing my master the letter, he offered him some advice also.

"If you do attempt this decipherment, then let me know how you fare. But always remember not to rack your mind over-anxiously, for too much brain work with these devices is ener-vating, so that the mind is fit for nothing afterwards. Also be mindful of what Signor Porta says, that when the subject is known, the interpreter can make a shrewd guess at the common words that concern the matter in hand, and in this way a hundred hours of labour may be saved."

"Thank you, Doctor Wallis. You have been most helpful to me."

"Then reconsider your decision about your *Opticks,* sir."

Newton nodded. "I will think about it, Doctor," he said.

But he did not.

After this, we took our leave of Doctor Wallis with Newton in possession of the new sample of enciphered material as well as several useful books; so that he was hardly able to contain his excitement, although he was very swiftly angry with himself that he had not thought to bring with him the other enciphered material that was already held by us.

"Now I shall not be able to work on the problem while we are in that damned coach," he grumbled.

"May I see the message?" I asked.

"But of course," said Newton, and showed me the letter that Wallis had given to him. I looked at it for a while, but it was no more clear to me now than it had ever been.

tqbtqeqhhflzkrfugzeqsawnxrxdgxjpoxznpeeqjtgmqlnliug
dxvcnfgdmysnroywpdonjbjmpardemgmqdnlnkfpztzkzjm
kgjhtnxqwxearowsualquwojfuidgrhjsyzzvccteuqzggfzqce
tydcjgessicisemvttajmwgciurgopmdcuydtgafyudnrdivux
gvhqtvgeoudkwvahhvxkjusukpwnvwcvedtqnljvhinmszpz
blkiabzvrbqtepovxlsrzeenongsppyoujyhwexpnakqlotvsm
curzybcstqqxfsxdihhbdlxfbtjymfvtubspvbxgftesuu

I shook my head. Merely to look at the jumble of letters dispirited me, and I could not see how anyone could enjoy cudgelling his brains with its solution.

"Perhaps you can read one of these books that Doctor Wallis has lent to you," I offered, which partly placated him, for he liked nothing better than a longish journey with a good book.

We were two or three hours on the road to London when Newton put aside the book for a moment and remarked most casually that it was now plain to him how Mister St. Leger Scroope had proved himself to be a liar.

"Do you mean the gentleman that presented your school with those very fine silver cups?" I enquired.

"I never liked the man," admitted Newton. "I trust him not. He is like a dog without a tail. Most unpredictable."

"But why do you say that he is a liar?"

"Sometimes," sighed Newton, "you are a most obstinately obtuse fellow. Do you not remember how he told us that Macey brought him a letter written in French, for translation? Why, it's as plain as the nose on your face that the letter must have been a cipher, just like the one he showed Doctor Wallis.

Perhaps it was even the same letter. There never was any letter in French."

"But why should Scroope lie about such a thing?"

"Why indeed, Mister Ellis? That is what we shall find out."

"But how?"

Newton pondered the matter for a moment.

"I have an idea how we might do it," he said at last. "Macey had no Latin. And yet by the account of Mister Lowndes, the bookseller, he bought a Latin book about secret writing that was a gift for someone. It cannot have been Doctor Wallis, who already possessed two such books. And Mister Lowndes's shop is but a short distance from the premises of Mister Scroope. Therefore I think that we shall visit Scroope again. And while I hold him in conversation, you shall find occasion to slip away and examine his bookcase."

"In search of the book by Trithemius?"

"Exactly so."

"An old book," I said. "It's not much evidence of a crime."

"No," agreed Newton. "That will come later. First we must prove things to our own satisfaction."

When the coach reached London, before night, we climbed down and found ourselves lousy, which only irritated my master a little, for he was in a mighty good humour at the prospect of solving the cipher. And straightaway he accompanied me to the Tower so that he might collect all his coded material and begin work all the sooner. Finding all well at the Tower and in the Mint, we went to the office, which had been newly painted and the windows cleaned in our absence, which helped to explain how it was that Mister Defoe had facilitated his entry and that we discovered him with the guilt of his intrusion still upon him.

"Why, Mister Defoe," said Newton. "Do you attend us?"

Mister Defoe laid down some Mint papers he had been examining and, stepping side to side like a dancing master, stuttered and stammered his crippled explanation. "Yes," he said, blushing like a virgin. "I only thought to await your return. To bring you information."

"Information? About what, pray?" Newton collected the papers Mister Defoe had been reading and perused their contents while our interloper tried to untie his tongue.

"About certain coiners," declared Mister Defoe. "I know not their names, but they operate out of a tavern in Fleet Street."

"Do you refer to The Goat?"

"Yes, The Goat," replied Mister Defoe.

Newton winced, as if he felt the pain of Mister Defoe's words. "Oh, you disappoint me. The Goat is in Charing Cross, between the Chequer Inn at the southwest corner of St. Martin's Lane, and the Royal Mews, farther west. Now if you had said The George—"

"I did mean The George."

"You would also be mistaken, for The George is in Holborn, north of Snow Hill. What bad luck for you. There are so many taverns in Fleet Street you might have chosen to mention: The Globe, Hercules' Pillars, The Horn, The Mitre, and Penell's. We know them all, don't we, Mister Ellis?"

"Yes, Doctor."

"Perhaps you meant The Greyhound? On the south side, close to Salisbury Court? Now that's a tavern that was always said to be full of coiners."

"It must have been that one."

"Until it burned down during the Great Fire. You did say you had some information for us?"

"I may have made a mistake," said Mister Defoe.

"You most certainly have," said Newton. "Mister Defoe, I

seize you as my prisoner. Mister Ellis? Draw your sword and command this rogue's obedience while I fetch a sentinel."

I drew my sword as Newton had ordered, and extended the point toward Mister Defoe.

"Upon what charge do you detain me?"

"Spying," said Newton.

"Nonsense."

Newton brandished the papers Defoe had been reading.

"These are confidential documents in this office relating to the security of the coin of this realm. I cannot think what else I might call it, sir."

"Is he serious?" asked Defoe when Newton had gone out of the office.

"He is so seldom anything else that I wonder if he knows one simple joke," said I. "But you will find out if this is raillery or not, soon enough, I'll warrant."

As good as his word, Newton returned in the company of two sentries and quickly wrote out a warrant in his capacity as a Justice.

"Mister Neale will not tolerate this," said Mister Defoe. "He'll have me out of here in no time."

Newton handed one of the sentries the warrant and commanded him to take the prisoner not to the Tower prison, as all of us had expected, but to Newgate.

"Newgate?" exclaimed Mister Defoe upon learning his fate.

"I believe you know it well enough," said Newton. "We will see what your friends can do for you when you are in there." And with that, poor Daniel Defoe was led out of the office, still protesting loudly.

"And now," said Newton, when we were alone again. "Let's have a fire and some supper."

After supper Newton commanded me to go to bed, which

I was glad to do, although I felt a little guilty leaving him at work; and so the next morning I rose early to do some paperwork of my own and found that he had not been home at all, and him being most sullen, it was evident how he had not yet made the progress he had earlier anticipated. His mood was not improved by the arrival in the office of milord Lucas, who loudly complained about my own conduct toward the late Major Mornay, and who proceeded to describe what had passed between us in a way that was quite contrary to the facts, so that I believed he had some ill will to me, or at least an opinion that I was guilty of provoking the Major to kill himself. But I cared not a turd—the more so when Newton defended me and took all the blame upon himself and said that Mornay had been murdered.

"Murdered?" Lord Lucas, who sat most stiffly as if he feared to ruffle his cravat or incommode his wig, and turned one way in his chair and then the other as if he did not believe what he had heard. "Did you say murdered, sir?"

"I did, milord."

"What nonsense, Doctor. The fellow hanged himself."

"No, milord, he was murdered," repeated my master.

"What, sir, do you contradict me?"

"It was made to look as though he had hanged himself, by them as I hope soon to arrest."

"I know your game, sir," sneered Lord Lucas. "It's your conceit to make men believe the very opposite of what their eyes and ears tell them to be true. Like your damned theory of gravity. I can't see that either, sir. And I tell you plain, I don't believe in it, sir."

"I wonder, then, that you do not fly off this earth, and into the heavens," observed Newton. "For I cannot think what else might detain you here, milord."

"I have not the time nor the patience for your blasted Royal Society sophistry."

"That much is obvious, in any case."

"Well, you may think what you like, Newton. If he's buried in this Tower—and it seems he will have to be, for his family don't want the disgrace—it'll be face down, north to south." Lord Lucas opened his snuff-box and smeared his lofty nose with a generous pinch which did nothing to lessen his obvious distaste for our company.

"Then for the Major's sake, I shall make a point of proving you wrong, milord."

"You haven't heard the last of this," said Lucas. "Neither of you has." And with a loud sneeze and a string of oaths he kicked the door open and marched out of our office.

Newton yawned and stretched himself like a cat. "I believe I shall take some air," he said. "Whenever I am in His Lordship's company I feel like I am a candle burning in Mister Boyle's bell-jar, which soon goes out for lack of atmosphere. Besides, I have not moved from this chair all night. What say you that we venture out to the Strand and call upon Mister Scroope?"

"I think that it would benefit you, sir," I replied. "For you are too much indoors."

Newton left off scratching Melchior under the chin and, glancing out of the window, nodded. "Yes. You are right. I am too much indoors. I should dwell more in the light. For although I have not yet much understood the Sun, I sometimes think its rays nourish all living things with an invisible light. I do not doubt how one day that secret light will be revealed as I have revealed the spectrum of colours; and when it is, we shall begin to know everything. Why, perhaps we shall even understand the immanent nature of God."

Newton stood up and put on his coat and hat.

"But for the moment let us merely hope that we may understand the mind of Mister Scroope."

We walked to the Strand, and along the way Newton outlined his plan in greater detail:

"Being a gold- and silversmith, Mister Scroope is obliged by law to keep a record of his stock of precious metals," he explained. "For it is of great importance that the Treasury knows how much gold and silver there is in the country. I shall say that the Mint has the power to inspect Mister Scroope's books. I shall inform him that I am handling the matter personally, in order that the inconvenience to his business shall be minimised. When I explain that such inspections often take a whole day but that I expect to complete my own within the hour, I believe that he will be more than pleased to co-operate with us. And while he is so diverted with appeasing me, you shall find an opportunity to slip away, perhaps to use the close-stool, and then to examine his library in search of the book by Trithemius."

"Is any of that true?" I asked.

"About the Mint? Sadly, no. But it ought to be. For much of the time we are making up our powers as we go along. Of course, as a justice of the peace I could easily obtain a specific warrant to inspect his books. But that would look wrong, for we must counterfeit the appearance that our actions are in Scroope's best interest, and he must apprehend that we are his friends."

Our walk took us along Thames Street and across the stinking Fleet Bridge with its many fishwives—where I bought threepence worth of oysters for my stand-up breakfast—onto Fleet Street and the Strand. I tried to raise the subject of Miss Barton, but when I mentioned her, Newton swiftly changed the subject and I was left with the feeling that I had done her greater injury than any that was ever done unto my master. That was what I thought. Later on, I formed a different impression of why he was reluctant to discuss his niece with me.

Near enough an hour's walking brought us unto Mister Scroope's place of business, close by the Maypole at the junction of Drury Lane. Scroope seemed most discomfited by our arrival on his doorstep, which Newton I think enjoyed, being now most convinced that a man who did not graduate from his university was likely a bad lot; and that this vindicated his own neglect of Mister Scroope when he had been his tutor.

Having heard Newton's most plausible explanation for our returning to see him again, Scroope ushered us into his office while all the while he grumbled that there was so much regulation for a man of business to take account of these days that he could wish all men who made laws might be ducked in Bedlam's night soil.

"Everything is regulation and tax. If it's not windows the Government wants money for, it's burial or marriage. It's bad enough that the closing date for the receipt of the old coin at full value is swift to be upon us. But so little new coin is produced."

"There's enough being produced," said Newton. "It's expected this month will see more than three hundred and thirty thousand pounds' worth of silver coin newly minted. No sir, the problem is that men hoard the new coin in expectation that its value will rise."

"That's an accusation I know well," lamented Mister Scroope. "I think I understand what it is to be a Jew, for the gold- and silversmiths of this city are most often thought guilty of hoarding. But I ask you, Doctor, how is a man expected to run this kind of business without keeping a certain quantity of gold and silver to smith that which a customer would desire? A man must have findings in this trade, or he has no trade at all."

Findings were what these goldsmiths called their stock of precious metals.

"Well, sir," said Newton, "shall we see what findings you do have? And then I promise to leave you in peace, for I like this task no better than you. When I left Cambridge for the Mint, I little thought I should become the money police."

"This is most inconvenient and aggravating."

"I came myself, sir," Newton said stiffly, "because I wished to spare you the trial of being examined by one of these other rascals. But it might be better if you spent a day or two with one of the inspection bailiffs, after all. I daresay you would prefer their careful scrutiny to the blind eye of an old friend and fellow Trinity man." And so saying, Newton made as if to leave.

"Please, sir, wait a moment," said Scroope, unctuous again. "You are right. I am most ungrateful for the service you do me. Forgive me, sir. It is merely that I was most occupied with something, and I am without a servant for an hour. But now I think that it can wait a while. And I should count it an honour to have my books inspected by you, Doctor Newton."

Scroope ushered Newton through to an even smaller office where, there being very little room, it was not possible for me to follow, so that I was obliged to remain behind; and as soon as I heard Scroope begin to explain his book-keeping to Newton, I excused myself and went to look about the house.

It was plain to me that St. Leger Scroope was a man of very evident wealth. On the walls were many fine tapestries and pictures while the furniture reflected the taste of a man who had travelled a great deal abroad. There was a library of sorts, with several handsome bookcases and dominated by the largest and dustiest binding press I had seen outside of a bookshop; but there was no time to wonder at it, for I was quickly in front of the cases and examining the spines of Mister Scroope's books; and finding these ordered according to the letters of the alphabet, I quickly found a copy of the *Polygraphia* by Trithemius. This book I removed from the bookcase and opened in the hope that Mister Macey might even have inscribed it, but there was nothing, and I was about to replace the volume when it occurred to me to look at some of the other books also; and finding many of these were on the subject of alchemy, I came away from that room with the strong notion that Newton's suspicions were correct: that Scroope did indeed have some involvement in the terrible murders at the Tower.

It was now that I made a most fortuitous discovery. Upon leaving the library, I took a wrong turn so that I found myself standing on the threshold of a courtyard that was enclosed on three sides by single-storey wooden workshops, each of which was topped by a tall chimney not visible from the street.

I crossed the open courtyard and stepped inside one of these workshops, which was arranged very like the melting-house at the Tower, with an open furnace and various forging tools. Not that there was anything very strange about any of this; Mister Scroope was a goldsmith, after all. Rather it was what Mister Scroope chose to smith that interested me, for all about the place were pewter plates, jugs and tankards, as well as the moulds from which these had been newly cast, since some were still warm. Others were already in packing cases that bore the official licence of the Navy Office.

First it struck me as strange that Scroope should be supplying tableware for the Navy Office, until I remembered that many smiths loyally manufactured all kinds of things for our army in Flanders, and that doubtless they had as much need of plates and tankards with which to carry their victuals as they had need of cannon and shot.

I was starting to leave the workshop when my eye caught sight of some empty Mint money bags lying on the cobbled ground. When full of silver coin, these bags were sold at the Mint and their dissemination among the people at large left to chance, for there was no public expenditure available for the money's distribution—which was, as every Englishman knew, a great fault of the recoinage. Rather it was the contiguity of these various items at the forge—the empty money bags and the pewter—that caused me to suspect that there was some bad business here; and examining one of the pewter plates more closely, I scratched the surface with the point of my sword, which prompted the discovery that the pewter was only a patina. For this tableware was not pewter at all, but solid silver, made of the melted coin that all those in the Mint laboured so hard to produce. What Scroope was evidently doing did not only undermine that recoinage, to the great disadvantage of the realm—to say nothing of King William's campaign in Flanders, for if there was no good coin, his troops could not be paid—but he was also making a profit by melting the coin and smuggling it across the Channel to France, where silver fetched a higher price than in England. What was more, the face value of the new coins was less than the value of the silver they contained. So that the mathematics of Scroope's scheme were obvious: Scroope bought a pound's weight of silver for sixty shillings to sell it in France for seventy-five.

It was a profit of twenty-five per cent. Not a great sum, perhaps, but if the main purpose of the scheme were not the profit but the advantage of the King of France, then it was clear to me how this treasonous act of economic impedition could easily pay for itself.

I returned to the clerk's office and found Newton still questioning Scroope most attentively, so that my brief absence had not, it seemed, been noticed; and after a while I was able to indicate to my master with a nod of my head that my task was accomplished. Upon which Newton pronounced himself easily satisfied with Scroope's books and, with a great effusion of continuing gratitude for Scroope's gift of silver for their old school, he bade him farewell; and eventually we took our leave.

As soon as we were gone, we went to The Grecian in nearby Devereux Court, where, over a dish of coffee, Newton made some enquiry as to what I had discovered; and I told him everything I had seen, which left him mighty pleased.

"Well done, Ellis," he declared handsomely. "You have excelled yourself. But did you see no signs of coining? No press? No guinea dies?"

"No," I said. "Although the book-binding press in the library was the largest I have seen outside a bookshop."

"A binding press, eh?" remarked Newton. "Can you describe it?"

"It was mounted on some small wheels so that it might be moved easily without lifting. Only I do not think it was used very much. I saw no loose quires of pages about. Nor any books that were new-bound. And the press itself was covered in dust."

Newton considered what I had said, and then asked me if the books in Scroope's library had been dusty, too.

"Not at all," I said.

"And this dust? What colour was it?"

"Now that I come to think of it," said I, "the dust was a strange colour, being dark green."

Newton nodded firmly. "Then I believe that you have solved this case. Half of it anyway."

"Me?" I said.

"Certainly. For that was not dust you saw, but Fuller's earth, a most absorptive and fine-grained substance and perfect for a *d'orure moulu* process of manufacturing false golden guineas. Which means there can be no doubt as to the true nature of that binding press."

"I understand," said I. "Scroope would not keep a coining press, for the Plate Act compelled anyone to surrender such a thing to the Mint."

"Just as you say," said Newton. "I have before heard of these rogues using a cider press to make coin; but a binding press would turn out guineas just as well."

Too excited to even drink his coffee, Newton's eyes were ablaze as he made his thoughts in the matter plain to me.

"Much is clear to me now," he declared. "Scroope is a most ingenious forger and smuggler and kept poor George Macey close to him, so that he might know who was being investigated by the Mint. Macey thought Scroope a good friend and an educated one, too, so that he confided in him. And Macey must have brought Scroope the ciphered letter and the book by Trithemius in the hope that Scroope might help him to understand it. And yet Scroope did not, or could not, devise the solution—it matters little, for it was certainly clear to Scroope that the cipher which had occasioned Macey's interest had no bearing on his own wrongdoings. Subsequent to this, Macey disappeared and Scroope continued to think himself safe. At least until I appeared in his life again. And grew close to uncovering Mister and Mrs. Berningham, and Daniel Mercer, whom I will hazard were Scroope's confederates in this crime.

"So Scroope, who knew my own rigorous reputation from Trinity, sought to be rid of those as might be able to testify against him. Doubtless Mrs. Berningham was ordered to take her own husband's life or to forfeit her own. For all I know, she may be dead, too. Killed by Scroope. Like Mercer and anyone else who stood in his way, such as Mister Kennedy. And by the manner of their deaths—the hermetic clues he fabricated and the enciphered message of which he had no understanding—he intended to divert me from my proper course of action. Until now."

"So Scroope killed Mercer and Kennedy," I repeated, so that it was clear in my own mind. "To cover his own tracks and to put you off the scent. But did Scroope kill Macey, too? And what of Major Mornay?"

"No, for it was not in his interest so to do. He enjoyed Macey's complete confidence, being sometimes an informer for him."

"Then only the murders of Kennedy and Mercer are solved," said I. "Who killed Macey and Major Mornay?"

"I think I will have to solve the code to know that," said Newton. "But before then we must decide what to do about Mister Scroope."

"Surely we must obtain a warrant for his arrest," I said. "The Navy Office will confirm the export licences for pewter tableware; and we shall arrest him in possession of illegal bullion for export to an enemy power. For all that we know, he is a French spy besides. In which case he may have intended to subvert the recoinage as well."

"You may be right," said Newton, in a voice that demonstrated some continuing source of concern in the matter of St. Leger Scroope. Usually he was most keen to see a man arrested as soon as he had sufficient evidence to obtain the warrant against him. But now he sounded strangely reluctant to proceed. And seeing my puzzlement moved him to explain himself to me:

"I hold myself partly responsible for Scroope's fall from grace. I paid him very little heed while he was at Cambridge. I failed him, Ellis, and I can see no excuse for it."

"No sir, not failed. From what you have told me earlier, Scroope failed himself. Even then he had perhaps the want of character that made him choose the wide and not the strait gate."

I also spoke some other things to assuage my master's sense of guilt; but it was to little or no avail, and while he sat in The Grecian, he drew up and signed a warrant for Scroope's arrest— which power he had as Justice of the Peace—with a heavy heart.

"Did we have but time," said he, "I would go to the Sessions House in Old Bailey to do this, for the history that lies between myself and Scroope persuades me that it would have been better if the warrant was obtained from a judge in the Middlesex court of quarter sessions. But there is no time. No, not even to fetch some sergeants and bailiffs to assist us, for this bird might fly the coop at any time; and needs must that we go and arrest him ourselves. Have you got your pistols, Ellis?"

I said I had, and within the quarter hour we were on our way back to Scroope's place of business at the sign of the Bell to arrest him.

Upon seeing our warrant, Scroope's Marrano servant, Robles, who had returned, let us in. A strange sight met our eyes: the furniture had been piled in front of the hearth, as if someone might have wished it to catch fire; but we hardly had time to pay this much heed, for Scroope met us from behind the door, with a pistol in his hand, which was levelled at us.

"St. Leger Scroope," said Newton, ignoring the pistol and more in hope than expectation, "I have a warrant for your arrest."

"Have you indeed?" said Scroope, smiling.

Seeing our situation, Newton sought to trick Scroope, promising that much could still be done for him, as if he still held all the best cards:

"I have men outside who are well armed and there is no way out of here. But it is in my power to plead for your life before the Lords Justices themselves," he explained. "There is every reason to suppose that you may not be hanged and that you may be transported instead. With a proper sense of remorse, some diligence, and the grace of Almighty God, a man might rebuild his life in the Americas. Therefore I entreat you to give yourself up, Mister Scroope."

Robles stared desperately out the window.

"I'll not go to Tyburn on a hurdle, sir," said Scroope. "To be untrussed like some spavined mare, and given my last suit of tar, and that's a fact. I don't fear death, only the manner of my dying. A musket ball has more attraction than putting myself in your bloody hands."

"I've not done murder," said Newton. "The Law is behind me, sir."

"The Law murders many more innocent than I am, Doctor. But I have no complaint against the Law. Only your religion."

"My religion? What, sir, are you Roman Catholic?"

"Aye, unto death." He glanced anxiously at Robles. "Well? What can you see?"

"Nothing. There's no one there," said Robles at last.

"What?" said Scroope. "You think you can cozen me, Doctor? You promise much more than you can deliver. Well, it was always thus. Despite your solemn oath at Trinity, it was well known you never performed a single act of divinity. You were always more interested in alchemy than you were in the affairs of the school. You were no pupil monger, I will grant you that, Doctor, but your own affairs did always tread closely upon the heels of your duty. Even so, I will regret having to kill one such as you, Doctor, for I believe you to be a great man. But you leave me with no choice. And it is very convenient that you have come by yourselves. Mister Robles and I were just about to set this house afire, in order to conceal our disappearance. But of course you would hardly have been satisfied, Doctor, without the presence of two charred corpses. But now you have solved all our problems. By killing the two of you, we can also furnish the bodies that will doubtless be taken for our own."

"Be assured that your position is hopeless," declared Newton. "The house is surrounded by my men. In our zeal to arrest you, we came but a moment or two before our men. Where can you go?"

Scroope glanced uncertainly at Robles. "Are you sure there is no one out there?" he asked. "For the Doctor's manner persuades me that there might be."

"There is no one," insisted Robles. "Look for yourself, sir."

"And take my eye off these two gentlemen? I think not. Light the fire."

Robles nodded and went over to the hearth where he produced brimstone matches from a tinderbox, and put a flame to some dry kindling.

It was at this point I did think Newton had suffered some kind of stroke, for he groaned and sank down to the floor on one knee, clutching his side.

"What ails you, Doctor?" enquired Scroope. "The thought of death? It will be quick, I promise you. A bullet in the head is better than what your justice would have offered me. Come, sir, can you stand?"

"An old ailment," whispered Newton, struggling painfully to his feet. "The rheumatism, I think. If I could have a chair."

"As you can see," said Scroope, "all our chairs are piled up for our conflagration."

"A stick, then. There is one." Newton pointed to a walking stick that lay against the wall. "Besides, if I am to be shot, I should like to meet death on my feet."

"Why, Doctor, you sound quite the bravo," said Scroope, and, backing up to the wall, took hold of the stick and handed it to Newton, handle first.

"Thank you, sir," said Newton, taking hold of the stick. "You are most kind."

But no sooner did he grasp the handle than he was flourishing a blade, and it was only now that I remembered, even as Newton did prick Scroope's ribs with it, that the ingenious walking stick concealed a sword. In truth, my master pricked him but lightly, although Scroope did let out such a shriek that you would have thought he had been killed. And the surprise of it made him let off his pistol, which passed harmlessly into the ceiling.

At this, Robles drew his own sword, and I drew mine, for there was not time to find and cock my pistol; and he and I set to it for a minute or so, while Scroope flung his own empty pistol at my master's head, which knocked him out, I think, and fled into the back of the house. By now the furniture was alight, and part of the house with it, so that Robles and I were obliged to conduct our swordfight against the flames, which were more of a distraction to my opponent, being at his back rather than mine. Newton lay still upon the floor, which was sufficient distraction unto myself; but finally I lunged at Robles, and pushed my blade straight through his side, so that he did let go of his blade and cry quarter. Forcing Robles through the door, I grabbed hold of my master's coat collar and dragged him into the street, for the house was now well ablaze.

Outside, I sheathed my sword and drew my pistols, in expectation that Scroope might yet make his escape. But it was not Scroope who soon came coughing out of the house, but the woman who had poisoned her husband and who had escaped us before. It was Mrs. Berningham, who would have run away, only I took hold of her, and held her until someone summoned a bailiff.

A fire-engine was fetched. And yet with an armed man still apparently on the premises, there were none of the fire-fighters who dared go inside; but by then the fire was out of control so that it began to threaten some of the other buildings; and it was only when I assured the fire-fighters that Scroope, who owned his building, was a felon and therefore hardly likely to hold the firemen liable for the demolition, that they fetched hooks and ropes to pull down the blazing edifice. By which time Newton was recovered from his blow on the head.

For a while I was uncertain whether the fire killed St. Leger Scroope, or if he had escaped; but Newton was in no doubt about the matter. For as we investigated the back of the house, he spied some blood upon the cobbles, which seemed to put the matter beyond all dispute.

After seeing a physician, Scroope's servant, Robles, was conveyed to the infirmary at Newgate with Mrs. Berningham, where, thinking himself close to death from the wound I had given him, although I had seen men recover from worse wounds than his, he confessed his own part in the murders of Mister Kennedy and Mister Mercer, and which had been done, as Newton supposed, in the manner being most provocative to the Warden's intellect:

"It is well known at the Whit, the pressure you're liable to put a man under, to peach. Mister Scroope feared you very much, Doctor Newton, especially after you got on the trail of Daniel Mercer, and John Berningham, for they could have told you everything about our operation that you would have wished to know. In short, that we were forging golden guineas and exporting silver bullion to advantage the cause of King Lewis of France in particular, and Roman Catholicism in general. It was certain that Mercer and Berningham had to be silenced, which meant that your own spy had to die as well, for he was watching Mercer. I just hit him over the head, trussed him up, and then introduced him to the lions, so to speak.

"That part was all Mister Scroope's idea. For he wished to divert you with a matter most intriguing to your fancy, sir. He said you were most interested in alchemy and that we would make it look as though it had been certain philosophers that had done the killing. But also that we should use a most secret cipher he knew with which to tickle you even more."

"But how did you come and go in the Tower with such facility?" asked Newton.

"That was easy. The first time we entered the Tower as two night-soil collectors. The sentry gave us a wide berth, for no one likes to get too close to the shite men. And while Mister Scroope distracted him with an enquiry, I lifted the key to the Lion Tower with a filch. We knew where it was because I drank with the keeper, and he told me. Your spy was already trussed up and waiting most patiently in Mister Scroope's carriage out on Tower Hill.

"The second time, we was delivering a cartload of hay. I killed Mercer in our own workshop and then put him in the cart while Mister Scroope went to Mercer's lodgings to leave some other diversions there for you. Then we drove to the Tower, put down the body, ordered the scene as you found it, left the hay, and then drove away."

"What about the book in the Tower library?" asked Newton. "Did Mister Scroope leave that there for me too?"

"Yes sir, that he did."

"I should like to know more about Mrs. Berningham," I asked Robles.

"She and Scroope were lovers, sir," said Robles. "She was a ruthless one, though. Poisoned her husband at Scroope's prompting her to do it, without a second thought."

Robles paused for a moment as he coughed a great deal; and still thinking himself dying, he said, "And there's a clean breast of it, sir. I ain't sorry to have it off my conscience."

For myself, I was sorry the poor wretch did not die then and there, as three months later Robles was dragged to Tyburn on a hurdle, where he met his death on his way to becoming one of London's grisly overseers, for his head was displayed in a place where he could see all of London.

Robles's death was cruel enough; but it did not compare to the fate that awaited Mrs. Berningham the following day.

She was conducted from the door of Newgate and, after a cup of brandy from the bellman at St. Sepulchre's, was led through an enormous crowd that had gathered, to a stake in the middle of the street. There she was made to stand upon a stool while a noose was placed about her neck and attached to an iron ring at the top of the stake. The stool was then kicked away, and while she was still alive, two cartloads of faggots were heaped around her and set alight. And after the fire had consumed her body, the mob amused itself with kicking through her ashes. Both Newton and I attended her execution, although I think there is something inhuman in burning to death a woman who, by being the weaker body, is more liable to error and therefore more entitled to leniency. A woman is still a woman however she may have debased herself.

Chapter Five

Michael Maier, *Atalanta fugiens*, 1618

Jesus said to them: "Whoever has ears, let him hear. There is light within a man of light, and he lights up the whole world. If he does not shine, he is darkness."

(The Gospel of Thomas, 24)

*N*ewton had solved the mystery of only two of the murders that were committed in the Tower by St. Leger Scroope and his accomplice and servant Robles; the unravelling of the mystery of the two other murders, and the great secret which they were intended to protect, still lay ahead of us. Now it must be explained what happened after Scroope's house burned down, and how Newton faced the greatest hazard to his person and detriment to his reputation since ever he had been born, for this university of London called Life provides its students with a more termagant variety of education than anything that is to be found at the Cambridge schools.

The day after Mrs. Berningham's execution, I arrived at the office to discover Newton sitting in his chair by the hearth with the air of a man most discountenanced. That he ignored my greeting to him was hardly remarkable, and in truth I was used to his ponderous silences which were sometimes very weighty indeed; but that he should have ignored Melchior's importunate suit for his attentions was strange indeed, so that gradually I saw how his black demeanour imitated Atlas with the vault of the sky upon his broad shoulders. Having questioned Newton several times, like Heracles, and even laid hold of his arm—for it was rare that I ever touched him, he being so shy of any physical contact—I saw how the matter seemed referable to a paper he held crushed within his fist.

At first I thought the paper was something to do with the code he still laboured hard to decipher. Had not Doctor Wallis warned him about racking his brains too much in search of the solution? And it was only when a closer inspection of his person revealed the shard of an official seal upon his breeches that I understood how the paper was nothing to do with the cipher at all, but rather some kind of official letter. Having questioned my master about its contents and still received no reply, not even a movement of his usually keen eye to make me keep my distance, I took the liberty of removing the letter from his rigorous grasp and perusing the contents.

What I read was most vexatious, and it was suddenly obvious to me why Newton gave the appearance of one who had received some kind of insult to his brain—even, perhaps, some kind of paralytic stroke. For the letter was from the Lords Justices inviting Newton to appear before them next morning in an informal and unrecorded private session, in order that he should answer affidavits *viva voce* that he was not a fit and proper person to hold government office, being of an anti-Trinitarian, Socinian, or Unitarian and therefore heretic disposition of mind most offensive to the King and the Church of England.

This was a grave matter indeed, for while I did not think that Their Lordships would have ordered Newton put to death, they might easily have sent him to the pillory, which would have amounted to the same thing, for, as I have explained, Newton was not loved by London's population, because of his diligent pursuit of coiners; and there were many pilloried who, pelted by the mob with brickbats and stones, did not survive the experience. Indeed, there were not a few prisoners who feared the pillory more than fines and imprisonment.

My first inclination was to fetch a physician straightaway so that some kind of cure might urgently be effected, enabling him to appear before Their Lordships and give a good account of himself. But gradually I saw how summoning a physician would only have served to create abroad some gossip about the state of Newton's mind. If he had suffered a stroke, then Newton was beyond any physician, to say nothing of Their Lordships. But if, as I hoped, the condition was merely temporary then he would not have thanked me for bringing a physician into his affairs. Newton disliked physicians at the best of times, preferring to treat himself on the very few occasions when he was ever ill. Besides, I knew he had suffered some previous breakdown, and from which he had, by his own account, recovered; and therefore I was encouraged to believe that my course of action was the correct one. So I fetched pillows and blankets from the Warden's house and, having made him as comfortable as I could, went to see if Newton's coachman still attended his master.

Finding Mister Woston beyond the Lion Tower, I spoke to him.

"Mister Woston? How was Doctor Newton when you brought him here this morning?"

"He was himself, Mister Ellis, as always."

"The Doctor has suffered an attack of illness," I said. "Some kind of fit or stroke, perhaps. I know not how best to describe it except to say that he is no longer quite himself, as you say. And that perhaps it would be best if you were to fetch Miss Barton. But try not to alarm her unduly. It would spare her much worry while she travelled here. Perhaps you might just inform her that her uncle urgently requires her presence in his office at the Tower, and she shall understand everything for herself when she gets here."

"Shall I fetch a physician, too, Mister Ellis?"

"Not yet, Mister Woston. I should like Miss Barton to see him first."

Upon her arrival in the Mint office, about an hour afterward, Miss Barton greeted me with a cool civility but then, seeing the attitude of her uncle, demanded to know why I had not brought a physician to him immediately.

"Miss Barton," I said. "If you will permit me to explain, summoning a physician may create some gossip about the state of Newton's mind. If he has suffered a stroke, then he is beyond any physician, to say nothing of Their Lordships. But if the condition is merely temporary, then he will not thank us for bringing a physician into his affairs."

She nodded. "That is true enough. But why do you mention Their Lordships so? Has my uncle some business with them?"

I showed her the letter I had found in Newton's hand, which seemed to occasion within her breast some kind of hysterical reaction against myself.

"You vile and despicable dog," she said bitterly. "I see your atheistic hand in this, Mister Ellis. Doubtless you have brought my uncle's reputation into Their Lordships' disrepute by your saying about him in public what you have said to me in private."

"I can assure you, Miss Barton, that nothing could be further from the truth. Despite what you may think of me, I owe a great deal to the Doctor, and would not injure his reputation for all the world. But even if what you say were true, none of this is helping him now."

"What do you propose, sir?" she said stiffly.

"Your uncle has referred to an occasion upon which he suffered some sort of mental breakdown once before," said I.

"Indeed it is so. It has always vexed him most considerably that Mister Huygens spread a rumour that my uncle's mind was lost to science. For he is a proud man and a most private person."

"Indeed he is, Miss Barton. The most private person I ever knew." Somewhat pointedly, I added, "There is so much about him that a person is never made privilege to, that I wonder how anyone can say he knows Doctor Newton at all."

"I know my own uncle, sir."

"Good. Then perhaps you will recall what happened before. Was anything done to promote his recovery?"

She shook her head.

"No? Then it is my own opinion that we should let this take its course. And that his great mind will heal itself of this malady. Until that happens, I believe we should keep him as warm and comfortable as possible."

Gradually she seemed to apprehend the wisdom of what I had proposed, and contented herself with arranging anew the blankets and pillows with which I had surrounded her uncle's person.

Miss Barton had visited the Tower before—to visit the Mint, the Armouries and the Royal Menagerie—but this was the first time in my presence; and saying very little to each other, for we were neither of us sure how much Newton could hear, we sat as stiff as any two statues, observing him and awaiting some change in his person. It was a most unnerving situation: Newton almost like a dead man, and yet not dead, perhaps seeing and hearing everything but unable to move or speak. And the two of us with full hearts and bittersweet memories.

"What could happen to him," she asked, "if Their Lordships believe him to be a heretic?"

"I fear he would lose all of his preferments," said I. "He might even be charged with blasphemy, pilloried, and then imprisoned."

"He would not survive being pilloried," whispered Miss Barton.

"No," I said. "That is also my opinion. If he is to answer these charges effectively, he must have all his wits, I think."

"We must pray for his recovery," she said, finally, and with emphasis.

"I am sure your own prayers would help, Miss Barton," I offered lamely.

Upon which she got off her chair and knelt down upon the floor.

"Will you not pray with me?" she asked. "For his sake?"

"Yes," I said, although I had little or no appetite for prayer. And kneeling down beside her, I clasped my hands and closed my eyes while, for more than an hour's quarter, she muttered away like someone most devout. For myself, I remained silent and hoped that she would assume that the hopes of my own heart were echoed in her prayers.

Toward the middle of the morning, she and I started to relax a little so that we began not to notice him. By dinnertime it was as though he were not there at all; and when Miss Barton's stomach rumbled loudly, I smiled and offered to fetch us both something to eat from The Stone Kitchen. When she agreed with some alacrity, so that I saw how hungry and thirsty she really was, I went to the tavern, returning quickly with our food. Alas, it was too quickly, however, so that I discovered Miss Barton doing something upon the pot, for which I felt some shame and pity to her poor blushes, not to mention some anger with myself. And when I returned to the office again after a decent interval, our conversation was stiff again because of our embarrassment.

But at last she permitted that I might have done the right thing by her uncle.

"I think you have done right, Mister Ellis," she said, "not to have brought a physician here."

"I am very glad to hear you say so, Miss Barton, for it has worried me this whole morning."

"I spoke unjustly to you earlier this morning."

"Pray do not mention it, Miss Barton. It is quite forgotten."

Day gave way to evening, with our vigil continuing, as if watching Newton were an act of religious observance. I lit a fire which warmed the room, and offered to fetch Miss Barton a shawl, which she declined; and as darkness finally chased off the last glimmers of daylight, I lit some candles and placed one close to Newton's face so that we might apprehend any palpable change in his physiognomy; and holding the candle up to Newton's eye, I saw the dark matter at the centre of his iris shift most perceptibly, so that I began to suspect that my master was not so very disturbed in his mind as to be reduced to the level of some living corpse. It was an experiment which I encouraged Miss Barton to repeat, to the satisfaction of her own mind that all might yet be well.

Sleep gradually o'ertook us both, and it was dawn when Melchior, leaping into my lap, awakened me. For a moment a rigidity of neck and limb kept away thoughts of any other than myself, and I forgot why it was that I had slept in the office at all; but when, a moment later, I looked for Newton in his chair by the hearth, I saw that he was gone from there, and, jumping up, I called out to Miss Barton most anxiously.

"It's all right," said Newton, who was standing by the window now. "Calm yourselves. I believe that I am quite recovered. I have been watching the sun come up. I recommend it to you both. It is a most enlightening spectacle."

Miss Barton smiled delightedly at me, and for a brief instant everything that was precious to me seemed to have been restored, although in truth Newton still seemed distant to us both. I think she even kissed him and then me, on the cheek;

and it was as if Miss Barton had drunk from that river in Hades which induces forgetfulness of the past; so that the two of us stood beside Newton, marvelling at his recovery and all the while grinning like horses and finding pleasure in each other's company.

"Why, sir," she exclaimed to him, beginning to sound an aggrieved note, "whatever was the matter? You have given us such a fright. We were sure your mind was gone."

"I apologise for having alarmed you both," he whispered. "There are times when my thinking so occupies me that it produces certain outward effects upon my person that give the appearance of my having suffered a stroke of God's almighty hand. The cause is quite a mystery even to me, and therefore I don't apologise for saying I have no other explanation for you, except to say that a great clarity of thought is usually brought about by this strange excursion from my own physical body, which, rest assured, is something I have encountered before."

But examining his face I saw that he looked pale and drawn, as if a great weight still lay upon his soul.

"But are you quite sure you are recovered, sir?" enquired Miss Barton. "Should a physician not be called to ascertain that you are indeed as well as you say?"

"'Tis true, sir," I said. "You look pale."

"Perhaps you should eat something," suggested Miss Barton. "Drink some coffee, perhaps."

"My dear, I am quite recovered," insisted Newton. "You did well to listen to Mister Ellis."

"You were able to hear our discourse?" I asked.

"Oh yes, I have seen and heard everything that has gone on in this room."

"Everything?" demanded Miss Barton. I could see by her blushing that she referred to that business with the chamber pot.

"Everything," confirmed Newton, whose confession had chased away every remnant of her smile.

"But, sir," I said, changing the subject for pity of her, "perhaps you are not as recovered as you think you are. For it was not earlier today that Miss Barton spoke of physicians, but yesterday. It is almost twenty-four hours since I found you seated in that chair."

"So long as that?" breathed Newton, and closed his eyes for a moment.

"Aye sir."

"I was thinking about the cipher," he said absently.

"This morrow you must appear before the Lords Justices," said I.

Newton shook his head. "Say no more on that for now," he said.

"Then what would you have me do, sir?"

"There's nothing to be done."

"I agree with Miss Barton," said I. "We should all eat some breakfast. And speaking for myself, I am uncommonly hungry."

I never ate so much as I ate that morning. But Newton sipped some coffee and ate only a little dried bread, as if he had little appetite for food. No doubt he was much preoccupied with his meeting with Their Lordships, which was now imminent. And, after breakfast, we took Miss Barton back to Jermyn Street, at which point Newton declared, most strangely, "It is my considered opinion, that girl is in love."

"What makes you think so, sir?" I asked coolly, although I felt myself blushing.

"I live with her, Ellis. Do you think my own niece is invisible to me? I may not read sonnets all night, but I think I can recognise love's peculiar manifestations. What's more, I'll warrant I know the lucky fellow." And with that he smiled at me, a most knowing smile, so that I found myself smiling back at him like an idiot, and thinking that perhaps there was still some hope for me.

⌒

From Jermyn Street, Mister Woston conveyed us both to Whitehall, and Their Lordships. Newton seemed more perturbed by the ordeal that lay before him than I had ever seen him; even when he had faced Scroope's pistol, he had not seemed so much affected as he was now.

"It is only an informal audience," he said, as if trying to reassure himself about what was to happen. "Their Lordships' letter was most specific about that. And I have every hope that this matter will be quickly resolved. But, if you will be so kind, I should like you to record my words, in case I have need of a formal transcript of these proceedings."

And so it was that I was permitted to enter the chamber where the Lords Justices who governed the country were assembled. Their faces did not encourage optimism, viewing Newton as if they wished to be elsewhere, and as if they had conceived some disdain for him, and would not suffer his renowned intelligence to make fools of them.

I was quickly able to perceive the true character of the allegations that were being made, and how perhaps my master had underestimated the gravity of his position—if one might say such a thing about Isaac Newton—for, soon after our going into Their Lordships, they touched upon the seriousness of the situation and their strong dislike of all religious dissenters and occasional conformists. After which the porter brought Count Gaetano into the room—he that had attempted fraudulently to deceive my master into believing that he had turned lead into gold.

Remaining on his feet, to make his statement before Their Lordships, Gaetano appeared nervous and most unpersuasive, but even so I had not expected the Italian to lie so egregiously, and there were moments during his testimony when I was so shocked at his testimony that I was almost unable to keep a note of what he said.

He charged that Newton had dishonestly solicited a bribe in order that that he should verify that the gold sample the Count had shown him was genuine. He also charged that Newton had threatened to go before the Royal Society and, upon his oath, to denounce the Count as a fraud if he did not pay my master the sum of fifty guineas; and that when the Count cautioned Newton against false swearing, my master had laughed and told him how he cared not what he swore upon the Bible, since he did not believe anything that was written in it anyway.

Reminding Newton that, by case of law of 1676, English common law was the custodian of Scripture and, to some extent, doctrine, Their Lordships said that these were serious allegations made against Newton, although he was not on trial; and that their only aim was to make certain that the wardenship of the Mint was entrusted to a fit and proper person. It was milord Harley who led the enquiry against Newton, and milord Halifax who did the most to defend him.

Newton rose to his feet to answer the Italian's charges. He spoke entirely without emotion, as if he had been debating a matter of science with members of the Royal Society; but I could see how shaken he was by these allegations, which did cleverly mix the circumstances of the Count's transmutation with the ambiguous character of Newton's faith.

"I should like Your Lordships' permission to lay before Your Lordships a letter that has been sent to me from the Dutch ambassador in London," said Newton.

Their Lordships nodded, at which point Newton did hand me the letter to convey to their table. I got up, picked up the letter, brought it to the table, bowed gravely, laid it before them, and then returned to my chair next to Newton.

"It will confirm that the Count stole fifteen thousand marks from the ambassador's cousin at the court of Vienna."

"That's a damned lie," declared the Count.

"Count Gaetano," said milord Halifax, handing the letter along the table for Their Lordships' perusal. "You have spoken. You must allow Doctor Newton the chance to refute your allegations, without interruption."

"Thank you, milord. The ambassador," declared Newton, "informs me in this letter how he is prepared to give evidence in person that the Count has travelled Europe obtaining money under the pretence of demonstrating the transmutatory art. In London he is the Count Gaetano; but in Italy and Spain he has been the Count de Ruggiero; while in Austria and Germany he called himself Field Marshal to the Duke of Bavaria."

Newton waited for the effect of this revelation to make its effect, before adding: "The truth, however, is that he is plain Domenico Manuel, the son of a Neapolitan goldsmith and the pupil of Lascaris, who was another great charlatan and mountebank."

"Rubbish," snorted the Count. "Nonsense. The Dutch ambassador is as wicked a liar as you are, Doctor Newton; either that or a drunkard and a sot, like the rest of his countrymen."

This last remark did not sit well with Their Lordships, and it was Lord Halifax who articulated their obvious irritation.

"Count Gaetano, or whatever your name is, it may interest you to note that, as well as being a distant cousin of the Dutch ambassador, our own dear King William is also a Dutchman."

All of which left the Italian in considerable disarray.

"Oh well, I did not mean to suggest that His Majesty was a drunkard. Nor indeed that all Dutchmen are drunkards. Only that the ambassador must be mistaken—"

"Be silent, sir," commanded Lord Halifax.

After this, Newton had little difficulty in discrediting Count

Gaetano's story even further; and finally Their Lordships ordered the Count removed, and conveyed under guard to Newgate, pending further investigation.

"We are not out of the woods yet, I fear," murmured Newton as the porters escorted Gaetano from the Whitehall chamber.

"Bring in the next witness," commanded milord Harley. "Bring Mister Daniel Defoe."

"How did he get out of Newgate?" I whispered; and yet while my bowels were wracked at what Defoe might say against my master, I let my face dissemble a different story, smiling confidently at him as he entered the chamber, so that he might apprehend the improbability of his doing any injury to the reputation of one so great.

It cannot be doubted how the Italian's arrest had a most palpable effect on Mister Defoe; and when he came into the chamber he seemed mighty put out by the other man's fate. But he soon recovered his composure, and proved to be a much more obdurate sort of witness.

The allegations he made against Newton were twofold: one, that he had entered a dissenting church of French Socinians in Spitalfields; and the other, that he was a close friend of Mister Fatio, the Swiss Huguenot to whom I had been introduced in the coffee shop, just before I became sick with the ague.

"This same Mister Fatio," explained Defoe, "is strongly suspected of belonging to a cult of extreme dissenters who believe that they can resurrect a dead man in whatever cemetery they see fit."

"How do you answer, Doctor Newton?" asked Lord Harley.

Newton stood and bowed gravely. "What he says is entirely true, milord," said Newton, which drew a loud murmur from their Lordships. "But I'll warrant that these matters can easily be explained to your satisfaction.

"I entered the French church in an effort to find information that might enable me to shed light upon certain murders that have occurred in the Tower, and which I believe are known to you. One of the dead men, Major Mornay, had been a member of this French church, and I went there in the hope that I might speak to the Major's friends and to see if there were any circumstances that might have led him to take his own life.

"As to Mister Fatio, he is a young man who holds certain views that are repugnant to me. But he is a member of the Royal Society and my friend also, and I am satisfied in time that his intelligence will allow him to appreciate his youthful folly, and to see the good sense of the arguments I have frequently advanced in opposition to his obviously blasphemous views."

At which point Newton did glance at me, as if his words were meant for me, too.

"For I believe it better that we live in a country where foolish men can be led out of their ignorance by the wiser counsel of their elders, than by torture and execution as still persist in less happier countries than ours, such as France."

"Is it true," asked Lord Harley, "that you, Doctor Newton, did order Mister Defoe thrown into prison?"

"Milord, what else was I to do with a man whom I caught in the very act of conducting a clandestine search of the Mint office, where there were many Government papers of a secret or sensitive nature affecting the Great Recoinage?"

"Is this true, sir?" Lord Harley asked of Defoe. "Were you apprehended in the Mint Office?"

"I was arrested in the Mint office, it's true," said Defoe. "But I was not searching the office for Mint papers."

"Then what was your business in the Mint office?" asked Lord Halifax. "Did you not go there when Doctor Newton and his clerk were elsewhere?"

"I did not know that they were elsewhere. I sought to bring before the Warden information regarding certain coiners."

"The Mint office is kept locked when my clerk and I are not there," said Newton. "It was not I who admitted Mister Defoe to the office. Nor my clerk. Moreover, his so-called information was no more than a lie to try to explain his unauthorised presence in our office. And can Mister Defoe now swear out a warrant against one of these coiners whose names he sought to bring to my attention?"

"I did not have names," said Defoe. "Only suspicions."

"Suspicions," repeated Newton. "I have those, too, Mister Defoe. Do not think that you can try to hoodwink Their Lordships as you tried to hoodwink me, sir."

"It is you who are the liar, sir, not I," insisted Defoe, who now played his best card. "Are you prepared to take the Test Act in front of Their Lordships, to prove that you are a good Anglican?"

This Test Act of 1673 required that a man, usually someone in public office, receive Holy Communion according to the rites of the Church of England; which was something I knew the anti-Trinitarian Newton would never do; and for a moment I persuaded myself that all was lost. Instead, Newton sighed most profoundly and bowed his head.

"I will always do what Their Lordships require of me," he said, "even if that means humouring a man who has been imprisoned for bankruptcy and who is himself a dissenter from the established religion."

"Is this true, Mister Defoe?" asked milord Halifax. "That you are a bankrupt?"

"It is, milord."

"And are you yourself prepared to take the Test Act?" persisted Lord Halifax.

"Doctor Newton plays a loose game of religion and Bo-peep with God Almighty," declared Defoe, and then hung his head. "But, in all conscience, milord, I cannot."

Perceiving this self-righteous and peevish streak in Mister Defoe, Their Lordships dismissed him with a warning to be more careful of whom he accused in future. After which Lord Halifax moved that Lord Harley offer Their Lordships' apologies for having had Newton endure such baseless charges by such worthless rogues as those we had seen. Lord Harley did so, but said that Their Lordships had only conducted this inquiry in the best interests of the Mint. And with that the hearing ended.

When we were outside the chamber, I congratulated Newton most warmly, and declared myself most mighty relieved at the outcome. "It is as Aristotle says in his *Poetics*," I said. "That the plot is the soul of tragedy. For this plot could very easily have succeeded and left you dismissed from your office. Perhaps worse."

"That it did not is partly thanks to your diligence, in discovering much about Mister Defoe," said Newton. "And Mister Fatio's, too. For it was Fatio who wrote to his friends on the Continent about Count Gaetano. But in truth my enemies were ill-prepared. Had they been stronger, they would have felt better able to reveal themselves."

I shook my head. "To think of what might have happened, sir. You must return home at once."

"Why must I?"

"Your niece, Miss Barton, will be most anxious to hear what has happened, will she not?"

But already his thoughts lay elsewhere.

"This has all been an unwelcome distraction from the main business in hand," he said. "Which is the decipherment of that damned code. I have cudgelled my brains and still I can make nothing out of it."

⌒

Over the next few weeks Newton continued to make only slow progress with the cipher, which moved me to suggest, when we were in the office one day, that he might seek the help of Doctor Wallis of Oxford. But Newton treated my suggestion with scorn and derision.

"Ask help of Wallis?" he said with incredulity, as he set to stroking the cat. "I should sooner solicit the opinion of Melchior. 'Tis one thing to borrow a man's books, but quite another to make use of his brains. Go to him, cap in hand, and confess that I am baffled by this cipher? Why, then the man would bend Heaven and Earth to do something which I could not; and, having done so, would tell all the world. I would never hear the end of it. It would be better that I stuck a bare bodkin in my own side than let him put a thorn there to plague me with."

Newton nodded angrily. "But it is right that you hold this up to me, for it serves to prick my thinking parts toward the devising of the solution of this conundrum. For I'll not be dunned like some vulgar arithmetician who can practice what he has been taught or has seen done but, if he is in error, knows not how to find it out and correct it; and if you put him out of his road, he is at a complete stand.

"Yes sir, you encourage me, by God you do: to reason nimbly and judiciously about numerical frequency, for I swear I shall never be at rest till I get over every rub."

Thus I observed that the cleverer the person, the more certain is his conviction that he is able to solve a puzzle which nobody else can solve; and that this goes to show the truth of Plato's theory that knowledge involves true belief but goes beyond it.

After that, Newton was almost never without a black lead and a sheet of paper that was covered with letters and algebraic formulas, with which he strove to work out the cipher's solution. And sometimes I altogether forgot that he did this work. But I well remember the time when Newton finally broke the code. All of a sudden there was great talk of a peace with the French near signing. Formal negotiations between ourselves and the French had been under way since May, at the Dutch town of Rijswijk. This was just as well, for it was common knowledge that the fleet was in a dreadful parlous state at anchor in Torbay, for want of provisions that was occasioned by the severe lack of good money. It was even said by my brother Charles that we had borrowed Dutch money to pay English sailors, and if so, then it's certain nothing but a peace could have retrieved our situation.

The date was August the twenty-seventh, 1697, and I can still recall how I was a little surprised when Newton ignored my news of the peace and instead informed me, most triumphantly, that the deciphering of the letters was done and immediately made pertinent sense.

I accepted his word on the matter straightaway—for there was no denying the look of immense satisfaction on his face—and congratulated him most warmly upon the solution; and yet he still insisted on demonstrating the ingenious construction of the cipher in order that I might be satisfied of the truth of what he said. Newton drew his chair up to our table in the Mint office and, pushing Melchior away from his papers, showed me the many pages of his copious workings.

"In truth," he explained, with much excitement, "a brief glimpse of how I might solve it presented itself to my mind just a few days ago, but only very vaguely. But now I see that it is all to do with constants and functions, which is but a cruder system of my own fluxions.

"The code is based in part on a system that uses a single short and repeating word, known to both correspondents, as the key to the cipher. Let us say that the keyword is your own surname. The encipherer repeats this keyword beneath his message, thus." Newton wrote two lines of text on a sheet of paper:

THE   LORD   IS   MY   LIGHT AND   SALVATION
ELL   ISEL   LI   SE   LLISE LLI   SELLISELL

"Observe," he continued, "how all the letters of the alphabet have a numerical value from one to twenty-six."

A	B	C	D	E	F	G	H	I	J	K	L
1	2	3	4	5	6	7	8	9	10	11	12

M	N	O	P	Q	R	S	T	U	V	W	X	Y	Z
13	14	15	16	17	18	19	20	21	22	23	24	25	26

"The letter T in our message is the twentieth letter in the alphabet," he said. "We add this to the key letter that appears below. This is an E and the fifth letter in the alphabet. The sum of these two letters is twenty-five, which is the letter Y. This becomes the first letter of our cipher. Of course the sum of two letters may easily be more than twenty-six, for instance with the letters T and S. Their sum is thirty-nine. Therefore, in order that we do not run out of cipher letters, we start the alphabet again so that after the letter Z, which is worth twenty-six, the letter A becomes worth twenty-seven, and so on. In this way, thirty-nine gives us the cipher letter M. When it is finished, the whole message in cipher would read as follows."

THE   LORD   IS   MY   LIGHT AND   SALVAT ION
ELL   ISEL   LI   SE   LLISE LLI   SELLISELL
YTQ   UHWP   UB   FD   XUPAY MZM   LFXHJMNAZ

"The person wishing to decipher the message," continued Newton, "executes the procedure in reverse. He writes out the cipher with the key word repeating underneath, and subtracts their numerical values. *E,* worth five, is subtracted from *Y,* worth twenty-five, which gives us twenty. Twenty-six is then added, to take account of any minus numbers. This gives us forty-six and the letter *T.* Equally, if we look at the cipher word *XUPAY,* we see that if we subtracted our keyword letter *S* from the cipher letter *A,* we would end up with one minus nineteen, which gives us minus eighteen. Minus eighteen plus twenty-six is worth eight, which gives us the letter *H,* from the message word *LIGHT.*"

I nodded as, slowly, I began to understand the character of the cipher he described.

"As I said to you before," explained Newton, "the code we have been dealing with here in the Tower is based on this general principle of a repeating keyword. But this makes it most susceptible to solution, for the key is always in full view of him who would make the decipherment. For example, you may perceive that in the cipher the letter *X* occurs twice in the cipher, and both times it conceals the same message letter *L.* Similarly the letter *U* occurs three times, and twice it conceals the message letter *I.* And it can be observed that one quarter of the time, common fragments such as the 'TH' in 'THE' will correspond exactly to 'EL' in 'ELLIS.' This is the weakness inherent in the system.

"Therefore the person who devised this key added an ingenious and numerical force that produced a motion within the key to hide those common fragments much more effectively. And yet so simple too, for the keyword itself changes based on the message, in a simple series progression. In this system, the keyword becomes a function of the letter *L.*

"The first five letters of the message would be encrypted in the normal way."

```
THELO
ELLIS
YTQUH
```

"But for the next five letters, the key changes based on the five encrypted letters—*Y, T, Q, U,* and *H*—according to whether or not the letters of the encryption appear before or after *L*. Any encrypted letters between *M* and *Z* cause the keyword to be incremented by one letter. But any letters before or including *L* cause the requisite letter of the keyword to remain the same. Or, to put it another way, *A* to *L* are our constants, while *M* to *Z* are our variables. For example, with:"

```
THELO
ELLIS
YTQUH
```

"*Y* occurs after *E*, which causes us to increment the key-word by one letter to *F.* This is true of *T, Q,* and *U,* but not *H,* so that our next keyword becomes *FMMJS.* This gives us:"

```
THELO  RDISM
ELLIS  FMMJS
YTQUH  XQVCF
```

"In the same way *X, Q,* and *V* modify the first three letters of our new keyword, *FMMJS,* so that it becomes *G, N, N.* But *C* and *F* being before *L* do not cause it to be incremented, and so we have a new keyword, *GNNJS.* Finally we end up with this:"

```
THELO  RDISM  YLIGH  T
ELLIS  FMMJS  GNNJS  G
YTQUH  XQVCF  FZWQA  A
```

"To undo the cipher you subtract the numerical values of the keyword from the numerical value of the cipher and add 26 each time. For example, *Y* equals 25, minus *E* equals 5, gives us 20, plus 26 makes 46 which makes the letter *T*; similarly, the last letter of our cipher *A* equals 1, minus *G* equals 7, gives us minus 6, plus 26, makes 20 equals *T.*

"It was a most brilliant mathematical variation, for the system becomes almost inscrutable."

"How did you solve it, sir?"

"Thanks to Mister Scroope's ignorant variation, I almost did not solve it at all," confessed Newton. "He was clever enough to introduce a small mathematical series into the sample he chose from the first message he had from George Macey. He simply added one to the first letter, and then subtracted one from the second letter; then he added two to the third letter, and subtracted two from the fourth letter; and so on. It was some time before I perceived that the message chalked upon the wall near Mercer's body was also the first line of the letter we found in Macey's message. And having seen this, I recognised how the cipher had been used ignorantly, without apprehension, and was intended but to further darken my own understanding. It was only when I dispensed with this message altogether that the other letters began to demonstrate some mathematical consistency.

"As to solving the rest, I must confess to an element of good fortune that came my way. Nothing works more to undermine the secrecy of a code than man's own frailty. For man is the natural enemy of mathematics, being most prone to error and habit. The plotters have consistently used two phrases as an exhortation unto their own inordinate zealotries and fanaticism. For, as you shall soon see, that is what they are: zealots and fanatics of a most egregious variety, mighty dangerous to the safety of the realm."

Newton tried to show me the many differentiations he had made during his months of work, but there were so many quadratic expressions that he only very slightly demonstrated to my understanding how the cipher had been solved. Later on I understood it better, for I copied a letter that Newton did write to Wallis, in which he explained the workings of the code in detail, but not his mathematics, for he said that would have been to show Wallis the workings of his own mind, and he had no mind at all to do that.

But at the time all that algebra made my head ache as if I had been back in school, or in my sickbed the time Newton had thought to stimulate my recovery by explaining to me his system of fluxions; and yet the messages were clear enough and revealed a glimpse of something dreadful that was still very much afoot in the Tower.

"The two phrases they used regularly and to their eventual detriment were 'Remember Saint Bartholomew's' and 'Remember Sir Edmund Berry Godfrey.'"

"That was the sentiment on Mornay's dagger," I cried.

"Exactly so," said Newton. "It was also part of the phrase that Scroope chose to embellish. Now the first message we had was upon Mister Kennedy's dead body, put there by Mister Scroope, who had it from Mister Macey, neither of whom had any apprehension as to what it meant. I do not suppose we shall ever know how Mister Macey came to intercept this message. But I suspect that the men who have been using this cipher are so confident of its Sphinxlike imperspicuity that they have taken few precautions with where they left their correspondence. And so Macey may simply have stumbled upon it accidentally."

Newton read out his translation: "'Remember Sir Edmund Berry Godfrey. Dear Doctor Davies, I do not think we should meet as you suggested. If you were recognised visiting my house, or we were ever seen together, the news might appear in every farthing paper in the land. But I would wish to know from you by what method Roman Catholics are to be identified. You may communicate with me by letter as always through Major Mornay. Remember Saint Bartholomew's. Yours, Lord A.'

"I believe 'Lord A.' is none other than Lord Ashley, the Member of Parliament for Poole, whom our spies reported that Major Mornay visited. He is the grandson of the Earl of Shaftesbury, Anthony Ashley Cooper, who once led extreme Whig opposition to the King. He was a notorious Green Ribboner and republican who fled to Holland after the Rye House Plot against King Charles."

"I have heard that phrase," said I. "Green Ribboner. My father used it as a term of opprobrium, but I never knew what it meant."

"During the reign of Charles II, the Green Ribboners posed more of a danger to this realm than the French," explained Newton. "They were a group of extreme Whigs who hated Roman Catholics almost as much as they hated monarchs, and wished to see the extinction of both in England. They would have restored the Republic and made Richard Cromwell Lord Protector once again.

"It is certain that the Green Ribboners fomented a number of plots to kill King Charles, or Roman Catholics, of which the Popish Plot of 1678, led by Titus Oates, that manufactured a false Catholic plot against the King, was the most vile—for many Catholic priests were falsely accused and put to death.

"But little or nothing has been heard of these Green Ribboners since Shaftesbury's death, in 1683, and the Glorious Revolution that deposed the Catholic King James. With so many real Catholic plots to depose King William—first Ailesbury, then Sir John Fenwick—what need would there be to create rumours of false ones?"

"Perhaps," I suggested, "Lord Ashley and his correspondent have endeavoured to discover if there are any more Catholics who plot against King William. I should think that every patriotic Englishman would wish to identify potential traitors among us."

"Suspend your judgement just a short while longer," counselled Newton. "Consider next this message we had from Doctor Wallis, which Macey gave him. I believe it provides the answer to the first message.

"'Remember Saint Bartholomew's. Milord A. We shall identify Roman Catholics as were the French Huguenots. From the tax rolls. Also I have lists from the last time that were made by constables for the justices of the peace; also a guide made by Mister Lee, a map by Mister Morgan, and a scheme by Mister King that shall show us where all these nests of Catholic vermin are to be found. None shall escape us. Your servant, Doctor Davies.'

"Now what is your opinion?" asked Newton.

"I confess it sounds like another Popish Plot," said I.

"It is much more serious than that," Newton said gravely. "'None shall escape us'? Is the matter not yet clear to you?"

"Yes, only I am afraid to say it, Doctor."

"Then I will say it for you, my young friend. It is a plan to massacre London's Roman Catholics that is here revealed. The tax rolls were how the Huguenots of Paris were identified on Saint Bartholomew's Day, in 1572. It was said that some ten thousand Protestant men, women and children in Paris were murdered in one night. And yet more in the country at large."

"But that was more than a century ago," I objected. "And Englishmen are not like Frenchmen. We do not murder people in their beds. Besides, there are not so many Catholics in London as there were Huguenots in Paris."

"Do you think so?" scoffed Newton. "London has many secret Roman Catholics—Church papists who pay only lip service to the Anglican Church, and celebrate their mass in private."

"But does not the Test Act demand that they take the oaths

of loyalty to the Anglican Church? A man may be fined for recusancy, after all."

"And yet few are fined," said Newton. "The law is a poor one, being seldom enforced."

"I still say that in this country people are not murdered in their beds, whatever their religion."

"Were not the Jacobite MacDonalds of Glencoe coldbloodedly slaughtered by King William's troops in Scotland? That was but five years ago, as I recall."

"They were Scotch," I said, as if that explained how such a terrible thing had taken place. "Scotch victims and Scotch soldiers. What else is to be expected of the Scots? Londoners are not so intolerant. Nor are they so barbaric."

"But if Londoners are provoked, albeit falsely," said Newton, "what then? You are too young to remember how the Great Fire of London was blamed upon a Catholic named Peidloe, who was hanged for it, although as every schoolboy knows, it was started accidentally by a baker in Pudding Lane. As was the Southwark Fire of 1676, although another Roman Catholic, this time a Jesuit named Grove, was blamed for that. Indeed the Southwark Fire was generally perceived to have been planned by Catholics as a prelude to a massacre of London's Protestants. And during the Revolution, did not Londoners expect to be massacred by King James's Irish troops with whom he hoped to keep his kingdom?

"No, Ellis. Londoners are like the people of any great city: most credulous and mad. I would as soon trust a dog with a foaming mouth as depend on the varied and inconstant opinion of a London mob. I wonder that any man who has been to an execution at Tyburn could hold such a good opinion of the populace as you seem to."

"I agree, sir, if the mob is provoked, then it is most ungovernable. But I do not see Englishmen being led by French Huguenots. How is the mob to be provoked?"

"It would not be difficult," said Newton. "But we must find out more, and quickly, too, for we have lost much time while I have been solving this cipher."

"I still find this hard to accept," said I.

"Then read the message that we found on Major Mornay's body."

> *To Sergeant Rohan.*
>
> *If I am killed in this duel, which I did not seek, I ask only that my murderer, Christopher Ellis, be slaughtered with the rest, for among so many, one more will scarcely be noticed, and it will doubtless seem that he was but a secret Catholic. I did my duty as a Protestant.*
>
> *Remember Sir Edmund Berry Godfrey. Remember Saint Bartholomew's.*
>
> *Major Charles Mornay*

"Does that not put it beyond any doubt?" asked Newton.

"Yes," I heard myself say. "And to think that I felt sorry for him."

Newton nodded silently.

"But were there not four messages, master? What about the message we recovered from poor Mister Twistleton? Did you not decipher that one?"

Silently, Newton handed over the decipherment and let me read the plain text for myself. It made alarming reading:

> *Remember Sir Edmund Berry Godfrey.*
>
> *Mister Twistleton,*
> *In this great religious enterprise, blessed of God, you are to assist Sergeant Rohan in devising a plan to assassinate Doctor*

*Isaac Newton, the Warden of the Royal Mint. All blame must
be seen to fall upon Old Roettier, the engraver, and a much suspected Catholic, and upon Jonathan Ambrose, the goldsmith,
who is a secret Roman Catholic, and who is know greatly to
resent Newton. Upon the return of King William from the war
in Flanders, this will help to stir up strong feeling against all
Catholics, as did the death of Sir Edmund Berry Godfrey
before. Therefore, acquaint yourself with Newton's habits, and
inform me by letter of how you propose to carry out this deed,
which will be at a more suitable time yet to be decided.*

  Remember Saint Bartholomew's.

Yours,
Doctor Davies

"I must confess that this one gave me a little trouble," explained Newton. "'Jonathan Ambrose, the goldsmith, who is know greatly to resent Newton'? That's bad grammar. Such a thing makes a decipherer's life most vexatious."

"But, sir, you understate the matter most egregiously. For, according to this letter, you are in mortal danger."

"I think that we are probably both in some danger," said Newton.

"But in my own case, I should only be killed with the rest. You, however, are to be killed first of all. Which might be at any time."

"Not until the King has returned from the war," said Newton. "That is what the message says, Ellis."

"It would explain why Sergeant Rohan was so curious about you," I said, unhappily.

"You spoke to him?"

"Once, when I had followed him to Westminster," I confessed. "I lost him for a while and then bumped into him. He was most affable. We had a drink together. At the time I thought that I might acquire some information about him."

"And now you discover that he may have gained some information about me, is that it?"

I nodded miserably, ashamed to confess that I had the suspicion that I might even have let slip Newton's address.

"No matter," said Newton. "Information about me is not so difficult to obtain. He would have found some other means, had you not told him what you did. Therefore, calm yourself. We are prepared for them and know them for what they are: ruthless men. Doubtless Macey was tortured and killed when he tried to understand their messages. Even Major Mornay, who was one of them, was not safe when the scandal of a duel threatened to compromise their plans. We must move very carefully."

"I wonder why they left Mister Twistleton alive," said I.

"Who listens to a madman?" said Newton. "You said as much yourself. It is a measure of their confidence in this stratagem and their cipher that they left him alive and in possession of a coded letter. It also explains why Mister Twistleton wished to attack me. But I wish I had possessed the wit to copy down what he said to us. For I've an idea that he actually told us the keyword to the code himself, when we visited him in Bedlam. Do you not remember what he said when I asked him the meaning of the letters?"

"Blood," I said. " 'Blood is behind everything,' he said."

"He meant it literally and cryptically," said Newton. "For *blood* is the keyword to this code." He shook his head sadly. "There are times when I seem very stupid to myself."

"But one thing I still do not understand," said I. "Why should this be happening here, in the Tower?"

"I have given this matter some thought," admitted Newton. "And I have concluded that if a mob must be armed, where better to do it than from the Royal Armouries?"

"Yes, of course," I said. "There are enough swords and guns here to equip a whole army. But what are we going to do?"

"We must insinuate ourselves into this secret correspondence," he explained. "Only then will we find the evidence to take to milord Halifax. To do that, we must know more about our plotters. Not least when they plan to commit their treason. I would know more about this Doctor Davies. Did not one of our spies follow Sergeant Rohan to the courts at Westminster Hall? Perhaps he was the man the Sergeant met there. Once we have discovered that, we shall play one against the other."

Our spy, Humphrey Hall, was a most diligent fellow, as I have said; and the next day I went to Westminster Hall with him to see if he could identify the man whom he had seen meeting with Sergeant Rohan. But the man was not there; nor the day after that. And it was Friday, September the third, before Mister Hall spied the man he had seen meeting with the Sergeant.

I had a good look at the fellow when we followed him to The Swan with Two Necks in nearby Tuttle Street. About fifty years of age, he was a tall man but bowlegged, with a bull neck, although not powerful, so that his head scarcely protruded from his body, and his abnormally large chin, which was equal in size to the rest of his peculiar face, seemed permanently bowed toward his chest. His eyes were small and quite feral, and his brow as low as his great hat, which darkened an already purplish complexion that was clearly the result of an overfondness of wine. Above one eyebrow was a large wart. His mode of dress was not only clerical but Episcopal, for he wore a cassock and, but for a long rose-coloured scarf and a way of speaking that better suited a costermonger or a Southwark porter—for we heard him speak to the tavern's landlord in a strident sing-song voice, so that he seemed permanently to complain rather than to speak—we might have taken him for a man of some learning, or even a lawyer, whose presence in the courts of Chancery was upon the instruction of his client, for there were many who attended that were never heard.

We followed the strange Doctor Davies to his place of lodging on the north side of Axe Yard, and collected some facts upon him from Mister Beale, who was the most talkative landlord at The Axe Tavern, farther along the street, and whose family had been in Axe Yard since before the Great Fire. He told us that Doctor Davies was a Cambridge man and the son of an Anabaptist chaplain in Cromwell's New Model Army; he had been a chaplain in the navy; he had written a book; he had been recently married to a wealthy widow who was away visiting her relations; he enjoyed a government pension; and he was a Baptist minister in Wapping.

Having thanked Mister Beale with five shillings for his information and his silence, it was to Wapping we now went to find out more.

I have never much like Ranters, and Baptists least of all, for what kind of sect is it that follows the precepts of a man as mad as John the Baptist, who lived in the desert and ate locusts? They must surely have been mad at Wapping, for only the Lord's fools and mad folks would have freely confessed that their minister's real name was not Paul Davies but Titus Oates, he of that notorious Popish Plot that had fabricated allegations that Jesuit priests were planning to assassinate King Charles II in order to place his Roman Catholic brother, the Duke of York, on the throne.

It was a great shock to Mister Hall and me that a man as malign as Titus Oates was at liberty, let alone that he was preaching the word of God; and Mister Hall was so shaken by this discovery that he felt obliged to go to a church and pray. Before Oates's vile lies were revealed, some thirty-five innocent men were judicially murdered.

The Duke sued Oates for libel in 1684 and was awarded damages of one hundred thousand pounds; and having no money to pay, Oates was cast into the debtor's side of the King's Bench prison. But for him, even worse was to follow. The next year the Duke ascended to the throne and Oates was put on trial for perjury before Mister Justice Jeffreys, whose declared regret was that the Law did not prescribe Jack Ketch himself; and the following day, whipped from Newgate to Tyburn—which is about two miles. He was also sentenced to be imprisoned for life and pilloried once a year—which has killed many a stronger man than he. And this was the last I had heard of Titus Oates until that September's Friday afternoon.

Wishing to discover how Oates had been set at liberty, I went to visit Mister Jonathan Taylor, a friend of mine who was a barrister in the Court of Common Pleas at Westminster Hall and whose reputation was that he was a veritable almanac of legal matters. And he quickly completed the legal history of Titus Oates until that same date. Taylor told me that when William came to the throne in 1688, Judge Jeffreys was imprisoned in the Tower and Oates petitioned Parliament for redress against his sentence. And it says much about the anti-Catholic sentiments that were once again abroad in the country that, in the face of all the evidence that he had conspired in the death of many innocent men, Oates was given a free pardon and quietly released from prison in December of that same year. According to Taylor, he was even granted ten pounds a week from the Secret Service money—which was no small sum. He then wrote a long account of his treatment that was published under the title *A Display of Tyranny*. Taylor told me it was a work that was reckoned to be a most villainous and reviling book against King James, by all who read it, which Oates then presumed to present to King William, although the King certainly could not do anything but abhor it, speaking so infamously and untruly of his late Queen's own father King James as it did.

When I informed Newton that Doctor Davies was none other than Titus Oates, he was as much astonished as Mister Hall and I had been; and yet he quickly declared that it all made perfect if unpalatable sense that Oates should be involved in a plot to massacre London's Catholics.

"Evidently prison and a whipping have taught Mister Oates very little," he said.

"Is it possible that milord Ashley does not know the real identity of Doctor Davies?" said I. "For I cannot conceive that milord Ashley would have any dealing with such a devil if he knew who he was."

"Was it not the Earl of Shaftesbury, Ashley's own grandfather, that helped promote Oates to inform the Privy Council of the Popish Plot? But for him, Oates would never have been heard of.

"I believe it is significant also," Newton added thoughtfully, "that this plot should be taking place when the country is trying to end a war. It was the same with the Popish Plot, which took place when King Charles was concluding a peace with the Dutch. There are some men for whom peace is always unwelcome, for peace means an end to lucrative government contracts for the supplying of an army and a navy. Worse still, it means paying off the army, and that means asking the Parliament for money, which always serves to increase its power at the expense of the aristocracy."

Newton shook his head. "There's much here that disturbs me greatly," he admitted. "But you have done well, my young friend. It is certain you have uncovered one of the ringleaders in this conspiracy. And yet I would know still more of their plans. I doubt that Sergeant Rohan or any of these other Frenchies could be persuaded to tell us more. And yet Oates might talk."

I frowned. "I don't see how or why," I said.

"I have met the young milord Ashley," said Newton. "At

The Grecian; and at the Kit Kat Club. I would say he is about your age and build, and a dreadful snob. Which may be another reason why he has not met Titus Oates. But we may exploit that to our advantage. We shall send Oates a coded letter inviting him to meet Lord Ashley at some place we shall appoint. And there Oates will tell us everything."

"But how? I still don't understand."

"Because you will act the part of Lord Ashley, of course," said Newton.

"I?"

"Who else? I am too old. But I may play the part of your manservant. We shall borrow a handsome coach and six from milord Halifax. And we shall hire you some fine clothes, as might befit the future Earl of Shaftesbury. We will arrange to meet Oates outside the Kit Kat Club in Hampstead where I know him to be a member. And the three of us shall go for a drive about the countryside, as if we were three men with much to hide."

"But will this work, sir? If you are marked for assassination, then perhaps Titus Oates knows your face."

"I am not such a remarkable-looking fellow," said Newton, "although I do say so myself. Besides, I seem to recall that Lord Ashley has a servant who wears an eye patch. As shall I. It will help to disguise me."

"So I am to be an actor, then, as well as a clerk?"

"Yes indeed, Ellis. Just like William Mountford, is it?"

"With respect, sir, that is a poor example you choose. William Mountford, the actor, was murdered."

"Was he?"

"Do you not recall it? Lord Mohun was tried for it."

"I do recall it now," said Newton. "And that he was not murdered for his acting, but for his association with a lady to which Lord Mohun objected."

"I had better keep a pistol hidden in the coach," said I, "so that if we are discovered, we shall be defended. For I believe your plan to deceive Oates and his Huguenot friends to be the most dangerous thing we have ever done."

"We shall do all we can to protect ourselves. Mister Hall shall be our postillion. And he too shall be armed. God willing, we shall prevail."

And, drawing up a clean sheet of paper, he wrote out the following message:

TBT QEQ HHFL ZKR FUG ZEQ SAWN XNIZAT PD GOD TLEW JKSZ HWJ LB GNLHK PBZI GAOAD I LOZ NKK LN KRR CRACSS NHGT VJ QAM FKML NAW CZAASF GWOD DHK VEN BP COKXS JDS LTH QB

On Monday morning we bought my suit of clothes at the second hand, from Mister George Hartley's shop in Monmouth Street, with the promise that he would buy them back from us when we had finished with them. I wore a silk suit, a pair of silk stockings, a velvet cloak, and a fine beaver hat that was trimmed with an ostrich feather; also a fine knotted cane with a silver head, a little sword with a gilt handle, a large *mouchoir* of scented silk, a silver periwig, a pair of soft, jessemy-scented gloves, a blue sash, and around my waist a large fur muff for my hands in which I did conceal a small pistol. It was as fine a set of clothes as ever I had worn, although I was somewhat discomforted by the information from Mister Hartley that my clothes had been stripped from the corpse of a dashing highwayman named Gregory Harris who had been hanged at Tyburn, and whose clothes had been sold by his executioner, as was the hangman's perquisite. I completed my lordly apparel with a good deal of powder on my face, my wig and my coat, a little snuff box, and a few affected airs. In truth I felt like a most modish creature, the more so when Newton told me that I went as handsomely as any lord he ever saw. And my only cause of regret was that Miss Barton could not see me and declare herself of the same opinion as her uncle.

In the evening, at around seven of the clock, milord Halifax's coach collected Newton and me from the Tower and drove us north up to Hampstead and the Kit Kat Club, which met at The Upper Flask Tavern in Heath Street. And while we drove through the town, people kept looking upon us, for the coach was very fine, with glass windows, two liveried coachmen and six black horses with their manes and tails tied with green ribbons that matched our livery.

At a few minutes before eight, our coach drew up outside the tavern in the village of Hampstead, which is a most fashionable part of London, being very high up on a pleasantly aired plateau. The Kit Kat was a most ardently Whig club that for a while was the most famous club in London, and its members included Mister Swift, Mister Addison, Mister Steele, Mister Vanburgh, Mister Dryden, Mister Congreve, Mister Kneller, Lord Ashley, and the same Lord Mohun who had killed the actor William Mountford, and who later killed the Duke of Hamilton in a duel. The club was lit up like a lantern and already noisy, so that I saw the wisdom of the club being here instead of in the City, for some of the younger members had a rakehellish reputation, and bonfires in Heath Street where the Pope was burnt in effigy were not uncommon.

For the quarter of an hour my master and I sat in the coach awaiting the arrival of the vile Titus Oates, and I began to worry that he would not come.

"Perhaps he suspects something is wrong," said I.

"Why should he?" asked Newton, who looked most threatening with an eye patch. "For all of the conspirators believe that their cipher remains inviolate. He will come. I am certain of it."

Even as he spoke, Mister Hall, who was acting as our postillion, saw a tall figure arriving up the hill and alerted us that
our man was coming, so that we had but a little time to prepare
ourselves for the dog's arrival.

"Remember," said Newton, "you are a Member of Parliament and the future Earl of Shaftesbury. You need never explain
yourself. Much of the time your conversation will have to
improve upon what he himself tells you. I shall assist you if I can,
but I cannot presume too much or it will look suspicious. We
must be exceedingly subtle with this fellow."

When Oates came alongside the coach, Hall stepped down
and opened the door, whereupon Oates, recovering his breath,
for it was quite a walk from Axe Yard, bowed gravely.

"Have I the honour to address Lord Ashley?" he asked in
his pompous, ringing voice, which reminded me of my choir-
master at school.

"This is His Lordship," said Newton. "If you are Doctor
Oates, come up, sir."

At this, Oates appeared taken aback, and then looked at
Doctor Newton for a moment, so that he seemed upon the point
of going away again.

"Is there something wrong, Doctor Oates?" asked Newton.

"Only that I do not go by that name anymore, sir," said
Oates. "At His Lordship's own suggestion."

"If you prefer, we shall call you Doctor Davies," suggested
Newton. "But you need not concern yourself on this matter. I
enjoy His Lordship's complete confidence in this matter. As in
all others."

Oates nodded and, climbing aboard, sat down heavily and
with evident relief. Hall closed the door behind him, and immediately I noticed how a strange, cloying smell did attach to the
person of Oates; and after a short pause to allow Hall to climb
up again, I rapped on the roof with my cane so that we should

drive back to London. Outside I heard the coachman crack his whip and we started south, down Heath Street, toward the City.

"This is indeed an honour, milord," said Oates, most unctuously. "I never met your grandfather, but from what I knew of him, he was a very great man."

I yawned ostentatiously and dabbed at my mouth with my *mouchoir* as I had once seen Lord Halifax do when we were at the Treasury.

"And I am happy to be of service to you, as I was to him," continued Oates. "Nay, not happy. Delighted and greatly honoured, too."

"*Façon, façon,*" I said with a foppish show of impatience. "Do let us get on. And pray do not call it my service, Doctor Oates, for this matter is too desperate to be done only on my account. In truth, you see me quite unnerved by the gravity of our design. So much so that I came up to Hampstead to take the waters. But now I desire that you might put my mind at rest that everything is made ready. It's not scruple of my conscience that made me write to you, sir, but want of confidence in our enterprise. I do swear I wish every Roman Catholic to the infernals, yet, *mal peste,* it's a beastly nuisance, for I still fret that something will go awry. But you have been through this all before, Doctor Oates. You are our Achilles in this endeavour, and because I am so *chagrin* and disquieted these past few days, I would have your counsel. That is why I wrote to you and summoned you, sir."

"Then be assured, milord," said Oates, "everything is just as it should be. Mister Defoe's pamphlet that will help to incite to anger all good Protestants is already printed and only awaits the proper occasion for its distribution."

"I should like to read that pamphlet," said I. And then to Newton: "Why have I not seen it, John?"

"You have not seen it, milord?" asked Oates. "I was informed that Lord Lucas had shown it to you."

I shook my head. "Perhaps he did show me something," I admitted. "But I'm afraid that I lost it."

"I have some more at my lodgings," said Oates. "I could show you one now if you wished."

"Yes, indeed you shall," said I. "We will take the coach to your lodgings, Doctor Oates, and you shall fetch me one of these pamphlets of yours."

Newton leaned out of the coach window and instructed the coachman that when we reached London we should drive to Axe Yard.

"And yet I am more concerned to know the mettle of our confederates, Doctor Oates," I told him. "Lord Lucas will vapour most hotly about the men of the Ordnance and how they are loyal to him. But after all, a lot of these are Frenchies. What of good Englishmen? And when last I saw him I said to him *à d'autre, à d'autre.* Tell it to the others, my lord, but not to me. For I thought him all bluster and grimace, and his explanations did not convince me. But I have heard you are a man of much subtlety, Doctor Oates. My grandfather always said as much. Which is why I have met you *à la dérobée,* which is to say secretly. That is to say, Lord Lucas does not know that I am speaking to you. Nor does anyone else for that matter, and I would prefer if it were kept that way."

"Your Lordship does me great honour," said Oates, bowing his head and trying to stop the self-satisfied smile that did appear upon his enormous chin, which was quite as big as the rest of his face.

"Subtlety and integrity, Doctor Oates. You are a man to call a spade a spade."

"Your Lordship is too kind," smirked Oates.

"So I would know how many we really are, and not what Lord Lucas sees fit to tell me. And what are our chances of success."

"We are not so many," said Oates. "But we are enough."

"Ods my life, Doctor, now you sound like Lucas. Not so coy, I pray you, or else I shall believe that this plot is mere fancy. The wise man builds his house not on sand but on a rock. So I would know who we may rely on, for I trust not men who have no names."

Oates's eyes narrowed and he stared out of the window for a moment as Hampstead became the manor of Tyburn, with its many dairy farms that supplied London's milk and cheese, so that I almost believed he suspected something was amiss, and I placed my hand on the loaded pistol concealed inside the fur muff that lay on my lap like a dead spaniel. Instead he nodded with much thoughtfulness.

"Milord," he said, most pleadingly, "it's safer that you do not know. And yet I wonder why Lord Lucas should not have kept you better informed. 'Tis most strange."

"Lucas is not a considerate man," said I. "Indeed I may tell you in secret that I do not like him."

"He is most impatient, and intemperate, it's true," agreed Titus Oates. "Why then, I will tell you as much as I know myself. Inside the Tower there's him, Captain Lacoste, Captain Martin, Sergeant Rohan, and several men of the garrison: Cousin, Durel, Lasco, Devoe, Harald. Then, in the Mint there's Mister Fauquier, the Deputy Master; Mister Collins, one of the assay masters, who did descend from Coligny, the great Huguenot admiral who was butchered by the French Catholics upon Saint Bartholomew's; Vallière, who works the melt, Mister Silvester, the smith, and Peter Bayle, the victualler. That's thirteen all told in the castle itself.

"Outside the Tower there are almost a hundred Englishmen in the barracks at Whitehall and at Somerset House; and among them several more Huguenots: Colonel Quesnal, Major Laurent, Major Sarrazin, Captain Hesse, Captain Popart, Lieutenant Delafons, and Sergeant Barre.

"Among the civilians there are perhaps a hundred more, including myself; Sir John Houblon at the Bank; Sir John Peyton; Monsieur Piozet, who's pastor at the Savoy; Monsieurs Primerose, La Mothe, Chardin, and Moreau, who are on the *grande comité français.* In Soho there is Monsieur Guisard, whose father was burned for heresy, and Monsieur Peyferie, as well as several dozen hatmakers, buttoners, silk-weavers, drapers, chandlers, apothecaries and wigmakers in the City that do number at least six or seven dozen.

"Last of all, there's Mister Defoe the pamphleteer, Mister Woodward the publisher, and Mister Downing, his printer; not to mention the several incendiaries who will help me to set the blaze at Whitehall, including young Mister Tonge, who knows much about raising fires.

"They are all good Protestants, milord," declared Oates. "Therefore be assured that our chances of success are high."

"For the conflagration," said Newton, "will surely be blamed upon the Papists."

"Aye," said Oates, "for it is only what they would do had they sufficient opportunity."

"Who would doubt such a thing after the Ailesbury Plot?" said Newton. "Or the insurrection of Sir John Fenwick?"

"And yet," said I, "so many Jacobites have been arrested this year that I fear they are driven underground and we shall find fewer Papists than there are. Were not all Papists banished ten miles from London, last February?"

"Aye, milord," said Oates. "But the measure was relaxed after only a month; and those few who were obliged to leave were soon back, like rats after the Fire."

"Then pray tell me, Doctor Oates, how accurate are your lists of who is to be killed? We do not want any Papists getting away."

"I'll warrant none shall escape, milord," said Oates, grinning most fanatically so that I saw how much he relished the bloody prospect that was plotted. "We shall begin with the Spanish Ambassador's house in Wild Street, Covent Garden, that bestows a Roman Catholic aura upon that whole area. I expect to find papers there that were compiled for the Catholic Minister Apostolic in Flanders as to how many Papists there are in England and Wales, and their names. I do not think we shall slaughter fewer Catholics than Huguenots were murdered in Paris, milord."

"It seems only appropriate that the number should be the same," murmured Newton. "But when will it be done?"

"Fool," said I, counterfeiting to Oates that I already had this knowledge, for I did not think it good that we should seem to know nothing. "I told you already. The damn fellow never listens, Doctor. Tell him."

"Why, when the King returns from Flanders, of course," said Oates. "What good is a Catholic plot to kill the King, if the King is somewhere else? It will all come out after this man Isaac Newton is murdered. For with his death, which will be blamed on the Catholics, the rest of their damnable plot will be revealed."

"How is he to be murdered?" I enquired. "I have heard he is a mighty intelligent fellow, this Isaac Newton. He may yet outwit you."

"I have not the precise details. But his movements are known to us. He will be assassinated in the street, and the blame put upon a notorious Roman Catholic who works in the Tower."

"After the peace is concluded, then," Newton said coolly, as if we were discussing the murder of some stranger.

"That is what we are waiting for, of course," said I. "Let me die, but you are an ass, John. A mischief to you. Of course it will be after the peace, for when else will the King come back?" I glanced at Titus Oates and shook my head wearily.

"Sometimes I wonder that I keep him in my service, Doctor, he abuses me so."

We spoke again, and gradually and with great subtlety, we learned much of their plans, so that when the coach drew up in Axe Yard, which was between King Street and the cockpit in St. James's Park, we knew a great deal except what was in the pamphlet which I now pronounced myself most eager to read.

"I will fetch it straightaway," said Oates and, opening the coach door, climbed down to the street and went inside his house.

"That is a foul, roguish fellow," remarked Newton.

"Most foul," said I. *"Un étourdie bête,* and no mistake."

"A senseless beast, yes, quite so." Newton smiled. "And you, sir, have missed your true calling. What an actor you would have made, my dear fellow. Your Frenchified English is most appropriate and aristocratic. *Bien tourné,* so to speak. I am indeed impressed."

"Thank you, sir. And now we shall find out what our Mister Defoe has been writing."

"That's another rogue," said Newton. "I hate all those who issue anonymously what they neither wish nor dare to acknowledge as their own. It's simple cowardice."

When Oates came back to the coach with one of his damnable pamphlets, I gave him a guinea, for which the wretched and loathsome fellow was most grateful, turning it over in his curiously blackened fingers, which made me think we had done well to have given him a real one instead of the false ones we had recovered.

"But I would you say nothing to Lord Lucas of our meeting," said I. "Or else he may think I go behind his back in this enterprise. And he is a person who gives off a most persecuted air, so that I do not want the fatigue of explaining myself to him. I swear he makes himself seem the most persistently wronged person I have ever met."

"I have seldom met His Lordship," said Oates. "Yet from what Sergeant Rohan told me, that is indeed his reputation. But Your Excellency may be assured that I shall say nothing to anyone of our conversation. And I look forward to making Your Lordship's acquaintance again, perhaps when we have made England a better place to live in."

"You mean without Papists."

Oates bowed his horrible acquiescence.

"Amen to that," he said.

Upon which Newton closed the coach door and we drove away, most horrified by what we had heard and much afeared of that knowledge to which we were now privy.

Newton often talked of the story of Belshazzar's impious feast and the secret writing that Daniel did decipher. Indeed the Book of Daniel was one of his most favourite in the Bible, being full of numerical prophecies. He wondered why those wise men of Belshazzar could not read the words: *mene, mene, tekel, upharsin.* "Numbered, weighed and divided." Perhaps they feared to give bad news to the King, whereas Daniel feared only God. Newton once told me that in Aramaic the words also meant three coins: a gold *mina,* a silver *tekel* (which was the Aramaic equivalent of a *shekel*), and the brass *peres,* which was worth but half a mina; and that this was the first recorded joke, being a pun on these three coins, and that I should imagine Daniel telling Belshazzar that his kingdom was not worth threepence. And why was it not worth threepence? Because Belshazzar was foolish enough to drink a toast to the gods of gold, silver and bronze using the metal vessels that his father Nebuchadnezzar had taken from the temple in Jerusalem.

This particular anecdote says much about Newton: herein may be found his interest in numismata that was stimulated by being at the Mint; but of greater importance is the meaning of the words themselves—"numbered, weighed and divided"— which encapsulate Newton's own philosophy and his contribution to the world. Now that I come to think of it, Newton's whole life could be compared to that disembodied hand whose writing so astonished all the king's own soothsayers and astrologers, for he had such little interest in his own body that it might not have existed at all.

Like the prophet Daniel, Newton had a low opinion of prophets and wise men in general; and he was especially scathing toward Mister Defoe's pamphlet that made much of a prediction by the French astrologer, Michel de Nostradamus—whose fame was widespread, although he was dead more than a hundred years—that there would be a conspiracy to kill King William.

"No man can prophesy the future," said Newton when we were back at the Mint, having read the pamphlet aloud in the coach. "Only God in Heaven can reveal the secrets of the world, through men, who are his chosen instruments. It is he that maketh known what shall come to pass. But it is given to man to understand God's world only by scientific inquiry and proper observation, and not by horoscopes or other foolish magic.

"And yet the common people are most credulous from their great ignorance," he said. "And readily believe in such nonsense. Therefore it's the proper job of science to exorcise these demon-haunted worlds, and to bring light to the regions of superstition. Until then, man will be the victim of his own stupidity, much preyed upon by the likes of Nostradamus, whose prophecies only seem accurate by virtue of their cryptic style and ambiguous content. Thus it seems to me entirely fitting that we should discover perjurers and villains such as Titus Oates and Mister Defoe making employment of the Frenchman's mountebankeries. For therein lies the true work of horoscopes, as fitting tools for liars and impostors.

"But our Mister Defoe's a clever man," admitted Newton. "A most skilful propagator. He blames the lack of coin on Roman Catholic goldsmiths that hoard much bullion. It was the same in Paris in 1572 when the currency was also much debased and it was suspected that the Huguenots hoarded money, for their good business reputation was well known.

"Also, Mister Defoe mentions that the Duke of Barwick comes from France with a Jacobite Irish army, which is sure to cause a deal of panic. There is nothing like an Irish threat to make Englishmen feel uneasy and resentful. And if Whitehall burns while this pamphlet be abroad, then there's no answering for what might be done in the name of Protestantism. Especially if there are arms made available to the people.

"We must stop this pamphlet and then alert Lord Halifax."

Early the next morning several of the money police accompanied Newton, Mister Hall and me to Bartholomew Close, by Smithfield. Armed with a warrant, we entered the premises of Mister Woodward and Mister Downing whom Oates had himself named as the printer and publisher involved in the plot, and, under the provisions of the Plate Act we impounded their printing press on the pretext that it was suspected of being a coining press. Protesting most vehemently, Woodward and Downing insisted that their press could not possibly be used for anything other than printing pamphlets, which gave Newton the excuse he needed to seize all of these pamphlets also, saying that Woodward's pamphlets would be required as evidence to support his contention that the press was being used for printing and not coining. It was a most ingenious albeit disingenuous course of action, and taken not a moment too soon, as it later transpired that a few dozen of these incendiary pamphlets were already being distributed in London.

A day or so later we went by coach to Bushey Park to see milord Halifax.

This was the first time that I ever spoke to His Lordship, although I had often seen him at the Treasury and in Whitehall, and Newton asked me to accompany him because of the gravity of what he was going to tell His Lordship—for he was worried that even he might not be believed, the story was so fantastic.

Charles Montagu, Earl of Halifax, was about thirty-five years of age. For a while he had been a fellow of Trinity College, Cambridge, which was where, despite the difference in their ages, he and Newton had become friends. Halifax had been one of those signatories to the Prince of Orange to pursue his own and his Queen's claims to the throne of England; and it is certain he was no lover of Papists. In appearance he was a very handsome man, and the manor of Apscourt very fine also, and I was very taken by him then, for he showed me much courtesy and remarked that one of his own names was Ellis and how we were perhaps once related. Which greatly enamoured him to me.

Lord Halifax listened most carefully to Newton's story and, when it was over, fetched us all a glass of wine himself.

"Monstrous," he remarked, "that such a thing should be contemplated here in England, and in this century."

"Monstrous indeed," agreed Newton.

"They have surely forgotten how France was condemned by all of Europe for the way that they butchered those poor Huguenots. If history is, as Dionysus tells us, philosophy from examples, then it's clear that the example has been forgotten, and the philosophy not learned."

"Your Lordship puts it very well," said Newton. "I have taken the liberty of preparing a list of those men we believe to be involved in this plot."

Lord Halifax glanced at the list and hardly got further than the two names that led it, before he spoke again, most soberly.

"I see that we must proceed very carefully," said His Lordship. "For Lord Ashley and Lord Lucas are powerful men and doubtless they would deny everything; and even against you, Doctor, their word would carry. And yet we have some time, you say?"

"Until the peace is concluded and the King returns home," said Newton. "I do not think they will act before then."

"Then we must bide our time," said Lord Halifax, "and make our preparations. I shall speak to milords Somers, Wharton and Russell. I should like the Government to act as one in this matter, the matter being most delicate. For the moment you may leave these matters to me, gentlemen. In the meantime, Doctor Newton, I would have you guard your own person most carefully, for it would go ill for all our preparations against these conspirators if some harm were to befall the uncle of the delightful Miss Barton."

This surprised me, for I had no idea that His Lordship was acquainted with that lady.

"I am beside him nearly always, milord," said I. "And I am armed with sword and pistols. So is Mister Hall."

"You see?" said Newton. "I am well protected."

"That is good," said Lord Halifax. "Nevertheless, Doctor, I should like you to stay away from the Mint until this business is over. If the Tower be full of such a dangerous contagion, it seems foolish to put yourself in the way of it. There is already so much feeling against Roman Catholics abroad in London that I do not doubt how killing you, Doctor, would work some dreadful effect upon the population. It would need only someone to come forward and swear Mister Ambrose and Mister Roettier out of their lives for the design of an assassination against the King to be the spark that would ignite the whole city in a more awful calamity than the Great Fire.

"Therefore I say to you, Doctor Newton, keep yourself from the Mint and leave these matters to me. I shall come to Jermyn Street if I need to speak with you."

"If you think it necessary, milord," said Newton, bowing gracefully. "We will do as you say."

The Treaty of Ryswick that ended the war was announced in the *London Gazette* on September the sixteenth, and signed on the twentieth. During the month that led up to the Treaty and the month afterward, things grew somewhat easier at the Mint, for, with the signing of the peace, the financial crisis that had afflicted the country for want of money to pay for the war eased most considerably.

Having to visit Newton in Jermyn Street so much, to conduct the business of the Mint, I saw more of Miss Barton again. I saw no sign that she might still be in love with me, despite what Newton had told me. Her behaviour to me was courteous but cold; not that Newton did perceive any difference between us, for he was quite blind to how things are between men and women. Besides, Miss Barton was often out, although I knew not where, since neither she nor Mrs. Rogers, nor Newton himself, saw fit to tell me; but several times Miss Barton and Newton were guests at Halifax's house in Bushey Park, while I remained in Jermyn Street, with Mrs. Rogers. But despite her apparent indifference to me, 'tis certain I was distracted by her, which is but a poor excuse how I managed to put the threat to Newton's life to the back of my mind; and how he was almost murdered.

One unseasonably warm day, my master and I were encouraged to walk instead of going about our business more safely by coach; but whatever the reasons, it is certain that we had relaxed our guard. We were coming away from Whitehall, where we had been interviewing Mister Bradley, who was an under-clerk in Lord Fitzharding's office, and Mister Marriott, who had confessed to a fraud involving the conversion of exchequer bills into specie bills, and were proceeding to The Leg, a tavern in King Street, to review our depositions, when two ruffians armed with swords came out of Boar's Head Yard and advanced upon us with very obvious intent.

"Have a care, sir," I yelled to Newton, and pushed him behind me.

Had there been just the one I should have drawn my own sword and engaged, but since there were two I had little alternative but to use my pistols. At the sight of these they fled into George Yard on the other side of The Leg, and believing I had them cornered, I started to follow until, thinking better of it, I turned back to King Street. It was well that I did, for both men had dived into the back door of The Leg and were now coming out of the front door immediately behind my master, with their swords raised. One of them lunged at my master, who, seeing his assailant out of the corner of his eye, twisted himself to one side, clear of the blade, which passed harmlessly through his coat.

I did not hesitate. Nor did I miss. The first man I shot through the side of the face, and though I did not kill him, it is certain he would have starved to death, such was the mutilated state of his mouth. The second I shot through the heart, which was to suppose that he had had one. Newton himself, although splashed with the blood of one of his attackers, was unhurt but quite shaken, for he trembled like a tansey pudding.

"See what he has done to my coat," he said, putting a finger through the hole his attacker's blade had left there.

"Better than your belly," said I.

"True."

At the discovery of the hole, Newton felt obliged to go into The Leg and take a glass of brandy wine to steady his nerves.

"Once again I am indebted to you, and the excellence of your marksmanship," said Newton, who still looked most pale.

He raised his glass to his lips and drained it gratefully. "I confess I little thought they would try to kill me in broad daylight."

"We do not know that they won't try again," said I.

"I don't believe that those two will try again," remarked Newton.

"Others may try," said I. "From now on, we must only move around the city by coach."

"Yes," he said, almost breathless with the fright of it. "You are probably right. A coach from now on, yes. That would be safer."

A parish constable arrived, and Newton said that our two assassins were ordinary footpads that had tried to steal Newton's purse.

"Why did you tell him that?" I asked when the constable was gone.

"Because it's what I would have supposed, had I not known of the Green Ribboners' Plot," he explained. "I see no reason to let it generally be known that there has been an attempt on my life. We must do or say nothing that will alarm the plotters until Lord Halifax is ready to move against them."

"Until this is over," I told him, "you must not be on your own."

"No, you are right. You must come to Jermyn Street. At least until this is all over."

And so for a while I lived at Jermyn Street again.

Mostly Miss Barton avoided being alone with me; but one day, while Newton was resting in his room, and it being a most inclement day, we found ourselves alone with each other. I had no idea how to broach the subject of her apparent estrangement from me, but I felt that I must say something, or die.

"Will you play drafts, Miss Barton?"

"No, thank you, sir, I am reading."

"Come, will you not play? I am much improved since our last encounter. I am learning much from the Doctor's style of play."

She turned her page, with eloquent silence.

"Miss Barton," I said at last, "I rely upon what once passed between us to justify my asking you now if you think it possible that you will ever look upon me as your friend again."

She said nothing, but kept on reading her book.

"If it seems at all likely that you will ever find it in your heart to forgive me."

Now she looked at me over the top of her book and beat me with her eyelashes. "It is not I who needs to forgive you, Mister Ellis, as I think I have made plain to you, but almighty God."

"But this is most unfair. Must we bring God into this?"

"Let me ask you a question, Mister Ellis. Are you still of an atheistic frame of mind?"

"I cannot, in all conscience, say that I am not."

"You are under my uncle's roof as a guest, Mister Ellis; as am I. We must try to get along as best we can. But I will tell you this, sir. I am a good Christian woman, Mister Ellis, and your views are repugnant to me. And your views being repugnant, it should be plain that you are also repugnant to me, so long as you shall hold them."

"Then surely it is your Christian duty to help me back to Christ," said I.

"It is not for me to show you the error of your thinking. That is not what is lacking in you, sir. Faith cannot be taught, Mister Ellis, like an alphabet. You must do that for yourself. I will not. I cannot."

That same night, alone in my room at Newton's house in Jermyn Street, my earlier conversation with Miss Barton, combined with a sense of apprehension that another attempt on

Newton's life might be made, made me restless, and finding it impossible to sleep, I resolved to go out and take the air of Hyde Park.

I had started down the stairs when I thought I heard a man's voice in the kitchen. Newton was already abed, and Mister Woston had lodgings elsewhere. Returning to my room for a pistol, I went downstairs to investigate, and about halfway down I heard the man's voice again. It was not a man saying anything that I heard, so much as a man groaning in his sleep.

Outside the parlour door I paused to cock my pistol, certain now that there was an intruder. And turning the handle, I advanced boldly into the room, with my pistol extended before me.

The sight I beheld was more terrible to me than any murderer could ever have been. In the candlelight which revealed her complete nakedness, Miss Barton knelt in front of Lord Halifax, who did serve her from behind like any common bawd. She stifled a scream as she saw me in the doorway. And seeing the pistol in my hand, Lord Halifax withdrew himself from inside her body, held his arms up in front of his head, and whimpered most piteously while Miss Barton tried to cover her naked parts with a tablecloth. And I stood there, saying nothing, but breathing like an angry bull. I almost put the pistol to my own head and pulled the trigger, such was the pain and disappointment that I felt. But after a moment or two I put up my gun and, begging their pardon for having put them in fear of their lives, explained that I thought I had heard an intruder, and then excused myself from their presence. Neither he nor she said a word; and yet by their situation all was suddenly plain to me. Newton had been right: his niece was in love; but not with me. It was Lord Halifax she loved.

I could not remain in that house. And not for the first time I walked from Jermyn Street to the Tower in a state of abject misery, hardly caring if anyone killed me. In truth, I would have welcomed death. For the injustice of it was only too painful to me. How could the she who had lectured me on a good Christian life give herself to another man within only a month or two of giving herself, more or less, to me? Of course the difference was plain; he was Lord Halifax and I was plain, poor Christopher Ellis. Better to be an earl's mistress than a poor man's wife.

After that terrible evening, Miss Barton was only infrequently at Jermyn Street when I called, and more often at milord Halifax's house, in Bushey Park, so that she and I were almost never alone in each other's company again.

Even now, thirty years later, it pains me to write about it. But this is small beer beside the main part of my story, which must yet be concluded; and I must relate how our spies and those of the Government kept close watch on Oates and the rest of the conspirators so that in early November, when it was given out that the King would return on November the fourteenth, the government was able to act in a most subtile way.

The very few copies of Mister Defoe's pamphlet, with its supposed prophecy of Nostradamus, that had got into circulation had still managed to raise a great public stir among Londoners, and there was much talk of conspiracy against the King; and therefore it was plain that a move against any shade of Protestantism, no matter how extreme or malign, would have been a source of real provocation to the mob. And so the Government was obliged secretly to bring down a regiment of soldiers from out of the north of England that it could trust. This being done, one night close to the return of the King from Flanders, finally we did act against the conspirators.

One evening, early in November, Newton and I were playing drafts at his home in Jermyn Street, when he received an urgent letter from Lord Halifax. As soon as he read it, Newton was all purpose.

"Come on, Ellis, get your hat and cloak, the time has come to arrest these traitors. A search for Jacobites has been undertaken," he explained. "Arrests are already being made. According to milord Halifax's letter, the Tower has been put under a curfew, with many men arrested both inside and outside its walls. We have been detailed to arrest that vile creature Oates."

"Sir," I said, arming myself to the teeth, as they say, "will you not take a weapon yourself?"

"If I did, I think I would have more to fear from myself than any rogue we might meet tonight," he said, declining my offer of a pistol.

We drove to Axe Yard, near St. James's Park, and along the way we saw London given the aspect of a city in a state of siege. Trained bands of men marched up and down the streets. The guards had been changed at Whitehall and Somerset House, with cannon placed around the former. The Temple gates were shut, the great thoroughfares barricaded, so that I did begin to worry that Mister Oates, hearing and seeing the commotion, would escape us.

"Do not concern yourself about that," said Newton. "He has been watched closely by Lord Halifax's men these past few weeks, and it only remains for us to have the honour of bringing the principal conspirator into custody."

"But will the mob permit the arrest of so many Protestants?" I asked.

"It has been put about that all those arrested are Papists," explained Newton, "being either disaffected Englishmen or French spies, although the truth is that these are the same French Huguenots or Green Ribboners that have plotted to massacre London's Roman Catholics."

Which, I confess, did seem to me to be a most dishonest and Machiavellian way of governing a country.

Outside Mister Oates's house, I removed one of my pistols from its holster and cocked it, before knocking loudly upon the door. By now I was an old hand at making an arrest, and had dispatched Halifax's men to the back of the house, in case Oates still thought to give us the slip.

"In the name of the King, open up," I called out, all the time pressing Newton back with my free hand in case any shots came forth. Finally, the door not being opened, Newton ordered the Treasury men to break in the door; and this being done, with a great deal of noise that did bring all the inhabitants of Axe Yard out of their houses, I entered the little house, followed, at a safe distance, by Newton and the rest. But the house was empty.

"I fear our bird has flown," I said, coming downstairs, having inspected the upper part of the house. "These fools have bungled it. Either that or they have been bribed."

Newton was examining the bowl of an old clay pipe most closely. "I wonder," he murmured, scooping the contents onto a fingernail, and tasting these.

"Bungled it," I repeated loudly, for the benefit of the Treasury men who were in the house. "For they would not dare to take a bribe."

"Not flown, I'll hazard," remarked Newton finally. "Merely gone out." He pointed to a handsome silver snuff-box that lay upon a table. "I do not think he would have left that behind if he intended not to come back."

"Then we may wait for him here," said I.

Newton shook his head. "All London is in a commotion," he said. "He will soon guess that something has gone awry with his plans. He may yet hear something that makes him bolt. No, we would do well to pursue him before he returns here."

"But how?" said I. "We know not where he has gone. Unless it be to Westminster Hall."

Newton shook his head. "It is long past nightfall. The shops will be shut by now. No, I have a mind he has gone somewhere else."

"Of course," I said. "The Swan with Two Necks, in Tuttle Street. Or perhaps the Baptist church in Wapping."

"It may be that we shall find him there," allowed Newton. "Or it may be that we shall find him somewhere else."

"I confess I am at a loss where else we may look," I said.

"This pipe is still warm," said Newton, handing it to me.

"Why, so it is," I said. "Then he cannot be long gone."

"Exactly so. But notice, more particularly, the thick black encrustation of the pipe bowl. That is not tobacco."

"It is like dried treacle," said I, examining the pipe bowl. "Is it charcoal?"

"No, not charcoal, either. Do you recall how when we saw Mister Oates, his fingers were quite blackened? And how a curious odour did adhere to his person?"

"Yes, it was most particular. For I did think I had smelt that smell somewhere else."

"In Southwark," said Newton. "At the place where you went when you did follow poor Major Mornay."

"Yes," said I. "How did you know?"

"This is opium," said Newton, touching the bowl of the clay pipe. "Paracelsus, and more recently an English apothecary, Thomas Sydenham, have learned to use opium in sherry wine for its medicinal properties. Here it is known as laudanum. The Dutch, however, have introduced the practice of smoking it; and in Turkey, where the practice has taken hold, it is called Mash Allah, which means "the work of God.""

"They were Dutch, the people who did keep that disreputable house in Southwark."

"That much you did tell me yourself at the time. Opium is most efficacious in the relief of pain, which is a mercy of God, of course, but when smoked it is also a most consumptive habit. A man, or a woman, might bear a beating more easily, having smoked opium."

"I see what you mean, sir."

"All of which makes me suppose that were not Mister Oates to be found at The Swan with Two Necks, in Tuttle Street, we would do well to look for him in Southwark. Did once you not lose Mister Oates while you were following him in Southwark, before you knew who it was that you followed?"

"Yes sir," said I. "And now that I come to think of it, it was not very far from that stew where Mornay went."

"It would also explain why Mornay did not recognise you immediately. He was probably stupefied with opium. You yourself remarked upon the fact that you thought he was drunk."

"I too would have been drunk if I had remained in that place. For the fumes were most intoxicating."

"Can you remember the place?"

"I think so."

"Good. We'll call in at The Swan and then, if he's not there, we'll head down to the river and get a barge across."

We took the Treasury men with us, although they must have wished they were elsewhere, such was the disdain with which Newton treated them after their letting Oates walk out of the house in Axe Yard right under their noses. Of that blackguard there was no sign at The Swan with Two Necks in Tuttle Street; and we were soon across the river and in Southwark where, as before, a fog was settling on the low roofs and jagged chimney stacks. There were few lights in the darkness to illuminate our way, and once or twice we slipped in the mud of the marshes so that we were thoroughly wet and mired by the time I had guided us, as best as I remembered, to the Dutchman's house.

Newton sent two of the Treasury men round to the back of the house, in case Oates should try to slip away, and warned them that if he did escape, they would pay dearly for it. Then, producing my pistols once more, I knocked loudly, in the name of the King.

At last the door was opened, and by the same bawd I recognised from before. And seeing my pistols, she called out some name—I still know not what it was—at which point a gigantic hound came scrambling out of another room, barking furiously all the while, which quite took me by surprise; and the animal would surely have torn out my own throat, or Doctor Newton's, had I not fired both pistols at its boxlike head and killed it. I was still trembling like a leaf as we entered the place, which was reeking of opium—for so I knew it now. Posting two more men at the front door, we searched upstairs and found several small cubicles, and in each of them, lying on a filthy bed, a man or a woman smoking a pipe full of that Mash Allah, that work of God, of which Newton had spoken earlier. Much to my relief, almost the first person I found was the so-called nun who had been whipped for the pleasure of the men in that room downstairs; she was alive, although so stupefied by the pipe she was smoking that hers hardly passed for life, and it was clear that she submitted to her degradation for the pleasures and oblivion of the pipe she now nursed in her blackened fingers.

Oates himself lay in the cubicle next to hers, wreathed in an evil spirit of white opium smoke. Seeing us, and hearing our warrant, he climbed slowly to his feet; but if we had expected the man to show fear and denial—and in truth we had grown used to fear and denial from the men and women we arrested— we were wrong, for Oates was all languor, submitting to the manacles I clasped around his wrists without demur.

"But we have met before, have we not?" said Oates, as we marched him outside. "I did believe that you were Lord Ashley, and you were his servant."

It was at this point that one of the Treasury men spoke to us.

"Where to now, Doctor Newton?" he asked.

"The Whit," said Newton.

Oates's near motionless eyes lit up like coals. "I am honoured," he said, inclining his head in Newton's general direction, "to be arrested by the great Doctor Newton." Oates smiled his smile, like a great sleepy snake, methought, which did prompt my curiosity as we made our way back to the river.

When at last we were in a boat, and on our way across the river, I could restrain my curiosity no longer. "You seem, Mister Oates, most sanguine about your arrest, the collapse of your plot," said I, "and the prospect of your imprisonment."

"Milord," he said, grinning, "for I know not what else to call you, the Whit and I are old acquaintances. But I think that I shall not be there for very long, this time, Protestant feeling being right now so strong against Roman Catholics in this country."

"We shall see," murmured Newton.

"Might I ask, were we betrayed?"

"Only by your own carelessness," said Newton.

"How so?"

"I deciphered your letters."

Oates looked disbelieving. "If that is so, Doctor, then I would simply ask you to name the keyword that we used."

"Willingly. It was 'blood.'"

Oates whistled. "Then it is true what they say, that you are the cleverest man that ever was."

"I deciphered it, yes," said Newton. "But I would still know more of how it was devised."

Oates waited for a moment as surprise gave way to recollection.

"The original cipher was devised by a French diplomat,

Blaise de Vigenère, in 1570. He was secretary to King Charles IX until it was discovered that he was a Huguenot, upon which he left the court and devoted himself to his ciphers. His work was taken up by Monsieur Descartes."

"Do you mean René Descartes, the philosopher?" said Newton.

"I do, sir. He lived in Poitiers as a student when Poitiers was still Huguenot. Which was where I came across it. When I was in a French seminary."

"But Mister Descartes was a Roman Catholic, was he not?"

"Mister Descartes's family was Roman Catholic, but Descartes had many close family connections with the Huguenots and was all his life a great friend to our Protestant religion. It was Mister Descartes who refined De Vigenère's code and made it impregnable until this day when you solved it, Doctor."

"Then my triumph is complete," said Newton. "For I would have defeated Monsieur Descartes above all men."

"No doubt you shall be well rewarded for your endeavour. By Lord Halifax."

"To know that it was the mind of Descartes I struggled to overcome is reward in itself," said Newton.

"Oh, come, sir," said Oates. "'Tis well known that you are much preferred by Lord Halifax. It is already whispered that when Mister Neale leaves the Mint, you will be the next Master."

"A false rumour, sir," replied Newton. "There, at least, you have the advantage of me, lies and false rumours being your own stock in trade."

"But does it not gall you, sir? To know that the reason for your preferment is not your fluxions and gravitation, no, nor even your excellent mind? Does it not sit badly with you, sir? To know the real reason you thrive?"

Newton stayed silent.

"Even in this poor light, I see the truth of it plain upon your face," continued Oates.

"Be silent, sir," commanded Newton.

"I don't say I blame you, sir. I would probably do it myself."

"Be silent, sir," insisted Newton.

"What man in our situation would not trade the virtue of a pretty niece, to the advantage of his own career? 'Tis given out that Lord Halifax is much taken with the girl. That he has made her his mistress and his whore. Lord Lucas had it from Lord Harley, who had it from Halifax himself. She is seventeen, is she not? Now that's a fine time for a girl. Her cunny is not too young. Nor too old. It's like a tomato when there is still a little bit of green in it. Sweet and firm. A girl of quality, too, so that her cunny is a clean one. For there's many a bawd that plays at being a virgin. But the real thing is something else. And who else could afford such pleasures as that but a rich man like Lord Halifax? For the price he has paid is your preferment, Doctor."

"That is a damned lie, sir." And so saying, Newton struck Oates, slapping him hard on the face, which was the first time and last time I ever saw such a thing.

Oates bowed his head. "If you say so, sir, I shall believe you, even if all London does not."

After that we all stayed silent.

I, most of all.

Yet it was already my opinion that Miss Barton was become Lord Halifax's whore for no other reason than she wanted to be.

⁓

Thus was a great disaster in the realm most narrowly averted. Although in the face of my own disaster I must confess I hardly cared. But what was worse, so little was done afterward to punish the principal ringleaders of these seditious men that a man might have thought there were some in the Government who were in league with those who had promoted this mischief. And which did explain why Oates had seemed so calm in the face of this disaster to his plans. At least that was what Newton thought when we discussed the matter afterward; and he said it was often thus, that the common people were held to account for themselves while their betters went scot-free.

Titus Oates was prosecuted not for treason or sedition, but for debt; in 1698 he was released and, most unaccountably, granted a lump sum of five hundred pounds and three hundred pounds a year on the Post Office in lieu of his pension. No explanation was ever discovered by Newton as to why this came about.

Or at least none that was vouchsafed to me. But that Oates continued his seditious activities seems most certain, for the Whitehall Palace was burned to the ground on January sixth, 1698, and only the Banqueting House survived. It was given out that a Dutch laundrywoman had been careless with a hot iron. Much later on, Newton had information that the woman was not Dutch at all, but a French Huguenot.

No action was taken against milords Ashley and Lucas. They were not even arrested. Lucas remained the Lord Lieutenant and welcomed Tsar Peter the Great upon his royal visit to the Tower of London in February 1698. Lord Ashley resigned as the Member of Parliament for Poole in 1698, and succeeded his father as the third Earl of Shaftesbury in 1699. He retired from all public life in July 1702, following the accession of Queen Anne. John Fauquier continued as Deputy Master of the Mint, while Sir John Houblon even became the first Governor of the Bank of England.

The King returned to England, landing at Margate on Sunday, November fourteenth, 1697. It rained almost continuously, but the weather did little to dampen the enthusiasm of all loyal Englishmen for the return of William; all over London, bells were rung, and it need hardly be said that guns were fired at the Tower, which brought down the ceiling in my house. Two days later the King arrived back in London, in a very pompous procession, although many who remembered it said that it was not as pompous as the return of King Charles.

Tuesday, November the second, was a Thanksgiving Day for the peace, and despite more wet weather, there were fireworks in the evening. The next day, many of the French Huguenots that were arrested as supposed Jacobites were tried for high treason. In courts that were closed to the general public, they loudly protested that they were no Jacobites, nor any Roman Catholics, but their offers to prove they were not Papists by taking the sacramental tests under the Act were ignored as being sharp and cynical—captious attempts to thwart justice. In truth there was precious little justice about, that December, and the trials were more show than substance, with the sentences, in Shakespeare's phrase, a foregone conclusion. More than one hundred men were transported to the Americas, but six, including Vallière and Rohan, were sentenced to death.

Sunday, December the fifth, was the first Sunday St. Paul's had any service in it since it was consumed at the conflagration of the City. The work was still not complete, with Sir Christopher Wren's great dome still not built; but the choir was finished and the organ looked and sounded most magnificent. Newton and I attended the service, with Mister Knight preaching on the Epistle of Jude, verse three, in which the brother of James exhorts that Christians should earnestly contend for the faith which was once delivered unto the saints. Mister Knight applied this text against the Socinian doctrine, which was only a short step away from the Arianism of my master.

Upon our return to the Mint, some days later, after an absence of several weeks, Newton received a message that

Sergeant Rohan—who was held in Newgate, where Newton's reputation for obtaining pardons for them that gave him information was well known—wished to meet with him in order that he might impart a great secret.

"What? Another damned secret?" I said.

"It is the Tower," said Newton, as if that were all the explanation needed.

Which was true indeed. The Tower was more than just a prison and a place of safety to mint the coin; it was also a state of mind, an attitude that affected all who came into contact with its walls. Even now I am haunted by its memory. And if you would speak to my ghost you must look for me there, for it was while I was in the Tower that I died. Not my body, it is true, but my heart and soul, which were most certainly murdered while I was in the Tower. Young ladies that wished to conceive of a child were in the habit of visiting the Tower armouries, intent upon sticking a bodkin into the large codpiece of King Henry VIII's foot-armour. It is too late now, of course, but I wonder that I did not think to prick his breast that I might have found myself a new love and, perhaps, even a new life in Christ.

We travelled to Newgate to find that James Fell, who had been the head keeper, was now dismissed. But all else remained the same, with the Whit still a place of much misery, although Sergeant Rohan was not as sorry for himself as I might have expected. He met us in the condemned hold, from which darkness the only escape was with a candle, with no resentment and much cheerfulness considering that he had clearly been beaten, and the awful fate that now awaited him. Since he had said nothing at his trial, he now began with a full confession of his crimes, all of which we heard with the lice cracking loudly under our feet; and it was the most extraordinary admission that I ever did hear in that dreadful place.

"That I did, I did because I believed it to be right," he said. "The Massacre of Saint Bartholomew's Day has hung over me all my life. And all Huguenot Protestants such as myself have better reason than any to hate Papists. I hate Papists as other men hate the clap or the plague, and I would willingly lose my immortal soul to see every one of them dead."

"George Macey was not a Catholic," said Newton. "No more was your Major Mornay."

"Poor Macey," said Rohan. "I'm sorry he was killed. In searching for coiners in the Tower, he stumbled upon our plot, as perhaps you did yourself, sir; and it was suspected that he would betray us, when he came to understand more of what we were up to. When he was found in possession of one of our coded letters, that sealed his fate. It was Mister Twistleton who, being the Tower Armourer, took charge of the torture, at the instruction of Major Mornay, so that we might find out exactly how much he knew and who he might have told; and if the code had been broken. I think it was Macey's screams that affected Mister Twistleton's wits, for his mind was never the same again."

I neglected to mention Newton's own diagnosis of Twistleton's madness—his syphilis—for fear of stopping the sergeant's explanations.

"Mornay was mad anyway," he continued. "A careless fellow, and even though we served on a French galley together, I don't much regret killing him. He was a perverted sort of man, and had become most unbalanced, so that he was a liability, as you might say."

After having seen what I had seen in the Southwark marshes, I found it only too easy to recognise the truth of this myself.

"You may as well know that you and the lad here were marked to die as well."

"I know it," said Newton. "Some of the letters we translated spoke of it."

"And yet you still came here?"

"We bear you no ill will," said Newton. "Do we, Ellis?"

"None at all, sir."

"But who were those two who tried to kill me?" asked Newton.

"Paid assassins, sir. Riff-raff. A couple of coiners who bore you a grudge. Mister Vallière was waiting inside that tavern to say that he recognised old Roettier and Mister Ambrose from the Tower as having killed you." The Sergeant spat. "Many's the time I've wanted to kill old Roettier. His whole stinking family's a nest of Catholic spies. The only reason he's not dead already is that it was thought he might be more useful to our cause if he was left alive to be blamed for this or that."

"But who would have believed that an old man like that would murder anyone?" I asked.

"In times like these, people will believe what they want to believe."

Newton nodded. "And what do you believe, Sergeant?"

"How do you mean?"

"You are a Socinian, are you not?"

"Aye sir. But that's still a good Protestant."

"I agree with you there. And because you are condemned, I will tell you that I do hold many of your own beliefs, for I am of the Arian persuasion."

"God bless you for that, Doctor."

"But I think we have chosen a bad time to reappear in the world, for it seems the world has grown tired of sectarian disputes."

"True, sir. Tired and cynical. I little thought I would ever be condemned as a damned Jacobite and Roman Catholic."

"Their Lordships would hardly have dared to condemn you as a Protestant," said Newton. "Not with all the feeling against Catholics there is in the country now. And yet I must also tell you I believe you are justly convicted. For you would have murdered so many that England would have been held in much opprobrium, as France was after the Huguenots were massacred. And I am firmly of the belief that such an atrocity would have given King Lewis an excuse to break the peace we have just made. But that you should be punished for the sins of your betters, as well as for your own, seems to me especially unjust. Christ asks only that we follow the example of his life, and not the meaning of his death."

At which I uttered some remark to the effect that the rich had fine scented gloves with which to hide their dirty hands. Which was a remark directed at Newton as much as Their Lordships in Government.

"And yet I am rich, too," said the Sergeant.

"Rich?" said I. "How so?"

"What else do you call a man who knows where the treasure of the Templars might be found?"

"You know where the treasure is?" said I, much excited by this news.

"I do. And I will tell you where it is to be found, if you can you get me out of here."

"I think I can do very little for you," said Newton. "Not even for the treasure of the Templars. But I shall plead for your life before the Lords Justices. I shall tell them that I do not think it right that you should be punished while others who did counsel you in this matter do go free. Not for any treasure, though. But because I believe you to be less culpable than several others."

"That's all I ask, sir. Why, then I'll tell you about the secret, sir. For there I take you upon your word. If you say you will do something, I know you will do it. That is your reputation in here, and in the Tower. But mostly I will tell you about the treasure because you are of my own religious persuasion and have no faith in the Trinity, and believe that the Father is greater than the son. For the proof of that, why, sir, that's the treasure I speak of."

"I would give much to see that proved to my own satisfaction," said Newton. "True knowledge is the greatest treasure of all."

Of this I was less than sure; had I not been happier when I myself was ignorant?

"But what is this secret and how did you come by it?" asked Newton.

Sergeant Rohan took a swig from the bottle of gin I had brought him out of charity.

"Bless you for this, lad," he said. "Well, sir, to cut a long story short, following the capture of Jerusalem in 1099, Count Hugh of Champagne, the patron of the Cistercian Order, went to Jerusalem and ordered his vassal Hugh of Payns to found the Poor Fellow Soldiers of Jesus Christ on the Temple Mount, this being the site of the Temple of Solomon that was rebuilt by Herod, and destroyed again by the Romans. Prior to this, it was said that the Cistercians sought the help of Greek scholars to translate certain texts found after the capture of Jerusalem that spoke of a buried treasure beneath the Temple Mount. And that the Poor Fellow Soldiers that became the Templars were ordered to look for this treasure.

"There have been many stories about what that treasure amounted to. Some have said it was the treasure of King Solomon that was Sheba's tribute. Others that it was the Holy Grail. Some believed they found the embalmed head of Jesus Christ. But it was none of these. Neither was it the Ark of the Covenant, the lance that pierced Christ's side, nor the blood line of Jesus Christ.

"It was the texts themselves that were the treasure, for these were nothing less than the original Greek texts of the lost Gnostic Christian texts, including those gospels that were regarded as heretical by the Apostle Paul, and which were later suppressed by the early Church, for these books prove that Christ was only a man, that he did not rise from the dead, and that the established Christian dogma is a blasphemy of the truth and evil teaching. That is why the Templars were accused of heresy and blasphemy: for possession of these forbidden books of the New Testament. And for translating them from Greek into Latin. That is the book of the devil they were accused of possessing. That is why they were persecuted throughout Europe and burned at the stake."

Newton looked thunderstruck, as if he had discarded darkness and clothed himself in light.

"That is the treasure," Sergeant Rohan continued triumphantly. "That is what the kings of Christendom tried so earnestly to find: the Templars' book. And that is why we hate the established Roman Catholic Church, for it is the Romans who have suppressed this truth for a thousand years. Many Huguenots were descended from Templars. And therefore we have a double reason to hate Papists, for they have persecuted us twice."

"But what other gospels can there be?" I asked.

"Did not Christ have twelve apostles?" Sergeant Rohan said scornfully. "And yet there are only three Gospels by apostles that are in the New Testament. Where is the Gospel of Philip, the Gospel of Thomas, the Gospel of Peter, the Gospel of James? For that matter, where is the Gospel of Mary Magdalene?"

"Mary Magdalene," repeated Newton. "Is there such a thing?"

"Aye," said Sergeant Rohan. "It was she who told the apostles the things that were hidden from them, that only Christ himself told her. But it is Peter you will want to read most of all, sir. For it is he who speaks strongest against the Christianity of Paul. It is Peter who refers to Jesus as a dead man. And learning this, you will know the truth at last, and be free."

"But where are these books?" Newton asked hoarsely.

"They are contained in one book in the library at the Tower," said Sergeant Rohan. "A copy of the book came to the Tower with the Templars who were imprisoned there, and was hidden under the altar in St. John the Evangelist's Chapel that is now a library. The safest place for the book was thought to be right under the noses of their persecutors. And there it has stayed ever since."

"But where is it now?" asked Newton. "For the altar is gone."

"On the tribune gallery, above where the altar once stood, is a window. In the window is a simple wooden box in which you will find the book. Many enlightened men who were in the Tower have read the Templars' book, for knowledge of its existence was only ever given to those who could not take the book away, and who were themselves educated or persecuted, or both. Sir Thomas More, the Wizard Earl, Sir Walter Raleigh, Sir Francis Bacon, to name but a few."

I could hardly believe what I was hearing; and I only wished that Miss Barton could have been present to hear what the Sergeant had to say, and see the look of keen fascination that illuminated Newton's face. I might have pointed to him and asked her if she still believed her uncle was the good Anglican she thought. "What?" I said. "No gold at all?" Which drew me a look of contempt from my master.

"Not all men who have known of the Templars' book were interested in the treasure it contained," said the Sergeant. "Sir Jonas Moore knew of the book, but he was not interested in truth. Only in gold. He found what gold there was, in the box with the book. But he thought there might be more."

"And what of the Saltire Cross?" asked Newton. "And Orion the hunter?"

Sergeant Rohan looked puzzled, and took another swig from the bottle.

"Was there not some significance in these for the Templars?" persisted Newton, who was referring to the cross that Mister Pepys had shown to him.

"Only that when Templars were buried, their arms were crossed across their bodies saltireways," said the Sergeant.

"That is common enough," said I.

"Aye, now. But not when the Order of Templars was first created," insisted the Sergeant. "As for Orion, in the Greek his name means a mount or mountain."

"*Oros,*" said Newton. "I did not think of that. Yes, of course. There have been several times during this case when I have been as blind as Orion. Only now does the darkness truly clear and I see all things in the light."

"Those upon whom the Spirit of Life descends," said the Sergeant, "when they are bound together with the power, will be saved and will become perfect and they will become worthy to rise upward to that great light."

"What is that scripture?" asked Newton.

"The Secret Book of John," answered the Sergeant. "The light is not the son, but Almighty God the father."

Newton nodded. "Amen," he said quietly.

"There is a Muhammadan mosque close by the Temple Mount in Jerusalem," said the Sergeant. "It covers the rock upon which Abraham prepared Isaac for sacrifice, and is the spot from which their prophet ascended into Heaven. I have not seen it. But I have heard how there is an inscription there which says, 'O ye people of the Book, do not exceed the bounds in your religion, and speak only Truth of God. The Messiah, Jesus, the son of Mary, is only an apostle of God, and his Word which he gave unto Mary, and a Spirit proceeding forth from him. Therefore believe in God and his apostles, and say not Three. It is better that you should do so. For God is only one God, and it is far from being his glory that he should have a son.'"

"Amen indeed," murmured Newton. For a moment he seemed almost overcome. Then he said, "I little thought when I came here, Sergeant, that my eyes should be opened so wide. All my life I have endeavoured to look upon the light of God, and I thought no man could see more of his truth than I do myself. But it is perhaps appropriate that it should be a man like you who reveals more of Him unto me. For God, who best knows the capacities of men, hides his mysteries from the wise and prudent of this world and reveals them unto babes. The wise men of this world are too often prepossessed with their own imaginations and too much entangled in designs for this life."

"Read the book," urged the Sergeant, "and you will know more."

The very next Monday, Newton went straight to Whitehall to plead Sergeant Rohan's life before Their Lordships; only they were not disposed to be merciful, despite Newton's eloquent entreaties, and upon the appointed day, Rohan and Vallière went to their probably well-deserved deaths, with mobs jeering them all the way to Tyburn as amidst the atmosphere of a bear-baiting. Neither Newton nor I attended the executions of these two criminals, but Mister Alingham, the Tower carpenter and undertaker who did, said that the hangman was so drunk that he tried to put a rope about the neck of the clergyman who went with them to their deaths, which doubtless would have amused that heretical pair of Protestants.

No men died so unpitied, for it was the common conception that these two had been involved in the very plot to kill the King which Nostradamus had prophesied in the pamphlet Titus

Oates had given to us. When Rohan and Vallière were at long last dead, their heads were fastened on two poles and pitched on the north end of Westminster Hall, to the great satisfaction of the people who saw it.

Newton spent the morning of the executions closeted with the lost gospels he had found in the Tower library, according to Sergeant Rohan's instructions. I thought the Templars' book to be in remarkable condition for a thing so apparently old, and I almost wondered if it were not some kind of fraud, as many of the supposed relics of Christ and the saints proved to be. The book was a codex bound in leather, with the constellation of Orion tooled most beautifully onto its surface—which was exactly like the cross Mister Pepys had shown us—and comprised beautifully illuminated pages of Latin.

When I enquired if these heretical gospels were everything he had expected, Newton said:

"Much is revealed of the nature of Jesus, the early Jewish sects, and the eternal conflict between light and dark. It is clear to me that we are forbidden to worship two Gods, but we are not forbidden to worship one God and one Lord: one God for creating all things and one Lord for redeeming us with his blood. We must not pray to two Gods, but we may pray to one God in the name of the Lord, so that we do not break the first commandment. Christ was not the son of God nor was he an ordinary man, but incarnate by the almighty power of God. He was the angel of God who appeared to Abraham, Jacob and Moses, and who governed Israel in the days of the Judges. Therefore it may be seen how prophecy is the most important aspect of Christ, and not his relationship to God; and that to the true worship of Noah, nothing more has been added." He smiled and after a moment or two added, "In short, I feel I will have the comfort of leaving Philosophy less mischievous that I did find it."

For ever after that he was evasive upon the subject of the Templar gospels, so that I soon ceased to mention it to him altogether.

The Templars' book is still in the chapel as I have described. Perhaps it would provide some people with the answers that they seek. I can only say that I did not find them for the simple reason that I never read the book. For what would a second Bible or a second Koran have told me? Only that the first one was wrong. Every sect contradicts another, which is why there have scarcely been any that did not spill blood.

All such man-made systems of religion are in error, for they presume to understand how God acts. I could not see how any of could ever hope to understand God, when most of us never manage to understand one another. What chance for a man to know the mind of God, when he cannot even fathom the mind of a woman?

Newton rarely spoke to me of Miss Barton after that; and I was never invited to his home while she was there. It was not a subject that could ever have been raised between us. Which is not to say that what Mister Oates had said was without foundation.

There is some uncertainty about precisely when Miss Barton was publicly the mistress of Lord Halifax, the first Lord of the Treasury; but what is beyond dispute is that by early part of the new century Newton's niece, who now called herself Mrs. Barton, and Lord Halifax were living together openly at his home in Bushey Park, despite his having a wife who was still alive. It was Lord Halifax who created Newton Master of the Mint, upon Neale's death; and when Newton was knighted by Queen Anne, on the same day as Lord Halifax's brother, in 1705, the honour was not for his services to science, nor indeed for his services to the Mint, but for his political services in Parliament to Lord Halifax—for Newton had become an MP and a supporter of Halifax in the House of Commons in 1701.

Naturally, I always remembered the words of Titus Oates: that it had been a pretty niece and not fluxions and gravitation that had furthered his career; and that Newton had traded her virtue to his own advantage.

What is equally beyond dispute is that Lord Halifax made a will leaving Mrs. Barton a bequest which, including the house, was worth, upon Lord Halifax's death in 1715 from an inflammation of the lungs, some twenty thousand pounds or more. Nor is it beyond doubt that Halifax's powerful relatives contested the will so that the house and most of the money remained in the Montagu family. It was only then that she married Mister Conduitt.

Thirty years have passed since then.

Newton was a good old man when he died. All the wise were his brothers. He admired Noah. Noah would surely have placed Newton in his Ark.

I was invited to Newton's funeral, and despite my feeling ill, I was determined to attend, for I did bear the man great admiration, as did all who had the inestimable honour to know the Doctor's mind.

Of wise men I saw a great many in the Abbey to see Newton laid to rest on the evening of his funeral, there being present almost every member of the Royal Society. While the Westminster bell tolled for Newton—nine times for his being a man, and then eighty-five times for his eighty-five years of age—Mrs. Conduitt (she that had been Miss Barton) presented each guest with a mourning ring while a servant handed about sprigs of rosemary, for remembrance, and to hide the smell of death, which, despite the best efforts of the embalmer, was beginning to be all too noticeable.

When she saw me, she coloured a little but maintained her

composure. "Colonel Ellis, I wonder that you can set foot in a church," were all the words she spoke to me.

To see Mrs. Conduitt again at Newton's funeral and have her speak to me thus was most painful. For she was every bit as beautiful as I had remembered, and even though she was in mourning I was quite distracted by her, for black suited her very much and served to contrast her own natural colours in the same way that ebony or jet will offset gold to best advantage.

I was still in love with her, of course. Even after all these years. I married, some years after I left Newton's service and took my commission; but my own wife died of the ague some ten years ago. It grieved me only a little to see Miss Barton married to Mister Conduitt, who was a Member of Parliament. Perhaps position in society was all that she ever desired. If so, then her uncle's funeral must have gratified her very much. Those six members of the Royal Society that bore her uncle's pall out of the Jerusalem Chamber, through a narrow door, and down a few steps into the candlelit nave of the Abbey, were the first in the realm. These were the Lord Chancellor, the dukes of Montrose and Roxburgh, and the earls of Pembroke, Sussex, and Macclesfield. The Bishop of Rochester, attended by the prebends and choir, performed the office while the mourners were led by a Knight of the Bath. Many more came than were bid, however, and by my own reckoning there were almost three hundred present that night to watch him laid, with every civility, in the floor.

It was a fine service, of infinite light, for there were so many candles lit which shone with such a triumphant splendour upon my head that it seemed to remind me of the absolute potentiality of infinity itself. And as I sat there, my thoughts returned to my conversation with Doctor Clarke and I wondered what satisfaction God could have in our having faith in the teeth of reason? What possible use was there in saying to God that I was convinced of something of which one could not rationally be convinced? Did this not make a lie of faith? The more I considered the matter in relation to Newton, the more I perceived his own dilemma. Faith required him to believe not that which was true but that which appeared to him, whose understanding was so great, to be false. The greatest enemy to his faith appeared to be his own genius. How could he whose whole life had been devoted to understanding, subordinate that which had defined him?

Perhaps alchemy provides the best metaphor for Newton's own belief in God. For it seems to me his religion was like a regulus—the purer or metallic part of a mineral—which sinks to the bottom of a crucible or a furnace and is thus separated from the remaining matter. This regulus is hidden, and the secret is only in the hands of those who are adept. It was wisdom not yet instructed by revelation; all other religions are good sense perverted by superstition.

Is that what I believe? I should like to believe in something.

When the service was complete, a black slab was laid upon his grave, which lies but a few steps from those of the kings and queens of England. And so all broke up and I walked to Hell, which was a tavern near the entrance to Westminster Hall, in Exchequer Court; and there I thought about these matters some more.

I am fifty years of age. My life grows short. Sometimes I seem to feel my own heart rub against my backbone. It is perhaps my own mortality. Soon I will have all the answers, if more answers there be than are on this Earth. Yet even now I do believe that Newton provided us with the greatest answers of all.

Author's Note

$\mathcal{A}$mong his other great discoveries, it was Isaac Newton who defined the modern concept of mass, essential for the development of matter upon which all of modern cosmology rests. Given knowledge only of the velocity of stars, Newton's laws have enabled scientists to deduce the distribution of matter in a galaxy, of which, typically, between eighty and ninety percent is to be found spread out beyond the spiral disk and not in the form of visible stars and gas. All that modern science knows about this kind of matter is that it does not give off or reflect much light. It is called "dark matter." And it may be of interest to the reader to note that this seemed to me to be a most suitable title for the tenebrous and crepuscular story that appears here.

The reader may also like to note that England's greatest scientist really did work for the Royal Mint. In 1696, after twenty-five years of distinguished academe, the Lucasian Professor of Mathematics at Cambridge University, better known to us today as author of the *Principia Mathematica* and *Optics,* accepted what was judged to be little more than a reasonably well-paid sinecure, as Warden of the Royal Mint, then located within the Tower of London, during the period of "the Great Recoinage." Four years later, he became Master of the Mint, and remained Master of the Mint until his death, in 1728.

In 1696, Newton threw himself into his new tasks with customary thoroughness, pursuing coiners and counterfeiters, taking depositions from witnesses, having himself commissioned as a justice of the peace in all of the home counties, maintaining a network of informers, and sending many men and women to the gallows. The London underworld had never known an investigator quite so thorough and incorruptible, and he was soon regarded among these criminal elements with real fear and hatred. We know a great deal about Isaac Newton's work at the Mint. But what do we know of Christopher Ellis, who is the narrator of the story contained in the book?

According to State Papers Domestic 362 (1696) in the Public Record Office at Kew, in London, the Lords Justices—the central body of government in the absence of King William III at the war with France—had agreed, on August 26, that an assistant clerk was needed for Dr. Newton following the mysterious disappearance of his previous clerk, George Macey. The clerk whom Newton chose was one Christopher Ellis, the younger brother of Charles Ellis, who, prior to his appointment as Comptroller of the Mint, was Undersecretary to William Lowndes, the Permanent Secretary to the Secretary of State for the Treasury, Lord Godolphin. (Godolphin resigned in the dying days of 1696 and was replaced by the Chancellor of the Exchequer, Charles Montagu, the future Earl of Halifax, who was also Newton's patron in the Mint.) Christopher Ellis's appointment was approved by the Treasury on November 17 (Treasury Books, 310, 325, 1693–96) to assist Dr. Newton's "extraordinary work" in detecting and prosecuting clippers and coiners, at the salary of sixty pounds per year, to be paid from September Quarter Day. But beyond these few facts, very little else of Christopher Ellis is known.

Newton's interest in alchemy, as well as his dissenting, not to say blasphemous, Arian views, which made him violently opposed to the ruling Trinitarian religious orthodoxy of the day, is also accurate. And anyone wishing to know more should read Richard Westfall's magisterial biography of Newton, as I have done. But any mistakes in the novel are my own.

I am very much indebted to Neil Agarwal of Harvard University for helping me with the code.

—PHILIP KERR, NOVEMBER 29, 2001

About the Author

Philip Kerr was born in Edinburgh in 1956 and now lives in London with his wife and three children. *Dark Matter* is his eleventh novel.

Michael Maier, *Atalanta fugiens*, 1618